BORDERLINE DECISION

HUGH SIMPSON

HAP STONER SERIES, BOOK #1

3Span
Publications

Borderline Decision
Copyright © 2018 by Hugh Simpson

Published by

3Span
Publications

website: 3spanpublications.com
email: hsimpson@3spanpublications.com

Cover Design: Marianne Nowicki, PremadeEbookCoverShop.com
Interior Design: Nick Zelinger, NZGraphics.com
Editors: Sarah Lovett, Cynde Christie

ISBN: 978-0-692-08298-0 (Paperback)
ISBN: 978-1-949393-02-6 (Hardcover)
ISBN: 978-1-949393-00-2 (eBook)
Library of Congress Control Number: 2018907610

First Edition

Printed in the United States of America

To my wife Mabel who allowed me to pursue my dreams.
To my Mother and Father who instilled this important
principal: "If not you ... who. If not now ... when."
Pop read my first stories in 1985, telling me how "good they
were." Now I know he lied being the supportive parent.
I only wish you were here to relish in this day
with Mom and I.

Cast of Characters

Nomads

Hap Stoner "Kang": Executive Officer 'XO" of HMLA 767 based out of Joint Reserve Air Base in New Orleans/ Co-Founder Vector Data Communications.

LtCol Chuck Warden "Tuna Man": Commanding Officer 'CO' of HMLA 767/International Airline Pilot in civilian life.

Jonathan Simmons "Jethro": Son of H.D. Simmons. 27 years old Captain United States Marine Corps Reserve. Two tour Combat Veteran and now attending Seminary in San Antonio, TX. Pulled between what his Father wanted him to follow… "the Corps" vs the higher calling continuing to tug at his heart.

Jim Bob Waters "Big Alabama": Marine Corps Aviator/ Offshore Helo Pilot in civilian life.

Paul Alessandro "Schlonger": Marine Corps Aviator/High School Math teacher in civilian life.

John Hancock "Hollywood": Marine Corps Aviator/ Attorney in civilian life.

Terrence LD Hicks "LD": Marine Corps Aviator/Flooring Executive in civilian life.

Terry Koch "Killer": Marine Corps Aviator.

Phantom: Marine Corps Aviator.

Major D.W. Eavers "Ambassador": Marine Corps Aviator/Airline Pilot in civilian life.

Blake Turner "Waco": Marine Corps Aviator/Software sales in civilian life.

Captain Arturo Parks "Meat": HMLA 767 Intelligence Officer/EMS Pilot in civilian life.

Sergeant "Little Ray" Martinez: HMLA 767 crew chief.
Corporal Lafleur: HMLA 767 crew chief.

Associates of Hap Stoner

Carla McCreery: Hap's live in for 6 years. Partner in high power Dallas Law Firm.

Peggy Smith: Hap's Secretary at Vector Data Communications Inc.

William Hunter Kellogg: Enlisted Force Recon Marine/Owner of Buccaneer Casino/Co-Founder Vector Data Communications.

Doc Benjamin Sherry: Black Jack dealer at Buccaneer who moonlights for Will Kellogg as hired mercenary.

Jeff Scharver: Former Marine Corps Aviator. Shadow Pilot.

LtCol John "Swamp Puppy" Stenson: LtCol in USMCR. F 18 Squadron Commander.

Rodney Reimnitz "The Roach": Former Marine Aviator. Expert in running operations for training/combat and independent global combat arms dealer.

Shadow Operatives

Thomas Lindblad Leffler "Blad": Co-Founder and CEO of Shadow Services with Global Reach.

Big Shadow: Former Nazi Agent, age unknown, as fit as Clint Eastwood.

Steve Smith: Shadow 28 Agent, is captured.

Jorge Gore: Servant to Scorpion and his older brother before him.

Bad Guys

Danny Boyd: Land developer/Businessman, CEO DL Boyd Associates International.

D L Boyd Associates International: Influenced Senator Jourdan III to slip a rider on Defense Budget to secure loan by US.

Scotty B Jourdan III: US Northeast Senator/Chair Armed Services Committee.

Colonel Ted Shank USMC "Bear": Marine Air Group Commander.

Charif Alawa: Son of Egyptian banking magnate.

Los Americana on the Lake: Syndicate structure loan led by Danny Boyd organization.

Drug Cartel/Muslim Movement in Mexico Jabhat al-Mahdi Operation Fer-de-Lance: Operation named after indigenous snakes that are excitable and unpredictable when disturbed. They can, and often will, move very quickly, usually opting to flee from danger but are capable of suddenly reversing direction vigorously to defend themselves.

Gregorio Moya "Scorpion": Head of the Black Stone drug cartel.

Geraldo Ponce Moya a.k.a. Muhammed Abu Moya: Considers himself the Caliph of Latin American Muslims/Scorpion's cousin.

Enrique Fuentes: Ineffective president of Mexico under Scorpion's control.

Maestro "The Teacher": Nephew of Saudi Prince, head of Saudi Intelligence.

Monday 1015; Richardson TX

Hap Stoner smacked the hand-carved gavel against a small block of Hill Country cedar, and closed his first board meeting as the chair of Vector Data Communications Corp. With the former chairman, Will Kellogg's resignation two months earlier, Hap, already the organization's CEO and President had assumed the role of acting board chairman.

John Hancock, the company's chief legal officer, gave Hap a single nod—*good meeting.* As they reached the elevator, Hap shook hands with each of the four external board members. He kept his goodbyes short. He knew the directors were anxious to catch the waiting limo for DFW International Airport and Love Field.

Back in the executive conference room, Hap stuffed documents into his leather portfolio. Before closing it, he caught sight of a grainy photograph of his mother that he intended to have framed. He thought about his roots, deep in the rock-hard foundation in a refining city on the Texas Gulf Coast. He smiled at the memory of the four kids in a 900 square foot, one-bathroom house. Lucky to have indoor plumbing, he thought. His mom had her hands full with her youngest son, Hap. A stay-at-home Mom, she had to pick up where a father working two jobs couldn't. Pop, as the Stoner kids called him, used his iron hand when Mom's velvet glove was not enough. Most of Hap's friends grew up the same.

"You about ready, Hap?"

Hancock's voice brought Hap back to the boardroom. He looked over and nodded. "Just about." He'd introduced John Hancock, call sign "Hollywood," and his Houston Law Firm to Will Kellogg, Vector Data cofounder and Hap's partner. The introduction turned out to be a Godsend for the company. As Vector Data grew, so did the demands for more in-house counsel to come onboard. Will had wanted to bring in one of his Vegas buddies, a corporate attorney. Hap intervened on the side of Hancock, who understood the company and could navigate the rocky regulatory environment. Hap had flown into combat with him so he knew he could trust Hollywood completely, even with his life.

Hap and Will had met at a local pub to deliberate seriously the choice of who would become VDC's in-house counsel. A round of three toddies each, followed by a forty-five-second arm-wrestling match, settled it. The next day, Hollywood formally became in-house counsel for Vector Data Communications.

Now, as he trailed Hollywood out of the boardroom, Hap felt good about the meeting and the last quarter, but he remained deeply concerned about industry regulations. Having passed on several purchase offers, Vector Data walked a tightrope over a hostile regulatory landscape. One particular attorney general from New York had established telephone companies while lining his pockets for a run at a governorship. The quid pro quo was to make life miserable for the smaller carriers like Vector Data, who were deploying cutting edge technologies. The AG used I-Commerce and payments for services as impetus to ask the Federal Bureau of Investigation for help. The Feds put constant pressure on the fledgling carriers and their young entrepreneurial owners. Enter John Hancock. Vector Data's chief counsel became the tip of the spear working the halls of Congress and the FCC, meeting with state regulatory authorities to ensure Vector Data's 350 jobs were secure.

"See you later," Hollywood said, as the two men reached his office.

Hap nodded, already turning toward his office located down the hallway. "I'll get my updated schedule from Peg and let you know when we can take off for California."

They were anxious to join the other members of HMLA 767 closing out the last two weeks of another JTF 6 mission. Hap enjoyed the dual roles: a Reserve Marine Aviator and a "member" of corporate America. What a life. Wearing fitted, suspended suits in the morning, but before noon, he and Hollywood would have wheels in the well taking the corporate jet to El Centro, California. Both would be in the cockpit of an AH-1W Cobra the same evening with a mix of Cobras and Hueys shooting live ordnance. JTF offered great training resources, plus free gas to hone night flying and aerial shooting skills using night vision devices. Training on the edge gave Hap much needed balance.

* * *

Peggy Smith looked up from a pile of messages on her desk. As always, she greeted Hap with a wide smile spread across her narrow face and a cheery "Good morning, Mr. Stoner."

"Morning, Peg."

She was the proverbial breath of fresh air no matter how bad the day. Her smile and blue eyes parted rain clouds. Not a day went by when she wasn't dressed to the nine's, her shiny brown hair bouncing off her shoulders. The day Hap hired her several years earlier he knew he could not get by without her. On more than one occasion, Carla, Hap's live-in girlfriend of six years and a high-powered attorney in a large legal firm, joked, "If I'm ever hit by a bus, Hap, you'll fall for the Mrs. Stoner in waiting."

"Good meeting?" Peggy asked.

"It's over, Peg, so it's a good meeting."

She nodded her head toward his office door. "Your Commanding Officer at the Squadron called. If I didn't know better, he wanted to interrupt your meeting. It sounded urgent."

Hap stepped inside his door, leaning back far enough to give her "the look," eyeball to eyeball, letting her know that he would return the call to his immediate report, call sign "Tuna Man," ASAP. He punched the speed dial on his console, and the Commanding Officer's mobile display appeared. As the phone rang, Hap noticed the empty place on his desk where his squadron cup—with a Camel wearing sunglasses and smoking a cigarette—normally sat.

Puzzling over the disappearance, Peg's voice startled him.

"Not so fast," she said as she handed him the cup, filled with steaming French Vanilla to the rim. Closing the door, she retreated from the office without saying a word.

"Damn," he said, bringing the cup to his lips, "How does she do it?"

2

Monday 1040; Calexico MX

From the second floor of the El Tigre Hotel in Calexico, Shadow 28 surveilled the busy scene through the room's grimy window. At the far end of the street, vendors offered food, wares, and trinkets to locals and tourists alike. Near his fleabag hotel, merchants, prostitutes and their johns, and kids running drugs and messages for the local cartel went about their day. Known in his old life as Steve, Shadow 28, six feet tall and fit, stooped a bit to place his eye on the scope of the tripod-mounted Forward Looking Infra-Red Camera, the "FLIR." While the 4.3" touch screen LCD displayed a constantly slewing image and the on-board 5MP camera recorded the action, the scope allowed him to see who'd forgotten to shave that morning and their contraband.

After seventeen years with the DEA, he didn't have to work very hard to spot illicit drug activity. Local authorities, many of whom filled the Cartel payrolls, did not interfere with the steady trafficking of drugs and human cargo. But, Shadow 28 didn't have to physically occupy room 2-A to watch the show; he had set up a dozen of the FLIRs, each in a room at other cheap, by-the-hour hotels in Mexican border towns from Calexico to Juarez. The T620, thermal-capable and better than boots on the ground, shot data to a "Shadow" operator embedded somewhere in the Caribbean. And, that remote operator could slew, elevate, and zoom any of the cameras 24/7.

Six Phoenix girls had vanished without a trace. That's what had brought him to Mexico this time. Missing five days now, the girls never made the five-block walk from their eighth grade dance to one of their homes where they all planned to spend the night. The dance at the school gym ended at 9:30 p.m. Shadow reported that a neighbor had spotted a white van with a broken antenna and a crumpled bumper cruising the neighborhood about that time. Less than 90 minutes later, a camera he had posted from a window at the Border Motel recorded a white van fitting that description crossing the border to Mexico. Shadow 28 had two teenage daughters. He couldn't let himself think about what those missing girls were going through right now. He had to stay focused to get them back safely. And, there was more. Two DEA agents had gone missing forty-eight hours earlier. The JTF-6 Operation taking place must be putting unrelenting pressure on the sector. "Thank God for the U.S. Marines," he said to himself.

He rubbed his eyes and refocused, catching a blur of kids racing across the rough streets below. He'd been staring at the same 180-degree view for the past hour after seventy-two hours in the field, and a long night working the streets would follow. He felt as if cotton filled his mouth. Fortunately, he still had beers. A half-smile crossed his weathered, unshaven face. He stretched to full height, dropped the shoulder-holstered 9 mm over the back of the room's lone rickety chair, and bee-lined it to the wheezing 70's-era Frigidaire. His Aunt Susan had the same model and he had fond childhood memories of sticking his head inside its cool interior on hot summer days in Enid. He reached in and grabbed two beers by their necks before closing the door with a soft soccer kick. Settling onto the room's funky couch, he swapped one beer for his laptop, and tipped the other bottle. The small chunks of ice that had formed in the beer soothed the inside of his mouth. After a long swallow, he activated the computer's decryption software with a password and a several keystrokes. An hour-old message from Shadow 6 flashed across his screen.

Begin Message. As Shadow anticipated suspect female arrived at ISIS checkpoint in Northern Syria 72 hours prior to kidnapping in question. Suspect female is high level 'messenger' who traveled "Underground Railroad" from Vera Cruz MX to Syrian border. Major concerns at Shadow: non-rank and file members can travel intercontinental network. Shadow 2 concurs. Shadow 2 believes meeting in Syria is preemptive action to begin funnel of human merchandise through covert network. Unknown at this time is 'intent' of end game. Verify messenger's arrival has to do with recent Phoenix kidnappings and put eyes on the missing girls. End Message.

He slugged down the rest of the first beer, then moved his weary frame and his laptop to the hotel room's queen mattress and stretched out, clueless of the dark blue Dodge Charger nosing its way to the hotel's front entrance. The ancient bedsprings squeaked mercilessly. As he drifted into sleep, Shadow 28 mused about disturbing the neighbors who were local prostitutes with their johns.

• • •

Three men armed with assault styled shotguns exited the Charger carrying Federales Insignia. To clear a parking spot in front of the El Tigre Hotel, the driver used the reinforced front bumper to smack a 1980's vintage Honda scooter beneath a Chevy van. One of the men carried a small kit containing an endoscope camera and lock picking utensils. He stayed a few feet behind the other two. The hotel proprietor turned from folding towels as his dark eyes focused briefly at the stack of hundred dollar bills, then over to the three men wearing black Federales' uniforms holding sawed off shotgun's pistol grips by their side.

"Si, Jefe, segunda planta, A-Dos," the proprietor whispered, gesturing overhead. Barely interrupting his work rhythm, the short fat man easily stuffed the bills into his pants before he returned to folding towels and minding his own business.

The three men climbed the wooden staircase with ease to the second floor, where they turned into the narrow hallway and walked as softly as if rice paper covered the linoleum floor.

• • •

Unbeknownst to the sleeping Steve, as the Cartel's thugs broke down the door of his room at the El Tigre Hotel, an important email came in; it read- Exit operating area immediately. Mission compromised. End message.

Monday 1130; Richardson TX

Six rings into the call, Hap's finger moved to disconnect when he at last heard LtCol Chuck "Tuna Man" Warden's groggy voice.

"Sorry about that XO," his Commanding Officer (CO) said. "Guess I fell back to sleep after leaving the message with Peggy."

"Hear you, Boss." Hap knew Warden flew Boeing 787s on international routes for a major airline, so jet lag was a constant. "Sorry I couldn't take your call. Board meeting. Peg thought best not to interrupt." Hap pulled from his mug, savoring the flavor. "What's going on with the mission?"

Warden paused. "Everything started out normal but as the mission progresses; things are getting, well…weird."

Hap rocked forward splashing coffee from the half-empty mug on the desk, and then eased back. "Never heard you use that word before."

"Well let me say it again. Weird. For the past few nights, we've had to drive cartel spotters from the ridges to place our OPs. Bastards are getting bold."

"Any fire exchanged?"

"Nope. Bad guys vanished into the night. Feds take the position, no harm, no foul. You know the ground element is unarmed except unit leaders have a magazine of 9mm. Air element has a magazine of 9mm for our side arms."

"Isn't this par for the course?"

"You say that, but the grunts found a prayer rug at one of the bad guy's OPs."

"Did Big Alabama leave it behind?" Hap asked, attempting to inject levity into an otherwise serious conversation. Hap tended to bring humor to any situation; Marines knew if LtCol Stoner wasn't joking around and laughing, they had better get the hell out of the way.

"I'm serious about this one, Hap. I don't like it."

"What about the bureaucrats? What are they saying?"

"Same old song, different verse. The senior official imbedded with us keeps vomiting about the *Posse Comitatus Act* and how if we engage, our jarhead asses are going to jail. There was a moment when I thought the Ambassador was going to level the dork."

"Good old Ambassador," Hap said, honoring the best Cobra pilot he had had the privilege of flying with in the Marine Corps. A fellow Texan as well, the Ambassador carried a black belt in karate and he wasn't half bad in judo.

Tuna Man continued, "Captain Simmons reported he believes he's on the trail of the rag heads."

"That wouldn't be Jonathan Simmons would it?"

"Yes, it is. Force Recon. Call sign 'Jethro,' inherited from his dad."

"I'll be damned," Hap said. "Knew he went in, but scuttlebutt had him resigning after meeting his commitment."

"He works with Force Recon Marines out of San Antonio. Regarding the bureaucrats, the Marines are not buying into their crap."

While Hap listened intently, the left side of his brain kicked in: Captain Simmons would make his father proud.

Considering the constraints of JTF-6 missions, *Posse Comitatus* acted as handcuffs for all the right reasons. The law limits the power of the Federal Government to enforce state law passed in 1878 at the end of Reconstruction. Congress updated it in 1981.

"Hear you loud and clear, Boss. Don't hesitate to contact me if anything changes. Peg will pass your calls through regardless of what I'm doing. Fly Safe! Semper Fi."

"Hey, Hap…before you hang up can I make a request?"

Hap leaned forward. "You know better than that. What are you needing, Boss?" No response. "Boss, you there?"

"Ammo. 5.56mm and 9mm."

"Son…of…a…bitch, Tuna Man. Did I hear you right? You do know what you're asking?"

"Hap, Jethro is chasing God knows who with 30-round mags full of ammo bought in Yuma. The boys all piled into a van for the road trip to buy ammo from Cabella's. I purchased a few boxes of 5.56 without telling anyone. Feds want our guys armed with only radios, flare guns, and a few rounds of 9mm. Fuck sticks even talked about giving our ground element Tasers."

Hap chuckled in a pissed off way. "May as well be shooting bean bags at the sons of bitches. How many rounds?"

"As much as you can get your hands on. Somebody might get hurt. I can feel it."

"*Semper Fi*, Boss." Resting the receiver into its cradle, Hap replayed his Commanding Officer's words. What in the hell was going on in the Imperial Valley? The Feds' activity was business as usual; fucked up with no accountability. After a moment, no smile on his face, he reached over to punch the intercom. "Peg, clear Hollywood's and my calendar for tomorrow. Inform Crash of our change of plans. We'll be heading out a day early."

4

Tuesday 1100; El Centro Municipal Airport CA

Hap Stoner walked off the Citation's bottom step at 1100, leaving John Hancock to complete the shutdown checklist. The Auxiliary Power Unit began winding down as a tug came to a stop off the sleek corporate commuter's rounded nose to tow the plane into the facility's lone hangar. Belonging to the airfield's Fixed Base Operations line crew, the tug bore the insignia of the Imperial County Airport. The young, sandy-haired driver jumped off the tractor, preparing to attach the tow bar to 421Vector Data's nose wheel. Bent over the nose wheel, the lineman looked sideways at Hap, asking, "How long will you be with us?"

Hap waited for the screech of the APU to wind down. "No more than two weeks. Top her off and put her in the barn." The kid looked to be working his way through college. Hap pulled a couple of fifties from his wallet and transferred them to the back pocket of his jeans.

"Let me guess. You flew in from Texas."

"That obvious, huh?"

"Only thing missing to go with those fine boots is the Stetson. The 421VD was on the board to arrive tomorrow, so you caught us off guard. Lucky we had hangar space."

Hap was pretty sure he told Peg to inform the FBO of their early arrival. That's OK, he thought. She is a busy woman. "I probably dropped the ball, forgot to tell my secretary to call ahead."

"Probably called and whoever took the message didn't change the board, most likely written on a sticky buried under a stack of fuel chits."

Hap grinned, watching the kid move from the nose wheel to the task of attaching the tow bar to the tug. No doubt about it, the kid knew what he was doing. "You working your way through school?"

"Yes, Sir," the kid said, as a flush crept across his cheeks. "Between the line and my flight instructing, I'm able to make my own way." Clearing his throat, he continued, "I sleep in the maintenance hangar."

Hap liked the story. There had to be more. "Parents not helping?"

The kid played with the grimy sleeves of his shirt. "I spent my whole life between foster homes and orphanages."

"Like flying?" Hap asked vectoring away from the direction the conversation was taking.

The kid's eyes brightened. "Want to fly for the Navy one day. Land on Carriers. I know I can do it."

Hap shook his head. He'd have to reform this one. "I could think of better services, son. Would you want to sit right seat in 421VD? It would be a paying job."

Stepping back in surprise, the kid reached out with his right hand.

Hap handed him a business card wrapped in the twin fifties. "Hap Stoner. The turd behind the controls is John Hancock." John stepped off the stair with an ear-to-ear smile.

"Billy Wayne Fritch." The kid quickly stuffed the bills into the front pocket of his jeans.

John reached across Hap to greet their new friend.

"Billy," Hap said. "If it's okay with you, I'm going to call you BW." With that blond hair touching his shoulders and those sparkling blue eyes, Hap thought the kid could be the spitting image of Chuck Norris if you went back about twenty years.

"BW's just fine, Sir," he nodded, letting a smile peek out. "But I still want to go to college."

Hap turned his head to frown at John. "Frigging squids." Turning back, he said, "BW, not only will you go to school, I will put this size thirteen up your ass if you don't."

BW eyed the polished leather gems. "Don't worry, Mr. Stoner. And I'll graduate, too."

"Call me Hap, BW."

"Yes, Sir!"

"I may need you to do me a favor," Hap said, thinking of the ammo in back. "There are wooden crates in the luggage hold. If you get a call from me, I'll want you to place them on the tarmac. They're heavy, but you're big enough to move them. You have any problem with that?"

"No Sir—I mean, yes, Sir, if it's drugs or something."

"No drugs," Hap said.

The kid handed Hap a card with the FBO logo on the front, his cell phone number penciled in on the back.

"No matter what time of night BW, U.S. Marine lives may be at stake."

"Sir?"

Hap pierced him with his deep blue eyes as he handed BW his United States Marine Corps Reserve business card.

Looking down to read the card, the kid's head moved

back and forth just slightly. Now he met Hap's gaze squarely, "Anytime day or night, Sir. Just give me a call!"

Hap drove the Plymouth Voyager allowing John to grab a fighter nap for the half-hour trip to join the Nomads of HMLA 767.

5

Tuesday 1135; Naval Air Facility El Centro CA

Hap slowed as he approached the front gate. A Petty Officer Second Class extended his arm and stepped into the center of the road. He wore the Navy's sharp working uniform, predominantly blue mixed with some gray, based on the Marine Corps' combat utility uniform.

As Hap braked to a stop, the petty officer stepped around to the driver's window. He kept his right hand near his sidearm.

"May I see your ID, Sir?" He accepted Hap's ID, his right hand still hovering near the pistol grip.

All business, Hap thought with a slight nod of approval.

After a close examination, the officer returned the ID to Hap, came to attention and snapped off a sharp salute.

Hap nodded. "Carry on."

Hap turned east at the Package Store, a small building the size of a 7/11 convenience market, which served as the Base Liquor Store. Extending for three hundred feet, the street then emptied into a mostly vacant parking lot adjacent to the Nomad flight line. Pulling into a spot with a metal sign marked HMLA XO 767, Hap exited the car, leaving it running with the keys in the ignition so Hollywood's face wouldn't melt to the passenger window. He was snoring like a baby and enjoying the air conditioning.

Hap placed the strap of his laptop's carrying case high on his shoulder. He covered the thirty feet to the guard shack in seconds thanks to his long-legged Texas stride. Shoulders pulled back and down, chest out, spine taut, and a grin that grew wider with each step that brought him closer to the Nomad flight line.

A guard shack the size of an east Texas two-holer outhouse was all that separated LtCol Hap Stoner from his civilian career. The Naval Air Facility was located in the heart of Southern California's Imperial Valley. A two-hour ride west landed the driver in San Diego, while Yuma, Arizona, was a one-hour drive to the east. Remote and yet allowing close proximity to the Mexican border, those specs were the basis for 4th MAW orders directing HMLA 767 to proceed directly to El Centro. Years of hard work by laborers, along with the miracles of irrigation, had transformed the city of El Centro and the surrounding desert into an oasis. Locals braved the sizzling temperatures for four months, the price paid for sharing ideal weather from fall through spring with snow-birds and military retirees. Before Mother Nature had time to break the century mark on the thermometer, I-8 was jammed with RV's heading east out of town.

Hap approached the gate, anticipating the menacing figure that stepped out of the guard shack. The MP, obviously seasoned in multiple tours in the war against terror, wore combat fatigues, 782-web gear, and a M16-A2 rifle slung across his shoulder. Chevrons attached to each collar indicated a Corporal in the U.S. Marines. At that moment, a smile broke out on his weathered face. "This is a restricted area; may I see some form of military I.D."

"No problem, Corporal." Hap reached into the front pocket of his Levis, retrieving his wallet. Fumbling briefly with its contents, he pulled out the pink Military Identification Card. Picture side up—denoting the rank of LtCol in the United States Marine Reserve—he handed it to the Marine. The Marine's gaze went from the card to Hap's angular mug. "Are you with the Marines on the line, Sir?"

"Yes, I am. If by chance a Marine gets out of the car parked over there…" Hap tipped his head back in the direction he'd come. "If he comes looking for me, let him know I'm in the Ops shop."

Satisfied, the Marine nodded, handing the I.D. card back to Hap with a smart salute. Hap returned the nod, adjusted the strap onto his right shoulder, and stepped onto the tarmac. Walking between parked AH-1W and UH-1N helicopters was like walking home, a breath of fresh air. Like worker ants, mechanics moved around and on top of the helos, checking off maintenance gripes from the previous night's launch. Missing a launch time is as bad as not launching at all in the U.S. Marines Corps aviation community. Tonight's launch would be a max effort so the day crew would be a stay crew until they signed off all the aircraft "clear to fly."

He peered into the partially opened hangar doors. Two Marine ordnance men, both grinning, clad in blue overalls approached at a fast-paced strut. The 80-pound M2-.50-caliber machine guns digging into their shoulders could not dampen the bounce and energy of their stride.

"Afternoon, Colonel," they said in unison, as they made their way to the UH-1N Huey helicopters parked down the line. Their job: to slap the guns into saddles located on either side of the aircraft. A tug pulling a string of trailers loaded with pods of 2.75-inch rockets raced around the corner of the hangar, steering toward the same section of aircraft. Eighteen months earlier the identical twins loaded the unit's Hueys and Cobras for missions in Iraq. The year before that, the unit had deployed for 12 months in Afghanistan.

The WWII era hangar would have made the Wright Brothers envious and an Air Force Pilot cry in his beer. Originally built to house propeller pursuit planes later called fighters, the Marines considered themselves fortunate to warrant a space like this. LtCol Warden—Tuna Man—had passed up deploying to Twenty-nine Palms Expeditionary Air Field, lobbying instead to operate in the kinder and gentler environment christened El Centro.

Twenty-nine Palms was a desolate training facility located in the Mojave Desert. Hotter than hell in the summer, the desert winters were just as brutal to the Nomad Marines working around the clock on the Expeditionary Fields tarmac. Ninety percent of the pilots and enlisted personnel served in Iraq and Afghanistan, making the unit very seasoned. Warden insisted that the unit would have gained little by adding another thirty days in Twenty-nine Palms. To a man, a Marine Reservist is the country's citizen soldier. Professionals in their civilian pursuits, many of the enlisted were college students, standby warriors who put it all on the line in both Iraq and Afghanistan. The Marines under LtCol Warden's command trained on the edge, and when called on, were unbreakable in combat. Another mission, another set of orders stamped JTF-6 meant damn good training would follow. Knowing the stakes, these guys gave it their all, every deployment.

Joint Task Force-6 was the designated code name for Anti-Drug and Illegal Immigration. Unsaid, except to the Command element, was that the military presence generated intelligence for the ongoing war against Islamic Fascism. Under Army Command housed at Fort Bliss, Texas, a small group existed to support units selected for JTF-6 operations all over the globe.

* * *

Hap entered the hangar steering toward a small group of pilots clothed in green Nomex flight suits and sipping steaming cups of coffee. Raising his brows, he announced, "Boys, boys, boys, kind of late in the afternoon to be drinking Joe."

"Attention on deck," Major Rory Hammer barked sarcastically. Locking arms to his side, hot coffee launched from his squadron mug, spattering across Hap's creased Levis. Major Turner and Captain Parks followed Major Hammer's gesture—but when they assumed the position of attention they managed fortunately, to keep what was left of the steaming brew inside their mugs.

"Who are you jarheads trying to kid," Hap retorted sarcastically. Looking around at their closely shaven faces he couldn't help but notice solemn expressions. "Who died?" he asked, thinking about the many combat missions he'd flown with these guys. He had become familiar with their facial expressions brought on by stress. He reached out his hand, and Captain Arturo Parks, call sign "Meat," firmly grasped it. Major Rory Hammer gave Hap a slap on the back, knocking the laptop strap off his shoulder. Extending his elbow, Hap trapped the strap just before the $1500 computer ended up in pieces on the hangar floor.

"Welcome to hell, XO." Major Hammer, call sign "Spanky," said. "Did you bring your sticks?"

"Unless Hollywood snuck my bag in with the luggage, negative."

Major Bobby Turner, call sign "Waco," stroked his salt and pepper hair as if he were the reincarnation of Elvis Presley. "By the looks of it XO, I won't have to be thinking about a haircut before we go home."

"Don't hold your breath, Waco; I want you with me when I make the walk of shame."

"Yes, Sir," Waco replied. Invariably, Major Turner was always the one officer other than himself, hounded about the length of his hair. By the time the CO instructed him to advise Waco that it was time to get a haircut, the Marine Aviator was overdue at the barber by at least a week. LtCol Warden was one of most liberal of the commanding officers Hap had served under when it came to hair length. He wore his hair in a crew cut, and his pilots knew not to push their luck because the man had his limits.

When it came to flying and tactics, every officer and enlisted Marine knew that LtCols Warden and Stoner trained hard and expected those within the command do the same. The word was out within the unit; any slacker gets nailed to the wall the first time they visit their shared office. A second meeting and the citizen Marine was well on his way to becoming a full-time citizen. Filling out the requisite paperwork needed for dismissal from the unit took less time than finishing four-finger scotch-rocks at Happy Hour. Nothing personal, the U.S. Citizens making up HMLA 767 were just dead serious when it came to their jobs as Marines.

* * *

When strapped into the aircraft Hap's good nature changed. He became an ever-hungry predator stalking prey. Nothing would stand in his way, except common sense and the realization that he would not ask any one of his Marines to go where he would not lead.

Hap looked over to Spanky, the squadron's Operations Officer, whose tenacity served him in the field and in civilian life. He was one of the Marines' top shooters in Iraqi Freedom as well as being a financial planning executive for Citibank. The man remained downright dogged.

"Hey Spanky, where's the boss?"

Spanky looked up from his cell phone. "Probably in his office, sleeping. By the way, it is your office, too. S4 dropped off a cot several days ago. Between events on the ground and being on the schedule tonight, he sleepwalks between office, ready room, and cockpit. Doesn't bother going to the "Q" except to shower and that's only because I complained he was beginning to stink up the ready room."

Hap nodded, thinking that whatever was going on, you'd never know it by watching the news. "I'll let him sleep."

"Squadron Intelligence Section received word you would arrive early so they've worked up a brief."

"Let's do it now." Hap looked around at the officers. "Spanky, Waco, Meat, and Hollywood's asses can join mine."

Major Hammer nodded and dropped the phone into his right breast pocket. "Fifteen minutes soon enough, XO?"

Hap nodded, already moving toward the ready room. "Send somebody out to my car, should be the only car with its engine running in the parking lot. Hollywood is sleeping like a baby in the passenger seat."

The Squadron Intelligence officer sitting on a bench of stacked MRE cases stared into his coffee and asked, "You going to pay off your gambling debts this trip, Hap?"

Showing his social finger, Hap said, "Meat, go wake up Hollywood and take him a Coke."

Captain Arturo Parks gave a thumbs-up. The unit's Intelligence and Tactics officer stopped at the Coke machine, plunking in a fist full of quarters. A can of Coke rattled down the chute just as Spanky passed by on his way to the ready room; he reached in and commandeered the icy can. "Thought Hap would want a Coke," he said, not bothering to look back.

Meat made a face. "XO is on 'Paleo,' Dip-shit."

Spanky turned and offered up a one-fingered salute with the hand holding the soda. "I'm not on 'Paleo'! Thanks, Meat!"

Grumbling, Meat fumbled in his breast pocket for more change, "You're welcome, Asshole."

6

Tuesday 1145; Naval Air Facility El Centro CA

Entering the ready room, Hap eased himself back in the wooden lounge chair with XO spray-painted on the backrest. He took a deep breath, closing his eyes for a second. Just as quickly, he blinked them open to see Spanky rounding the corner holding up a glistening can of cold soda. Hap waved him off. "You know I don't drink that shit."

Spanky shrugged and popped open the can. "I didn't think so, XO."

Nothing more than an abandoned maintenance room from an earlier time, now the ready room held an assorted mix of chairs and metal cruise boxes set neatly in four rows of six, lining one wall of the dusty room. A path between chairs and boxes ran front to back. The wooden walls screamed out for a coat of paint, with a dry-erase board screwed into the wall at the front of the room. A ready room could be a tent with a sand floor, but it was always home for a Marine Aviator.

Hap flashed back to the day he first crossed paths with Spanky. It was between HMLA 767 deployments to Iraq and Afghanistan, the night before Spanky's formal interview, and Hap threw back cocktails in the All Ranks Club in Marine Aviator fashion. He couldn't help but notice the Marine in Summer Service "C's" uniform adorned with rows of ribbons.

The Marine was a beast, drinking like a sailor, talking it up at the bar with a pair of attractive Navy nurses.

"Hey, 'Waaar Heeero'," Hap called out. What happened next made the following day's interview a formality. Introducing himself, Hap's offered hand met a firmer handshake. Minutes passed while the men discussed where their paths might have crossed. Never in their brief conversation did Spanky let on that he would be interviewing for a position, nor did Hap let him know he would be part of the decision-making process to allow or disallow the other man to join the NOMADS.

When Hap bumped a polished flight boot against the Marine's Corfam shoes, he glanced down to inspect the damage. The Marine officer looked straight ahead. Testicles protruded from the aviator's zipper like rooster waffles, although the zipper was not taut enough to rupture him. Senior officers scorned the act of "ball walking," even though some had taken "the walk" themselves during their formidable "Lieutenant Years." Belly laughing, Hap blew a mouth full of beer all over Spanky's crisp uniform. Having already indulged in a couple of toddies too many, Spanky thought it best to retreat to the BOQ to preserve his uniform for the next morning's interview and grab some shut eye.

"Take your seats, gents." Hap said. "Please don't rip a seam out your flight suit in the process." Spanky grabbed the empty chair to the left of Hap's wooden lounge chair.

"S2," Spanky barked, the words being generated somewhere from within his protruding midsection.

Waco sauntered in, nodding to all. Meat entered the room with a groggy-looking Hollywood in trail. Hollywood sent a screeching sound throughout the room as he slid a metal chair across the floor.

Spanky yelped, Meat cringed. Hap looked straight ahead.

"Now why did you have to go and do that, Hollywood?" Meat asked, shaking off the noise like a dog shaking off a wet pelt. "Of all the things you could have done, you had to go and do that. Try farting next time."

Hollywood leaned back, his grin spreading cheek to cheek. "You woke me up from what was about to become a Grade-A wet-dream."

Meat made his way to the front of the room and ran his fingernails along an ancient blackboard mounted on one of the sidewalls. Spanky slid further down into his chair grimacing as if gut-shot, both hands raised to cover his ears.

Rubbing his slightly out-of-reg mustache with the thumb and forefinger of his left hand, Hap waved off the stunt, gesturing with his right. "One more stunt like that will get you two days in the penalty box, Captain."

The "penalty box" that Hap was referring to was the squadron's Operations Duty Officer position, manned from the time the first crew was briefed until the "last plane was on deck," or LPOD. As important as the job was for aircrews and command, the poor bastard that stood that generally 16-hour watch was normally bored to tears. Time in the penalty box typically precluded the ODO from joining the boys lucky enough to land earlier in the evening for drinks at the bar. The post had to stay manned until LPOD, which during JTF-6 operations was usually around 0300 hours.

"Anything but that, Skipper," Meat replied, jokingly. But his grin evaporated as fast as it appeared when he caught a quick glimpse of Hap's glaring blue eyes.

"Get on with the brief," Hap said.

"How about it," Spanky parroted.

As if someone had just kicked him in the balls, Meat did a quick quarter-turn to the left directing a red beam at a point on the chart designated A3, or in military jargon "Alpha 3."

The chart denoting the operational area was divided into six sectors, encompassing all the area west of Yuma, Arizona, to San Diego, California, along the southern boundary, while a line due east from Los Angeles southeast to the northern edge of the Salton Sea delineated the northern boundary. Each sector had an alpha designator accompanied by a numerical value placed to the right of the letter identifier. Months earlier, staff planners at JTF-6 Headquarters designated the alpha points based on prominent terrain features, which usually meant the points overlooked high density and illegal human traffic crossing points along the border. Because both ground and air assets used the sectors and alpha designators as control points, civilian assets working with military assets could quickly respond to points of incursion when Nomad crews called them in. Those crews might be in the air or might be Marine grunts living in the dirt.

"Sir, Alpha 3 had a minor incident last night, though local enforcement agencies do not foresee—"

"Stop it right there, Meat," Hap cut in. "Enlighten me on this minor incident."

"*Reader's Digest* version?" Meat asked.

Hap nodded. "Cut to the chase and just give me the meat and potatoes."

"Three Observation Points operate in Alpha Sector. Each outpost is in good hands, manned by Marine Force Recon assets. We discussed the change of command that occurred within the cartel. Also, two DEA agents have been reported missing." Meat flashed the red beam and quickly bounced the light around to the three small triangles labeled within Alpha Sector. "Scout vehicles approached the border from the Mexican side at Alpha 3. The water is roughly knee-deep with a rocky bottom allowing the vehicles to cross the border with little difficulty. The vehicles were observed crossing the river and pushed to within 100 meters of our southernmost OP." Meat circled the light around the OP, and then shifted to an old miners' trail that ran from the stream into the mountains on a north-south line.

"The vehicles—a recent model Suburban and an F-50 4x4 with a heavy weapon mounted on a pedestal—rolled across to rendezvous with a panel truck from the American side." Meat's voice had deepened and he sounded grim. "We called in LEA as individuals exited the vehicles. They kept a man behind the heavy weapon at all times and we reported this to LEA as well. Crates from the American truck were loaded into the Suburban and the 4x4—all the while under cover of the heavy weapon. After 15 to 20 minutes all vehicles retrograded from where they came."

Hap's mouth creased into a frown. "I didn't read about the incident in the paper this morning. Did LEA attempt an intervention?"

Meat shook his head. "As far as the local law enforcement agencies, Feds, and now the DOD are concerned, the incident never occurred."

Hap rubbed his chin back and forth with the fingers of his right hand. "So if I understand you correctly, this operation isn't really taking place?"

"Don't shoot the messenger, XO, but that appears to be the government's position for now."

"This is way over my head, Meat," Hap said, slowly.

"Colonel," Spanky interrupted in a firm voice. "Damn," he said softly, as he pushed himself up from the chair next to Hap's chair.

. . .

Hap cut his eyes to his operations officer. "Go ahead, Spanky." Meat took his cue and stepped around the Operations Officer to grab the empty chair. Spanky strolled to the podium.

"Damn it, Colonel, the mission sucks. It's as if the government wants to demonstrate effort. It appears we're the proverbial check in the box, nothing more, nothing less."

"Hell, Major, tell me something I don't already know." Hap replied. "The boss has said as much, but he and I hadn't talked about last night's flights."

"Sir, it's much different this time around, and it revolves around three critical items. We have choked the border to such a point that very little is moving within the Op area. The druggies have recently replaced their head operations man in Calexico and are not paying the mules. Desperation is beginning to set in. From our vantage point we could see groups of people moving south across the border. We think some of them may have been young females being led against their will."

Hap leaned his right elbow precariously on the chair's rickety armrest. He found himself twisting his out-of-reg mustache again. "I can understand the border situation, but how do we know the operations person has PCS'd out of

Calexico, and please expound on desperation theories." PCS, a term used by both the Marine and the Navy side of the house meant that a person has received a Permanent Change of Station. Or, to put it in layman's terms, a transfer.

"Sir, the operations person we worked against for the last year was Miguel Moya. Mr. Moya was not PCS'd out of Calexico, he was offed. The Mexican Military found his headless corpse a few miles outside of Mexicali. CIA believes they capped the piece of crap because he disapproved of the Middle Eastern ties that the various cartels have established. Apparently, Mr. Moya was showing a tad bit of nationalism and paid for it with his life."

Hap made a mental note to reach out to his Shadow Services contact, "Continue."

"We have no confirmation that any Middle Eastern personnel are operating in our sector, although Captain Simmons came across a prayer rug south of Bravo 6," Spanky said. "The American bureaucrats haven't been made privy that Captain Simmons broke up the four-man team and left two Marines to man their post atop Bravo 6. They are now trailing the contact with ammunition Warden purchased."

Hap nodded. "The boss told me about the ammo purchase. Continue."

"It is only my opinion, Colonel, but if we do not clear out of the area soon, somebody is going to get hurt. For the past week, I've seen vehicles gathering on the Mexican side of the border, and damn, it seems all the trucks have some form of heavy weapon mounted for all to see. Each had a 14.5mm pedestal mounted machine gun with a belt of ammo hanging from the feeding chamber. One night there was only one, but now there are three and I have it all on disk."

Hap raised his hand to silence Spanky and turned to Meat. "So, what about the heavy weapons, Meat?"

Meat chose his words carefully. "Sir, I have witnessed the vehicles and just like Spanky said, we have it on the FLIR disks. We turn the disk over to the LEA's and we'll never see or hear of it again. This bullshit is frustrating the hell out of the boss. There is no mention, much less discussion between S2 and the LEA Intelligence Section. If I didn't know better, I would think that we have two fighters squared off in the center of the ring. One of the fighters began jabbing before the bell. The other fighter has to stand and take the punches. It's as if the judges mandated the other fighter neutered."

Hap turned his gaze to Spanky. "Do you concur with Meat?"

"Not only do I concur, I believe the neutered fighter has both arms tied behind his back."

"I guess you are referring to the good guys?" Hap asked.

"Yes, Sir, and I don't like going into a fight with nothing on board the aircraft except a damn 9mm and two magazines of ammunition in my pocket. I purchased one of the magazines and its ammo. The heavy weapons mounted on the trucks were 14.5mm. My experience tells me the guns were not mounted to show off to the local populace." Spanky turned slowly and placed his forefinger on B6. "And this is where Meat and I believe the next incident, or should I say the 'big push,' will occur."

Hap raised out of his chair and focused on the mountainous terrain located around Bravo 6. "I am not going to question the logic of my staff in that the incident at Alpha 3 was a mere demonstration, but why Bravo 6? Hell, there are a hundred or more crossing areas in our AO." AO was military jargon for Area of Operations.

Meat leaned back in his chair, balancing on the back two legs with his arms crossed. "Sir, I have a disk from last night that I think you might want to see. Since all of mine and the Ops O's DVDs were never returned by LEA, I thought it best to keep this one for you to see."

"Well, then, let's see it." Hap asked.

Meat let the chair fall forward, pointing a clicker to the TV with the DVD player sitting on top. "Spanky has already seen it."

"Better than Debbie does Dallas, Ops O?" Hap asked attempting lighten the mood in the room.

"Sensitive material," Spanky cut in. "The boss was flying with Meat when the film was shot. I was with Phantom as their Dash 2."

Hap was the picture of relaxation, his sharp blue eyes, and thin lips revealing nothing of his inner state. His first active duty CO told him that the active Marine Corps could not handle his adventurous and entrepreneurial spirit. The words remained engrained in his mind. "Hell, Hap, what the Marine Corps wants with folks like you is to wrap you up in a mausoleum and save you for the next war." The CO's comments did not make him happy back then, but ten years later, they suited him just fine. He was ready for action. "Clear the room, gentleman."

Hap waited through the screeching noise of steel chair legs scraping against cement as the pilots pushed them aside and made their way to the door. Meat stood by until Waco and Hollywood left the room, then closed and locked the door.

Spanky picked up the remote from the podium and pointed it to towards the DVD player. He hit the power button. "Lights, Meat."

Meat hit the light switch and waited the few seconds for the screen on the TV to cast enough light around the room so he could find a chair next to Hap. Hap watched the numbers on the top left hand corner of the screen scroll through as Spanky fast-forwarded the film.

"436, Meat?" Spanky asked.

"That's correct, Ops O," Meat replied.

Hap watched in silence as four sets of headlights appeared on the disk well inside the Mexican side of the border pushing north, following a heavily used paved road frequented by drug traffickers. Hap could detect the Cobra positioned northwest of the target. The range finder on the screen displayed 6700 meters.

"Is this why the disk wasn't turned over to the feds?" Hap asked, not noticing that no one answered his question.

The outline of the vehicles appeared black on the screen, with the area beneath each vehicle's hood emitting a white glow from engine heat. With a flick of a switch inside the cockpit, the front-seater could convert the white heat to black heat, and the screen jumped from white to black heat a couple of times as Spanky's crew attempted to achieve the best resolution for the camera. They settled on white heat, showing the humans inside the vehicles ghostly white and their cigarettes glowing red.

Hap could make out the lead vehicle now, a Suburban, as the caravan approached the intersection to the highway that ran east-west along the U.S. border. Instead of turning, the vehicles rolled straight ahead onto a dirt road that wound its way to the stream. The Suburban slowly approached the river, stopping fifty yards short. A van and two open-bed trucks equipped with mounted weapons and gunners, pulled abreast of the Suburban, switching headlights to bright. The ground in front lit up like a stage. The rangefinder displayed 1250 meters.

"Is the wind coming from the north?" Hap asked.

Meat answered. "Yes, north-north-west and brisk. Unless the sons of bitches were deaf and wearing ear plugs, I'd say they heard us."

Two figures wrestled someone clad in orange scrubs out of the van and pulled him around front until the headlights lit him up. They'd bound his hands behind his back so when his captors slammed him down; he hit the ground with his face. The bigger man started kicking him viciously, the smaller joined in, kicking a half-dozen times. Then, as quickly as they'd started, they stopped and walked back to join the dozen or so spectators now gathered in front of the van. They spent a few minutes drinking and smoking before the bigger man walked back to the prone victim, grabbed him by his hair, and yanked him to his feet. He pulled the man around to where the mob had gathered to enjoy the show, and then kidney punched him to the ground. The dazed and damaged prisoner inched himself slowly to his knees where he wavered.

Suddenly another man emerged from the parting crowd. He wore a hoodie and made a show of his running start to deliver a brutal kick to the prisoner's exposed belly. Crumpling to the ground, the prisoner lay motionless.

Jaw clenched, Hap watched the footage, his lower stomach churning. The man in the hoodie, the leader by his body language, strutted back to the van where he issued orders. His enforcers pulled another bound individual from the van and dragged him by his scalp, pushing him on top of the first prisoner, who lay still. The leader pulled a pistol from his shoulder holster and placed the muzzle hard against the back of the first victim's head. The flash made Hap wince—he knew what would come next. The leader moved to the next victim, killing him with two shots to the back of the head. Hap resisted the urge to look away from the executions; he needed to sear the details to memory. He barely noticed when Spanky stopped the footage and the image froze.

After about half a minute, Hap spoke slowly. "So…do you give the show an academy award?"

"You agree it was all an act in a play for the Marines to see free of charge," Spanky said. "But to what end?" Questions raced through Hap's mind and one took precedence: how many more acts remained before the final scene?

"That's not all, Hap." Meat clicked the remote to play. The leader holstered his gun and pulled a large knife from a sheath. Wrenching the first corpse halfway up to its knees, he sliced into the body's lifeless neck until finally the headless body slumped over. The leader displayed the cranium for the gathered mob. After they'd appreciated his efforts, he turned, deliberately, and looked up toward the sky and the helos. He raised the head in his hands, the way somebody might raise a glass in a toast, and then he swung it like a lunch pail. The screen went dark. It took Hap a moment and then he spoke through gritted teeth.

"Has the boss seen this?"

"Affirmative," Spanky said. "The Group Commander is on his way out to join us. Unless you saw this for yourself, you would never believe it."

"There is a war going on," Hap said.

"The President says the bad guys are on the run and yet we may have just witnessed a terrorist beheading on our border." Meat's voice was rough and low.

"He'd say it was one of the cartels. If I hadn't seen it for myself, I would be inclined to agree."

Meat ejected the DVD and returned it to its case. "Kind of why we haven't turned this over to LEA. Midterms are around the corner."

"Did you notice the gunners manning the trucks stayed behind their mounted weapons the whole time?" asked Spanky.

Spanky switched the lights on, temporarily blinding everyone but Hap who had closed his eyes in anticipation. His vision adjusted quickly enough to see Meat drop the DVD into his ankle panel.

"Did they bury the victims?" Hap asked quietly.

Meat turned to his CO. "No Sir, left them for the buzzards to pick on."

"I want the LEA notified about this so they can coordinate with the Mexican authorities to pick the bodies up."

"Right," Meat nodded.

"And, Captain," Hap said, stopping the Intelligence Officer as he reached the door. "No mention of the disk, okay." It wasn't a question. Snapping his fingers, he reached out with an open palm. "The DVD please."

Meat reached down to retrieve the disk. Handing it to Hap with a nod, he then turned and exited, closing the door behind him. A heavy silence filled the room. Finally, Spanky cleared his throat and said, "So now you know what has been wearing the boss down so hard."

Biting into his lower lip and drawing the faint taste of blood, Hap said, "So the pricks put on a show. The leader used a knife for a beheading. I'm inclined to call this thing off."

"The boss wanted to talk to you about the possibility," Spanky said. "If tonight plays out anything close to last night, then the boss is going to knock it off."

"Something's up and we know it ain't good." Hap took a deep, almost shuddering breath. "I sure as hell agree with the boss, no guarantees about further operations after tonight's launch."

7

Tuesday 1145; Scorpion's Penthouse Juarez, MX

Gregorio Moya, aka Scorpion, awoke at his customary time, a few minutes before noon. The daughter of one of the maids slept peacefully beside him, but he barely allowed himself a glance. This was no day to get distracted, not with this afternoon's meeting with Salman Abdullah bin Al Saud "El Maestro" and an unknown guest. Sticking to his daily routine, he rolled from the bed using his hands to cushion the fall. Slowly he pushed his body up into a rigid plank position and he began to crank out pushups, determined not to stop before completing one hundred fifty.

Thirty-one, thirty-two, thirty-three—

With legs and back in a straight line, chin raised and eyes fixed forward, the 37-year-old executed the same number of reps at the same pace he'd drilled as a young enlisted Marine at Paris Island, South Carolina. Even after twenty-one years, the bitter taste remained; They'd tossed him out of boot camp after two weeks. He replayed it in his mind. *Sure I got caught rifling through a Marine's footlocker two racks over, so what? Frigging jarhead owed me money. Anybody owes me pays up, one way or another. But, that DI and I didn't see eye to eye.*

*Seventy-five, seventy-six, seventy-seven—*his body still hadn't broken a sweat.

The 15-year-old on the bed moaned in her sleep and rolled over, revealing her curves beneath the silk sheet. His thoughts moved to her perfect ass and the way she naturally knew how to please a man.

One-hundred-one, one-hundred-two, one-hundred-three—his piston-like biceps pumped with almost perfect precision.

One-hundred-thirty, one-hundred-thirty-one—sweat now beaded on his forehead and he grunted with each rep.

He counted aloud: "One hundred-forty-seven, one-hundred-forty-eight, one-hundred-forty-nine, and one-hundred-fifty."

Coming lithely to one knee, he placed one hand on the side of the bed. Slowly he slid back the sheet, and eased his fingers to the small of her back, slowly, gently guiding his touch down and over the curves of her buttocks. Her soft skin enchanted him, one of the many reasons he preferred young girls. Now, as he moved his fingers in small concentric circles, she began to respond. Still half-asleep, she rolled onto her stomach with a soft murmur and with eyes still closed; she shifted again to face him. He eased himself up onto the bed.

He watched as she placed a small hand to his chest urging him on to his back. Kissing him softly around his neck, she slowly slid her tongue along his chest, continuing down his torso. He closed his eyes, resting the back of one hand against his sweaty forehead, massaging the back of her neck with his other hand. For these few moments, all thoughts of business and the upcoming meeting left his mind.

•   •   •

With the city of Juarez stretched out below him, Scorpion stood on the 15th floor balcony of his condo, sipping a third glass of orange juice. Breakfast was to arrive at 12:30, en punto. The staff knew what any breach of routine would cost them. He ran a finger along the tall-stemmed and highly polished crystal glasses resting on the granite tabletop. Frowning, he flicked away the few specks of barely visible dust between two of the four place settings. Peeking through breaks in the overcast sky, sunlight reflected off the hand-polished silver placed around each fine china plate.

Scorpion, now clad in a white silk robe cut above the knee, took his seat in one of the handcrafted iron chairs. He chose the one that positioned him at an angle to the bulletproofed glass on the balcony but gave him a direct view of his front door and living room. Poring over the latest report, Scorpion was like any other international business executive grinding it out on Wall Street. There was one significant difference, however. He took things personally, taking decisive, sometimes violent actions to reverse trends that chipped away at the bottom line of Black Stone, his business empire.

The oldest of twelve children, Gregorio grew up in a 20' x 20' mud and corrugated metal shack in Juarez's biggest slum, Anapra. The shack's floors were dirt and the toilet was a stinking outhouse used by six families. By the time he turned five, he worked seven days a week selling sodas, Camels, Chiclets, and newspapers while hustling softhearted tourists in town. The two American dollars he gave to his mother each evening after a ten-hour day helped keep food on the table for his siblings. The head count grew almost every year, straining an already impoverished family.

At fourteen, Gregorio attempted to move in on a rival gang's turf, killing one of the gang members in the process. Thinking back, it was the easiest $25 American he ever earned. To get him away from the cartels, his family sent him across the border to the Imperial Valley to live with an uncle and work in the fields. At seventeen, he enlisted in the US Marine Corps with fake papers showing him to be eighteen. He liked the weapons and the regular meals but he hated the pendejo DI and the stupid grunts who took orders like babies. Overall, he lasted just two weeks in the Corps.

Gregorio did not bother to return to the Imperial Valley to pick vegetables. Instead, he returned to the Mexican streets on the bad side of town. And, he never looked back. By the age of twenty-five, he'd earned his Scorpion alias and controlled all of the drug traffic in and around Tijuana. He mounted his competitors' heads atop stakes on the southern edge of town. Word on the street: "Want to stay alive? Don't target Black Stone's business."

Black Stone's intelligence network encompassed Mexican citizens, any age, gender, or status, who liked the protection and gifts offered by Scorpion. Its tentacles seemed to reach around every street corner and down every alley. The network thwarted most attempts to knock off a Black Stone drug deal. The few who were stupid enough to try and actually succeeded never lived long enough to spend the first dollar, and their families never saw another sunrise.

Sipping his café Scorpion perused the report. It was clear the Marines operating in the El Centro sector had overstayed their welcome. Normally operations headed up by Joint Task Force 6 lasted only thirty days; then they would pick up and move to a different sector. Typically, Scorpion shut down the flow of drugs and humans until the Task Force 6 units completed their short deployment and returned to home base. It was a nuisance, but workable.

Now however, Scorpion's informants, operating in the bars of Calexico and El Centro, reported that the Marines' presence was permanent. Scorpion set down the report, jaw clenched.

* * *

Jorge Gore exited the penthouse elevator into the hallway. Walking the thirty paces to the balcony, he balanced a heavy, silver serving tray and dishes bulging with Scorpion's breakfast. He kicked himself for not bringing the cart. Too much on his mind and that could be dangerous.

Each morning, the chefs hired and trained by Jorge prepared a morning feast for two or more. The Scorpion ensured his female guest or guests were seated at the table. Three over easy eggs, four ounces of hash browns, two sausage links, and two slices of Canadian bacon. Jorge always gave everything an extra effort, especially the four slices of wheat toast. He toasted each piece of bread perfectly, and then smothered it with honey butter and finally served the toast on its own piece of china. Jorge's chest felt tight. He knew that one mistake—one extra ounce of hash browns or one punctured egg yolk—meant harsh repercussions, verbal if not physical.

Escorpion Loco, Crazy Scorpion, a tag used by the staff behind Scorpion's back, was earned after the grounds' gardener trimmed the azaleas lower than Scorpion liked. The gardener swore he trimmed them with a ruler every time, but his pleas made no difference to the Crazy Scorpion. Jorge had watched the boss's hammer-like fist smash the gardener's jaw, breaking it after the third punch.

The gardener and his contemporaries knew there was no other job in Mexicali where they could earn $850 American each month. Jorge moved to the table and began to place the Scorpion's meal in a careful constellation: eggs centered perfectly on the plate, toast at ten o'clock, coffee cups at two o'clock, and the small cream pitchers at three o'clock. The guest's plate remained covered to keep it warm.

"Your breakfast, Sir," Jorge said, removing the cylindrical plate cover. Filling the juice glass, he couldn't help but eye the pretty adolescent entering the balcony through the open French doors.

"It appears it's going to be a warm afternoon," he said, attempting to make conversation. Earlier in the morning, he read Scorpion's daily intelligence report end-to-end before sliding it into the manila envelope. Scorpion would not be in the best of moods.

"It's those damn Marines," Scorpion said, his head hovering over the plate taking in the aroma.

"Ah," Jorge said, pulling the chair out for Scorpion's guest. "Weren't you a Marine once?"

"A long time ago, Jorge. I got out of there quick. Sons of bitches couldn't fight their way out of a wet paper bag. Besides, the pay sucked."

Jorge gently pushed in the girl's chair. "Shall I leave the pitcher?" he asked, not wanting the conversation to go any further.

"Yes, and I'll need strong coffee and clean linens for my meeting later this afternoon." Scorpion reached for the fork to dice his eggs into the hash browns. The pupils of his dark eyes dilated as he remembered details of the report. His mind swam in the ocean of ideas. He had to knock the U.S.

Administration on their heels. Doing so would make the fast-talking President order the Marines off the border in fear the U.S. would appear racist to the rest of the world using U.S. Military assets to block immigration. Scorpion picked up his mobile to issue the order.

As Jorge leaned over to remove the cover on the girl's food, he scrutinized Scorpion closely from the corner of his eye. Turning his attention to the girl, he saw she was a fresh face. If she had treated the Scorpion to his liking last night, he would see her again. The girl dug into the scrambled eggs and buttered flour tortilla as if she hadn't eaten a real meal for a week. Perhaps she hadn't.

Seeing an opportunity to excuse himself, Jorge issued a half bow and retreated to the elevator.

Tuesday 1600; Breckenridge, Colorado

Lindblad P. Thomas, known as Blad to his friends, sat behind the kidney-shaped control console in the oversized basement of his Breckenridge, Colorado, home. Four 22-inch status monitors formed a half-moon around his desk, which faced the 8' x 14' video wall. One level below the basement, and guarded by an old bank vault door, all the servers used to run the system rested in a half-dozen computer racks. Behind the desk, two chairs marked either side of the safe-housing backups, passwords, and hardware cryptographic devices. A satellite surrounded on four sides by an eight-foot-long cedar-plank wall, received intelligence, surveillance and reconnaissance information.

At work well before the sun appeared over the Ten-mile Range, he had not slept more than thirty minutes since Shadow 28 failed to check in. As he glanced over his shoulder to grab the coffee pot from the warmer, he noticed a photo from an earlier era. A couple of Marine Corps buddies—the inseparable Hap Stoner and H.D. Simmons, call sign "Jethro"—were immortalized as they leaned over the Kadena Air Force Base Officer Club bar holding up warm shots of gin. Blad couldn't help but smile at the mustaches Marine aviators sported in the photo taken soon after 9/11. Maybe it was because the style was reminiscent of 1980s' porn stars, but for whatever reason, the ladies seemed to migrate to the look. He vowed never to let his crew cut get out-of-reg for more than a couple of days and made a mental note to grab a haircut.

Hap was the youngest of the three men, and tortured Jethro and Blad with his worn out pick up line. With the ladies gathered around their table, he would say calmly, "Ladies…I know you are looking at my small hands. Rest assured my feet are extremely long and wide." The game was over and the ladies were in love. Blad, alone in his office, shook his head and smiled. Hap Stoner had the skinniest feet he had ever seen on any man. They'd all had good times together, Blad thought, but the ending wasn't always happy. Eighteen months after taking the photograph, Simmons died flying a combat mission with Hap in support of operations in Iraqi Freedom. Hap was still flying, acting as Charlie Warden's Exec in HMLA 767.

The unit was currently operating out of El Centro, and Blad was fully aware of the situation brewing along the border in 767's sector. The Shadow agent operating in the Mexicali/Calexico area who had been missing more than a day was taking up most of his time.

One of the four handsets hanging above the safe lit up like a Bat Phone. He returned the picture to the corner of the desk and quickly donned a headset lying on the desk. Recognizing the caller ID, he jacked in his headset to the port above the phone. Flipping the switch to the right of the handset, he said, "What's up, Hap?"

"Drop your cock and put on your socks!" the voice on the other end said.

Blad grinned. He didn't need caller ID to know that voice. "I've seen better excuses for a Marine Cobra pilot than your dead ass."

"Maybe some active duty Cobra pilot, no way would you be referring to a Reserve Cobra pilot," Hap retorted.

"You got me on that one, Hap, how in the hell are you?"

"I was taking a crap when low and behold your ugly mug was on Page One of the *Wall Street Journal* for busting the espionage ring at Langley. Hell, I decided to see if you needed any help spending all your money. At least I don't have to worry about *this* mug on *Time* or *USA Today*. A little liberal for my blood anyway and they have no interest covering a broke dick telephone man."

"The door is always open for you to visit, Hap. And as if you never knew, yes, I will spend some of my hard-earned cash on dinner and a couple of beers and—"

Hap cut him off. "I need some help."

"Now I have heard and seen everything. The great Hap Stoner calling for advice before knowing my billable rate?"

Hap didn't hear the last comment. A five-ton military truck was rumbling slowly across the tarmac of the Naval Air Facility and he was trying to stick his finger in his other ear to keep out the noise.

"There's a critical flash drive arriving at your office scheduled for a 10 a.m. delivery tomorrow morning. Run all your traps now, DEA, FBI, DIA, and Military Circles, and see what's going on in the Calexico/Mexicali area we need to know about," he shouted.

"Just happens I have an agent overdue checking in." Blad didn't try to cover the concern in his tone. "He was operating in the Juarez area, and we expected to hear from him more than 24 hours ago."

"Sorry to hear about the agent, Blad. Hopefully it's nothing more than being shacked up with a hooker." A section of Cobras flew low overhead and in formation, their blades cutting the air—whop, whop, whop.

This time attempting to talk over the helos, Hap shouted, "Run the traps with your contacts also."

Listening intently, Blad nibbled on the last of the eraser attached to the pencil he was using to scribble his notes. There are friends, and then *there are friends*. Blad could count on two hands the guys for whom he would put his life on the line. His friendship with Hap Stoner fell into that category. Hap's tone told him that he was deeply concerned about whatever was in the package. "Where can I reach you if something surfaces?"

"My cell phone is primary. I'm staying at El Centro Q, room 121. You know my email address."

Blad closed his eyes rubbing his temples. "You okay, Hap? Sense you're a tad bit anxious."

"View the footage ASAP, and then you'll understand. Note that the sons of bitches knew full well they were putting on a show for my Marines on each of the incidents. Had the area under full surveillance from both ground and air assets. I do know this is not the end. What I don't know is if this is the end of the beginning, or the beginning of the end."

"Can't comment now, Hap. Hate to be rude, as I would love to chat, but I need to do a little work before your package arrives in the morning." Dropping the call, Blad tossed the headset to the side and began working the keyboard and mouse.

Eight computer systems and the multi-screen, wall-mounted system flickered to life.

Typing "Tequila Sunrise" in the subject line, he tapped the send button. Hopefully, all twenty of his Shadow agents would receive the message regarding Shadow 28's absence. Together, they played a critical part in the intricate and privately owned global intelligence network, headquartered on an island in the southern Caribbean. Upon receipt, each contact knew to check in with Shadow Ops as soon as practical. An exclamation mark trailing the code word would expedite that response. Shadow 28 was solid, a pro, and a master of the trade. He also had a name, Steve Smith, and a family.

Now the waiting began. Families in the U.S. were missing their teenage daughters for over a week, and Shadow was missing an agent. The DEA was missing two of their own and Blad had to ask himself, was all this misery tied together?

9

Wednesday 0300; Bravo 6, Mike Team

Captain Jonathan Simmons USMCR peered through Anvis 6 Night Vision Goggles at an empty desert divided into two countries by the shimmering ribbon of a slow moving stream. On the last half hour of Simmons's watch, his relief, PFC Ball, slept like a baby just outside the two-man fighting-hole. Roughly 30 feet away, the Team's two other members were asleep under a patch of creosote bush a few strides from their fighting-hole. A solid overcast warded off a half moon's glow. West of Bravo 6, San Diego reflected enough light off the overcast to turn the night into a greenish landscape. North and to the West, Staff Sergeant Barton and his four-man team were set up on Bravo 4. The trail they were observing snaked into the mountains dead-ending into Bravo 4's position, south of Interstate 8. As the crow flies, 2500 meters separated the two positions. Travelling the winding trail, the distance turned into a 5000-meter journey.

Headlights from the Mexican side of the border caught Simmons's attention. He didn't need goggles to spot them, roughly 1500 meters away approaching on paved road with their brights on, as if they didn't give a shit who had eyes on them. Sliding his hand along the side of the fighting-hole, he wrapped his palm around the barrel of his M4 rifle. He still couldn't figure out why he remained in Force Recon, having just entered the Seminary in San Antonio. He was called to leave active duty, but he was beginning to realize that he had two callings, both strong. His father seemed to whisper in his ear to stick with the Marines, but for Jonathan there was an equally strong message from the man upstairs. At this moment, he was answering the call of the Marines as he followed the vehicles with his goggles, counting four still across the stream and still moving. This stretch of public road normally had traffic, but he kept his M4 close. If the vehicles continued on their way, he would allow the three Marines stretched out next to their fighting-holes to grab a few more winks of sleep.

"Keep moving, Boys," he whispered, barely blinking through the goggles.

It was a long shot that the vehicles had anything to do with the prayer rugs they came across two nights earlier when they were occupying the OP. He and Ball tracked the owners of the rugs, but the trail went cold after 24 hours. Having only moved back into Bravo 6 at 2200 hours, Captain Simmons did what any Marine leader would do; he sucked it up pulling a five-and-a-half-hour watch. The team needed to recharge their batteries.

The caravan was slowing and the first two vehicles, dark Suburbans, were similar to those used in last night's grisly festivities.

"Show yourselves, A-holes," he whispered.

"Got something?" PFC Ball whispered back, still half asleep, still stretched out on the ground, his head resting on a crushed empty case of MRE's.

"Looks like we got company," Simmons said quietly. The Suburbans were now only one thousand meters from the stream, making good time, and trailed by two more vehicles that looked like small pickup trucks.

Simmons glanced over to the second fighting-hole where LCpl Eddie Schmidt USMCR was awaking from his sleep, but not before pushing half a can of Skoal into the front of his lower lip. Reaming the bottom with a forefinger, Schmidt dropped the empty container into the side panel pocket of his desert fatigues. Simmons shook his head. Schmidt was one hell of a Marine. The situation sucked but he knew Schmidt was considering leaving the Corps after his enlistment was up in the fall. Marines came and Marines exited the Corps, but the one constant was they were always Marines. Schmidt swiped away sweat collecting on his forehead, and whispered to the Marine who'd risen to a low crouch a few feet away.

"Hey Jocko, what's up?"

"Captain says vehicles approaching." LCpl Sands sounded sleepy.

Schmidt palmed a pebble, tossing it at the feet of PFC Albert Ball who seemed to have gone back to sleep fifteen feet away. When it fell short, he picked up another and gently tossed the pebble, which passed to the right of the sleeping Marine. Picking up a handful of small pebbles, he unleashed them in the general direction of PFC Ball shotgun style. One smacked him in the face, and he shot up onto his elbows, the M16-A2 rifle in his hands.

"Get your ass to your position, Ball," Schmidt barked, not bothering to keep his voice down. "There's movement to our front."

Simmons remembered PFC Ball the day he walked into the Reserve Center six months earlier. Having completed his first semester at St. Edwards University in San Antonio, Ball made it clear to everyone during their weekend stints that he contemplated trying Officer Candidate School.

Wiping the sleep out of his swollen eyes, Ball tossed aside the camouflage poncho liner. He rolled into his fighting hole, just as the last vehicle, a half-ton truck, entered the stream and slid under water momentarily.

"What's up, Captain?" Ball asked, sliding next to Simmons.

Simmons remained silent as the vehicles touched the American side. The Marines watched the convoy push up a narrow dirt road passing below the OP, hunkering down a bit lower into their holes as the last two vehicles, both half-ton trucks with mounted heavy weapons, came into sight. A gunner leaned back behind each gun clutching the weapon's twin handgrips.

Three weeks earlier Simmons was studying in the Seminary's Library. Tonight he was clad in desert cammies, face darkened with black cammo paint, about to take part in something that was never part of this JTF 6 mission.

Sands turned towards Simmons's position. "Any contact with Mother?" He spoke firmly, not really concerned about the bad guys in the truck hearing him over the racing engines.

Captain Simmons removed the handset from his ear and directed a beam from his flashlight at the frequency window to ensure he had the proper frequency dialed into the PRC FM radio. "Damn it, Jocko, the son of a bitch is on the fritz," he barked. Emphasizing the urgency of the matter, he slapped PFC Ball's shoulder. "Get another battery and load it. The battery may be dead."

"The battery in it now, I replaced it before turning in," Ball said.

"Damn it, Ball, you better put a battery in this radio before I shove this piece of shit up your ass." Simmons dropped the radio at Ball's feet and ran low out of the fighting-hole to join Sands and Schmidt in their position. Sands and Schmidt were watching the situation develop through their goggles when Sands heard Simmons drop to a knee next to their position. Sands spoke without looking up. "What's up with the radio, Skipper?"

"If I didn't know better, I'd say the frequency is being jammed," Simmons said. "Ball is replacing the battery, and if the new one doesn't work, I'll give the secondary frequency a go." He hesitated before speaking again. "Jocko, we'll use the emergency flares if these Bandits as much as wink and our radio stays down."

"And give away our position?" Sands asked. "Damn it, Captain, have you lost your balls?"

"Use the flares, Jocko," Simmons ordered anxiously. "Bear in mind, if these are the same sons of bitches that put on the horror show last night, I would think they know damn well who and where we are." After a moment's silence, he added, "No knee jerking on my watch. And, let's not forget what happened to the team in Texas. Hell, they thought they were doing the right thing and the Jarheads killed a sheepherder."

Simmons raised the goggles as the lead Surburban came to a sliding stop behind a small stand of trees about one hundred meters in the draw to their front. Within just a few seconds, the second Suburban vanished behind the trees and both vehicles cut their engines.

The two half-tons, with their weapon mounts, were moving west along the U.S. side. Both trucks turned right past the finger the Marines occupied. With no road or trail to travel, the vehicles were moving up the wash. Within two minutes the two half-tons had negotiated the terrain and come to a stop. There was plenty of noise as the occupants of both Suburbans poured out of their vehicles. Moving up the finger, the Bogeys oriented their movement to engage both flanks of the OP. Simmons's jaw went taut. He knew what had happened to the team operating out of the Texas Big Bend area. They would not be repeating history. What Simmons didn't know was that the bad guys the team was trailing had used Satellite phones to report the location of the Marines who had run them off, and would more than likely set up shop on the point.

He lowered his goggles and called out, "You get that damn radio working, Ball. If I didn't know better, I'd say we're about to be in one hell of a firefight. And based on what they put the team leader through in Texas for following rules of engagement, we're going to have to let these guys shoot first."

Simmons moved bent at the hip sprawling back into the fighting hole he shared with Ball, raising a cloud of dust. Ball turned on the radio. A loud squeal emitted from the headset.

"Go to the alternate frequency," Simmons said.

Ball punched in 36.80 into the screen but all they heard was the loud squeal on that frequency as well. The young Marine looked up to see Captain Simmons slamming the handset against the dirt wall.

Simmons's cupped right hand touched his mouth to muffle his voice. "Jocko, they are jamming us; one frequency maybe, but both frequencies? So, the bad guys must have somebody on the inside." Simmons wiped the dirt, cammo, and sweat, from his narrow eyebrows and reached into the side panel of his Alice pack, removing two hand-fired flares. "Schmidt, pull your flares from your pack and stand by."

"Will do," Schmidt called back.

The Marines heard the crunch of shale and sliding rock as the bad guys moved up the hill toward their position.

"These sons of bitches are serious," Schmidt said, sliding the thirty-round clip into the magazine feed. Pulling the charging handle back, the bolt slammed home.

"Hold your fire. Fire on my order," Simmons said. "Damn it, there must be some asshole leaking on the inside." There were more sounds of men scrambling up the finger, clearly in total disregard for noise discipline.

"These guys are charging up this hill like they're the Rough Riders," Simmons said. "Got to let them know we're up here and mean serious business," he said, thinking aloud.

He shouted out his next command loud enough for the benefit of the individuals stumbling over rocks and each other, aiming to storm his position. "Lock and load!" He prayed that hearing the unmistakable sound of bolts going home would make them think twice before advancing. After that, the flares, yeah, the flares would surely defuse the situation.

"Schmidt, fire both your flares!"

Schmidt laid his weapon on the ground in front of the position. Pulling the safety cover from the top of the flare containing two tits, he turned the small plastic cover into a firing pin by placing the cover on the bottom of the flare. Gripping the flare with the thumb of his right hand down, he used the open palm of his left to launch the red parachute flare out of the tube. It went airborne with a *swoosh*. The sound of the flare leaving the tube was distinct and Schmidt cast the empty container aside, already placing the cover on the bottom of his last flare.

Simmons launched a second flare sending it arcing across the sky. Then he watched in horror as Schmidt stood, preparing to launch another flare. Before he could shout for his Marine to take cover, a short burst of automatic weapon fire stitched Schmidt's waistline from one side to the other. Simmons watched him spin and scream at the same time, thrown back against the fighting-hole and landing across the back of Sands' legs. Sands looked down at Schmidt, bit down on his rage, and cut loose with a full clip of ammo, spraying the rounds to the right of his position. He hit the ejector button on the magazine feed, ejecting the spent magazine and quickly inserted another.

"Conserve your ammo," Simmons shouted, attempting to gain control of the situation. Bringing the goggles to his eyes, he quickly swept his immediate front, and for good measure swept once more to his right.

Sands crouched low in the hole, only the tubes of his goggles and bush hat appeared over the rim. The quiet that followed made the hair on the back of Simmons's neck stand straight. It was as if he were back in Iraq. Pressing back against the wall, he fired his second flare. The Marines kept up their terrain scan, not bothering to watch the flare climb into the overcast. Within seconds, the silence was broken when automatic fire to Simmons's immediate front raked their position. Rounds snapped passing inches over the top of the hole as other rounds tossed dirt and rock on top of the Marines. Silence followed.

"Is everybody okay?" Simmons yelled out.

Sands slumped back in the bottom of his hole across the top of Schmidt's corpse. Blood poured from the gaping wound in his right temple mixing with Schmidt's blood already pooling in the bottom of the hole.

Ball glanced over toward Schmidt and Sands' position, catching a glimpse of movement to his left. Two greenish figures ducked below a small scrub followed by a third figure. "Contact left," Ball said. The thumb of his right hand pushed the selector switch down to semi, squeezing short bursts into the base of the scrub. His first pull of the trigger exposed the position and suppressing fire would follow at any moment.

Captain Simmons knew that the issuance of grenades would have equalized the situation. Too bad they weren't. He worked on getting another flare into the sky as Ball squeezed off another short burst. The entire front erupted as the flare left the hole. Ball screamed, propelled out of the hole, rolling down the backside of the finger. Using short burst, Simmons covered the entire frontage and both flanks. Inserting another clip, he wheeled to his right, firing three quick bursts. Both the attackers backed down the hill. But, the captain's position was untenable.

As if his Father was whispering for him to check his six o'clock as his life might depend on it, he swung around wildly, putting two bursts into his would-be assailant's chest, driving the corpse into the dirt.

Halfway down the slope, lying back against a three-foot-high boulder, Ball fought off the shock from his wounds. Fighting off the effects of serious blood loss, he pulled himself on hands and knees and crawled to the sound of the guns. Slowly, painfully, he pulled out his Ka-Bar knife and crawled up the hill to rejoin the fight. Simmons looked back for Ball. No good, he thought. Have to find Ball. He had to check on Schmidt and Sands. *Can't just leave them.* A burst of fire passed a couple of feet left of the ground he was peering over, sending him down to the bottom of the hole. Acting on instinct now, he brought the M4 to his shoulder, rose up on one knee, and let off four three-round bursts into the base of the shrub where the last burst had come from.

A burst of fire came from his right, bullets entering the meaty part of his right arm close to his shoulder. Spinning from the force of the round, he toppled over the dead assailant. Screaming at the top of his lungs, he called to Schmidt and Ball. He was so caught up in the fight he hadn't even noticed if they had been firing. Screaming for them one more time, he crouched in the hole and quickly dove head first out and rolled across the level ground for fifteen feet before spinning down the hill to the spot where he calculated Ball had fallen.

At the rim, he came across Ball's M-16. Clasping the weapon, he flung headlong down the hill and after only traveling another seventy-five feet he crashed into the half-conscious Ball trying to crawl up the hill. Both Marines tumbled over each other, not coming to a stop until rolling onto the same trail they'd been observing only moments before.

Gaining his composure and shaking off the cobwebs that choked his thought process, the Captain of Marines grabbed two fists full of bloody cammies and pulled Ball to standing. Ball gestured wildly with his Ka-Bar, pointing in the direction of the OP. No words, only gurgling sounds, but Simmons knew Ball wanted to go back up the hill and check on Schmidt and Sands.

"Let's get the hell out of here, Ball," Simmons hissed, squatting slightly to let the limp Marine fall onto his left shoulder. The Ka-Bar fell to the ground. Grabbing both weapons, the wiry Captain ran up the trail deeper into the foothills. 5000 meters down the trail, another OP was in position. As Simmons jogged down the trail, he heard the grunts and gurgling sounds emitting from Balls lips, signaling that Ball was alive, for now. He kept the pace. The bad guys were dangerously close and he didn't know if they were pursuing. All he could think of was that Ball needed medical attention.

Surely, Barton's team had heard the commotion. Team Rules of Engagement ordered all teams to proceed to sounds of gunfire if no communications existed with the engaged position. Barton would go out of his way to look for a good fight. There was no reason to believe that he wouldn't stumble into Barton's team shortly.

"Hang on, Marine," he said, between gasps for air. Simmons, with Ball bouncing over his shoulder in a fireman's carry, vanished into the shadows.

Wednesday 0300; Flying On Patrol West of El Centro

Moving lazily 20 feet over the southwest Arizona desert, the Section of AH-1W ATTACK helicopters patrolled within eyesight of the Mexican border. Hap piloted from the back seat of Nomad 21, adjusting his helmet with both hands to ease the hot spot halfway between forehead and crown. It felt as if someone had wedged a piece of steel wool between his helmet and head, and the extra weight of the Anvis 6 Night Vision Goggles only made it worse. He found himself concentrating on the increasing irritation instead of leading his section of two attack helos on the last half of their scheduled three-hour patrol. He wasn't any more superstitious than the other guys, but the headache didn't seem like a good omen.

Both Hap's knees cuddled the cyclic, allowing Waco, who was strapped into the front cockpit, to observe the terrain through the Night Targeting Systems Multi-Function display.

Waco manipulated the Track Control Stick (TCS) with the index finger and thumb of his right-hand-mounted center mass on the right side of the Telescopic Sight Unit (TSU). Good gunners manipulated the TCS with two or three fingers to operate the optics, or aim the BGM-71C Improved Wire Guided TOW missile or laze for a Hellfire shoot. When directing the TOW, corrections needed to be small and over-correcting was a common mistake for young officers.

Mounted on the front of the aircraft and extending into the front cockpit, the TSU forced the gunner to sandwich himself between the Scope and the back of the seat. The Left Handed Grip (LHG) mounted on the left side of the TSU allowed the gunner to shoot ordnance, range targets, and laser designate with the 13 switches making up the grip. Optical fields of view offered 39X magnification on Direct View Optics and a 50X magnification when utilizing the FLIR device. The eyepiece, which only the gunner could use, was monocular and allowed the gunner to use either eye when viewing. Most of the time the gunner would use the small television screen above the eyepiece called the Multi-Function Display (MFD), which allowed him to maintain a constant scan outside the TSU's field of view. When utilizing the eyepiece, the gunner dropped his head to the eyepiece and his field of vision became one with the capabilities of the TSU, which took away one set of eyes from tracking the goings on within and around the aircraft. This was especially hazardous when the aircraft was hovering in mountainous terrain with the gunner's head in the eyepiece, commonly referred to by Cobra gunners as "going into the bucket."

Hap looked through his goggles to the west and couldn't help but notice the scud layer building west of the 45-mile-wide mountain range separating the California desert from a plush California coast. Glancing underneath his goggles, he grabbed a quick look at the clock on the right side of the instrument panel. It was 0320 hours.

"Kind of slow tonight, Waco," Hap said, speaking through the aircraft's intercom system.

Waco rubbed his fingers around tired eyes, "The bad guys must be taking a night off, Hap."

Hap's thoughts, however, were on the helpless figures being brutally executed he'd seen on the surveillance footage. It made his blood boil to think that U.S. Marines had been only seconds away flying unarmed aircraft. Rules of Engagement. "Frigging ROE," he muttered. Hap's mind swirled. Maybe he was making something out of nothing. Maybe the individuals executed were nothing more than dirty DEA. Or, maybe they were unfortunate individuals caught up in a drug deal gone badly.

Most of the pilots in the unit considered drugs in America a clear and present danger, understanding that the danger might be the product of government policies influenced by moral considerations of the voters. One could see what the American Left called immigration as desperate people paying to make it to the U.S. border. The Left was all about helping the oppressed, what they called "refugees," but the unintended consequences only added to the human misery. In the Marine Corps, this line of thinking is "good initiative, bad judgment."

Hap could justify legalizing drugs, though he firmly believed legalization did not justify usage. The country was spending billions in this war and losing ground every day. Every night, as the Nomads of HMLA 767 put it on the line attempting to interdict, almost fifty U.S. citizens lost their lives to prescription opioid overdoses. Was this all God's way to thin the herd? Hap wondered. In any case, trafficking humans for profit he was sure deserved the death sentence.

"How we doing on fuel, Hap?" Waco asked

LtCol Stoner snapped back into the cockpit. He glanced underneath the goggles to the dimly lit instrument panel. Reading the blue light of the fuel gauges, he passed on the number of pounds of fuel remaining. A quick scan over his right shoulder confirmed Spanky in position off his right wing, anchored like any good Marine Corps wingman would be. Within moments, trusty Spanky would swing the Cobra in a wide arc passing from the 3 o'clock to Hap's 9 o'clock, clearing the flights 6 o'clock in the process.

"You sure are being quiet tonight, Colonel," Waco said.

Hap remained silent, his mind busy. Why in the hell did the Nomads receive orders to go out on this JTF 6 Operation? Was this nothing more than the administration checking boxes to show the voting public that they care?

"Not to interrupt Hap, but I have a heat source 12 o'clock three thousand meters."

Without asking, Hap knew Waco was gingerly milking the joystick, centering the heat source on the MFD. Within a couple of seconds, the thumb of his left hand would depress the auto lock button. Four dots would encase the target indicating the FLIR had locked on the heat source. As long as Hap did not put the Cobra into an abrupt maneuver, the scope would hold the lock.

"Just when you think everyone is asleep," Waco said.

"So we have a target?" Hap inquired. He glanced through the Heads Up Display, where a symbol on the HUD depicted the quadrant in which the FLIR was pointing. "Can't put eyes on it. No joy."

"Wouldn't think so," Waco said. "The target is underneath some overgrown trees and it appears to be two people standing in front of a vehicle. Hasn't been parked long, the engine is still hot."

Hap eased back on the cyclic, putting the Nomad 21 in a fifty-foot hover attempting to minimize the chances of kicking up a dust cloud. He said, "Kang flight, target 11 o'clock about twenty-five hundred out."

Spanky replied. "Tally ho! I am at your nine o'clock."

Hap swung his head to the left for a second to verify Spanky's position, while Waco focused in on the MFD, observing the targets for hints that would identify them as either drug related, illegal immigrant, or civilian.

"What's the verdict?" Hap asked.

Waco watched intently as the two figures grappled with each other.

"Hap, the smaller of the two appears to be losing. Whoever it is, one is lying face down on the hood. The larger figure appears to be standing behind the smaller figure. Just can't tell if the larger figure is about to bre…."

Spanky's voice interrupted. "Number 1 says we are about to witness some real good sex."

"Talk to me, Waco," Hap said.

After a few seconds, Waco replied. "I concur, Colonel, looks like we have front seat tickets to a good old fornication session."

"Just how good is it?" Hap inquired, pissed he wasn't sitting in the front seat.

"I've paid for less revealing shows, Hap."

The flashing strobe of a Huey appeared, working over the border and moving slowly to the west, probably the CO's bird. Hap was thinking Warden might want some entertainment. He keyed the UHF Radio. "Tuna Man, Kang. Have eyes on a situation you may want to look at. A real pounding matter going on. We are at your 4 o'clock. Will throw on our beacon for you."

"I got it, Kang," Spanky said.

Hap watched the CO's green position light located on the right side of the aircraft vanish from sight. The rotator beacon mounted atop the twin exhaust rapidly transitioned from casting its flashing light parallel to the ground to moving to perpendicular.

"On my way, Kang," LtCol Warden said, piloting the Huey with Meat strapped into the left seat, angling towards the Cobra's position.

"Tally ho, Kang. Leave your IR beacon flashing."

Hap keyed the mike twice indicating Spanky would comply. The couple was now obviously in the act. The larger figure had joined his mate on the hood of the car and they were busily, and apparently consensually, copulating. Hap wondered if it would be best to climb up to three or four thousand feet and come spiraling down over the lovers, lighting up the position with the IR searchlight. IR searchlights were invisible to the naked eye but for those with Night Vision devices, really lit up an area. The whining and whopping engines would offer up a grand coitus interruptus.

Suddenly one red parachute flare popped out of the overcast on the western horizon trailing smoke and sheets of flame as it shot upward. After a few seconds, the flare reached the peak of its climb, deployed its small chute and began slowly swinging back and forth before settling out of sight into the overcast. Hap watched tensely as a second red flare burst above the clouds, although not as high as the first one. Drifting down, trailing smoke it passed out of sight. Then, a third.

11

0320; *Flying Over Bravo 6*

Hap sat up sharply in his seat, speaking to Waco. "You see what I see?"

"Tally, I believe the flares are red, Sir," Waco said.

"Concur," Hap snapped. He dropped the snout of the Cobra, pulling in military power. Accelerating, Hap steered directly for the flailing couple, roaring over, just above treetop level, before banking in the direction of the last flare.

"Spanky, we have red flares to the west. Join on us and Tuna Man can follow in trace if gas allows." Glancing back over his shoulder, Hap saw Spanky accelerating with him, banking right to the 3 o'clock position. Nomad 21 skimmed over the ground at 165 miles per hour. Peering through the heads-up display, Hap maintained the Cobra 125 feet above the ground.

"Waco, check the map," Hap ordered. "Confirm flares came out of Bravo 6."

Hap thought back to Captain Parks' in-brief, shooting the laser pen at a spot on the map to emphasize that the next incident would occur at Bravo 6. He punched the GPS, bringing up the waypoint labeled Bravo 6. Hap punched another button, direct loading the coordinate into the previously programmed navigational system.

Waco laid open the tactical map and pressed his lip up against a small plastic lever mounted on his mike, energizing a lip light mounted to its end. After a quick glance, he spoke. "Hap, flares could be from Bravo 4 but would bet originating from Bravo 6."

Hap glanced down at his kneeboard, at the frequency card, and noted the tactical frequency for Bravo 6 and transmitted, "Hap, flight go lavender."

A short burst followed over the radio—"Two, Three"—as Spanky and Tuna Man verified receiving the directive to switch frequencies. In pilot lingo, this act referred to a front-side check. To be certain the flight was on the same frequency, there was also a back side check, which Waco would initiate once he punched the frequency into the radio. The Cobra was equipped with three radios and typically, the number 1 radio supported elements working frequencies, while the second radio handled inter-flight communications. Abruptly, a deafening squeal came across their headset. It was Waco keying in the frequency.

Hap reacted instinctively to clear the flight from the annoying squeal, foregoing the back side check. He said, "Flight go gray." Immediately, the flights' headsets went quiet except for the whine of the turbo shaft engines driving the blades overhead.

Hap looked down for a backup frequency for the grunts, running the index finger of his left hand down the laundry list of frequencies; wouldn't you know, the next to the last line of the page contained the backup frequency, labeled with the color code Silver.

Hap broke the silence over the net. Each cockpit within the flight needed to know what the hell was going on. At the moment, Flight Lead was in the dark. Silence would not render situational awareness (SA) on events on and around Bravo 6, which was now a mere three miles to their front.

"Kang Flight go Silver!" The front side check quickly followed the command. Seconds later Hap initiated the back side check, and, like clockwork, the flight checked in.

He exhaled. He was about to initiate a fuel status check, but the piercing squeal rendered the backup frequency untenable. As before, Hap switched the flight back to button Gray, his command barely audible over the squeal.

His mind was racing about as fast as the Cobra was covering ground, and now the ridge forming Bravo 6's eastern boundary was clearly visible barely a mile away. "Hap flight, say fuel." He needed to know how long the flight could stay on station.

Spanky quickly chimed in over the radio, "Twelve hundred pounds for dash two."

"Tuna Man has 900 pounds," Tuna Man said, his demeanor as calm as the day Hap had to inform him that the business deal they'd both thrown over one hundred thousand dollars into had gone bust.

Hap quickly computed fuel burn for both types of aircraft. The flight only had 45 minutes on station. He watched the high terrain race towards them. Only one hundred feet separated the cloud layer from the top of the ridgeline, and again like clockwork, both Hap and Spanky initiated a gentle bunting maneuver to lower the aircraft over the back side of the ridge.

"Bravo 6 off the nose about two thousand meters," Waco said.

Hap pulled the cyclic back into his lap while simultaneously lowering the collective to the stops working to break the aircraft's forward motion. Shouldn't have done that, Hap thought. Looking left, he saw the nose of Spanky's aircraft arced towards the overcast all the while maintaining position. Always has, always will. Even if caught in a lurch, Tuna Man will go high to avoid the midair while staying clear of the goo.

Both Cobras came to a stop 200 meters east of Bravo 6. Hap pulled on the collective, placing the bird into a high hover hold north of the OP. Waco swept the FLIR along the entire finger and then traced the dirt road east of the finger.

"Hell, Colonel, there are multiple targets. I have two vehicles stationary in the draw off the nose. They're parked alongside the road just below the OP."

Waco moved the TSU to the right against the slope and concentrated his search in the area of the OP. "Shit Colonel, multiple targets moving down toward the vehicles to our front, and multiple targets moving down the back side of the finger. No doubt there are vehicles waiting for them."

"Got 'em," Hap replied into the intercom. Switching over to the UHF radio, he began barking orders to his flight. "Spanky, you have the targets moving down the back side of the finger. Tuna Man move north along the road I am currently hovering over, and keep your six o'clock clear. All aircraft ensure all exterior lights secure." The last order had all aircraft dim exterior lighting, which on a dark evening made the aircraft almost invisible to the naked eye. They were still loud as hell and could be heard a couple of miles away. But, it's hard to shoot a target you can't see.

Spanky responded immediately. "Tally, we are moving past your 6 and will set up on the west side of the finger."

Seconds passed after Spanky's reply before Tuna Man reported moving north along the road.

Wednesday 0400; Flying Over Bravo 6

LtCol Warden piloted the UH-1N just over the tops of the trees and shrubs while Meat manipulated the FLIR. Handling a device similar in appearance to controls that operated Nintendo games, Meat searched both sides of the road for any heat source. The FLIR's monitor was located above the console so both pilots could observe.

Two deer darted across the scope's field of view and vanished into a dry streambed that snaked off to the left. A lone long-horned bull strolled into the middle of the road. As Warden's Huey's massive rotors cut the air with a *whop-whop* sound, the bull froze, head cocked to the side, four legs poised to react, not sure which way to run. Gaining its senses the bull bounded down the road, throwing its hind legs back rodeo style.

A shape—barely more than a shadow—caught Meat's eye. "Tuna Man, I have movement to our front on this side of the bend in the road, and it ain't an animal."

Warden focused in as directed. "Keep me clear of the trees, boys," Tuna Man said, addressing the two aircrew positioned aft on either side of the aircraft's cabin. With the two sliding doors pinned back, the aircrew maintained excellent visibility giving the cockpit two additional sets of eyes. Positioned on the left behind Meat, Sergeant "Little Ray" Martinez swung most of his body out of the aircraft to ensure the main or tail rotor remained clear of any entanglements. Tethered to the aircraft by a gunner's belt secured around his barrel chest, he watched for tree limbs, rocks, and power lines. "All clear, Sir." he said speaking through the aircraft's intercom system.

Cpl Lafleur, positioned on the right side behind Tuna Man, did a quick check to his side of the aircraft, hanging precariously out of the aircraft to check the tail rotor. "All clear." Lafleur's French Cajun accent made Little Ray's Cajun accent sound plain old east Texas.

Tuna Man nodded and noticed the lone figure standing in the road. He nudged the cyclic forward. The Huey moved slowly up the road.

"Kang, we have a target 500 meters north of OP."

Meat nodded and kept the FLIR zoom function focused on the unidentified target. The figure was carrying a body on his back.

"Shit, Colonel, it's got to be a Marine carrying an injured Marine."

Tuna Man asked, "Are you sure that is an injured person and not a mule lugging a couple hundred pounds of weed?"

"Damn it, that's an injured Marine up there," Meat said.

Tuna Man heard the urgency in Meat's voice. He dropped the Huey's nose and accelerated. "Find me an LZ, boys," he said, sharply.

"Roger that," Little Ray replied, hanging out of the aircraft and straining his neck around like a crane, looking for a safe place to land the helicopter.

Tuna Man reported, "Kang, it looks like we have two Marines. One appears injured."

* * *

Hap's mind raced. Wounded Marines to my rear, I don't know if they were shot from the road, which puts bad guys to my six. Were they driven from the OP and making their way to the hard surface road for help? Poor bastards' radios were jammed. They used flares. Need to give the team leader a medal. Multiple targets are to the front. Oh, to have ordnance on these gunships!

Tuna Man flipped the IR searchlight switch and Meat immediately aimed it at the area the Marines were occupying. One of the Marines lay against the base of a small boulder and the healthier of the two began signaling wildly with both hands above his head.

"Find me that LZ, boys," Tuna Man repeated.

Meat pointed to a spot 50 meters west of the road. He would have liked to find something closer but it wasn't in the cards. Trees had overgrown too much of the road.

Tuna Man nodded and pointed the nose of the Huey towards the clearing with a little cyclic and rudder.

Lafleur watched the tail swing around, missing a branch by a mere 10 feet. No sweat. No need to tell the pilots right now, he thought, and he gave the "All clear" over the intercom.

Tuna Man piloted into a ten-foot hover over the designated spot. Hearing the all clear from the crew, he settled the skids onto the rocky ground and heard the banging sound of two metal couplings on the gunners belt drop to the cabins aluminum floor.

Little Ray and Lafleur bounded out of the aircraft vanishing into the vegetation.

Tuna Man drummed his thighs with his fingers. Minutes dragged on...two...three...

At five minutes, with the tension almost unbearable, the two crewmembers finally moved into view. They were carrying a Marine on a doubled-over poncho functioning as makeshift stretcher. A second Marine appeared. He moved painfully, bent at the hips and knees, covering the Medevac with his M4 and a M16 over a shoulder.

Little Ray and Lafleur carefully loaded the wounded Marine onto the cabin deck.

"Wounded Marine on board," Little Ray reported.

Warden glanced back at the lifeless figure and the wind-blown poncho flapping against the Marine's unresponsive face.

Warden saw one of the crewmembers gesturing wildly with a flashlight towards the Marine covering the Medevac. He had gone to a knee, and was trying to gain his feet using the two rifles as crutches. "Go get him," Tuna Man said, growing impatient. The bad guys could appear at any moment. An unarmed Huey spinning on the ground is defenseless against heavily armed aggressors.

Little Ray lowered the flashlight, bent over and raced to the Marine who was down on one knee, still attempting to cover the Medevac. He grabbed the Marine by the collar, but the grunt fell face first into the rocks. Without a thought, Little Ray swept the Marine into a fireman's carry. He picked up both rifle's, ran under the rotor arc and helped him into the cabin. "This one is routine, Colonel. Clear to lift."

Tuna Man pulled the helicopter out of the LZ and raced for the only hospital in El Centro reporting his intentions to Hap. "Go to Air Traffic Control, Meat."

Meat's head went down toward the console and a gloved hand punched in the radio frequency to Approach.

Warden spoke calmly. "Request vectors to El Centro's hospital. One priority medevac and one routine."

Five miles from the hospital, Tuna Man glanced back and saw the Marine who'd covered their withdrawal tending to the wounded Marine. Little Ray reported quietly to Tuna Man and Meat, "the injured Marine will not last long."

Air Traffic Control continued passing vectors, apprising Tuna Man that a trauma team would be standing by on the helo pad. With the LZ now in site, Tuna Man lowered the collective and brought back the nose of the Huey slightly to set up for landing.

Hap and Spanky were still out there. There were two Marines missing and maybe needing help. He would get gas and return to Bravo 6.

13

Wednesday 0410; Near Bravo 6

"Lead's moving forward," Hap said over the radio. "Spanky, work your way down the western slope of the finger and if fired on, disengage."

As Spanky inched the Cobra forward, the heat sensors picked up a collection of human figures. "Kang, the bad guys are moving the dead."

"Tally," Hap replied, grimly watching two men clasping the lifeless figure underneath each shoulder. It looked as though two KIA's were being muscled into the back of the lead vehicle, a dark Suburban.

Hap said, "Looks as though the Marines gave something back."

"Or they're dragging away Marines, dead or alive," Spanky said.

The thought of this trash hauling away Marines caused Hap and the Cobra to close the ground, separating the gunship from the two Suburbans at an even faster rate. At a mere fifty yards, he pulled up into a 75-foot hover. Three men raced from behind the lead vehicle. Dropping to a knee, each put the butt of the weapon to his shoulder.

Looking quickly to the right and rear, Hap saw no terrain to put between themselves and the threat. Their only advantage of darkness was lost when the lead vehicle's headlights flashed on bright and lit them up.

"Climb—" Waco said.

"—Pulling power." Hap cut off Waco in mid-sentence.

The headlights washed out their night vision devices. Hap put the Cobra into a max power vertical climb. Passing one hundred feet, he mashed on the right rudder pedal to the stop, swinging the beaklike nose violently to the right. Looking underneath the goggles, he saw flashing muzzles of the assault rifles flickering death, fortunately missing the mark.

"Spanky is inbound."

Hap watched Spanky steer the Cobra over the crest of the finger, its two skids seeming to scrape the ground. Bunting over the high ground, the Cobra lowered its nose accelerating toward the shooters.

Nice move Spanky, Hap thought. Now close the ground between you and them.

The Suburbans were in a small clearing void of rock and shrub.

Spanky lined up the nose of the aircraft a couple of feet in front of the shooters' shoulders, his left skid now in line to skewer them. Two of the shooters went to the ground while the man on the left side of the line stood turning to fire on Spanky's Cobra in the off-hand position. Bad mistake, Hap thought.

"You going to climb?" Hap asked over the UHF radio.

Spanky bore down on his prey like a lion pouncing on dinner. The toe of the skid caught the shooter just below the right shoulder, tearing him almost in half. On impact, the aircraft yawed slightly left. Spanky pushed the Cobra into a max climb, and then entered a hard right turn.

"Spanky breaking right. I got you in sight, Kang."

"Roger, Spanky, coming left."

Hap ducked into the draw to the east, remaining below the crest. The Suburbans were heading south at a high rate of speed. Popping up, Hap came over the crest as the vehicles bee-lined for their sanctuary, the Mexican border. Hap brought the Cobra back to the south with a hard-banking turn, descending to thirty feet above the ground, accelerating all the while.

"What in hell are you doing?" Spanky called out over the airways.

A grin appeared below Hap's goggles. Within seconds after crossing the border he gained a visual on the vehicles that only moments before had attempted to shoot up their aircraft. Moving fast, the Suburbans worked to gain the hard surface road paralleling the border.

"OK, so we catch them. We have no ordnance to shove up their ass," Waco said.

Hap reached for his 9mm. "Take the controls and catch the sons of bitches."

Waco grabbed the controls. "I have the aircraft."

Hap tapped the barrel of the pistol against the canopy. The slide of his Beretta came to the rear before he let it ride home chambering a round. He said, "Pass just to the left of the rear vehicle."

Waco dipped the rotor slightly passing the trailing vehicle offset no more than ten feet to the left and paralleling their track. The hard surface road was only a half-mile away now. Hap reached over with his left hand, twisting up the canopy lever. Air rushed in filling the cockpit. Loose papers and maps twirled around both cockpits before getting sucked out into the cool night air. Wrestling with the canopy door, Hap had to work hard to keep the Plexiglas bubble from flying into the rotor disk. Unable get a bead on the truck without shooting through the canopy, he shook his head. "Come a little right and back."

Waco steered the Cobra a mere twenty feet above the rear Suburban, drifting slightly behind it.

"Hold it there." Hap's left hand passed underneath his right arm. Squeezing the trigger, he heard the distinctive *pop, pop, pop.* He emptied the magazine of the 9mm through the top of the vehicle. "Maintain your position Waco," he said.

Hap reloaded and within seconds, the pistol was spraying death into the rear of the Surburban. *pop, pop, pop.*

The Surburban angled 30 degrees to the right and suddenly turned hard, sending the vehicle into a deadly roll. The SUV rolled over and over, enveloped in vaporized gasoline and dust. A tire kicked off into the air, spinning, barely missing the Cobra. A body ejected before the vehicle bounded fifteen feet into the air and exploded in a pirouette of death, raining down on the desert floor in a blazing heap of scrap metal and billowing black smoke.

"Good shooting, Hap," Waco said.

"Get us back on the American side of the border. *Muy pronto,*" Hap said.

Waco banked the Cobra hard left, breaking away from the burning hulk.

"Since we're here, how about the other vehicle?" Waco asked, "We can be on them in a couple of minutes and I can pass back my magazines."

Hap deliberated the possibility of taking out the second SUV. The vehicle was on the hard surface road heading east, probably for Mexicali. The situation reminded Hap of the old

John Wayne movie where the Duke contemplates raising his hand to halt the line of cavalry at the Rio Grande, as he watches the Apaches escape across the border into Mexico. Hell, I've gone this far, why stop now? Hap thought, and then "Let's do it!"

Waco banked hard to the right heading east towards Mexicali.

Allowing common sense to trump valor, Hap shook his head and slammed an open palm against the bubble canopy. "Take us home, Waco," he said.

Keying the radio, he transmitted: "Spanky, we will be crossing the border. Join on us." There was no need to push their luck.

He reached back and flipped on the Cobra's infrared exterior lighting, which for those wearing goggles, lit the aircraft up like a Christmas tree. Placing the pistol on safe, he holstered the weapon and regained the controls.

"I got this, Waco," Hap said, adjusting the shoulder harness and shifting lightly in his seat. Snap-rolling the aircraft to port, he picked up Spanky moving east on the U.S. side of the stream. Deflated and definitely concerned about the debriefings soon to follow, he questioned if any of the LEA or Marine Corps high brass would share in "Kang Flight" reacting to the situation. Whoa, I am in a world of shit, he concluded.

"Tally ho," Spanky transmitted. "Spanky bingo fuel."

Moments later, Spanky gave two clicks over the UHF radio. Looking back, Hap confirmed that Spanky's Cobra on his left wing. Easing back into the seat, he questioned if tonight's response would have any impact on the bad guys' future considerations. If nothing else, he hoped they would realize that Marines in this sector would fight back if pushed into a corner. They had drawn Marine Corps blood and the Marines gained a little payback, but as Hap saw it, they had a lot more coming. Something tugged at his gut, telling him that the Nomads would get a second crack at them. But first, upon landing at El Centro, the bureaucrats and the brass would begin their second-guessing. No doubt.

14

Wednesday 0515; Returning to Bravo 6

"Ready to lift, Sir." Sergeant "Little Ray" Martinez was hanging halfway through the open cabin door.

"Clear right," Corporal Lafleur confirmed, stretching his neck around to clear the whirling tail rotor. The Huey idled on the red X of the hospital's landing pad.

LtCol "Tuna Man" Warden rolled both throttles to fly. While the hospital staff offloaded the wounded, Little Ray and Lafleur used what little time was available, to wipe up as much of the coagulating blood as they could with a wire brush and shop rags borrowed from the ER staff.

Keeping the goggles flipped above his brow, Tuna Man pulled into a six-foot hover. As he scanned the instrument panel, Meat leaned over the center console gesturing thumbs-up with his right hand. Tuna Man acknowledged with a nod and climbed, ensuring altitude over airspeed for the 5-minute flight to Navy El Centro.

Warden transmitted to the ODO: "We will be hot pumping and returning to Bravo 6. Two Marines remain in the field."

Seconds passed before Meat said, "The crew is behind you, Colonel."

Little Ray followed with "*Semper Fi.*"

"Switch to base," Tuna Man said.

Meat switched primary transmission to radio 2, following with a thumbs-up.

"Nomad base, Nomad 22," Tuna Man said.

"Go ahead, Colonel," the Squadron Operations Duty Officer replied.

"We will be coming in to hot pump. I want two Ma Deuces uploaded with three hundred rounds per gun."

"During fueling, Colonel?"

"Do I stutter, Captain? Switch Tower, Meat."

Pulling the collective to his armpit Meat dove the now armed UH1-N to the deck, clearing the city's lights. In the distance flying low and fast, Hap's lit up Cobra was returning to base.

"Kang, Tuna Man. Sit rep."

"Spanky has shut down on Bravo 6," Kang reported. "Two Marine KIA. The zone is socked in and Spank is at bingo fuel. Have all the shooters RTB'd?"

"Affirmative. Aircrews have put in for the evening. Something tells me, Kang, it's probably for the better."

"We are bingo. Do you want me to reconstitute...armed?"

"Negative, XO. I'm the only one putting my career on the line tonight. We are armed and LEA has been notified."

"Do you want me to hot pump and join unarmed?"

"Negative. Will bring the Marines home. Spanky can escort."

Tuna Man rocked his wings as the helos approached merge.

"It might be a while before you can get in," Spanky said, monitoring the radios with one engine shut down to conserve fuel. "There is just enough wind to stir this soup. Shutting down and will use hand held radio from my vest."

"Understood, Spanky," Tuna Man said. "Come back around to the left, Meat. I want to take a look at the road near the stream to set down."

Nodding, Meat pulled into a hard left turn. Minutes later the Huey was below B6 trying to crawl into the zone.

"Rotary Wing in the area of B6, switch to guard."

Recognizing Spanky's voice, Tuna Man said, "I have the radios, Meat. Spanky, I'm on the American side of the border, now crossing over to the Mexican side to see if we can find another path."

"Contact right," Lafleur yelled.

Tuna Man snapped his head over his right shoulder. The goggle's 40-degree field of view was chock-full with tracer rounds. Each glowing slug seemed to be coming directly at his head. "Break plane, Meat."

"Sir, are we cleared to engage?" Little Ray asked, both bolts of the .50's slamming home a round audible over the screaming engines and twirling rotors.

"Hold your fire. Meat, get us out of here," Tuna Man said demonstrating little emotion in his tone. With no John Wayne ambitions, Warden hoped first and foremost that he and his Marines woke up in the morning to find their names blessedly absent from every English-speaking newspaper in the free world.

Meat banked hard into a climbing right turn.

Bang Bang Bang Bang! Lafleur rolled left shielding his face with both forearms from the incoming fire slamming hard against the deck. The Number 2 Fire T Handle illuminated.

"Hold the Number 1 throttle. I'm rolling 2 closed." Tuna Man cranked the lower throttle to the high side stop. Flipping a switch with his thumb, he quickly rolled the throttle closed. "I'm dumping the extinguishers." Reaching up he pulled the illuminated handle and toggled the switch injecting the fire retardant into the engine compartment.

"Fire secured on number 2," Little Ray reported.

"Number 1 is smoking," Lafleur added.

Although continuing to fly, Meat could not be as aggressive with the loss of power. "Number 1 engine temps are going through the roof."

Tuna Man looked down just as the Number 1 Fire T Handle illuminated and then said, "Can we make the American side?"

"Negative," Meat replied

"Go wings level and straight ahead into the meadow. I'm going to leave Number 1 up to give you something besides inertia on the bottom. Mayday, Mayday, Mayday! Nomad 22 going down south-south-east of Bravo 6."

Nomad 22 began an autorotation the moment Meat bottomed out the collective. With the Huey falling out of the sky for the short fall to the sticky ground of the marsh, Tuna Man called out, "No forward airspeed, Meat."

"Brace," Meat called, as Nomad 22 stood on its tail, bleeding off airspeed a mere 75 feet above the ground. Rocking forward, leveling the skids, Nomad 22 settled into mud with no forward airspeed.

Rolling the engine off, Tuna Man secured Number 1. Upon pulling the fire T handle and throwing the toggle switch, fire retardant dumped into the Number 1 engine. Both aircrews grabbed fire extinguishers located behind the pilots' seats and sprayed down both engines as the rotors flexed into the muck, snapping off the rotor mast. Tuna Man felt heat burning the back of his neck. Small-arms-fire raked the fuselage. The assailant's shouts drew closer between lulls in trigger pulls. Reaching back to disconnect the ICS cord, Tuna Man unbuckled his harness.

Rolling out of the seat, he fell into the rear cabin. "Lafleur, take the bolt out of your gun and get rid of it. Meat, take the boys and make your way to Bravo 6." Lafleur worked feverishly to remove the bolt to his .50-caliber, tossing it into the marsh.

"What about you?" Meat said.

Spinning out of his seat, Tuna Man settled behind Lafleur's gun. "I'll throw out some cover fire. Get going. I'll follow shortly."

Meat led Little Ray and Lafleur through knee-high water and reeds the 200 meters to the border. Tuna Man placed and held the circular rear sight on a group of greenish tinted figures as he pressed the toggle trigger with both thumbs. Two of the figures spun to the ground. He unleashed a short burst in the direction of anything moving. The shouts grew closer. The gun went silent.

Throwing the empty ammo can to the rear; he placed a fresh one into its saddle, raised the cover, laid in the linked rounds, and slammed the cover home. Charging the weapon with his right arm, he was back in the fight unleashing longer bursts now, preparing to retrograde to the American side of the stream. All the bad guys' heads were down. Apparently, he'd stopped them in their tracks. He threw out a long burst until the ammo can emptied, then jumped from the port side landing face down into the bog. Pulling himself up, he swept away the mud caked over his eyes.

Smoke curled from the barrel of the .50cal while a layer of acrid smoke drifted around the crash site. Barely able to see, he came face to face with the barrel of an AK-47. Slowly raising his arms, he could make out the assailant behind the rifle. Another gunman appeared, and then another. Black and white *kufiyahs* covered most of their faces and the man who appeared to be the leader grabbed the military issue 9mm.

Speaking in broken English, the gunman stuffed the pistol in his belt and gestured with the rifle, as if pitching hay. "Take off your helmet."

Tuna Man dropped his hands slowly, undoing the chinstrap of his flight helmet.

"Jes, jes," the man said, nodding as others wearing identical kufiyahs gathered around him.

Removing his helmet, Tuna Man tossed it to the side showing no emotion. Before his headgear hit the watery bog, the Commanding Officer of HMLA 767 caught the butt of the AK-47 against his temple. He dropped like a sack of wet cement face down in the muck.

The assailant stepped onto the unconscious Marine's back. Bubbles surfaced as the full weight of his boot bore down before he reached down into the dark water and dragged the American's limp body by the collar to dry ground.

● ● ●

Lying in some underbrush on the US side of the border, Meat and Nomad 22's aircrew waited for their Commanding Officer to join them. They brandished their government issued 9mm pistols as they eyed the dark restlessly. Gunfire on the Mexican side of the stream had gone silent. Hearing sounds of someone approaching from their rear, they slid deeper into the brush. The noise of careful footsteps grew closer. Meat raised his head just enough to see four figures come out of the darkness. He aimed his pistol at the point man. Only six feet away before the trigger pull, Meat could see they were US Marines.

"Night." Meat called out with the challenge.

"Cruiser," came the reply. "Is that you Nomad 22?"

Meat came out of the brush followed by Lafleur and Little Ray.

* * *

Hap heard Nomad 22's Mayday call as his unarmed Cobra turned in the fueling area referred to Marine Aviation as the hot pits. Switching on his flashlight, he crossed the beam across his throat several times toward the fueler controlling the tank farms fuel pumps as the helo's tank topped off.

"Base. Nomad 26."

The ODO's voice responded. "Go ahead 26."

Hap heard Big Alabama, booming expletives in the background.

"Big Alabama, can you put a Huey crew together?"

"Do they have to be sober?"

"I would hope one of the pilots could pass a Breathalyzer."

"I can make that happen. Local Law Enforcement is still an hour out."

"I want door guns on a Huey. See you at Bravo 6."

"Do I get to bring bullets, Colonel?"

"Let me make it easy. It's a direct order, arm up! Now get on it! Switch ground, Waco."

15

Wednesday 0630; Naval Air Facility El Centro CA

Thirty minutes after circling Warden's crash site, Hap's Cobra's skids touched the Nomad flight line. Big Alabama, diverted to Bravo 6 on orders from Hap, had brought back their KIA. No need to put another aircraft and crew at risk with LtCol Warden MIA.

With Ambassador on the warpath, Hap didn't bother entering the ready room. Handing off his vest and helmet to Waco to drop at flight equipment, he slid into a waiting car driven by Hollywood. "Let's put eyes on the Ambassador."

"No need," Hollywood said. "Got word he's in the weight room beating the crap out of a heavy bag." He squinted at Hap, motored down the street making the first right, and moments later pulled the vehicle into the deserted BOQ picnic area. "Where to now?"

"This'll do," Hap said, already sliding out of the car. I've got a call to make and I'll need some quiet." With his cell phone in hand he strode toward the lone picnic table and the small charcoal grill stuck on the end of a recently painted pole that served as Building 270's picnic area. An older structure remodeled years earlier, the building served as the Naval Air Facility's Bachelor Officers and VIP Quarters. Against a backdrop of an eastern horizon, the sun cast another magnificent desert first light. When they reached the table, Hollywood sat, but Hap couldn't settle himself. He punched in Blad's number and, when his old friend answered, filled him in on events as quickly as possible.

Rubbing chin stubble 26 hours in the making, Hap heard Blad's words, but thoughts of a world gone mad filled his mind. Top of the list consisted of 2 KIA's, 2 WIA's and LtCol Warden was MIA—last heard from three hours ago! Where in the hell was LEA?

"Hey, did you hear me, Hap?" Blad asked now.

"Sorry, Blad," Hap said, pacing. "I didn't catch the last few statements."

"I said I'm missing an agent myself, Hap, but you know that. He was conducting surveillance along the border and came up missing in Mexicali."

"So what the hell is going on? We gave our DVDs to the LEA and Feds and nothing happens. LEA and Feds receive the calls for help and retreat. And my aircraft are unarmed!"

"Speaking of being unarmed, I have reports of an incident further inside Mexico from where Tuna Man went down."

"What have you heard?"

"Tell you what, Hap, after we hang up turn on cable news. Turds are claiming an international incident has occurred. Knowing you, I would say a good attorney might be in your future."

"Not sure where you are going with this, Blad. I have dead Marines and Tuna Man is missing. At this point, I'm assuming he is alive. For Christ sakes, H.D. Simmons's boy was shot."

"Jonathan?"

"The Captain is one of our WIA's."

"Sons of bitches."

"What about your guy? Anything?"

"Silence is deafening, Hap. Retired DEA. Before DEA he wanted to be a beat cop in Texas. My guy was no slouch. To answer your question my contacts are digging deep. I have got to find my guy."

"So why did they hit us?"

Blad answered with silence.

Hap's voice came deep from within his diaphragm, as it did when he was irritated, "Hey, you bastard! Shit is flying and you've got no answers?"

Blad chuckled. "You haven't changed Hap. Grasp some SA. Did you take notice of anything I said?"

"So you're an advocate of cable news." More silence. Hap knew exactly what his old friend said. It wasn't as if Hap had just fallen off the turnip truck. "Sorry about that, you prick. I'm tired and want some bad guy ass."

"Based on my reports, Hap, you already got a bit of payback. There are a bunch of dead bad guys."

"The turds were probably drinking and driving and flipped their Suburban. As far as the bad guys on the OP, they probably tripped high on meth."

"Hap, I never said it was a Suburban. But, between you and me, it was a Suburban that was destroyed. Do me a favor. Don't you or any of the other pilots beat the hell out of—or *shoot*—any of the LEA. I mean not one."

"And why the hell not?"

"A couple of them might not like what is going on within the Fed, Hap. Can I say it any clearer? You might silence someone who may be slipping me information."

Hollywood pushed a Styrofoam cup of coffee across the dew-covered fiberglass tabletop. Hap nodded thank you, pressed 'speaker,' and placed the Samsung on the table. He waited for Big Alabama's Huey and Spanky's Cobra to pass. Spanky's Cobra flew directly to the taxiway. Big Alabama banked the Huey crossing Spanky's 6 o'clock to set up on final to land at the Base Infirmary helo pad to offload the body bags.

Frowning, Hap said, "Follow up in four hours, Blad. Keep me posted. I'm calling an all hands at 1200 hours for a memorial."

"Hap, you do the same if you hear anything regarding a Steve Smith from the locals or the Feds?"

"Semper Fi."

"Semper Fi, Hap," as Blad killed the call.

Exhaling, Hap looked into Hollywood's bloodshot eyes.

Hollywood stared back. "Hey, Hap, take a chill pill, and let's get our arms around this situation. You know, we give the administration and the authorities a chance, Colonel America."

"In my mind they had their chance and they didn't show up," Hap growled.

"So we don't take our eyes off the clock. We're going nowhere until we get a location on Tuna Man."

Hap blinked. The son of a bitch was right. Hell, he was always right. There was a lot to digest but the main thing was to get Warden back. The last rays of sunrise and desert air seemed to clear his head.

"Group CO stood us down for the next two nights," Hollywood said slowly. "Rumor has it Shank may have us fly back home in 72 hours."

Hap's jaw visibly tightened. He would give LEA their chance to do right, but their clock was ticking and if they…

"What's up Colonel?"

Hap gave one quick nod. "The memorial. Could you have the base Chaplain present?"

"Why bother, Colonel? Preacher will do just fine."

Hap scratched his ear. Captain Steve Tyler, call sign 'Preacher.' "How could I forget Preacher? He is the one pilot in Iraqi Freedom that Big Alabama refused to be scheduled with."

Hollywood ran both hands through his thick mane. "Probably the one sea story I haven't heard."

"According to Big Alabama, Preacher was ready to meet his maker."

"What is wrong with that? I would think, doing what we do, we're all in that mode."

"Apparently Big Alabama wasn't quite ready to meet his maker. According to Preacher, Big Alabama was threatening the schedule writer to ensure there were a few more happy hours on his calendar."

Hollywood bit his lip.

"It's okay to smile, Hollywood. Will you see to the memorial? Call the ODO and have Big Alabama wait for me at the helo pad. Want to catch a ride to the hospital to check on our wounded Marines." Getting to his feet with the cup of coffee in hand, Hap began the four-block walk to the base infirmary.

On the move, he dialed Carla's number. After a few seconds, the call went to voicemail.

16

Wednesday 0715; Naval Air Facility El Centro CA

Walking briskly towards the athletic facility, which was nothing more than a football field sandwiched between two softball backstops, Hap finished leaving his message to Carla and then signed off. As he turned the corner of a small maintenance building, he stopped in his tracks.

Four Marines waited, standing at attention beside two gurneys, while Big Alabama secured the engines and engaged the rotor brake of the Huey. Hap came to attention as the rotors turned to a drooping stop. The Marines repositioned front and aft of each gurney, rolling slowly side-by-side, stopping short of the helo's open cabin door. Head down, Preacher, clad in desert cammies, stood at the head of the gurneys reading from an open Bible. Each Marine grabbed one corner of the thick plastic, removing the first Marine and carefully placing his body on one of the two gurneys. They placed the second Marine's corpse on the other gurney. Preacher made square facing, ceremonial movements, repositioning behind the gurneys for the journey to the infirmary.

Snapping a salute, Hap let the phone fall from his right hand to the grass. He held that salute while the Recon Marines presented as the deceased Marines' escort. In step, the escort slowly pushed the gurneys past a Marine color guard detail.

At the head of the detail, a wounded Marine in freshly press cammies barked, "Order H-h-h-a-a-a-arms!"

Hap held the salute for five minutes. He remembered throwing back scotch at the club with H.D. Simmons, who told the story of an entire Marine flight line stopping all activity to honor comrades. Hundreds of Marines conducted a face turn, some holding wrenches, others spare parts, standing at a position of attention as Brits carried their dead to a line of waiting C-130 transports for the long flight to Great Britain. For one hour, they ceremoniously carried the flag-draped coffins between an honor guard of fifty men and a detail on the bagpipes.

Now, as Hap stood next to the Huey, Captain Jonathan Simmons approached pale as an apparition. Stopping in his tracks, giving his best attempt at pulling up to a position of attention, he raised his right hand in a salute. Seconds later, he collapsed into Hap's arms.

Cradling young Simmons, almost as he'd done twenty years before when the Captain was a baby, Hap climbed aboard the helo.

"Get us to the hospital, Alabama," Hap yelled over the noise of rotors. Leaning over the seemingly lifeless Marine, he placed his ear to Simmons's chest and his hand to the Marine's mouth. Simmons's heart was beating and he was breathing. Thank God, the helo pad was only minutes away.

As soon as Big Alabama brought the helo down on the hospital pad, Hap carried Simmons out, placing him gently on the waiting gurney. With his flight suit now covered in the Captain's blood, Hap stayed by Simmons' side as they wheeled the gurney into the emergency room.

A brash, tough-looking nurse stepped in Hap's path, the emergency room doors closing behind her. It didn't take a genius to know she was upset with the Captain's recent activity. As other hospital staff attempted to intervene, Hap apologized emphatically to them all for the actions of the unconscious Captain Simmons.

"Good initiative but lacking sound judgment" is what Hap said.

Hap heard somebody from the trauma unit call out, "Stat!" A flurry of activity sounded from behind the closed doors.

"You will have to leave, Colonel." The order came from the rough and tough nurse, who bore the looks and build of Arnold Schwarzenegger. Pushing him away from the door, she ran him into Big Alabama, coming around the corner.

"What in the wide world of sports is going on, Colonel?" Big Alabama asked. Eyeing the nurse muscling up on Hap, he did what Alabama always did when confronting any female. He widened his eyes and asked, "Do you have a cell phone number?"

"Both of you out, now!" she yelled.

"Does this mean I'm not getting your number?" Big Alabama replied with an innocent smile. Hap would find out later that H.D. Simmons' son had snuck out of the hospital to a waiting cab, in order to head up the detail.

· · ·

During the short ride to the flight line, Hap began multi-tasking in his brain as he strapped into one of the jump seats. As Big Alabama rolled both throttles open, Hap's thoughts seemed to spool faster than the rotors, jumping between the pending memorial, his speech, and Colonel Ted Shank, the Marine Air Group CO, who was, with Warden's absence, Hap's direct line in the chain of command. Hap shook his head sharply, pulling his attention back to situation basics: what and why.

When Big Alabama set down on the Nomad flight line minutes later, Hap had calmed his thoughts. Entering his office for the first time since coming on station, he grinned at the small desk the CO used. Against the wall next to the boss's cot rested a folded-over sleeping bag. Catty-corner, Gunny Milligan had placed his field desk, made of sturdy wood painted olive drab, with the desk's edges and corners lined with reinforced metal. A kick-out leg provided support and a place for Hap to slide his own legs under, next to two wooden letter-size file drawers filled to overflowing.

Dropping his flight bag on the secretary's chair, he admired the ripped backrest, the ancient Naugahyde, and the squeaky wheels. Warden had mounted a small dry-erase board above the cot; it was still marked up from an earlier gun hop. The drawing was crude, but Hap recognized the terrain feature used for the IP. Half of the board had the target area marked up with pairs of circles, each with a tail signifying Hueys. Lines with a hockey stick for a tail represented Cobras. Run-in headings were off to the side of each section of stick drawings. This diagram depicted an L-attack, a section of Cobras attacking from the south simultaneous with a section of Hueys from the west.

A rap on the door took Hap's attention away from the board. The Squadron Administration NCO stuck his head inside, "Sorry, Sir."

Hap pivoted. "Yes, Gunny?"

Closing the door behind him, Gunnery Sergeant Milligan gestured with his head toward the next room. "We have a bunch of FBI agents, a County Sheriff, and NIS agents wanting to talk to you, Colonel." Hap made an unintelligible noise. "Excuse me, Sir?"

Hap frowned. "Nothing, Gunny, send the FBI agents in." A minute later, two agents entered flashing credentials.

"Agent Gordon," the older of the two agents announced himself and held out his badge. Hap shook hands, and then gestured for them to grab a seat on the cot. He did not offer them the CO's chair, not wanting them to get comfortable and stay longer than necessary. The agents' timing nixed the idea of fitting in a fighter nap prior to the memorial.

The lead agent, wearing a crew cut and carrying a slight bulge around the waist, opened the interview. "Colonel, can you describe what you saw this morning? We haven't been able to speak to any of the ground units. You are the first of the aircrew and we hope to obtain statements from all. We were hoping you would facilitate the interviews and arrange a flight to the OP in question."

Hap began with the sighting of the flares that interrupted their front row seat of the sex show. He briefly described their taking fire and Spanky's killing one assailant with a well-placed left skid to the man's upper body. He told them about Warden conducting the medevac of Simmons and Ball and passing Warden's aircraft when he was returning to evacuate the KIA's.

"Colonel," said Agent Gordon, "we have a report that multiple aircraft within your flight crossed over into Mexico. The Mexican Ambassadors to both the UN and United

States are raising hell. Our Administration, as you can well understand, doesn't like the publicity surrounding Marine Corps aircraft conducting combat operations within Mexico's border."

Hap's left elbow propped atop a crossed right arm. With his free hand, he rubbed the stubble on his chin. He continued to massage his square chin as he watched both agents squirm on the cot, trying to get comfortable. He remained silent for a moment before sounding off.

"So excuse the hell out of me if I don't give a shit what any politician in Mexico has to say about last night. Not sure if you two have heard but politicians, especially Mexican politicians, always have opinions—after the fact. The turds also have assholes, and most of the time, both stink. And by the way, where in the hell were the Feds when the call for support went out?"

Gordon came off the cot. "Colonel, in times like this you shouldn't be talking down the leadership of our southern neighbors. One would think talk like this wouldn't further your career."

Hap was quick in shutting down the agent. "So you think saying what is right should get in the way of doing what's right?"

Flustered, the agent settled back on the cot. "Not exactly Colonel, but we are conducting an investigation and we will be submitting a report. I would be derelict of my duty if I left out your last statement. I'm beginning to think your narrow-minded feelings could have instigated what occurred last night."

Hap maintained his poker face. Clearly, these two had instructions to find a scapegoat. Hap knew that "Mr. Big

Stuff" would eventually find out that he had led the flight south of the border. If he didn't, Hollywood would let him read about it in his book.

"Look," Hap said. "I will facilitate your interviews and get a hop to the crime scene. I need to put eyes on the scene myself."

"Nobody said a crime has been committed, Colonel."

"If I'm not mistaken we have two dead Marines, two wounded Marines, and my boss is MIA."

"Maybe your Colonel died after the wreck. His body is probably lying in the swamp."

Hap rose halfway out of the chair, blood boiling and about to let his mouth get him in trouble, when the Group CO entered, slamming the door behind him.

Seating himself behind Warden's desk, Colonel Ted Shank grasped a manila file between his bony fingers. Removing his wire-framed glasses, he turned to Hap. "Stoner, why does crap seem to follow you around?"

Hap chuckled through clenched teeth, "Colonel, I'm not sure what you were doing last night, but we were knee deep in shit. Is there any word on Tuna Man?"

"I'm catching so much shit from Wing, DHS, and the Feds for this international incident. I'm not concerned about LtCol Warden. I have no doubt he will end up on the United States side of the border any moment."

Hap blinked. "You kidding me, Colonel?"

"Do I sound like I'm kidding? Mexico's UN Ambassador will be speaking in front of the UN Assembly any moment."

"With all due respect Colonel, we have two KIA. Hell, H.D. Simmons's oldest is one of the wounded."

"Not surprising, Hap. H.D. was even more aggressive than you were. Where is that Marine now? Let's see. That's right, dead. His boy is WIA. Fruit doesn't fall too far from the tree."

Hap gazed over to the agents, who seemed to be enjoying what they were witnessing. "Would you mind allowing the Colonel and me to speak alone?"

Looking at each other, both nodded. Maybe they seemed relieved to leave the two sparring Marines to their own devices.

Hap cut his eyes toward Shank. "I'm not sure what is in the folder, but the United States was attacked last night."

Shank shifted his skinny ass in the chair. "Give me a break, Stoner. According to the Mexican authorities, US Military aircraft were doing God knows what on the Mexican side of the border last night. Who attacked whom?"

Hap took a deep breath. "LtCol Warden is a friend of ours. If I didn't know better, I'd say because of this political climate, the Administration is going to flush him—and you're okay with that?"

"Not before they flush your ass in the process. Look Stoner, I didn't want you to have the executive officer job. Tuna Man insisted on it and what did it do for him? This incident could cost me my star."

Hap sat and took the browbeating as he used to take it from his high school principal. Between both Marines, there was no love lost, no shared professional respect. They were polar opposites in the universe of the Marine Corps.

Under different circumstances, Hap might have pile-driven the chrome-dome bastard. But, if the Administration was going to throw Warden to the wolves, it would be over

Hap's dead body. He had to stay in the cockpit and retain command of the Nomads for a few more days. Shadow Services would have to come through. He would also need to bring Will Kellogg in on this one.

17

Wednesday 1000; Breckinridge, CO

In his subterranean office in Breckinridge, Colorado, Blad lowered the volume on his headset just as the young, energetic-sounding female inside the State Department said, "How could the engagement be denied?" She'd been covering the same conversational ground for the past six minutes, repeating her explanations that the Administration would meet the incident "head on."

Blad played five fingers hard against the surface of his desk. The mission of the country's lead foreign affairs agency was to shape a freer, more secure and prosperous world by developing and implementing the President's policy. Along with a friendly press corps in step with the Administration, the Secretary of State was the master in defending the indefensible.

"Sir?" the woman asked. "Are you still there?"

"I'm here."

As she chattered on, Blad reminded himself that she was simply doing her job, passing along the Department's primary talking point, which would hit cable networks within the hour:

International incident along the US-MX border. In support of Joint Task Force 6 operations along our southern border, a rogue Marine Corps officer was in direct violation of the Posse Comitatus Act. The Department of Justice will conduct a thorough investigation, and,

*if any laws or civil rights of any person have been violated,
the responsible party or parties will be prosecuted to the
full extent of the law. The penalty for Posse Comitatus
violations consists of a fine, and imprisonment for not
more than two years, or both.*

"If you have further questions," she said, cheerfully, "then
I can refer you—".

Blad disconnected, flipping the headset to the desk in
disgust. On earlier calls, CIA and DEA contacts in D.C. and
Mexico had instructions to stand down. The trifecta came
from inside the Pentagon, corroborated by a Marine One Star
and Colonel. A team of State and Marine Corps brass were
airborne, destination Naval Air Facility El Centro. All Marines
involved in the JTF-6 operation were to sign documents
compelling silence.

LtCol Warden was on his own. A snort of disgust slipped
out from between Blad's gritted jaws. None of the contacts
within the Administration seemed to care if Warden was
dead, much less innocent of the charges bandied about. It was
obvious to Blad that many officials wished Warden were dead
to avoid further embarrassment to the Administration and
the Marine Corps.

Replacing his headset, Blad dialed Big Shadow's direct
line. The next call would be to LtCol Hap Stoner USMCR. He
only hoped Hap would be sitting down when he received the
news.

A voice with a hint of a German accent answered on the
third ring.

"Yes Number 6. "

Blad appreciated the quiet confidence communicated by
the voice. The man on the other end read every report coming

over the organization's intranet. At a cost of $1,500,000 monthly, Shadow Services' private network operated with security in mind. They took hacking incursions seriously, and on more than one occasion, they physically terminated would-be hackers in the act. Two hours and forty-five minutes was the record for timing between the beginning of a particular international intrusion and its end, including exterminating all participants (except the lucky ones).

"You know why I'm calling," Blad said.

"Unfortunate incident," came the casual reply, as if he were ordering an after dinner Schnapps. "Did you know any of the injured?"

"Everybody I knew is alive, I think. LtCol Warden and I have shared drinks and women in our younger days. He is MIA."

A short chuckle followed. "That is good to hear, Number 6. Perhaps you'll share a story one of these days. Right now, I would like to hear your thoughts regarding Shadow 28. He was a good man."

Blad's partner and confidante always asked his opinion on situations outside of finance. It was rare for him to interrupt. "It looks like we have a Middle Eastern influence in one of the cartels. They go by the name of Jabhat al-Mahdi Americanos. Actually, we have a picture of their flag. It's Black over red with the Shahada in white. They're heavy into human trafficking. I will get that file over to you."

"That would be useful. Do we know which cartel?"

"Scorpion, Sir," Blad answered.

"I was going to suggest that it was Scorpion but held back at the thought you might believe I was profiling."

Blad snickered. "Gut tells me the piece of shit is responsible for Shadow 28's disappearance. Scorpion is probably behind the missing cheerleaders from Phoenix, too. I suspect Shadow 28 got a little too close for Scorpion's comfort." "We do know he purchases a lot of weapons and pays for them by moving narcotics across the border into the U.S. and a dozen other countries. Since we know why he brings the human column to the border, any ideas why he'd be moving humans out of the U.S

"Sir, I'm sure the case of the cheerleaders and others are not kidnapping in the usual sense. If it were me, I'd grab somebody who is loved and who has a family with deep pockets, a family willing to pay almost anything to get their loved ones back."

"Then why bother? I have taught you that with every risk there is reward. The only difference is the amount and who pays."

"Yes, Sir, and at this point I don't have a motive. Without a motive, I'm clueless as to who is writing the checks for the human merchandise. We do know the UAE royal family and other Middle Eastern royalty write checks for desirable female merchandise. The younger and most attractive girls draw the largest payments. But at this time I have no hard evidence of the incident being tied to the missing teenagers or Shadow 28."

"Are you thinking it's coincidental?"

Blad thought about the question posed by the man who was not only his boss but also his mentor. "Don't like coincidences and neither do you. I will let you know after Hap's package arrives."

18

Wednesday 1000; Paradise Island, Bahamas

Senator Scotty B. Jourdan lazed back on the chaise on the eastern promenade overlooking Danny Boyd's pool, the remnants of breakfast on the table beside him, his cell phone in hand, Missy Ann's trebly voice in his ear. Letting his bathrobe hang loosely open, he savored the heat of the sun stinging his very pale skin.

"Scotty?" Missy Ann's voice still surprised him, even after 25 years of wedlock.

"I've got to go, Honey, love you." Scotty disconnected abruptly, knowing Missy Ann wouldn't mind. The four-term United States Senator from the state of Vermont made certain that Mrs. Jourdan heard what mattered most to her—the well-rehearsed words and trappings of a happy marriage and solid family. The Senator's salary provided adequately for his wife and six children, even with private school tuitions rising and his third child entering an Ivy League school in the fall.

Damn, he'd needed this solo vacation. He sighed, almost shuddering. He felt as if he'd lived beneath the rotunda for the past forty-five days, making the hard push to pass this year's National Defense Authorization Act. Riddled with controversial riders—the usual public land and energy provisions—the bill drew indignation from the right side of the aisle.

His colleague, the senator from Colorado, wanted to designate new national parks and wilderness areas. The honorable senator from Wyoming, joined by senators representing North Dakota and Louisiana, needed to accelerate the permit approval process to facilitate fracking.

To protect the Jourdan way of life, Scotty had worked tirelessly to push U.S. Treasury loan guarantees, which included a U.S. guarantee for the construction loan for the Los Americanos resort in Mexico. It would be the fourth (and last) time he pulled this off, and it would reap him a larger financial benefit than the previous three combined. Failure was not an option.

Quid pro quo was Capitol Hill's gas, and Scotty found himself in and out of senators' offices from both sides of the aisle, which was no easy feat for a man with a bad hip who walked with a cane. Thanks to his diligence, the head of the Senate Armed Services Committee would ensure delivery of each respective senator's pork, artfully buried beyond page 432 in the thousand-page bill. Following the Committee's blessing, the bill would attach to this year's National Defense Authorization Funding Act DOD budget, and then it would go to the floor of the Senate for a vote.

The last days of pushing the bill through had been the worst. Scotty had worked up a sweat while attempting to ward off a Texas Senator arguing that a provision inserted by Senator Jordan would be an extreme injustice to American citizens. With his eyes closed, he could still conjure up the image of the Texan pounding the podium with his open hand, yelling into C-Span cams, "With the military's budget dwindling, Senator Jourdan's $600 million loan guarantee for a resort in Mexico is the rawest kind of pork! It's incomprehensible and self-serving!"

In the end, the bill had garnered the necessary sixty votes by the narrowest of margins. A last-minute compromise with members from the minority side of the aisle sealed the deal, thanks to a behind-closed-doors negotiation promising that the defense budget would see a sizable increase. After the vote, an ecstatic Jourdan had dialed Danny Boyd and announced, "It's done!" He could hear Danny take a satisfied sip of what was probably a 25-year-old cabernet. "When will you call our 'friend'?"

Charif Alawa of the First Bank of Panama would act as the mandated arranger for the Los Americanos Resort's syndicated loan. The bank would reap huge fees structuring the finances to completely buildout the 1200-acre project. What was more impressive, it was legal and approved by both houses of Congress. This was easier than robbing a bank and less risky. Assuming Danny Boyd could complete the development on budget, the U.S. Treasury would guarantee every penny for the project. As with the previous loans attached to the National Defense Authorization Act, persistence would once again pay huge dividends for the Senator. Sweet, Scotty remembered thinking *I love this country.*

But, hours later, watching CNN, Scotty had barely recognized himself on screen—the double chin, the deep shadows beneath the eyes, the extra pounds, damn he was a sorry sight. He couldn't believe the man looking back at him was only 55 years old. His pug nose had begun to sag after the first election. The droopy bags beneath his bloodshot eyes had appeared after his run for a second term. Even after his reelection, they hadn't gone away. The thin, spidery veins spreading across his rounded cheeks appeared after he began depriving the public of honest services, soon after the third reelection. It was easier than he ever thought to use his official position to line his business associates' pockets, along with his own.

But based upon the figure staring back at him, the deceit, the anxiety, the constant fear— always looking over his slumped shoulders—all of it was taking a toll.

"Earth to Scotty…"

At the sound of his lover's voice, the Senator half turned in his chaise. "Danny?"

Danny Boyd motioned from the opening of the "dog run." A folding glass wall enclosed either end of the room. On glorious mornings like this, all seven units were in their cubbies, creating a 35-foot opening to the Caribbean breeze.

"Hurry, you have got to see this," Danny gestured with both arms. "Leave your place setting. I'll have Stephan move it to the dog run."

Scotty, waddling past Stephan, clutched a coffee cup made of English bone china. All this luxury gave him a tinge of jealousy in the pit of his bulging stomach. Danny had the 84-inch TV screen divided into four separate screens. Each cable network was breaking the story about an incident that occurred only hours earlier on the southwest border with Mexico. All four networks were questioning state and executive public relations spokespersons about a possible incident along the US/MX border. Each expert spouted the same talking point about the rogue Marine Corps officer and an altercation. They touched on the dead and wounded Marines and the fact that the rogue Marine officer was missing. The Department of Defense was withholding all names until next of kin notification.

Scotty's cell rang; the opening of Beethoven's Fifth vibrating from the low pocket of his bathrobe. With phone to ear, his eyes remained locked to the TV. "Yes, Gary," he said, to his chief of staff.

"There are dead Marines in Southern California, Senator.

Nodding, the Senator said, "I'm watching the report on TV now."

"The Administration is flying personnel into El Centro. I'm reading the reports issued to the Senate Armed Services Committee. There are even reports of possible Middle Eastern ties associated with the incident. There is a Senate hearing tomorrow morning with the Commandant and senior officer conducting the investigation, a Colonel Ted Shank. You will need to return to Washington, Sir."

Scotty knew exactly to what his chief of staff was referring. Scorpion's brother had secretly introduced him and Danny to leaders of the Jabhat al-Mahdi last year. Scotty knew how to get his hands on weapons, while Danny only had to see the human cargo transported safely out of Latin America. A long journey would follow, marrying up with freighters owned by Boyd. Hidden away among concrete and heavy machinery in the freighter's holds, Boyd's top line of revenue for the human cargo and drugs carried much higher margins than the construction materials.

For some of the human cargo, it would be a round trip ticket. Young warriors accepting Sharia law were just now beginning to return to the Americas, final destination Los Americanos in Mexico and future resorts/secret jihadi training camps.

The senator's Swiss bank account grew exponentially as a result.

The U.S. Administration's allowing carte blanche access to the U.S. through its open border policy played right into Jabat al-Mahdi Americanos' hand. With open arms, the leaders of Catholic and Baptist charities met the indoctrinated allowed to enter the U.S. Hundreds of millions of dollars found its way to the charities' coffers. Danny Boyd and the senator were now making money coming and going.

"I will return to Washington immediately, Gary. Regarding the hearing tomorrow, not to worry, Colonel Shank is willing to throw his own mother under the bus for a general's star."

19

Wednesday 1245; Naval Air Facility El Centro CA

Deliberately running a Nomex-covered finger down each line of the open pocket checklist resting atop his kneeboard, Major Dick Calder called out each procedure. The mood among Nomads was tense, and Major "Goose" Heimlich responded sharply to each directive with *on, off,* or *check* as he touched each switch as directed.

Standing outside of the rotor arc at the Huey's 12 o'clock position, GySgt "Mad Dog" Bodette's hand circled above his head before he pointed directly at the crew with one finger raised.

Goose reached up, throwing the battery toggle to the on position. Dropping his left hand to the collective, a quick counterclockwise turn of both throttles followed, confirming both throttles remained closed.

Goose thumbed the start switch to the left, initiating the Number 1 engine start sequence. Upon the compressor stage reaching 12 percent on the Ng gauge, Goose rolled the upper throttle to the lower side stop, introducing jet fuel in the form of a spray into the hot section. The rotors, at first turning as slowly as a man could walk, gradually began to turn faster. With the Number 1 engine idling and all gauges in the green, Goose thumbed the start switch to the right, repeating the same sequence on the Number 2 engine.

Hap had just stepped away from the podium centered in front of the formation of Marines who made up HMLA 767 at the memorial, when the Huey began turning on the line. Exiting the hanger, he removed the piss cutter, sliding it into his right ankle flight suit panel as he walked toward the bird. The ride to the hospital would be short. His narrow face wore a fixed expression, signaling to all "stay clear."

Hap ducked below the drooping rotor arc, stepped onto the skid with his left boot, and took a large step up with the right, entering the wobbling aircraft. With throttles rolled on line, the rotors spun up to 100%, stabilizing the aircraft as Goose checked out with the ODO.

"Go ground," Goose said. Calder looked through his shaded visor to switch the preset frequency, a move followed by a "thumbs- up."

Goose nodded, squeezing the trigger switch past the first detent. "Ground, Nomad 24 taxi for takeoff. Westerly departure. 1+30."

"Roger, Nomad 24. Taxi to Helo Spot 2 at the intersection of Golf and Romeo, contact tower."

"Roger, Ground," Goose replied. Calder stuck his left hand out of the open window to signal thumbs-up. Mad Dog returned two thumbs- up. To lift the bird, Goose pulled the collective, matching the rate of speed set by Mad Dog's gesturing arms. Delivering a safe signal like a baseball umpire, Goose stabilized the helo in a hover. Mad Dog's palms began gesturing toward his chest.

Goose eased the bird forward until Mad Dog crossed his forearms over his head, fists clenched. Easing in the right pedal, he followed Mad Dog, who was pointing the left forefinger to the ground and gesturing with his right hand like a traffic cop. Stabilizing, Goose landed and Mad Dog ducked underneath the rotors to find a seat across from Hap.

"I'm secure, Sir," Mad Dog said over the intercom.

Goose lifted and taxied to the intersection. "Go tower, Dick," he said.

Calder came back with thumbs- up.

"Tower, Nomad 24 is holding at helo Spot 2. Ready for takeoff, Spot 2, westerly departure with a turnout to the south."

"Roger, Nomad 24. Clear for takeoff. Westerly departure with turnout to the south is approved."

Hap heard the conversation through the headset, but his mind was somewhere outside the aircraft. Leaning partially from the cabin, he was hit with a blast of wind against his face that felt better than coffee. Peg was going to call the parents of the KIA's upon notification by Marine Corps. She would place a day and time for him to visit on his calendar. Having spoken to Warden's wife, he'd said the only thing he could say. "We'll bring him back one way or the other." Hap had also warned her to stay away from cable news and the papers at least for the next 36 to 48 hours. The news outlets would put her through hell; no way he wanted her listening to them lambasting her husband unchallenged. Peg had engaged a security firm to post guards in front and back of the Warden residence to keep out overzealous reporters.

Hap owed H.D. Simmons's widow, MC, a call. The Marine Corps had probably notified her about her son's injuries by now. Knowing MC, she was already on an airliner to San Diego or Yuma. This was the one call Hap wouldn't allow Peg to make. He was in the cockpit when MC's husband died and whatever needed saying now, he had better do it in person. When provoked, the lady was a fire-eating dragoness and she would surely track him down the moment she left her son's hospital room.

Hap watched the Hospital LZ come into view as the engines decelerated and Goose began final approach. Even as he'd agreed to give authorities the chance to make good on Warden's rescue, to Hap each heartbeat felt like precious minutes lost. He was formulating a plan for Warden's extraction, but he had to have a fixed location first. Whatever Blad's organization was, it had better get on the stick. In any case, LtCol Hap Stoner and select Marines were going to make a run at the border.

20

Wednesday 1245 Breckenridge CO

Even though Blad was surrounded by technology and unlimited financial resources, the knot in his stomach wouldn't go away. Now he wished he had kept the room above ground to enjoy Mother Nature in moments like these. Instead, he would look past the elevator and take the three flights of stairs, leading to the homemade retreat room. Lined in concrete, the room also contained an arsenal James Bond would envy.

As Blad felt the pressure of his slacks from taking the steps two at a time, he told himself he would not go past the size 38's purchased last month. Gaining the retreat room, he slipped through the opening bookcase and strode through the master bedroom. He poured a four-finger scotch from the small bar to the right of the 84-inch smart TV hanging on the wall. Then opening the French doors to the back porch, he stopped to take in a deep breath of Colorado mountain air. After half a minute, he eased back in his favorite Tommy Bahama deep leather chair.

Taking in all of Mother Nature's magnificence helped ease the nerves. When nature alone would not lower his blood pressure, an 8-year-old cabernet usually did the trick. But today, it took an 18-year-old single malt scotch. He sensed isolation. Hap Stoner, being the tip of the spear, would feel the same after they spoke.

Since Blad had spoken with Shadow, several reports had come in from multiple Shadow Services' sources. As he pieced together the intelligence, it seemed clear that the Nomad's San Antonio-based Recon Unit had stepped smack into a buzz saw. Based on his sources, and listening to the government PR mouthpieces, it was clear they intended to deem LtCol Warden the responsible party for the incident. Hap Stoner would call it "thrown under the bus." "Careerists," clawing their way up the military chain of command or bureaucratic hierarchy, would call it "covering one's ass."

Marines expected politicians to blather. Members of Congress didn't have to write the first letter to the parents of Marines KIA. But, for a group commander with lives on the line, putting your Marines first shouldn't be an afterthought. To do otherwise was a sacrilege, yet this was what Ted Shank did every day of his career. Tapping his fingers on the heavy aluminum armrest, Blad shook his head. No love lost between Hap Stoner and Ted Shank. Through the years, the careerist knew to stay on the other end of the bar from warriors like Hap and Warden. Yet, Blad knew that in spite of this, Hap and Warden would both give their lives attempting to save the life of that same careerist.

Tracking news and intel feeds, Blad worked his way down his four-finger single malt scotch. Rare indeed, but today was no ordinary day. Everything confirmed LtCol Warden's fate as the administration's fall guy. Blad would talk to Hap in person. And, he'd keep his handcuffs at the ready to make sure Hap didn't go hunting humans.

Blad took another pull off the scotch and pressed 3 on his cell.

"I need the plane ready within the hour," he told his pilot. "File for El Centro. And pack for a few days, extra skivvies and socks."

Blad drained the glass and typed the final message to Hap:

Coming your way. Will be at club 1800 hours. You buy the scotch.

21

Wednesday 1345; Scorpion's Villa MX

In his private gym, Scorpion lay on his back on the bench, positioning his grip on the straight bar and staring up at the mirrored ceiling that offered an expansive view of the room as well as the inspiring reflections of his two female personal trainers. Both were clad in low-cut, form-fitting workout apparel designed to show off muscles and curves. Each woman packed a 9mm stowed in a black leather shoulder holster, and each clutched one end of the straight bar, which was weighted with one 25-pound- and two 45-pound steel plates per side. Beginning his second set, Scorpion allowed his thoughts to stray for a few seconds from counting reps.

Despite going against his better judgment, the past week's work would pay well. His concern was the added attention, the last thing the organization needed. He had hidden the American teen-age girls safely away on his ranch in Sinaloa, tagged by the jihadists "Mecca II." The spying American agent was on his way there to join them, and when the Saudi "teacher" applied his special tools and skills, they would soon learn if the agent was working for the DEA or some other agency.

Most interesting and surprising was the unexpected acquisition of a second male hostage, a gift from the sky, literally. If played well, some Salafist jihadist Saudi prince would pay $15 million, maybe more, for this high-profile captive. Perhaps that Saudi prince would be a relative of the "teacher." After all, his uncle was Crown Prince Sayed bin Sultan bin Al Saud, the head of Saudi Intelligence.

Scorpion let his thoughts linger a bit longer on the Saudi "teacher," an interesting man. The Arabic word for teacher was *mudarris*, but the Saudi had adopted the moniker "El Maestro" after several of Scorpion's most beautiful women (presented to the Saudi as gifts) amused him with some lessons of their own in Spanish.

Breezing through the last reps, Scorpion was feeling a little bit richer than when he went to bed. He bridged his shoulder blades against the bench, pushing 275 pounds into its cradle without his trainers' assistance. Both of the lovelies, born and raised in Fallujah, came as gifts from El Maestro and Crown Prince Sayed bin Sultan bin Al Saud. Sunni warriors, they were part of a religious enforcement unit before El Maestro plucked them out of western Iraq to bring them to Mexico and to Scorpion. At his every beck and call, even in his bed, the agile jihadists always kept their weapons within reach.

Now, they removed the 25-pound plates, and added a 45-pound plate to each end, the weights clanging against each other. Sitting up on the end of the bench, Scorpion took several deep breaths, shifting his focus to the upcoming lift. He positioned himself underneath the straight bar. His two spotters each used both hands to lift the bar from its cradle. Scorpion cranked out another set of seven reps. After two short breaths, he lowered 315 pounds to his chest, squeezing out the final rep with a scream. He allowed his spotters to secure the bar back into the cradle. When they were finished, Jorge approached quietly, respectfully. "Sir, your guests have arrived."

Sitting up, Scorpion gestured with his head for his trainers to leave. He waited until they were out of earshot before speaking. "El Maestro?"

Jorge nodded, "And a female guest."

"Another gift, Jorge?"

"Not sure, Sir, but she is clothed in a burka," Jorge said. "And there is someone else accompanying El Maestro. He calls himself Muhammed Abu Moya. If you ask me, he looks like a Mexican in Muslim attire with a beard dyed salt and pepper."

"That would be my cousin," Scorpion said. "His real name is Geraldo Moya." He shook his head, sneering. "The loser calls himself El Caliph de America Latina.

Jorge chuckled. "Where would you like me to seat them?

Frowning, Scorpion closed his eyes. El Maestro's 'gifts' were always desirable, and always willing when it came to performing after-hour collateral duties. "The dining room will be fine. Have the kitchen prepare a tray of fruit for our guests."

"Will that be all?" Jorge asked.

Scorpion nodded. "That's all, Jorge."

Bowing slightly from the hip, Jorge turned toward the doorway to attend to his duties. Scorpion watched him: he moved with surprising grace for a muscled three-hundred-pound man. Scorpion thought of Jorge as a 'gentle giant,' one of very few men he would trust with his life.

* * *

El Maestro posed at the far end of the 20-place teak banquet table, standing in a wide-legged stance with hands on hips. A female figure cloaked in a purple burka sat silently by his side. Poised with her spine pressed straight against the high back chair, her delicate hands clasped in her lap, Scorpion found her oddly intimidating, certainly mysterious. Scorpion's cousin, Geraldo Moya, aka El Caliph, was sitting across the table from El Maestro. Apparently, he was dressing to match his new name these days: in long cloth, turban, coat, and baggy pants. Scorpion suppressed a sneer; whatever his costume, Geraldo would always be a two-bit hustler.

As Scorpion approached casually, El Maestro held the pose that showed off his summer weight, navy blue thobe and dark turban, its loose ends resting atop his shoulder length hair. Scorpion knew the royal Saudi was avoiding the dress of the kuffar (unbelievers), while maintaining the standard of the People of Excellence. The turban indicated good character, intelligence, and patience, or at least gave the appearance of those positive qualities. Like many Saudi men who did business with the West, El Maestro kept his beard manicured.

Scorpion puffed a bit with pride. His guests sat in the formal dining room, illuminated by an immaculate, imported 19th-century wrought iron chandelier suspended from the domed ceiling. On the 15th of every month, two of his staff dedicated the entire day to fastidiously cleaning the crystal and its complement of seventy-two lights. He greeted El Maestro with a nod, extending his hand.

"So good to see you again, my friend," the Saudi said smoothly. "My uncle, Crown Prince Sayed, sends his condolences on the untimely death of your brother."

Scorpion kept his expression masked even as he went cold inside. "Please relay my gratitude to your uncle." He did not say that it had been extremely unwise for some members of El Maestro's inner circle to fraternize with Scorpion's cousin, *El Caliph de Pendejo—Caliph of Stupidity*. Geraldo could hold neither drink nor tongue, and, in a drunken stupor, he had revealed to one of Scorpion's most beautiful spies that the murder of Scorpion's brother had been ordered by none other than El Maestro's uncle, the Crown Prince Sayed bin Sultan bin Al Saud.

Scorpion's world was a brutal one, and he ruled it with extreme violence, retribution, street smarts, and wisdom. A devotee of Sun Tzu's "The Art of War," he had trained himself to be patient, a trait he did not naturally possess. He considered himself an artist when it came to his empire. Each action he took was a "brushstroke" applied to "canvas" with meticulous attention and execution. No stroke gave away the stroke to follow. No single line revealed the entire pattern. Therefore, everything he and his brother put in place before his brother's assassination aligned to trigger the next phase of operations. He would have his retribution, when the time was right.

"*Ashkirak sadiqi,*" El Maestro said in Arabic, then: "Thank you, my friend. *Allah 'akbar.*"

"*Allah 'akbar,*" Scorpion returned.

Scorpion knew that El Maestro used the concept of Salafist Islam as a tool and dealt promptly with anyone who stood in his path to power, either through manipulation or through elimination. In this, he was no different from his uncle, Crown Prince Sayed, or, for that matter, from Scorpion.

Squeezing his guest's hand, he praised Allah. "*Subhan 'Allah.*"

El Maestro replied, "*Subhan 'Allah.*"

Arms by his sides, Scorpion greeted the woman with his best smile. "Subhan 'Allah," he said. The woman looked straight ahead without speaking, but Scorpion, who always expected a positive response from the opposite sex, caught the fluttering of her eyelashes and hoped that she was sending him an invitation.

Ignoring his cousin, Scorpion returned his attention to El Maestro, whose "versatility" intrigued him. But, as head of the largest cartel in Mexico, the Black Stone Cartel, Scorpion knew that America's democracy would be what ultimately allowed him to reach his objective. In contrast, Islam was Islam and had no modifiers.

"A political movement masquerading as a religion," El Maestro had said weeks earlier, speaking candidly in front of his uncle, the Crown Prince, as the three shared a $2800-dollar bottle of *AsomBroso Reserva Del Porto*. "The battle that unites all Muslims and leaders of Islamist groups is jihad. Instead of living in misery, many Latin Americans, as well as others around the world, see the concept of jihad as a way out of their misery. A lesser of two evils is how we discuss it among our kingdom's elite."

Scorpion had taken over as sole leader of the Black Stone Cartel after his brother's assassination and had no problem brandishing a banner of religion to make a buck. Radical Islam attracted many followers and it attracted cash. Scorpion's oldest brother had been a true convert to Islam, but he had also been immensely practical. Before his murder, he passed on a valuable reminder. "In the great Gold Rush, most miners in the United States went bust," he told Scorpion one night when they shared an evening alone. "It was the man who sold the pickaxes, shovels, pans, and food who got rich."

Posing as true guardians of The Faith, Scorpion invoked the banner of religion to allow Black Stone to take control of drug markets. Since it was permissible to lie to infidels to advance the cause of Islam, Scorpion took it one step further and lied to Muslims. But one thing for sure, if the information regarding El Maestro's uncle turned out to be true, by initiating Fer-de-Lance, a river of blood would flow throughout the organization, ultimately purging all Islamic members.

Meanwhile, Black Stone trafficked in humans as if they were cattle. They skimmed off the healthiest boys for the voyage east, where eventually they would undergo indoctrination into the Islamist faith. Black Stone looked first for people with trades such as auto mechanics, carpenters, electricians, and welders who could undergo and withstand military indoctrination. They would remain in the Middle East to use their trades to help build the Caliph's brick and mortar infrastructure.

They also shipped some of the young girls, several only fourteen years old, to the Middle East. For many it was a one-way ticket. Some would serve as jihadi wives and nurses. Others would return home to complete jihad, becoming prostitutes for other cartels and embedding Black Stone's tentacles inside competing organizations. Under the guise of furthering the religion, the girls would give up their bodies willingly, while feeding Black Stone new intelligence 24/7. Human trafficking was lucrative, whether to the east or the west, but El Maestro was beginning to make bad decisions, first, with the kidnapping of the American girls in Phoenix, and then, the killing of US Marines.

Scorpion took his seat next to El Maestro at the end of the table and gestured with his hand towards the empty crystal glasses. "Would you and your guest like anything to drink?"

Jorge entered the room carrying a large, beautifully arranged fresh fruit plate. Leaning delicately between El Maestro and Scorpion, he placed the platter of sliced watermelon, red and green grapes, avocado, and pineapple on the table.

He neatly turned four crystal glasses upright, one in front of each guest. Walking over to a serving table placed below a 12 x 12 arched window, he retrieved a pitcher of ice water and filled each glass, beginning with the woman. Obviously perturbed by the act, El Maestro's gaze hardened. El Caliph, in contrast, seemed oblivious to everything but the food.

Removing each of the folded napkins propped in front of the plates, Jorge handed one to each diner, ladies first. He was very careful not to even brush the sleeve of the female. With cheeks reddening by the second, El Maestro's dark eyes cut toward Scorpion.

"Thank you Jorge," Scorpion's tone was cool and polite.

Seeing the servant as a mere slave and infidel, El Maestro refused to acknowledge him in any way.

Placing a pressed cotton napkin on the table, Jorge set the pitcher of water within Scorpion's reach. "Will you need anything else, Sir?"

Scorpion glanced at El Maestro, who gazed toward the window, declining to engage in conversation.

"That will be all. Thank you, Jorge."

Responding with a curt nod, Jorge left the room.

Gesturing towards the platter Scorpion said, "Please, fill your plates. There is more where this came from."

"*Bismillah*," El Maestro said, stabbing some pineapple slices and chunks of watermelon. Using his right hand, he selected a batch of red grapes. He spoke again as Scorpion filled his own plate. "I understand you have another load ready to ship east?"

Scorpion recognized the brief prayer alternative, *Bismillah*, "In the name of Allah." Although he was famished from the workout, he ate lightly. El Caliph, his cousin, disregarded etiquette. After a quick, "*Bismillah,*" he began grabbing fruit by the handful building a small pyramid on his plate.

El Maestro continued. "My uncle would like me to visit the facility to inspect the merchandise." He plucked a green grape with his teeth.

Scorpion took a long drink before replacing the crystal glass on the table. "I will be visiting tomorrow." His cold, dark eyes passed over his cousin, who had his face almost buried in his food, apparently to minimize the travel time to his mouth.

"Will El Caliph de America Latina be joining us?" Scorpion asked, not bothering to cover his derision. "Better yet, El Maestro, please, invite your uncle. I would like him to see how his money is being spent."

El Maestro nodded. "I will ask. Zaida will be accompanying us."

Scorpion's gazed settled on the woman. His male sense told him she was attractive and wearing little beneath the tent-like burka. "Our next move?"

"Within a week we will be moving the merchandise to the City of Nifaq. We will send as many of the infidels as possible to see *Munkar wa Nakir* and let the angels of Allah sort the faithful out."

"A city I know?"

Steely-eyed, El Maestro met Scorpion's gaze, "Washington D.C., of course. We will bring jihad to the school where the children of the Great Satan attend. Their seed will be sacrificed and many of their classmates and teachers will bow before Allah."

Gesturing with his head toward the woman, he continued, "Zaida will complete our martyrdom operation by leading the attack on the *Shahe Najaf Islamic Center* and all present at the afternoon prayer."

"Don't you think the retaliation against Mexico will be quick and decisive?" Scorpion said, concerned by this news. "This could put me out of business."

"No need to worry. The jihadists chosen for the assignment at the school are from Germany and France," El Maestro said, pausing to sip some water. "The weapons used will come from caches purchased from the U.S. infidels in their so called "Fast and Furious" operation. The leader of the infidels will have only himself to blame as he watches mothers and fathers crying over their children's caskets.

Scorpion's cousin looked up from his almost empty plate. "El Maestro," the self-proclaimed El Caliph de America Latina said. "Allah has blessed us with weak US leadership. But do you believe the President's wife will allow her husband to stand idle even if the martyrs fail?"

"Saudi Intelligence will leave a trail a blind man could follow. It will appear our mujahedeen warriors entered the lands of Al Kuffar through several infidel charities. The enemy of Allah fears our culture of martyrdom. Our warriors fear nothing."

Scorpion nodded slowly. He prided himself on being the first to enter a fight, always expecting Black Stone members to follow. He doubted that El Maestro had participated in anything more than a playground fight. And, Scorpion knew firsthand how fast his cousin, the so-called Caliph, would begin to blubber and beg for mercy. All it would take was one light slap to his fat cheek. Scorpion cut his eyes away from El Caliph's face and his unkempt beard currently decorated with an assortment of food remnants.

El Maestro's Swiss bank accounts had swollen over the past 14 months. Scorpion had also done very well. For now, all he had to do was pretend that nothing had changed and Black Stone would continue to do Islam's bidding to spread the religion further. Nothing more, nothing less. But, with the sacrifice of his brother, and now this, the end of the business relationship had arrived.

* * *

Standing alone in the butler's pantry, Jorge removed the earpiece, placing it in the secret cubbyhole carved out of the bottom of a vase. Next to it was a pair of AAA batteries, a small receiver, and a motherboard, accessible by removing the false bottom. He had built listening and recording capabilities into the base of the wooden flower vase, an ancient Mexican artifact that only Jorge was allow to touch. A planted microphone, half the size of a pushpin also lay hidden inside a tiny hole carved into the dining room's 24' x 24' cedar arch connecting the chain and chandelier. Given the room's acoustics, Jorge never missed a word.

22

A good jukebox at the OC can amp up certain characters, flooding high levels of testosterone throughout their systems. In most circumstances, a Naval Aviator would fit that category of character. But then again, under the right circumstances, Shamanic flute music could rev LtCol Hap Stoner's mojo, while Squadron mates, lacking his musical soul, would simply call him a pussy. That he might get them laughing to the point of puking—many of the Nomads did just that—didn't bother Hap a bit.

Hap leaned against the jukebox, fumbling around in his left breast pocket for loose change, staring at pretty much the same selection of tunes from his two previous deployments to El Centro. And, despite the recent and ongoing adversity, tonight looked to be magical. The officers and enlisted Marines of HMLA 767 needed to blow off a head of steam. Soon enough they'd be moving into action.

This night, there would be no shamanic flutes. Hap slipped three quarters into the jukebox. By memory, he punched J then up to 3. Christopher Cross's "Ride like the Wind" would be the first song. Going down and left he punched G then up and right to 2. Steppenwolf's "Born to be Wild" would follow. Even on his most tipsy nights, his hand traced up and left to A, then right and down to the number 2. Jimmy Buffet's "Let's

Get Drunk and Screw." Running a well-manicured finger down the alphabet, he pushed the H then up and right to 7. Alan Jackson's "Remember When." Then came the Romantic's "What I Like About You." No hip-hop or rap music from this jukebox tonight.

The Officers' Club had "Rules of the Bar," carved on a large piece of wood and hanging behind most bars in the Military Club System. A bell hung nearby.

Glancing left, Hap saw the maintenance man bent over the ice machine behind the bar. Hap noticed that he appeared to be more interested in the dice game going on at the end of the bar than with tinkering with the ice machine. He contemplated inviting the chap to join the game. But, he decided to leave it alone. Money was changing hands at lightning speed. The liquor was disappearing down the boys' throats just as fast, in an effort to blot out the reality of "payback."

By the time "Born to be Wild" was shaking the jukebox speakers, Hap was nuzzling against Carla in the darkest corner of the O' Club. He loved the way she whispered in his ear, even when she relived events inspired by an incident on the border west of San Diego.

Since Hap wasn't answering his cell phone, Carla had jumped the first plane to San Diego's Lindbergh Field. After four beers during a 90-minute layover, she endured the short hop in the twin turbine commuter over the mountains to El Centro. Ten minutes into the flight, she was digging her fingernails into both armrests as if her life depended on it, wishing she'd rented a car.

Hap could never get out of her how she continued to gain access to the Nomad flight line. Tonight, after Gunny Milligan directed her to Hap and Tuna Man's empty cubbyhole of an office, she demanded, and he courteously offered, the duty driver to transport her to the Officers' Club. Minutes later, she found Hap alone at the bar.

They were bemoaning the way the press secretaries for the state and executive branches spun the story, even while Jimmy Buffet sang, "Why don't we get drunk and screw, I just filled up a water bed made up for me and you." She explained how she cringed hearing that "overzealous Marine pilots, trying to be heroes, have infringed on Mexican sovereignty."

The music continued. Carla clutched Hap's forearm. "Have you spoken with Tuna Man's wife?" Hap shook his head; not wanting to face the urgency that he knew was very real. He and the boys could not do anything until they had his location, damn it. He took a breath. "The next of kin have been notified. I was hoping the bad dream would end, and Tuna Man would be sitting across the table."

Alan Jackson's "Remember When" began. Carla rose to her feet grabbing the collar of Hap's flight suit. He allowed her to pull him onto the small dance floor in front of the idle DJ equipment. She pulled him close. The boys stopped the dice game and watched the two twirling around.

With his attention on Carla, Hap still caught sight of the maintenance man circling from behind the bar, lifting a glass of spirits in a toast. The face behind the beard looked familiar to Hap. With an obvious hiccup, the jukebox flipped back to "Born to Be Wild," and on the opening beat, the boys, including the maintenance man, joined Hap and Carla on the floor. When Hap reached out again for Carla, he saw that Phantom and Spanky had her off to the side, and they were rocking as only Marine Aviators could do. Off by a beat, trying to sing, and not even close to hitting the notes.

Then, it all stopped abruptly and Major Dick Calder was tapping on the DJ's microphone. Phantom unplugged the jukebox, and raced over to Dick, wrapping an arm around his buddy's shoulder. The music to The Doors "Roadhouse Blues" followed, the two Marines started singing, following the words on the Karaoke screen, and although they were two octaves off, all the Nomads in the bar moved to the floor to pay homage. Hap moved back to the table and picked up drinking where he'd left off. Carla stayed on the dance floor, swaying with the other pilots to the singing coming across the Club's sound system. Hap had heard Dick and Phantom's shitty singing before but tonight actually seemed to be one of their better efforts.

His thoughts returned to his missing friend. The Administration and possibly the Marine Corps were ready to sacrifice his boss. Neither one seemed to care about the Marines engaged at Bravo 6. The Administration press secretary stated the Marines should not have had live rounds, but instead, should have carried beanbag shotguns. Pressed by the Administration, the Pentagon pressed the Commandant, who raised hell with MARFORCOM, the commander of all Marine operational and shore-based commands in CONUS, less IMEF Forces. The generals of 4th MAW and division were trying to explain the incident. The group commander, Colonel Ted Shank, would act as the senior Marine investigating the incident, reporting directly to the 4th MAW commander.

Hap reviewed the Administration talking points. *LtCol Warden accidentally—or possibly intentionally—entered Mexican airspace. Mexican authorities responded by chasing down the perpetrators and taking fire from the crash site. Captain Simmons's recon team engaged Mexican citizens while protecting the Marines' escape.* Grinding his teeth, he vowed to ensure their biggest mistake would be the cover up.

Draining the last of the scotch, Hap rested the empty glass on the tabletop. As a habit, the Administration apologized to the Mexican Government, and within the same hour, asked for forgiveness from the UN. Thinking about UN Ambassadors from Venezuela and Nicaragua (to name a few countries) railing on all the cable networks regarding the United States Military overreach, made Hap's stomach churn.

Completing the last line of "Roadhouse Blues," Dick and Phantom picked up the Marine Corps hymn. Motion on the dance floor ceased immediately as all present locked up. Carla joined in assuming the position of attention, tears streaming down her reddened cheeks. Hap came to his feet, pushing the chair back in the process. Out of the corner of his eye, he could see the maintenance man locked up, as well.

Big Alabama, Goose, and Ambassador barreled through the club entrance, heads on a swivel. Big Alabama and Goose had flown the Huey, landed, and then gone through the normal post-flight procedure. Giddy as a kid in anticipation of the evening's events, Ambassador joined them on the way to the club. As their eyes adjusted to the dimly lit bar, the three came to the position of attention, Big Alabama still covered. The bell rang and Hap saw the maintenance man holding the cord and pointing in Big Alabama's direction.

The big guy shrugged, removed his cover, and pulled out his wallet at the same time, knowing the rule carved above the bar: *"He who enters a bar covered buys the house a round if the bell is rung while covered. He who rings the bell and the person in question is uncovered, buys the house a round."*

With the steam building in him like a pressure cooker, Hap wanted to find a bureaucrat to hit. He warbled, attempting to sing through a clenched jaw.

> Here's health to you and to our Corps,
> Which we are proud to serve;
> In many a strife we've fought for life
> And never lost our nerve.
> If the Army and the Navy
> Ever look on Heaven's scenes,
> They will find the streets are guarded
> By United States Marines.

Each officer on the dance floor had arms around the man's shoulders next to him. The circle drew tight around Carla, heads bowed. Raising his empty glass to the fallen, Hap gave out a healthy "uhhhhhhhhhhrah, next round's on Big Alabama!" The others responded in chorus. The need for sleep popped him between the eyes, just as someone, not Carla, forcefully took a fist full of his collar.

"Okay, asshole. That's enough."

The voice came from behind Hap. Barely able to keep his footing, he thought about a half turn, and a well-aimed quick jab. Whoever it was had a scotch bottle with two glasses teetering atop the neck in the other hand, so he held his punch and instead followed him out to the veranda. Both stopped and a Mexican faceoff ensued. Now Hap recognized the eyes, the rounded cheeks that the cheesy beard couldn't disguise, and the fifth of Johnny Walker Black.

"Nice choice, Blad."

Holding a glass bottom up, Blad flipped the glass to bottom down. "It's on your tab, Hap."

Hap couldn't hold back the snicker. Catching Carla standing in the doorway, he gave her a certain look. She nodded and returned to the dance floor. Hap gestured to one of the many unoccupied tables, and he and Blad sat opposite each other, with the bottle of Black between them. The mountains overlooking San Diego cast their creeping shadow across the veranda as the sun touched their peaks. Sitting on topography twenty feet above the runway elevation, both watched a section of Marine Reserve F-18's rotate, their turkey feathers expanded, easing off the runway on a night low altitude run. The mission would end with both aircraft emptying all their ordnance on a target of tires, plywood, or, if lucky, a rusting tank, before both crews ended up at the bar.

"So you weren't lying," Hap said.

Blad shook his head filling both glasses. "Too much work to do, Hap. This incident is as personal to me as it is to you."

"I know. So what have you learned?"

"Administration is covering their ass, Hap, but we knew that would happen." Blad leaned across the table. "Press and Administration claim LtCol Warden took out a vehicle on the Mexican side of the border."

Shrugging, Hap frowned, forming wrinkles across his forehead. "I wouldn't know anything about that."

Blad threw back the Scotch and lowered the glass holding only ice to the table. "I would've loved to be a fly on the wall when you and Shank were discussing the matter. I know Bear is crawling up your ass looking for answers!"

Hap pulled a long sip, "I'm surprised Shank isn't at this table sponging drinks while he tightens the noose around the Tuna Man's neck."

Blad settled back into his chair. "Hap; piecing this event together, there is no way Warden's bird took out the vehicle. It was you or Spanky. So who was it?"

Hap tried to maintain his best poker face. Blad frowned, seeing right through it. *Son of a bitch used to do the same, staring me down during poker games on the boat.*

"It was me."

Blad nodded slowly, having figured this out the moment he received the news. "You guys weren't armed. How in the hell did you pull it off?"

Hap went on to tell the story that he'd pass on to children, grandkids, deer lease buds, and, one day, God. Starting with the couple on the car, the red flares, getting jumped by small arms fire below Bravo 6, Tuna Man's medevac of Captain Simmons and Ball. Hap's jaws tensed as he described the "Broken Arrow call" and the voice telling the LEA to stand down moments later.

"Wait a minute," Blad interrupted. "I never heard about the Broken Arrow call."

"Made it myself, Blad." Hap held up an empty glass, "Freshen me, *por favor.*"

Blad nodded, silently thanking the hostess for the bucket of ice she had left at the table. He gave a judicious pour. Setting the bottle down, he dropped a couple of ice cubes into Hap's glass, and then into his own. "What the hell was the 'stand down order' all about?"

Hap took a long pull, savoring the soft, nutty flavor. "Your guess is as good as mine. At this juncture, I don't really give a shit. What I do care about is getting Tuna Man back to his family ASAP. I owe the man and his family that much."

Blad's fingers strummed across the table. "So when are you going in to get him? And, how're you going to do it, and how can I be of assistance? Remember, I'm also missing a man."

Hollywood came around the corner toting an empty glass. Leaning down, he feigned a whisper into Hap's ear. Dropping a couple of ice cubes into his glass, he clutched the bottle, pouring his glass to four fingers. "Nice disguise, Blad," he said, walking away.

Hap's bloodshot blues burned through Blad. "Bear is flying to D.C. tonight. Son of a bitch will be sitting to the Commandant's right at the Senate Armed Services Committee hearing tomorrow morning. That frigging prick Senator Scotty B. Jourdan heads up the committee."

Blad shrugged and rolled his eyes. "You knew that was coming. So how are you going to do it?"

"Do what?"

"Bring Tuna Man home?"

"First of all, you prick; you're going to have to tell me where he is. After that, I'm going to go get him."

Blad's cell chirped. Retrieving it from his blue denim overalls, he thumbed to his email and read silently.

Almost positive Black Stone is involved with Islamo Fascist organization. Attempting to find the organization name but Scorpion keeping all activities close to vest. Have seen Islamic target but have neither pictures nor a name. Scorpion and Islamo target accompanied by a guest will be traveling to Camargo City tomorrow. Suggest converge all available assets to this location. End of message.

"Guess it's going to be a long night," Blad said. "Before I forget, you should know Shadow has operatives deep inside the Black Stone Cartel and another moving within the Jihadi'

s. Shadow has been working to get inside Black Stone for years. By the way, I'm going into Mexico tonight."

"Tonight, Mexico?" Hap shook his head. "I got that right?"

"You ever seen a fat ass with a few drinks fast rope?"

Hap recoiled, picturing the helo in a hover, with Blad's guys wearing heavy-duty gloves and riding thick rope to the ground. "Sounds potentially messy, big boy, have you considered driving in?"

With a last long pull of Black, Blad pushed the empty glass against the ice bucket. "Wish me luck. I will be in contact." Rising from the chair, he flipped the tab into Hap's lap.

23

Wednesday 1900; Naval Air Facility El Centro CA, OC

Hollers of "Dice on the floor, buy a round!" reverberated from inside the club.

Hap ducked in to grab a drunken look, and saw Carla standing among a dozen Nomads gathered over the bar, keying in on a competitive game of Klondike. It was not hard to miss the pile of strewn bills building up at the corner of the bar. Each participant leaned over, under, and around the other to catch the next roll. Watching the magic, Hap chuckled. Local talent from the village entered the bar wearing heels better suited for a pole dance show, swinging their buttocks side to side, strutting down the aisle of Nomad Aviators. It was Wednesday night at El Centro and that meant one thing, *Ladies Night*.

Shouldered up next to Carla, Major Kennard, the "Wrapper," leaned back, obviously checking out early prospects. Big Alabama turned away from the bar, shaking the leather cup next to his ear, as if he were Tom Cruise mixing up a dirty martini. Carla rattled a second leather cup in hand before slapping it upside down on the bar. Then, slowly and sensuously, she removed the cup to reveal a six and a two. Carefully picking up the dice she gently placed the two cubes on the bottom of the turned down cup.

"Come on, Jimmy," she said. "There are twenty of my dollars in the pile of cash."

"Beat an eight. Ain't shit. Pot!" Big Alabama shouted. Throwing the cup face down onto the bar with a leathery splat, he didn't hesitate to remove it quickly. A roar erupted from the officers, and Carla joined in, all of them high fiving one another. Pulling out his wallet, Big Alabama removed two "C" notes, dropping them on top of the growing pile of cash.

Big Alabama and Wrapper followed Major Faulkner, call sign "Love Doctor," who was already nestled in with three lovelies. One woman was a pretty Native American, and Wrapper settled down into her generously large lap, introducing himself with a kiss to her cheek. Big Alabama was down on a knee, begging the second for a dance. Love Doctor seemed to be in good form, his arm was around the third, whispering God only knows what. Hap did notice she replied with a wink.

Whatever it took to take their minds off the events from the previous morning worked just fine for Hap. He downed the backwash in his cup before inverting it over the neck of the half-filled bottle of Black Label. He scooped up bottle and ice bucket and walked outside and down the stairs to a small sitting area. Two concrete benches overlooked a horseshoe pit and sand volleyball court.

Removing the cup from the top of the bottle, he dropped in two ice cubes followed by a pour of four fingers. He fumbled for his cell phone from the flight suits left breast pocket, punched 1 on his keypad, speed-dialing Will Kellogg. On the first ring, Will's gruff voice answered, backed up by at least two different women's giggles. "You miss me already?"

Hap grinned, tears welling up. It was as if he were talking to Pop. "Need some guidance, Will." Hap heard some rustling about.

"You know what I'm looking at, Hap?"

"Now, or a few seconds ago?"

"I'm watching the last of the old Spanish Fortress' shadow on San Andres Bay. So you're involved in the incident flashing all over cable news?"

"Unfortunately yes, with two KIA, two WIA, and the MIA, who happens to be my CO. One of the WIA was H.D. Simmons's boy. And, my CO, the MIA, you know him as well. LtCol Warden."

"I do remember meeting Warden once. Did I hear you right, little old J.D. is WIA?"

"Affirmative. The Marine is fit to be tied. The KIA's and WIA were under his command. He'll be fine."

"What in the hell happened on that hill, Colonel?"

Hap threw back another long pull, thinking how to respond. "Hell, Will, the sons of bitches crossed the border and assaulted the OP. They knew exactly what they were going to do and where to do it."

"Colonel, the DOD is going along with the Administration, crying out that the incident was caused by a rogue LtCol."

"Scapegoat, Will. A cartel is working side-by-side with jihadists. Just can't prove it. Seems pretty damn clear the Administration is throwing Warden and our dead to the wolves."

"Well then, Colonel, it appears, the one thing we both know, the assholes involved should die. You're right on one thing; this pussy president of ours is not going to lift a finger to get Warden back. When do we start and what do you need from me?"

"Assault teams armed to the teeth, Will."

"I have 30 commando types available at a moment's notice. They should, I pay their salary at the Casino. Well trained."

"Of course," Hap said, beginning to feel a little bit better.

"I will pay twenty big ones per man. Hell, I will pay you my share for giving me the opportunity."

"Thanks, Will. But, that won't be necessary. I just need some boots to put on the ground."

"Colonel, in all seriousness, you okay?"

"I will be when the plan is in place, and that can't happen until Warden's position is confirmed. Where do I need the C-130 to pick you and your team up?"

"That wouldn't be a Marine Corps bird?"

"I wish. Have a friend you need to meet who doesn't know he is about to loan the plane to me."

"He must be a good friend, Hap. Pickup will be at San Andres, Columbia. Fly into the private airfield next to the Fortress. I know the owner and will set everything up."

"Bird will need fuel upon landing. ETA in twelve hours." Hap paused, "Will, you wouldn't happen to have parachutes?"

"Everything will be ready on our end, Colonel, to include an insertion by parachute if need be. Get a good pos on Warden."

Hanging up from his old friend, Hap settled his ass into the hardpan, leaning back against the concrete bench. Slipping on wire-rimmed aviator sunglasses to darken an already dusky surrounding, he leaned his head back allowing his tired eyes to rest. Clutching his scotch, thoughts of putting together a strike package seemed, on the surface, easy enough. Possibilities raced around his brain a mile a second as he surveilled aircraft parked on the flight line a few hundred yards away. Militaries around the world could only wish to have the air assets that Hap had at his fingertips. The ordnance was on site, stored in ordnance bunkers, which became available simply by putting together a flight schedule.

But, putting together air and ground crews would be tricky. Outside of locating Warden's position, manpower would be the largest obstacle. Shank grounded only Warden's crew before flying back to D.C., leaving the Nomads the ability to launch ordnance missions for training purposes, just no scheduling of JTF-6 missions. He knew the ticket to get the strike package in the air and off the base was a flight schedule. Once the package launched, the mission had, on the outside, a three-hour head start before people started asking questions. Rumor had it their orders would be to fly back to New Orleans within seventy-two hours.

Savoring a long pull, Hap calculated that a 48-hour window existed for Blad to locate Warden and identify volunteers without landing in the brig with severe charges to follow. A dishonorable discharge and prison time would be swift in coming.

Hap shifted on the concrete bench to keep his ass from going numb. The Administration would do nothing except send their propagandist talking heads to all the daily cable networks' newscasts for as long as it took this story to go away. Sunday was three days away. Oh, sweet justice, if he could only have the Administration dinks walk in to find Tuna Man back in his office. Talk about swallowing a mouthful of crap dry, with nothing to wash it down. Hap smiled.

Most, if not all senior-level military officers and enlisted personnel were aware of Senator Scotty B. Jourdan. A real pussy in their eyes, and Hap's feelings were no different. The marshmallow man would be satisfied with a national police force doing away with all branches of the military. Definitely a kumbaya kind of guy. Strip the U.S. of its military muscle and the world would be one big happy place. "What a douche pump," Hap thought to himself, shaking his head back and forth, working the knotted muscles in the back of his neck.

His gut screamed that Tuna Man was within range of a Marine Corps vertical assault. Would Swamp throw in some F-18's from VMFA112 for what he had in mind? Nicknamed the Cowboys, the squadron currently based out of Ft Worth Joint Reserve Base. He had no doubt several of the Cowboys would be throwing back drinks with the Nomads. With only one section of F-18A's scheduled tonight, several of the pilots would be enjoying Ladies Night.

He texted the Roach:

Need to ask a fav. U have a C-130 laying around? Need the bird in San Andres Columbia 12 hours. Bill me for the gas.

He pushed send.

Will's commandos were seasoned combat veterans; he'd discussed their Special Forces background with Hap many times. Marine Close Air aside, the assault carried one hell of an edge with Will's ground assets. Will proudly boasted contracting out services, primarily in Latin and South America. Coffee Growers of America, DEA, and his old employer, the CIA were repeat customers.

Hap considered all contingencies, including marrying up Will's ground element with the strike package. Probably best to have the ground element marry up with the vertical lift component outside the target area. Damn, he hoped a Forward Arming and Refueling Point "FARP" would not be required. One thing was certain; it would be a night action. And, if the deal went down as mapped, all Marine volunteers would have flown their last flight in the Marine Corps. Now he had to start putting the crews together without the world getting wind of their intentions.

Hap's chin hung, touching his chest. Mentally kicking himself, he thought, "What the hell are you thinking Hap Stoner? Talk about a hell of a lot of initiative and very bad judgment. You're sitting alone, next to a vacant sand volleyball court and horseshoe pit, planning a strike, and you're the only pilot.

Granted, if successful, the mission would be the talk of the Marine Clubs for decades to come. He stared into a cloudless night, and laughed. One thing he knew, LtCol Warden was coming home through hell or high water. *Semper Fi.*

24

Thursday 0530; Mecca II MX

They'd pushed him, allowing gravity to propel him down the hard limestone steps carved from the wall. Barely conscious then, Steve Smith remembered dropping eight feet like a wet bag of cement. And, maybe he remembered young American girls huddled down the trail.

Now, through swollen lids and the semi-darkness of the cave, illuminated only by what little moonlight passed through its canopy, his gut told him that he had found the missing girls from Phoenix. Age was about right and he had counted six in the scrum. He stared down at his own body splayed across the limestone floor. The fall added fresh injuries to a body already battered by blows from Scorpion's thugs and his interrogator who'd used a bat and their fists. He yearned for his cellmate's comforting presence. Maybe after this job, after he got the girls back—or at least got a viable lead—it would be time to think about retiring. After his years with the DEA, another organization with an almost invisible profile recruited him. He was proud of the work he'd done for the last three years for Shadow. But, maybe his days in intelligence were drawing to a close.

Steve ran both hands slowly across his body. Nothing critical broken, maybe two ribs on his right side. Even with the sharp pain, he could still breathe, so at least the last beating didn't result in a punctured lung. Although he was no doctor,

Steve questioned if the next beating would be his last. Maybe a piece of one of the broken ribs would puncture a lung. Gritting teeth now fractured and splintered, he slowly eased his bruised and battered shoulder blades up the limestone wall, left shoulder blade first, then a push with both of his bare feet, working to the right shoulder blade. Complete focus and all his energy were required for each movement, which he repeated a half dozen times. Every other breath, he coughed and spit out blood and teeth fragments onto his ripped pants and the dirty floor.

Attempting to keep his airway clear, he ran a disfigured finger across what was left of his upper and lower teeth. Discovering anything loose, he pressed the social finger against a crooked thumb to flick a tooth fragment six feet against the opposite wall. Spitting up blood and snickering at his private joke: the experience gained from years of slinging beer tops actually came in handy.

Since the three beatings, and getting knocked cold several times, the six-by-six limestone cell was home. Even in the dim light, he could tell it had been hand-carved and enlarged from an existing grotto created by Mother Nature thousands of years earlier. The ceiling and walls leached water. With his head leaning against limestone, the cool water seemed to sooth his body's pain a bit. Reaching out, it took most of his strength to collect a few teaspoons of moisture in his twisted hand and bring it to his cracked lips. It tasted only slightly salty and he could keep it down.

He didn't have the strength to reach the clay pot placed strategically against the wall to collect drinking water. Oh well, he'd get it later. Drifting toward unconsciousness, he made an effort to focus, puzzling over the men he'd seen guarding the cave. Heavily armed, they were wearing mask-like *kufiyahs*, and praying to Mecca. What the hell were Islamo Fascists doing in Mexico? ISIS or al-Qaeda or Al-Shabaab, it didn't much matter. They were all part of Islam and all totalitarian terrorist groups. They seemed quite interested in his cellmate but the end game wasn't clear. Steve and his cellmate were clearly in a terrorist training camp, but where? Surely he was in Latin American, but was he still in Mexico?

"Damn, my head hurts," he muttered aloud, spitting out more blood between swollen lips. It was good to hear a friendly voice, even his own. The butt of the shotgun into the side of his head had made lasting impressions. He continued to reposition his ass, shoulders, and head until he found a semblance of comfort. Within minutes, the pain returned and he found himself shifting yet again.

Based on his absence, the Marine Aviator must be taking his turn in Scorpion's chamber of horrors. The Administration, wanting their Marine back, must have reached out to Mexican authorities. Maybe they would include him if they returned the Marine. If it was going to happen, it had better happen quickly. Each episode lasted at least a couple of hours and at that rate, neither of them was long for this world.

What, he wondered, were their plans for him and the Marine? Commandeering a Marine LtCol must be a real prize for the Islamo Fascists, one they had not been able to obtain in all the years since 9/11. If Steve thought like them, they would ship this LtCol to Southwest Asia, post haste. What a great recruitment tool. The Marine officer's picture and video would be on every Islamo Fascist website. If they didn't behead him in the next few days, the Marine had a one-way ticket to hell in his future. Then they would behead him. He'd often wondered if they gave drugs to the unlucky individuals prior to the beheading to calm their nerves for social media. Grim thoughts…

Through limestone, he could hear heavy foot-traffic overhead and a man speaking harsh Spanish. Half asleep, Steve translated, but needed only to hear the sounds of small children crying, then curses and shouts, "*Pronto!*" A woman's voice desperately hushed the child, each voice a part of a faceless human convoy of misery. *Stone cold bastards, I'd slit their throats if I got a chance.*

Blood spattered across Steve's face and then a massive weight slammed down on his body. A dream or had the beheading begun? Warm fluid splattered his skin as he struggled back to full consciousness. He rolled, pushing away the heavy object on his chest, forcing it to the floor. It was a man, maybe one of the jihadis! He reached around to pound the attacker's skull into the limestone wall.

A shaft of light from the high oblique moon poured through the grotto entrance, illuminating a lifeless man and his disfigured face. Steve fell back. This was no attacker. The barely conscious Marine had survived another vicious beating. The Marine clawed at his own throat, gasping for air.

Steve forced his mouth open, reaching in, sweeping out teeth and blood from the airway. Seconds passed before he felt the faintest breath passing across his blood-soaked fingers. With an adrenaline rush, he ripped the green T-shirt from underneath the Marine's torn flight suit, and dipped it into the clay water pot. He used it to wipe away some of the blood, while the Marine struggled to lift his blood-filled eyelids.

"Don't try it, friend. It will be a while," Steve told the Marine. He did his best to comfort him before the man slipped into blessed nothingness.

Although he already beaten to mash, Steve could only wait for his invitation to the next party. Apparently, the stakes were rising. By the looks of it, the Marine was receiving more than his share of "special attention."

Above, the human chain had started moving again. The vibrations reached the floor of the cave as the individuals passed the opening, blotting out the light. A sharp bark escaped Steve's throat as an image of the lights and vibrations of discos from his college days flooded his hallucinating mind. He realized he was going a little bit over the edge.

He focused on counting the shadows and made it to 35 or 36 before he started to fall into his own stupor. He forced himself to confirm the Marine was still breathing before dropping all the way down the deep well of unconsciousness.

25

Thursday 0530; Naval Air Facility El Centro CA,
Behind OC

The moment the sun's upper crest peaked above a cloudless eastern horizon, Hap felt perspiration begin to bead on his closed eyelids. He gently moved his hand to his lap and felt the familiar contours of cheek and chin. Carla was using his body as her pillow. He remembered drifting off solo, and wondered when the others had joined him.

Cracking open one eye, Hap saw a drop of his perspiration fall onto one of Carla's rounded cheeks. Purring like a kitty, she nuzzled her head deeper between his legs. Opening his other eye, he found himself staring at a close-up of LtCol Johnny Stenson's ear. Sometime during the night, "Swamp Puppy" had borrowed Hap's shoulder for a pillow. He grabbed the sleeping jet puke by the cuff of his flight suit, gently lowering his face onto the hard pan.

Hap looked around to see the large deck and yard behind the OC littered with Nomads who, like him, refused to take the walk of shame. Big Alabama was snuggled around one of the poles that held up the volleyball net, snoring like a Cummins diesel. A god-awful retching noise came from Schlonger, on all fours, barfing like a dog. Just beyond Schlonger, Wrapper lay almost hidden behind his ample and pretty date. Only his hand was visible, moving across the fabric of her blouse from her belly to her breast. Sleepily, patiently, she pushed Wrapper's hand away repeatedly, as if brushing off a pesky fly. Hap marveled that even in a drunken stupor, Wrapper's carnal instincts remained intact, proving Wrapper's steadfast assertion (usually expressed while the Nomad bent across a bar), that his Momma didn't raise a quitter!

Love Doctor was nowhere around. The Marine must have made the walk of shame or the lucky lady had driven the lovebirds to the BOQ. Coming out his stupor, Swamp Puppy raised up on one elbow, gazing up at Hap with a bewildered expression that clearly read, *where in the hell am I?*

"I feel like you look, Swamp," Hap said.

Swamp chuckled. "If it wasn't for you, Hap, Carla would have made the walk of shame with me."

Hap pushed the Paul Newman lookalike back to the ground. "Hell, Swamp, chew some gum or something. Your breath smells like crap from way up here."

"I'm feeling like I have the blue flu, Hap," Swamp said, rolling back onto both elbows. "There was a lot of crap being thrown about last night while you were outside. I have to ask. You're going in to get Tuna Man?"

Hap didn't answer right away. Instead, he watched a groaning Schlonger crawl away from the pile of vomit, only to roll into a ball and fall fast asleep facing west.

Hap turned, gently stroking Carla's long flowing locks. "Sooner rather than later if I have my way."

"If you're thinking like I think you're thinking, I can get you a bunch of F-18's," Swamp said, his Mississippi drawl intensified by a hangover.

"You're drunk," Hap answered, narrowing his eyes. Carla purred and rolled until her forehead butted up against his midsection. She wrapped her arm around his backside.

Swamp looked up with his coal black eyes. "If by chance you get wind of where he is, the Cowboys are in."

Hap stared straight ahead. "You know what that means."

"Prison possibly, last flight in the Marine Corps, for sure. Do believe if it were me, or any of my pilots, you would do it for them, no different than Warden would do it for you. There would be no conversation. Besides, the derelicts splayed around you will be going as well. Kinda feel sorry for the sons of bitches on the receiving end of this decision, Hap."

Carla continued to sleep peacefully, emitting an occasional snore. Hap tipped his head, kissing her forehead gently. When he looked up again, he saw Swamp had dropped to his back, fast asleep.

On the surface, it appeared the die was cast. The strike package was coming together. In between the pounding going on inside his head, Hap wondered if the U.S. taxpayers knew how their tax dollars were about to be spent, would they say it was a worthy cause? You bet. When you got past the politicians, the bureaucrats, and their bullshit, the people would stand on the side of right.

The window was closing fast and they only had hours before it locked shut. Shadow Services had to find Warden, and Hap needed to get to the BOQ to catch the Senate hearing on C-Span.

26

Thursday 0900; Washington, D.C.

General Russ Verbie, Commandant of the U.S. Marine Corps, fingered the microphone resting on the stained oak table in Room SR-22 of the Russell Senate Office Building. Suited in his Marine alpha uniform, his body ramrod straight, his naval aviation wings positioned above the shooting badges and five rows of ribbons. The chair pressed sharply against his rigid spine. "Thank you Mr. Chairman, Ranking Member Johnson, members of the Senate Armed Services Committee, I appreciate the opportunity to appear before you this morning."

Verbie's hard gaze never left Chairman and Senator "Scotty" Jourdan's face, whose soft features had disdain smeared all over them. It was no secret that Jourdan had no love for the military. Verbie had lost count of how many times he had heard his insulting catch phrase, "With the United Nations' immense capabilities, why do we need an overpowering military with a bloated budget?"

These thoughts ran through Verbie's mind even as he continued to brief the committee. "Chairman Jourdan, the units in question in the recent incident were from the Marine Corps. They were participating in a Joint Task Force 6 operation. Each unit had previously operated in numerous JTF-6 Operations. Most of the Marines were seasoned combat veterans, spending multiple deployments in the war on terror."

Verbie took a breath, maintaining his stony calm as he continued, "Earlier today you heard Secretary of Defense Mack describe the matter in detail. Job One is to see to our wounded, bury our dead, console the fathers and mothers, and for Christ's sake, bring back LtCol Warden. I will touch on my last point later." Verbie paused for emphasis, maintaining command of the room. He barely acknowledged Colonel Ted Shank, seated to his left, as he went on.

"At this juncture, Colonel Shank has been on site, leading the investigation, and he will speak of his initial findings shortly. We have sent NIS to help the Mexican Military investigators. I understand the FBI has sent assistance as well. With coalition partners, including local and county law enforcement, we should be able to release our findings in short order." Verbie scanned the faces of each committee member, and more than one man squirmed beneath his razor gaze. "I want to emphasize that if our military has done wrong, those accountable will be punished to the highest extent allowable by the Uniform Code of Military Justice "UCMJ." That being said, the Marines leave no man behind."

As the Commandant spoke, Senator Jourdan met Ted Shank's eyes with a barely visible spark of acknowledgment. To most of the participants seated in Room SR 22, and to much of the C-Span audience, Chairman Jourdan appeared to focus intently on every word of the hearing. But, in truth, his mind was thousands of miles away, somewhere along the southwest border.

With breaking news of the incident, Jourdan's first thought was, what the hell has Scorpion done now? As if kidnapping the Phoenix schoolgirls wasn't bad enough, now his men were somehow involved in combat with the U.S. Military, and damn that LtCol Warden. By playing John Wayne, he'd just jeopardized everything for which Scotty had worked.

Scotty snapped back from his thoughts when he heard Verbie say, "Cartels, the drug trade, and their unholy alliances, are bound by no laws, God's or man's." The Commandant maintained his deathly calm, his clear voice. "As the JTF mission evolves and continues to demand our attention, we should expect JTF's adversaries to adapt their tactics as we adjust our approach. Through all of this, we must not lose touch with the situation in the Middle East and the jihadist militant influence as the conflicts evolve and continue to demand our resources. We must be prepared and not be stretched thin. Bear in mind our southern border is wide open. People come and go freely, although in some instances, against their will. Let me remind all in this room of the recent disappearance of the teenagers whom I refer to as the 'Phoenix Six.' It may surprise some of you in this room that a Marine general is a caring parent, even the Commandant of the Marine Corps."

Clearing his throat, Scotty Jourdan straightened in his chair, befitting his stature as a U.S. senator. "I, too, am a caring parent, as are the other members of this committee. While this Committee understands the Commandant's many concerns, we respectfully request that General Verbie stay on topic. If this incident is not properly and quickly addressed, it may become an international incident." Scotty sniffed, tipping his head toward Colonel Shank. "Perhaps this is a good time to let Col. Shank enlighten us with his findings. The Chair recognizes Colonel Ted Shank, USMC."

The best news Jourdan had received in the past hours was the report that one of his aides had accompanied Colonel

Shank on the drive from Andrews to the Russell Senate Office Building. Shank, as a high-ranking military officer, only needed to deflect the Commandant's assaults, no matter the direction. And, with each word, he would be making huge strides toward his goal of becoming General Theodore W. Shank, USMC.

After Jourdan's initial shock watching the story unfold, he'd called the half-dozen members from his party sitting on his Committee. So now, here they all were, because someone had to screw a lid on this thing. Scotty, aka Chairman Jourdan, had the most to lose, and Shank was his weapon.

Continuing to clasp the microphone, General Verbie's gaze turned inward even as he faced the committee members boldly.

"General..." Jourdan repeated. "With all due respect, the Chair recognizes Colonel Ted Shank, USMC." Committee members and spectators shifted nervously in their seats, but Shank smacked a folder on the table, eyed the room, and cleared his throat sharply, a signal he now had the floor.

"Thank you, Mr. Chairman, Ranking Member Johnson, members of this committee. I appreciate the opportunity to appear before you this morning. Arriving at Naval Air Facility El Centro hours after the incident, I gained a good understanding of what occurred Tuesday night and into Wednesday morning..."

As Shank adjusted his wire-rimmed glasses and scanned ahead on his prepared statement, Jourdan thought back less than 24 hours to when he was boarding Danny Lee Boyd's private jet to return from Paradise Island. Accompanying him to the jet's air stair, Danny had assured the senator that, within 24 hours, a breaking news flash would shift the media's attention away from the cartels and the American southwest. Now, with the lead investigator's testimony and first public announcement transmitted worldwide courtesy of C-Span, the networks would have their news flash.

Colonel Shank swallowed deeply, his Adam's apple sliding as he paused. "As sad as it is for me to report this, it does appear that certain Marines under my command acted with total disregard for Mexican sovereignty. Two Marines were KIA, while two other Marines were WIA. However, we do have the squadron commander who crossed into Mexico with an armed aircraft, completely unauthorized. LtCol Warden is MIA. We believe the actions of LtCol Warden incited the incident causing the Mexicans to shoot Warden's aircraft down. All aircrew retreated to the US side of the border, while Warden provided cover for their escape by manning a .50 caliber machine gun. We are still investigating, but it appears that by LtCol Warden's actions, Mexico protected their sovereignty and that led to the deaths of the Marines on the ground and total loss of an aircraft." Shank scanned the committee members, before cutting to the C-Span cameras. "I'm open to field any questions."

A low rumble filled the room, signaling rising tensions. General Verbie shifted forward slightly so the bottom row of his ribbons brushed the table's surface. He kept his eyes straight ahead, jaw taut, lips tight.

"Thank you, Colonel," Senator Jourdan replied, holding his index finger above the microphone. "I'm sure our wounded Marines are being properly cared for, and our fallen will be properly honored."

Shank, leaning close to the mic, avoided all contact with General Verbie. "Senator Jourdan, as a member of the U.S.

Armed forces, I appreciate your concern for our Marines. The wounded are being cared for, Senator," Shank replied.

Jourdan nodded somberly. "Do you have any idea where this LtCol Warden is being held?"

"We do not, Senator," Shank answered. "Once Warden is found, or by chance appears, know that he will be placed under arrest and read his rights."

Jourdan caught Senator Murphy raising his hand. "The Chairman recognizes the Senator from Texas." Republican Senator Murphy leaned forward on both elbows, looking toward the Chairman.

"Thank you, Mr. Chairman. First gentlemen, I want to thank you for your service. My question is for Colonel Shank. Do you find it odd the Mexican Military has not officially acknowledged an incident actually occurred?"

Shank leaned forward, mirroring Murphy. "Senator, we all know that back-channels run swiftly even as the public is left out of the flow of intel. I believe Mexican authorities are conducting their own investigation. In saying this, I'm confident they will come away with similar conclusions."

Senator Jourdan was surprised to see General Verbie turn toward Shank, his eyes boring into a subordinate officer even as his face showed absolutely no emotion. Sweat broke on Jourdan's bald pate and his stomach fluttered uneasily. Was the General perceptive enough to pick up that he and Shank had...certain agreements?

"Does it disturb you at all, Colonel Shank," Senator Murphy asked, looking down at his notes, "that reports indicate LtCol Warden's aircraft was shot out of the sky after the incident at Bravo 6? For what it's worth, Colonel, this information disturbs me and other members of this Committee."

Jourdan felt perspiration beading on his face as the Republicans appeared to be ganging up on the Colonel. Just then, General Verbie pulled the mic to his mouth with one finger. Always at odds with the Administration, the Commandant of the Marine Corps maintained a good poker face looking back towards the Committee. But, at this moment, Jourdan almost imagined he saw steam coming from the General's nose.

General Verbie's voice had dropped to a deeper tone with an ominous rumble. He spoke very slowly. "Mr. Chairman, if I may be so bold, I first met LtCol Warden as a young 1stLt, when he was checking into the squadron I commanded 20 years earlier. I have *never* known LtCol Warden to be the type of officer who would bring disgrace to himself or to the Corps. Never. Again, I want to emphasize, the Marines leave no man behind." His finger still gripped the mic.

Jourdan could swear he saw Verbie's lips curl in disgust at the corners. The Senator frowned at Shank, who sat stoically, eyes straight ahead, wiping both lenses of his glasses before putting them on again.

Jourdan coughed, prompting, "Colonel Shank, would you like to add to General Verbie's comments?"

Shank set down the glass of water, adjusted the glasses perched on his birdlike nose before shifting towards the mic. "Not much to add to the General's comments. I'm proud to say I served under General Verbie in the same squadron with LtCol Warden."

"Colonel Shank," Jourdan prompted. "How would you explain LtCol Warden's actions?"

The Senator from Texas tapped his microphone sharply, signaling the senator had gone over his allotted time. Eyebrows raised, Jourdan looked to his colleagues in the Democratic caucus signaling that he required some of *their* allotted time.

The Senator of Maine took the cue. "I yield my allotted time to the Chairman."

"I want to thank the Senator from Maine." Nod. "I'll repeat my question, Colonel Shank. How would you explain LtCol Warden's actions on the night in question?"

Shank took in a deep breath, shaking his head slowly. "Mr. Chairman, I can't say for sure. Every man is different. Maybe Warden broke under pressure. It has happened to men who are the equal of LtCol Warden."

27

For the past 90 minutes, the men hurled insults and trash at the 52-inch screen hanging in Hap's VIP quarters. An empty water bottle bounced off Shank's face as the Group Commander vomited televised lies, throwing their boss under the proverbial bus. Meat, Little Ray, and Lafleur would be sucked into the vortex in due time. Anything either Marine said would sound like so much ass covering.

"Incoming," Schlonger announced, lobbing a water bottle in Hap's direction.

Reaching up to catch the bottle, Hap used his free hand to remove the towel around his neck and wipe the perspiration from his three-mile run. As small as the accommodations were, the amenities included a private bedroom, adjoining sitting/living area, which the men were occupying, and a private head. At the moment, the room reeked of alcohol pouring from the occupiers' pores.

The door to the room shuddered with sudden, heavy, and insistent noise—*bang, bang, bang.* None of the officers took their eyes off the screen, including Spanky, who simply reached over and turned the door handle.

Ambassador stepped into the doorway wearing P.T. shorts and holding a sweat-drenched T-shirt in his hand. "Can you believe the frigging Bear?" he blurted. "I want some ass, Hap." With his eyes locked on Shank continuing to hold forth on the TV screen, Spanky pushed the door closed. Hap never saw him as he read the text on his telephone.

Urgent. Need eyes. OP 1 SW of Camargo. My organization can handle OP 2 in the vicinity of Anapra and OP3 south of Santa Teresa NM. No Shadow air assets available to transport to El Paso. Good chance missing Marine is captive inside one of these compounds. Respond with intentions.

Hap's gut hollowed out. *Tuna Man held captive...*

Pressing the forward button, he sent the text message to the Roach.

Punching in the distance between Camargo and the base, he frowned at the display: 854 miles. OP 3, the closest, was still 690 miles. Sons of bitches didn't wait long to move the boss east, Hap thought. Why east and not south?

"What's up, Hap?" Spanky asked.

Hap leaned over the map spread open across the coffee table and ran a straight edge from El Centro in a southeasterly direction.

"We going to shee-it or get off the pot, Colonel?" Ambassador demanded in his south Texas drawl.

Looking up, Hap suddenly felt punch drunk. He had no answers. Listening to the testimony, Warden was guilty, sentenced, all before the trial. And, 900 miles could very well separate Warden from the Nomads. Maybe it was time to stop thinking John Wayne shit and involve the Administration.

The phone vibrated and Hap pulled up the text. Blad's second message breathed life:

Have your eyes at Cutter Aviation El Paso International by Midnight. Need a pilot to ride shotgun and a crew chief. Acknowledge.

Hap didn't have to look around the room to know the officers' eyes were burning through him. A decision had to be made, and, as Pop Stoner always told him, "If not now, when? If not you, then who?"

He looked up with an expression the boys knew so well. "I need Captain Simmons out of the hospital post haste."

"I'll get him," Love Doctor replied. "Need a crew to shuttle me to the hospital."

"Use the SAR bird," Spanky said, cutting his eyes to Hap.

Hap said, "I have to get five Marines to volunteer to complement his team."

"I'll take care of that," Spanky said.

"Just like his old man," Big Alabama said, allowing the words to slide off in an accent honed in the deep South. Hap looked over to Schlonger.

"You want to fly with one of Blad's crew and insert Simmons's team into Mexico?"

Schlonger stood shirtless with crossed arms leaning against the door opening to the shitter. "Is the mission fraught with danger? Will the Bear want a piece of my ass if he finds out?"

"Does your question require a response?" Hap replied.

"That's why I will fly it, Colonel."

Hap looked over to Hollywood lying shirtless on the floor with his hands behind his head. "Hey, Hollywood, you mind if I take you off orders effective immediately?"

Hollywood tilted his head, baffled. "I'm not going to miss this rodeo."

"Take the corporate bird to El Paso. You will meet the Roach at Cutter aviation tonight. Schlonger, Captain Simmons, and five Recon Marines will be on your manifest."

"Shit, Hap, I feel like I'm missing the fun." Hollywood frowned.

Both sides of Hap's mouth turned up slightly. "You are a warrior, my friend. I want your attorney skills, plus, I need the jet on strip alert. Something tells me you are going to be one busy boy for the next couple of days."

Sitting up, he rested his square chin on a knee. "Hell, Hap, whatever I can contribute...I'm in."

"As soon as we get Simmons on station, you and Schlonger join me for the ride to the airport. I will brief the Captain on the way. Time your departure to arrive at Cutter Aviation at El Paso International by 2200."

Hollywood nodded. "Roger that, Hap."

"And Hollywood, ensure half the ammo is on the jet."

"What about the other half?"

Hap's blue eyes appeared to come to life. The dark bags below, so pronounced earlier, were now long gone. "Something tells me there will be other Marines needing use of it."

28

Thursday 1300; El Centro Regional Medical Center

The Huey settled into the Hospital LZ using a no-hover technique. Love Doctor's spit-polished boots touched ground before Goose could roll the throttles to idle. He ducked under the rotor arc wearing camouflaged utilities and walked deliberately past emergency room personnel rushing towards the helicopter.

Upon entering the door, he grabbed a white jacket left hanging over a chair. Slipping it on, he continued past the nurse's station where he hooked an unattended stethoscope on the desk around his neck. A nurse came around the corner, drawn by the commotion outside.

"Good afternoon, Doctor," she said. "Did you just start at the hospital?"

Love Doctor winked. "You could say that." Entering the elevator, he punched the fourth floor. On the second floor, the elevator stopped, and a middle-aged male nurse entered pushing an empty wheel chair. "Fifth floor please."

Love Doctor punched the button, rolling his eyes to the ceiling.

"I haven't seen you before, Doctor. Are you new to the hospital?"

"You could say that," he repeated as the elevator stopped. Stepping out with a smile he asked, "Could I relieve you of the wheel chair?"

The nurse pushed the chair out of the elevator just before the doors closed. Love Doctor pushed the empty wheel chair briskly down the hall, passing at least a dozen hospital personnel. He fought back the urge to stop and chat with the eye candy. He knew that if he surrendered to temptation, somebody other than H.D. Simmons's oldest boy would end up riding in the chair. Hearing the door swing open, Captain Simmons cut his attention away from a Fox News broadcast on the TV.

"Drop your cock and put on your socks, Captain," Love Doctor said, grinning ear to ear. Grimacing in pain, Captain Simmons sat up.

"Doc, I'm not in the mood to take a push about the hospital."

Love Doctor began removing IV's from the left arm, letting the elongated needles fall against the stand. "You wearing a catheter?"

Perplexed, Simmons said, "Yes, I am."

"You will have to remove that yourself, Devil Dog. A quick jerk is all it takes," Love Doctor said, going through the small closet and holding up a wallet. "This is yours."

Simmons's chin didn't have a chance to nod all the way, when his wallet landed on the bed. Love Doctor removed a robe and draped it over Simmons's shoulders.

"Where you taking me?"

"If I didn't know better, LtCol Stoner is having you and a recon team inserted into Mexico tonight. They need eyeballs. Warden may be in the position, then again, maybe not. Are you going to be able to make this trip drug free?"

"Urrrah," Simmons grunted, settling into the wheel chair.

Simmons pushed back into the seat and rested his bare feet on the footrest as Love Doctor turned the corner, entering the empty hallway. The attendant at the nurse's station didn't even look up as the two wheeled past.

"Good afternoon, Doctor," she said, her nose buried in a patient's report.

"Afternoon, nurse," he replied, suppressing a laugh.

The attendant rose from her chair and followed them around the corner to see the doctor backing the patient into the elevator. Settling back into her chair, she kept thinking that the patient in the wheel chair looked like Captain Simmons, but that couldn't be because he wasn't due to be released for at least four days. She shook off the thought that the good-looking Marine was attempting to make an escape. Besides, in a couple of days, she planned to hit him up for a drink.

He changed his route to avoid the emergency room and wheeled the chair out the front door without incident. Straight ahead, tracking down the sidewalk at a good clip, was a gorgeous nurse with flowing dark hair and a perky topside who approached from the opposite direction.

"Oh shit," Simmons said. "The nurse coming this way works my floor. We are busted." Love Doctor kept a straight face, even while the nurse blocked the sidewalk. Clearly, she recognized the occupant in the wheel chair.

"Do I know you, Doctor?" she inquired. "And what the hell are you doing with this patient?"

Simmons braced himself as the wheelchair came to an abrupt stop. He watched as Love Doctor's dark eyes met her baby blues. Damn, he thought, under any other circumstances Love Doctor would be working her for drinks.

"Today is my first day. Let me introduce myself. I'm the Doctor of Love."

Bewilderment spread across her face, as the wheel chair rolled by. Rounding the nearest corner, Love Doctor began double-timing it towards the helo pad. The crew chief stood underneath the rotor arc, arms crossed, thumb on ICS button, dark visor down.

Sprinting now, Love Doctor heard Simmons grunt in pain, as the chair bounded across the walkway. Goose opened the throttles as Love Doctor ducked underneath the rotor arc. The crew chief and Love Doctor shoved Simmons into the cabin. He slipped a knot with the white jacket securing it to an arm-rest and laid the stethoscope in the seat. Love Doctor kicked the wheelchair off the helo pad where it fell to its side. He sat on the cabin floor, both his boots resting atop the right skid as the Huey broke ground using a no-hover takeoff technique. The hospital personnel racing for the helo pad stopped halfway between the emergency room doors and pad. Love Doctor waved and blew the nurses a kiss as they climbed out over them. Then he rolled inside the cabin.

"Base, Nomad 24. Cargo on board. Will be on the line in five minutes for pax pickup."

29

Thursday 1345; Naval Air Facility El Centro,
Nomad Flight Line

Five Marines, dressed in loose fitting flight suits concealing desert cammies and covering the tops of their combat boots, bent over bloated rucks. Conducting final equipment checks, the Recon Marines awaited the arrival of their team lead and chariot. Flight line personnel moved hastily to next tasks, asking no questions, entering and leaving the building more concerned about a Staff NCO crawling up their asses for slacking off than anything else. Their collective goal: to have all Nomad aircraft on the maintenance control board with a green arrow pointing up next to the aircraft side number, signaling cleared for flight.

Checking the rucks' contents for the third time, the team organized the packs on the plywood floor, one item at a time. Each of the team knew what the other carried, and where the specific piece of gear was located. Some rucks contained communications gear; others held antennas, while others contained scopes used for observation. Each Marine carried Night Vision Goggles, extra batteries for the goggles, scopes, and PRC-119 Radios. Add in four-days-worth of MREs, two pairs of clean socks, six canteens, poncho, and poncho liner. All items, along with side arms and assault weapons, would go back into the ruck, and finally packed into a parachute bag. The Marines would then walk the gear to the helo. Ammo issuance would take place at a location TBA.

Waiting in the afternoon sun, on either side of the steps leading into the flight line shack, Hap and Schlonger said nothing as they watched over Captain Simmons's parachute bag. Nomad flight line personnel passed them without speaking, sweat soaking their suits, clutching tools and copies of Maintenance Action Forms to work from, checking off each action when completed.

Goose brought Nomad 00 to a hover over the helo spot on the other side of the steaming tarmac. Still, Hap and Schlonger waited on the steps, only gaining their feet as Goose made the last pedal turn to enter the taxiway, passing in front of the shack.

Corporal Sullivan leapt from the steps, racing by and coming to a stop over the center strip of the taxiway. Holding his arms out, as if clutching a baby, he brought both hands in, flipping thumbs-up, until he was crossing arms above his head. Goose brought Nomad 00 to a hover. Sullivan gestured with palms down for the helo to land.

Hap could see Simmons seated in the back. The crew chief stepped out, visor down, gesturing the men under the rotor arc, while keeping his thumb on the ICS button ready to take on pax. Throwing the P-Bags over shoulders, the men's legs gave a bit due to the weight and clumsiness of the load. They walked in column, not speaking a word, ducking under the spinning rotors.

As soon as the skids settled onto the tarmac, Love Doctor squeezed Simmons's hand, and then jumped off the bird. The crew chief relieved each Marine of his P-Bag. Allowing each to step up into the bird, he slung their bags like bales of hay, to the waiting Marine.

Hap and Schlonger each grabbed one of the P-Bag's handles, before making their way to the idling helo. Hap and Love Doctor exchanged a thumbs-up in passing. Dropping the bag at the crew chief's flight boots, they wedged themselves in, packed like sardines for the short ride to El Centro International.

As Goose taxied to the helo spot, Hap burned with the prospect that the bad guys were going to move Tuna Man out of country and transport him to the Middle East. Shadow Services had not ruled out the possibility.

Goose tipped the nose of the weighed-down bird, inching forward. Suddenly shuddering, the Huey passed through translational lift, its rotors clawing sky. If they were going to move Tuna Man, interdiction would be the only way to bring the Marine home alive, and that meant effectively invading a neighboring country. None of the volunteers had hesitated to give a thumbs-up, many adding a "frigging A," knowing they could be tossing their Marine careers in the proverbial shitter. Bringing their boss to safety was everything.

Hap fully anticipated that the Squadron would have 5 Cobra's and 3 UH-1N's ready to fly the mission by sunset. Swamp would round up F-18's, but ultimately how many would join the fray? Roach and Blad had air assets, arms, and ammunition. Shadow Services had humint assets on the ground and Will would bring 30 highly trained and well-armed warriors to the fight. With proper Forward Air Control from both ground (FAC) and air (FACA), the bad guys would learn to understand the meaning of Marine Close Air.

Hap knew the legal shit storm to follow would be intense, but that meant nothing when it came to doing the right thing. The Administration, including the Marine Corps "Head Shed," played politics sitting comfortably behind their desks in D.C. The die was cast, the talking points sent to the media; Warden had gone rogue and would have the full weight of the Uniform Code of Criminal Justice dropped into his lap. Any prosecution initiated by the DOJ would be just piling it on.

It was becoming obvious to Hap and others that the Administration did not want Warden back alive. Off the top of his head, Hap could think of a half dozen articles that members of the Strike Force would face. Though General Verbie appeared visibly agitated with Bear's testimony, the Commandant of Marines was probably putting the pieces of the puzzle together. Hap knew Verbie dressing down the Colonel would roll off the Bear like water off a duck's back. Shank knew Verbie would not be writing his fitness report, and any Marine officer worth his salt knew Shank would throw his mother to the lions if it meant he'd gain a star.

Hap also knew that if he were fortunate enough to walk away after "Mission Complete," he would toss his wings into the Bear's lap with pride, after seeing that the casualties were in good medical and legal hands. Hollywood would have already contacted the best criminal attorneys in the Country. *Semper Fi.*

30

Thursday1345; Mecca II, MX

Nestled between mountains in the eastern part of the Mexican state of Chihuahua, Santa Rosalia de Camargo sprang up around the old Mission Santa Rosalia. Established by the Spanish during their march across Mexico, the city has a long and bloody history. Armor-breasted soldiers on horseback and on foot usually carried the day, wielding lances, finely crafted steel swords and even an early musket called the *harquebus*. With no such weapon to penetrate armor, the native dead and wounded littered the ground. Those who survived shook their heads in agonizing defeat, and shouting in a language the Conquistador couldn't understand, ended it all with a coup de grace sword thrust to the heart.

Other invaders included Apache Indians who used the Ojinaga and Rio Conchos to ride their horses into the region and wage war against the Conchos Indians and other local inhabitants. Pancho Villa invaded the municipality during the Mexican Revolution.

Today with a population of over 40,000, the municipality is known for its agriculture, cattle, corn, pecan trees, and surrounding mountains. Tarahumara Indians still travel from the mountains and canyons to sell their goods inside the city.

DEA knew the area situated between Camargo and Lake Boquilla all too well. Mexican Federales and Military shielded from intrusion the 60,000 acres set inside a high fence more effectively than a force field protecting the Starship Enterprise.

With the Rio Concho running through the heart of Scorpion's Mecca, he hid the trafficking operations and drug business behind the high fence, with video surveillance, drones, and aggressive roaming foot and mobile patrols. Stalin could only have wished the Berlin Wall were as effective. Across the river from Scorpion's country house, limestone cliffs climbed 250 feet above the Black Stone compound. Amid a stand of drooping junipers, tangled vines, and remnants of a 19th century stone cabin, Shadow 22's perch offered a great view, well concealed. Down river, the branches of century-old hardwoods growing out of the sides of the bluff draped almost to the ground masking five cabins tucked in against the 250-foot bluff. Human formations snaked along the narrow paths cut into the limestone bluffs. Armed guards prodded them along with the barrels of the AK-47's they carried. All of the guards were dressed in black with *kufiyah* scarves wrapped tightly around their heads, revealing eyes only.

Agent 22 drained the last of a canteen, suppositions running through his mind. Caves carved into limestone walls; lines of humans filing in and out of the second cabin, the one that belched smoke from what must be very large ovens. Women urged children to stay in line. Teenagers took charge of younger siblings as if they knew what would happen to those who became a nuisance. Guards looked away as children filed from the eatery, nibbling on or clutching tortillas. They knew well enough to carry their next snack with them.

Unaccompanied children, some as young as six or seven, used both hands to carry the heavy buckets filled with water from the river that vanished under the tree canopy. They were probably working for only a few pesos a day. Scooping the water from the river, the smaller children moved maybe 15 feet before letting the bucket fall to the ground, having to stop and rest. It seemed to take them ten minutes to cover the 150 feet from the river to the cabins. Minutes after vanishing under the canopy, the same children reappeared with buckets emptied, to repeat their labors.

South of the cabins, terrorists in platoon-sized elements traversed what Shadow 22 would describe as a Marine Corps obstacle course, an agility course, and a confidence course, customized for terrorists. Retired from Marine Intelligence, Shadow 22 noted that they altered the course's obstacles by lowering walls and removing ropes, he supposed to preserve their delicate machismo. Farther up river, hand-to-hand training was taking place, but what the agent saw would not pass frat house standards during rush. Beyond was a class within the confines of a four-foot high berm. The instructor stood surrounded by a circle of kneeling students, apparently receiving grenade and explosives training. Shadow 22 made a mental note to target the explosives instructor.

Across the river, a hacienda constructed around a mid-19th-century log cabin, was cleverly built with the structure modestly designed on the outside so as not to draw attention from the authorities. The driveway vanished underneath the structure, probably into a basement carved from the limestone. Agent 22 would have given a month of *per diem* to know what was below the hacienda. South of the hacienda was a large barn, built atop an old tennis court. Gators and four wheelers motored in and out of the barn. Many of the ATVs towing small trailers bulging with supplies traveled across the river or made a left turn passing out of sight to locations west.

Shadow 22 feverishly punched up a message into the pocket size lightweight transmitter, sending the data via satellite down to a location above a junior agent's paygrade.

● ● ●

The crunch of tires turning off the hard-surface road onto the drive leading down to the hacienda echoed through the canyon. A minute later, an F-150 rounded the bend.

The shiny F-150 4x4 pulled to a stop roughly ten yards from the porch. Jorge watched from the corner of his eye as El Maestro exited the F-150, trailed by a woman wearing a familiar purple burka, the one he'd seen in Scorpion's dining room earlier. A man stepped around from the rear of the truck. Plump and short, he wore a dark jubba, and a close-fitting prayer cap called a taqiyah. The robe-like garment had long sleeves and a collar wrapped around the Mexican man's neck. It was Muhammed Abu Moya, the Mexican Caliph who styled himself after the movement's First Caliph, Abu Bakr. An Anglo, wearing loose fitting blue jeans topped by a neon-colored Hawaiian shirt trailed behind the Caliph. Jorge knew the group would be touring Black Stone's Underground Railroad.

Jorge had concluded that Scorpion really didn't care if the shipping of humans to the Middle East stopped tomorrow, as long as the cash continued to flow in by other means. And, Black Stone could continue to cull the most attractive girls for the cartel's prostitution rings. Scorpion, being the kind of man he was, made a habit of sampling the sweetest fruit. His lust for young women gave Jorge the chance to put eyes on the unfortunate victims. He was certain that, so far, none of the "Phoenix Six" had shown up. More mystifying, he'd heard no small talk within Black Stone's circle that the cartel bore any responsibility for the girls' disappearance.

Now Jorge's eyes followed the men as they greeted each other with firm handshakes and "*as salaamu alaik,*" a salutation that enabled them to include the woman without touching her.

Scorpion gave his unwelcome guest a half-hearted embrace, and an unenthusiastic "Welcome cousin," adding, "the woman can remain on the porch. Jorge will see to her needs."

El Maestro turned to the woman with a curt nod, and then fell in behind the Mexican Caliph and the gringo in the loud flowered shirt. Jorge knew if the woman was slated to undertake a suicide mission inside the U.S., then disrobing her would be Scorpion's pleasure. The leader of Black Stone presented few mysteries to Jorge, who knew that the woman's deadly intentions would only make her more attractive to Scorpion.

"Attend to her with care, Jorge." Scorpion said. "If she needs to rest, give her the guest room next to mine."

"Yes, Sir," Jorge said, stepping back in a half bow and grazing his right arm across his chest. His thumb brushed across the top of the pen in his vest pocket, activating the hidden micro-cam. A hotspot connection would ensure the upload of the digital imagery to the Shadow Service's Operations Center.

Scorpion led his guests inside the hacienda. Only members of Black Stone's inner circle had permission to enter the rooms resting below the hacienda. Even Jorge hadn't earned Scorpion's trust in that regard.

Alone with the woman, Jorge offered her a chair in the shade of the portal. "Is there anything I can do to make your visit...cooler?" he asked, modestly indicating the burka's head-to-toe coverage.

Now he shifted from perfect English to perfect and rapid Spanish, "*Yo se, hace mucho calor.*" She remained silent, but beneath the burka, she shook her head, declining the offer.

The throaty revving of a Gator's engine coming from the riverbed caught Jorge's attention. The four-wheeled recreational vehicle rounded the corner, bouncing fore and aft. The road, used a century earlier for horse and wagon travel, was now used to transport personnel and supplies across the river to occupants of the barracks and caves built against the cliffs. The driver of the Gator pulled up just a dozen yards from the portal. The armed guard gestured for water. Jorge pegged them Laurel and Hardy. Quietly excusing himself to the woman, he filled and carried two glasses toward the vehicle.

Perhaps showing off, the driver accelerated rapidly and then slammed on the brakes just shy of Jorge. Something heavy thudded against metal in the Gator's bed. Jorge brought the water close enough to glance into the vehicle bed, gaining a visual with the mini-cam of a man face down and brutally hog-tied, wrists trussed to ankles so they met in the small of the prisoner's back.

"Who's the *pendejo*?" Jorge inquired, feigning half-hearted interest.

"Marine, *Americano*," the overweight driver tagged Laurel boasted, "Scorpion's present for El Maestro and that weird

Caliph," He guzzled his water and handed the empty glass back to Jorge. "He is about to get another workover from El Tigre."

Jorge nodded. El Tigre, who always wore a large diamond earring to show off his wealth, had a bad habit of taking things personally when any of his victims survived his interrogations.

"Maybe you won't have to bother with a return trip to the caves," Jorge asked, working to make the harsh joke sound authentic.

"Hope not," Laurel replied, sneering. "This one is a real tough hombre, but El Tigre doesn't like to be shown up. Besides, we hear that Scorpion will receive a big check when this *pendejo* gets handed over to El Maestro's friends."

"Really," Jorge said, in a 'you've-got-to-be-shitting-me' tone. "I heard we have some hot teenage girls from Phoenix bedded down in the compound."

Laurel shook his head puffing out his thick lower lip as if he didn't know about what Jorge was talking. When he laughed, he jiggled the flesh around his abdomen, which spilled over his trousers. Laurel then released the brake, shifted into reverse and eased down the accelerator, pushing the vehicle back. Each time the Gator jolted over another large rock, the Marine's face slammed against the metal bed. Through it all, the man remained silent. The vehicle made a hard 180 degree turn. Following the drive, it curved below the hacienda and pulled to a stop in front of the service entrance.

Jorge returned to the porch to check on the woman. She had made herself at home, pouring carbonated water into a tall glass, and settling into the hand-woven loveseat. Jorge made his way into the house carrying the empty water glasses. He had an urgent communication to send.

31

Thursday 1700 hours; Naval Air Facility
El Centro, Airfield

Talking since 1400 hours, the four Marine aviators were acting out of character. Cell phones turned face up on the table, resting next to glasses of ice water instead of Black Label. Bravado cast aside, they discussed "what if's" all the while Hap had his Pop whispering into his ear again. The warriors kicked the tires on how far they would take their planning.

Hap, Hollywood, Spanky, and LtCol Swamp Puppy Stenson spoke quietly over dinner. Colonel Shank would return on station tomorrow evening. The mission to return Warden would have to commence before the private jet's landing gear touched the runway, no, ifs, ands, or buts. Otherwise, the mission would be aborted.

Hap's phone vibrated, skittering slightly across the table. "Shadow" appeared across the top of the screen. George Strait's "Living for the Night" suddenly played in Hap's mind. Picking up the phone, he remained silent, not breathing, waiting for Blad to say his old friend was dead.

"We found him. The son of a bitch is still alive Hap. Big Shadow is en route to Mexico City to speak to the President. My boss will feel the bastard out. The son of a bitch may very well be on the take. Big Shadow will be able to sniff this out."

Hap sucked in a deep breath. "Should we take this up the chain?"

"Your call, but I wouldn't until we find out where the Mexican President stands."

"So we continue contingency planning?"

"And launch before Bear returns. The son of a bitch is in such a cover-his-ass mode, I'm surprised the turd hasn't grounded the squadron."

"Hey, Blad...."

"Get on with it, Hap. My God, I already know you're putting together a package, a Marine air, and ground task force."

"Swamp will give us as many as six F-18's."

"What type of ordnance? Anything worth talking about?"

".20mm, Zuni, and Mark 82."

"You sure you want the suck and blow guys to go in without precision ordnance?"

"Swamp's Cowboys would take them as fightin' words, Blad. Remember you're talking about guys who trained dropping bombs with iron sights. I've controlled enough of those missions to know what they can do." He knew they could drop bombs on target without precision weapons. Required bigger balls, sure, but every Marine on this mission toted around balls made of brass.

"Helo assets are going to need to fuel twice to get to the target."

"That bad, huh?"

"It could be three stops if you don't get favorable winds," Blad said. "For sure, one stop north of the border, one stop south."

"What about gas, hoses, and security on Mexico side. I'll bring the ordnance men with me for arming."

"I'm working on that, Hap. I'll be on the ground south of the border with some of my team. Roach will have 9mm, 5.56, 7.62, .50 caliber rounds and tripods. Roach said to bring your Ma Deuces. Let the ground element put them to use. He believes your Huey gunners would just waste the ammunition."

"No comment on your last. Enlighten me on our target for our last flight as Marine Aviators."

"*Delicias* will be the FARP south of the border, a little over 40 nautical miles from the compound southwest of Camargo where they're holding Tuna Man."

"*Gracias*, Blad."

"I'll get a call to you by midnight. Don't lay your head down. We have work to do."

Hap raised an index finger, punching the end call button. Resting his elbows on the table, he clutched onto an over-stuffed shrimp po' boy with both his hands; a million thoughts ran through his mind. Shrimp and red sauce dropped down on the greasy fries. He took a large bite that tasted like crap. Chewing in a deliberate motion, he thought about the 2 am arrest in Thailand. Hap could still remember the two police officers who manhandled him into the rear of a Jeep and took off for the magistrate. The local police had an easy time of it since Hap was holding a boxed-up, extra-large Canadian bacon and pineapple pizza. He would always remember the takeaway from the shakedown.

The middle-aged magistrate looked like he wanted to be anywhere but on the bench at this hour. "Sir," he mumbled, "apologize, and you are free to go."

Hap remembered nodding as he choked down the last of the pizza and slowly approached, still clutching the empty box with both hands. The arresting officer leaned in to hear the Captain of Marines express regret to the upset business owner. Standing in front of the accuser, Hap leaned over to apologize, Patton-style. "You can kiss my ass, you low-life fuck."

Wide-eyed the police officer broke down, hands on knees, laughing. The Magistrate slammed the gavel down, "Maline, you are free to go. God bless you and all like you. You keep my countrymen safe."

Looking around now, trying to choke down the bad chow, Hap came face to face with the look of determined Marines. Nothing he hadn't seen before, flying with Marines in combat. I almost feel sorry for the bad guys, Hap thought. These guys are going to be like chickens on a lizard.

Hap turned to Spanky. "Ops O. I want a midafternoon launch, eight planes on the schedule. Five Snakes, three Hueys." Spitting what was left of the po' boy onto the mound of fries, he added "Swamp, give me what you can. Ops will have a plan memorialized sometime this evening."

A grin spread over Spanky's square jaw. "We have air crews who will fight each other to make the schedule."

Swamp dropped a balled fist on the table, presenting a thumbs-up. "The Cowboys are on board, Hap."

Hap was stoic. "Whoever does not have the stomach for this fight, we will let them depart, as there is no dishonor in saying no. None of us wants to die. Whoever lives to tell about this borderline decision, will rouse himself every waking day. He will tell embellished stories to his sons and daughters."

Tears leaked from the sides of both eyes, but there was no holding back. These sons of bitches had never seen him show such emotion. He spoke lower, leaning farther across the table. "Whoever sheds his blood with me shall be my brother. Those Marines who pass, I will kiss their forehead. Those men from the Administration, who would throw Warden to the wolves, are lesser men. They will hear how we fought and maybe died, but they will know that in the end we brought our Commanding Officer home. Last…loose lips sink ships."

Thursday 1900; Mecca II MX

Trainers shouted into bullhorns urging trainees to pull themselves over or crawl underneath final obstacles, their voices bouncing off the steep canyon walls. The last echo of gunfire faded, marking the end of the day's training. Standing between the barn and the portal, Jorge watched as the trainees filed from the facilities to the front of the line of cabins, tucking under an arm a prayer rug, given to them by a familiar figure in a purple burka. An NCO positioned himself on either end of the four rows of trainees for the fourth of the five Muslim obligatory prayers.

El Maestro appeared on the top step of the middle cabin, joined by the Mexican Caliph who opened his arms, and welcomed the jihadi trainees. Each member stood with his mat to his front, facing in the direction of the Holy Mosque in Mecca, home of the *Kaaba*, the giant black cube that is pilgrimage destination for all devout Muslims. Each man raised both hands to his ears in prayer, the right hand following the left.

All kept their gaze lowered, focused on the place they were standing. Then, moving as one, they bent at the waist and then stood. The group went to their knees placing head and hands on the prayer rug. Rising to their knees, they each kept their left foot, from ball to heel, on the rug, while only the toes of their right foot made contact with the rug. As they all stood, Jorge knew that one rakat was complete, and, depending on time of day, up to three more rakats might be required. Now they all sat on their knees, every head turned to the right. Moments later, they turned their heads to the left, reciting from the Koran in Spanish. Jorge watched knowing that both El Maestro and the Caliph were spewing Wahhabi ideology, instilling hate.

A Gator motored out of the riverbed, slowly rounding the corner. Jorge recognized driver and passenger as Laurel and Hardy. He gestured to them, as if drinking from a tequila bottle, bringing a wave from the driver. Walking quickly into the hacienda, he returned with a bottle of Scorpion's house tequila, just in time to see Laurel brake in front of the underground entrance. As he approached the Gator, both occupants were already reaching for the bottle.

"You here to pick up the Marine?" Jorge asked in Spanish.

Holding the bottle, Jorge allowed the driver to chug down three long gulps while nodding. When he pulled the bottle away, tequila dribbled over Laurel's heavy chins. Hardy's hand grasped for the bottle. Catching the movement out of the corner of an eye, Jorge stepped back, wagging a forefinger at both. "Let me spit on the body, and you can have the bottle."

The two thugs stared at each other in confusion. "Which one, Jorge?" Laurel asked, wiping a dirty wrist across his mouth.

"You know," Jorge replied.

Hardy leaned forward, resting both elbows on the small dash. "Jorge, we have two enjoying the pleasures of the chair right now."

Jorge masked his surprise. It seemed he had missed some activity in the last few hours. He smiled. "Did you take the two men and the lady across the river?"

Motioning with both hands in a snakelike gesture, Hardy said, "You like the girl, Jorge?"

"Not really. Looks like a folded up umbrella. Who's the other guy who's gonna be hurting?"

Again, the two looked at each other, confused. "You know what Scorpion would do to us and our families if he heard us gossiping," Laurel said, licking his lips.

Jorge pointed to the bottle with two fingers. "Yeah, he would be pissed you two made off with two bottles of his favorite tequila."

"You're not bullshitting us, Jorge?" Hardy said, wide-eyed.

Shaking his head slowly, Jorge pressed two fingers against the bottle.

Laurel jumped into the conversation, talking as rapidly as the passenger, even as he glanced around furtively, checking if anybody was listening in. "Two bottles plus what is left in your hand."

Jorge nodded knowing he would have this part of the disk erased before the wheels of the Gator met the stream. "Don't worry. Scorpion already has you on video. I will explain what happened if he asks me."

Both men bit their lower lips, looking at the other before Laurel answered, "It's an Anglo captured in Mexicali a few days back. Black Stone and one of El Maestro's fighters kicked in a hotel door."

Jorge laughed. "Why do these people go against the Black Stone? So futile. Go get the Marine so I can spit on him, and I will get your bottles for you."

Walking to retrieve the bottles, Jorge calculated that Shadow 28 was somewhere inside the compound, that is, if he was still alive. Reaching for two bottles from the liquor cabinet, "What the hell," he murmured to himself and tucked another bottle under his armpit.

Minutes later, he could hear groans come from the still body in the back of the Gator. He handed Laurel and Hardy the original bottle, and the two passed it back and forth between them, taking long chugs.

Jorge eased to the back of the Gator, pulling out a bottle of water from his jacket. Curled up in a ball, the bloodied and bludgeoned body lay motionless. Slowly lifting the Marine's bruised head; he made sure the camera in his breast pocket captured the scene as he began carefully dripping water to the swollen lips. Jorge saw several jagged dark spaces where teeth once were and met the Marine's eyes peering through slits, sending out signals that he was at peace and Jorge was Jesus Christ.

Jorge poured water onto the Marine's battered forehead. He removed the bloody nametag from the flight suit and slipped the half-empty bottle into a tattered pocket. Despite the blood, he could make out the name WARDEN. He dropped the nametag into his pocket not realizing the blood leaked through his white pants.

Walking back to the front of the Gator, he handed each man a bottle of tequila, keeping the third tucked visibly under his armpit.

"Hey, what do you have in your pocket?" Laurel asked.

Jorge looked down. "Shit," he said to himself, and then with a damn good poker face, he smiled. "I like to frame mementos of Scorpion's victims."

Puckering his lips, Laurel nodded.

He held up the third full bottle next to his right ear and issued a crooked smile. Come on, Jorge, give it to us."

Jorge slowly held out the bottle. Laurel clasped it by the neck and Jorge almost pulled him from the driver seat when he yanked it back. Laurel maintained a death grip around the bottle. Looking the man in the eye, Jorge smiled. "Where is this other Anglo being held?"

Laurel kept a firm grip on the bottle, "With the Marine."

Jorge released his grip. Laurel sprang back into the seat clutching the bottle of spirits. "Keep the bottle," Jorge said walking away. "You earned it."

33

Resting an elbow in the palm of his opposite hand, Hap scratched the stubble sprouting from his chin between thumb and forefinger. He slowly shook his head.

"Hate giving up a weapon station for an external fuel tank, Spank."

Leaning over the map, both palms on the coffee table of Hap's BOQ room, Spanky studied the route. "We have no choice, Hap. A 318 nautical-mile leg is a lot to ask from an armed-up Cobra. We can't afford to come up short on this one."

"Refuel and 284 miles to the FARP," Hap said. "Give the Hueys a thirty-minute head start on the second leg, the flight should arrive at the FARP within minutes of each other."

Big Alabama entered the room, closing the door behind him. He dropped the flight schedule for the next day on the side of the table. "Hap, five Snakes, and three Hueys will launch for the Strike Package. Two Cobras and one Huey for the training mission."

Hap tapped the eraser on the take-off times, while he penciled in the blank slots- 1500 for the Hueys and 1530 for the Cobras. The second flight he penciled in for a 2330 launch. Return time for the first flight was marked TBD, "to be determined." The second flight he marked in 0115 hours.

Spanky and Big Alabama waited. The signature line was still blank.

"How about it, Colonel?" Big Alabama asked.

Hap quickly scrawled his name across the signature line. Handing it back to the Operations Officer, he grinned. "So, you think Station is going to have issue with this? What about Group?"

Spanky shook his head. "Good news, Bear is still in D.C. Station may have a question. Hell, if nothing else, we can always say after the shoot we will overnight in Douglas or Station can give us permission for closed field landings. Colonel, at this juncture, we only need to be able to depart to the east and have a little bit of wiggle room and lots of luck. Once we enter Mexico airspace, there will be no turning back."

Hap traced the line from Douglas to the FARP, ticking off fifty nautical-mile increments. "Special Ops would think twice flying this mission."

Spanky picked up the flight schedule. "Nothing against Special Ops, Hap, but the Nomads are better. If you don't believe me, ask the world in about thirty hours."

Hap returned a grin like a father standing over his first-born son. The acting commanding officer of HMLA 767, walked over to the couch. "What a way to close out a career, Spank," he said, falling back onto the cushions.

Spank could only nod. "Ironic isn't it," he said. "The only upside to our mission is getting Warden back along with the entire package. Mission accomplished, and then the real fight begins, protecting our Marines from the JAG and Justice Department. Only under this Administration."

"Only in America," Hap parroted.

Spanky turned to leave, "Gotta go talk to the combat crews and ordnance. Be back in a few."

"I'm with you, Spank," Big Alabama said.

Hap replied with a wink and interlocked his fingers behind his head. As Spank closed the door, Hap's thoughts returned to the mission. He could see the birds making both legs. With any luck, they would launch from the FARP with 80% of the package. F-18s could come in two flights of three, 45 minutes apart. There would be a TOT assignment and Swamp would only have to ensure the F-18's were overhead at that time. Marines would have eyes on the target soon enough. As Captain Simmons's team fed intelligence, the ground scheme of maneuver would come together.

Without bothering to knock, Swamp entered the room at the same time Carla walked out of the BOQ bedroom clad in an oversized T-shirt. He waved the coiled up sheet of paper at Carla before handing it over to Hap. She acknowledged the gesture with a smile and ducked back in the bedroom closing the door gently.

Hap reached out, uncoiling the document using both hands. Looking over the top of the Cowboys' next day flight schedule, a grin flashed from ear to ear.

34

Friday 1945; Mecca II MX

Danny Lee Boyd watched Scorpion stroll with a deliberately lazy stride across the small, subterranean conference room. He stopped in front of a white board, where he began to doodle a crosswise track, overlaid with a circle.

Now he sketched a structure that Danny Lee thought resembled the Leaning Tower of Pisa, adding a column of wavy lines resembling seagulls—the kind a kindergarten kid would draw. The leader of Black Stone enclosed the seagulls into an oblong circle, sketching a boat-like contraption with a small smokestack.

Boyd interrupted raising an index finger to the ceiling. "What's with the seagulls?"

Scorpion shot back a 'how stupid are you?' look. "They are floors of the Los Americanos, dumb ass."

Danny resisted the urge to fidget in his chair. He actually wished El Maestro had joined them. Scorpion was becoming drunk with power. With a single swipe, Scorpion drew a curvy mark above the initial drawing with "US" printed above the new stripe. Pointing at the bottom of the grease board, he half turned, looked over his shoulder, and caught the eyes of his audience of one: Danny Lee Boyd.

"Black Stone's Underground Railroad culls from the human wave we move to the north." His index finger ran laterally across the bottom line, he said, "Product that can bring the best price, we cull for Black Stone operations. The others we move to the Gulf Coast states for the benefit of Mullahs and their jihadi warriors. Kidnapped girls north of the border bring a premium and will be transported south across the border and moved across Black Stone's Underground Railroad."

Scorpion beamed with pride, gloating, "Black Stone has just moved over two dozen jihadi 'wannabes' across the border using the railroad. Let me add, these efforts bring handsome payment. With the US southern border wide open, our jihadists returning from the East can enter the US with little chance of interdiction. So you can see why our profitability will increase twofold over the next few months."

Boyd raised three fingers of his right hand. "Treason was never part of the deal."

"Unless you want to get your Senator indicted, you will do as I say." Scorpion turned to a map draped across an 84-inch flat-screen mounted on the wall behind the grease board. He circled the real estate on the southern shoreline of El Cuchillo Lake. "The Resort's employees will be El Maestro's jihadists in waiting."

Boyd shook his head. "As much as I like the scratch, it's all coming too close to home."

Scorpion looked into Boyd's dull brown eyes. "I suggest you and your boyfriend find a way to cover your tracks."

Boyd kept his alarm at bay and his expression cool, massaging the bridge of his roman nose. How could Scorpion know about Jourdan and him?

Scorpion smirked. "Are you washed in the blood of the lamb, Danny Boy? My people will take back their stolen property. This past weekend, Black Stone coordinated violence near Guadalajara and Jalisco. As much I hated to give the order, Black Stone shot down one of Mexico's Government helicopters, killing five soldiers. We burned a dozen bank branches and half dozen gas stations across the state. Now, the New Beginnings Cartel has to fight against a government military operation intent on taking it down. They were becoming militarily powerful, and jeopardizing my loan guarantee for the Puerto Vallarta resort. Obviously we have taken care of the issue and the road is open for the Senator to bring across the loan."

Boyd's thin lips twisted into a leer. He looked forward to telling Jourdan about how Scorpion mugged like Mussolini at a Fascist rally. He said, "So, who did the Mexicans take from? The Spaniards? Let me see, the Spaniards took the land from the Indians, who kicked out the horny toad. Kiss my ass, Gregorio!"

Bent back with hands on hips, Scorpion let out a thundering laugh. "You ready to fly away, Danny Boy? In the past three months, Black Stone kidnapped the students, implicating the Spanish Templar Cartel in those actions. The military is taking down my enemies for me. They are mortally weakening my rivals. The President of Mexico has twittered warnings that those criminal groups behind the atrocities will be dismantled."

Beginning to cower, Danny said, "You will get your loan guarantee. I thought this was all about money and status." He tried not to squirm.

"You are still alive, Danny, because I need that loan guarantee." He shrugged. "At least for this month, anyway. More so, the movement needs that loan guarantee. Don't make me go find another senator. It's surprisingly easy, you know."

Danny gestured with his palms towards Scorpion, feeling ridiculously small, like a deer standing alone on the tracks, attempting to stop a freight train. "Calm down, Gregorio. I have always delivered the goods. Besides, Black Stone would never assassinate a U.S. senator."

An annoyed scowl crossed Scorpion's broad face. "The United States leadership is fickle. We would never kill your President or his Vice President. Doing so would jeopardize the movement and naïve participants. But I damn sure have no problem eliminating a problematic senator."

"Even this Administration has a line that would be dangerous to cross, Gregorio. I would stick with trafficking and not cross that line."

Scorpion waggled an index finger like a first grade teacher in the direction of a belligerent student. "It's the movement, Danny Boy. Never forget about the movement. I have to ensure the startup factions never have the time to set roots. The Mexican Military—with U.S. financial aid and military assistance—will cast aside Black Stone adversaries."

Boyd turned, showing Scorpion an aristocratic profile, hoping the look would distract from the fact he was about to shit his pants. "You wouldn't know anything about the missing U.S. Marine?"

"Who, me?" Scorpion said, using both hands to touch his chest. "Can you say a quick $15 million, Danny Boy? Transportation along the Underground Railroad FOB your basement. A Saudi Crown Prince will wire you and the Senator $2 million each the moment his jet's wheels go into the well."

Danny Lee Boyd prided himself on never committing treason, but two million wasn't a bad day at the office. What the hell, it was just one dumbass Marine.

Scorpion continued the verbal mugging, "Danny, you can't leave the family. You and the Senator are in waaaaay over your head and making waaaay too much money. You see, I am simply a man willing to kill to maintain status. Status, you see, is survival for people like me." Scorpion jabbed a finger in Danny's direction. "You on the other hand are just acting like a good capitalist. It is all about the money, baby, and staying alive."

Boyd sat with his back erect, arms crossed; attempting to demonstrate something he knew he didn't have—moxie. He knew that Jourdan would let the one Marine die for two million cash. But, the fact that he and Jourdan had become part of a business deal that allowed jihadis to pass back and forth over the US-Mexico border possibly leading to the death of US citizens…everybody had a limit.

He said, "I can't speak for the Senator, but can we stop with the jihadis moving north across the border?"

Scorpion offered a questioning look, the corners of his lips turned down. "So you are worried about the jihadis and El Maestro? Don't be. Though they wire me funds like a slot machine, I have a few surprises for those assholes. It is all in the timing, Danny Boy."

Boyd squeezed his lower lip between his thumb and index finger, trying to get his mind around the ramifications if this operation went south. "We can handle shipping product east, but bringing them back, and pushing them north, appears problematic, Gregorio. Can't we just divorce El Maestro and go back to the old way of doing business? You know we did pretty well just moving human mules carrying backpacks of narcotics north into the U.S."

Chuckling, Scorpion shook his head. "Have you ever considered I will plant enough of the jihadis in my competition's backyard? Create a few incidents with Black Stone personnel dressed as jihadi's and kaboom! U.S. Military will work side-by-side with the Mexican Government, eliminating the cockroaches and my competition off the face of the earth. Don't think the Mexican Government isn't concerned with the Muslim movement spreading its roots throughout the country."

Boyd nodded, allowing a smile to sneak out from one side of his mouth. "Then it's all yours."

Scorpion nodded. "Something like that. Hitler started World War II similar to this sham. Most people don't know Gestapo officers impersonated Polish Military to raid the German radio station. Similar to Hitler, we will drop a few dead bodies dressed in jihadi attire where we need to create hysteria. Of course the United States Administration and the Mexican Government will be able to prove they trained in the Middle East and here." Scorpion returned the marker to its holder at the base of the white board.

Turning now to face Danny head on, he said. "I would think we will have an 'International Incident.' They will kill El Maestro and others like him. Black Stone will probably end up fighting alongside the Mexican Government. Naturally, we will retake Mecca II from the jihadists. Dead men tell no tales and they will all be put to the sword. No pun intended."

Boyd felt his head begin to bob in agreement, and, oh so slowly, he twisted his lower jaw to the side. "What about retaking what Mexico used to claim on the U.S. side of the border?"

Scorpion laughed. "You didn't buy that garbage. I have to preach this kind of garbage to my lieutenants to get them to go along with all this jihadi crap. Don't want to piss off a bunch of Texans. If you want to know the truth Danny Boy, their thinking is close to yours."

35

Thursday 2000; Washington D.C.

For the best power lunch in Washington D.C., those inside the Beltway sit down at the Palm Restaurant. Commonly known as the Palm, the owners literally papered the walls of the restaurant with the faces of Washington powerbrokers as well as small portraits of politicians, journalists, lobbyists, and other notable figures.

This day, after hours, was no different from any other Thursday, except that General Verbie, accompanied by his military secretary, Colonel George Mislick, sat drinking at the bar. A direct advisor to the Commandant, Colonel Mislick, call sign "Slick," filtered and directed the flow of information, keeping General Verbie abreast of all situations affecting the Marine Corps. Analytical in his thinking, Slick always collected everything pertinent to the upcoming discussion, and then analyzed the data until the wee hours of the morning. Regardless of the time Slick turned in, the early risers on the road to beat rush hour would see the Marine running the streets around 8th and I at six a.m. After completing up to 9 miles, he would be sitting in front of the Commandant's desk at 0730, providing sound guidance and counsel to his dear friend.

Verbie tossed back a Jack Daniels over ice, while Slick sipped a cabernet from a long stem wine glass. Both anticipated the President would nominate the Marine Commandant to succeed General Arthur Rosales as the Chairman of the Joint Chiefs within days. As the top military advisor to the President and Defense Secretary, Verbie would influence the President as to when and where to use U.S. armed forces. Earlier in the week, Verbie had informed Slick that, if nominated, he would put the Colonel up for deep selection to Brigadier General and make him his adjutant. Neither Marine anticipated the announcement until Monday.

Slick leaned on the bar with both forearms, speaking as he swirled the wine around the crystal glass. "General, somebody got to Shank."

Verbie lowered his head in frustration, "You saw it too. For a moment, I thought it was me. I have known the son of a bitch since he was a junior captain."

Slick chuckled. "You know as well as I do, Shank wants a star. Hell, give the bastard a star and, sure as I'm standing, he would stab his own mother in the back if she stepped in his way for the second star."

"So what do you think happened with Warden?"

Biting his lower lip, Slick gestured to the attractive bartender, ordering another round. "Is that OK, General?"

"You have got to be shitting me, Slick. The way I'm feeling right now, you could stack my side three-deep. I have two dead Marines, two wounded, and a very good friend missing, and the frigging Administration is blaming my Marines."

"We both know Warden and Stoner. Warden is even keel and goes by the book. Provoke Hap Stoner, and get the hell out of the way. I believe Stoner's and Captain Simmons's account."

Verbie tossed back his drink and pushed the glass to the side. Grabbing the fresh drink, he stirred the ice into the whiskey. His eyes narrowed. "Concur, Colonel. So what's with Shank's story?"

"General, someone has promised the turd a star. Why? Your guess is as good as mine."

Verbie hesitated, took a sip, enjoying the sting of the whiskey in the back of his throat. "Damn, Slick. I remember telling Hap Stoner when he was a captain the active duty Marine wanted no part of his ilk. I went so far as to tell the Kang Cobra the Marine Corps wanted him stored in Cosmoline. Go to the Reserves and pursue the business career he longed for. The Marine Corps would bring him out in the time of war. Fortunately for the Corps, the man has seen three conflicts and was staring at another rotation to Southwest Asia as Warden's Exec."

"So much for the Cosmoline, General, although I do remember raising my glass of wine at the Futenma O'Club, after hearing Hap Stoner submitted his resignation from active duty." Rolling back against the bar, Slick propped back on both elbows. The toe of one of his Corfams locked atop the polished foot rail. He scanned the sparsely occupied dining room and saw an opportunity.

A lobbyist, wearing a Michael Andrews Bespoke two-thousand-dollar suit, leaned across tables, aiming to influence a congressman, a senator, or one of their staff, in an attempt to swing a vote on an upcoming bill. One vote could mean the difference between landing a $2 billion contract and nothing. Some might call this power brokering but Slick and the Commandant of the Marine Corps called it crap. The two Marines spent many an hour after meetings within the halls of Congress and the White House closing out the evening at the Palm. Lobbyists knew to steer clear of General Verbie, and didn't waste their time attempting to go through Slick to get to the Commandant.

Cutting his brown eyes across the crowd, Slick gestured with his chin, "Speaking of Shank…General, the bastard is tucked in the corner with Senator Jourdan."

Verbie turned, holding his drink. "Where is the Bear?"

"Two o'clock long, General."

Verbie focused in on the table where a Marine Colonel sat with none other than the Chairman of the Senate Armed Services Committee. "What the hell is that all about?"

"Nothing stupid now, General, you do have a confirmation hearing coming up."

"I have a missing Marine, Slick. You can take that confirmation hearing and shove it up your ass."

Slick gestured at the bartender to close the tab. He watched Verbie, drink in hand, move toward Shank's table as if vectored by ATC. Short in stature, Verbie, even at his age, could hold his own in any bar skirmish. While the General maneuvered between tables, Slick signed the tab and picked up the General's braided barracks cover. Even from the bar, Slick could see Shank's eyes widening, as if he were watching a ghost approach. Summarily pushing off the bar, Slick made his way toward them to protect General Verbie's career.

Shank came to his feet assuming the position of attention. "Good evening, General." Senator Jourdan remained seated and offered a limp handshake.

"Take your seat, Shank." The Group Commander eased uncomfortably into his chair. Verbie sat in the empty chair, resting his drink on the table, cutting his brown eyes between the two. Silence followed, with the three men swapping gazes like the characters in the final scene of "The Good, The Bad, and The Ugly." Instead of drawing his pistol, Verbie spoke firmly. "Did I interrupt something?"

"Would it matter if you had?" the Senator replied.

Verbie took a slug from his glass. Returning the glass empty, shaking his head, he said, "Not really, Senator."

Perspiration beaded on Shank's brow. Well-manicured fingers picked up the cloth napkin. Patting above his brow, it was obvious Shank wished he was anywhere but the Palm.

"Nervous, Shank?" Verbie asked.

Shank shook his head. "No, General. Lack of sleep I believe," he said, faking a chuckle.

One side of Verbie's mouth cracked a smile. "The Palm is not a place one visits to catch up on sleep, Colonel."

The junior Marine at the table looked straight ahead, "Yes, General."

Slick could see that Shank was uncomfortable and probably thinking his career was on the line.

Jourdan's Chief of Staff appeared out of nowhere, leaning over the table. "Pardon me, General, for interrupting, but you are acting like an ass in front of the Chairman of your confirmation hearing."

Slick watched Verbie's narrow face turn slowly, giving the staffer an incinerating gaze.

"Senator Jourdan. I'm not sure what you promised the Colonel to entice him to stretch the truth." The Commandant pointed his index finger in the direction of the Committee Chairman. "I know LtCol Warden, and the Marine I know would not have done what I heard in the hearing today. LtCol Warden is missing and could very well be dead." Verbie's next words came from somewhere below his stomach. "Just how in the hell am I supposed to feel, Senator?"

Jourdan patted down his wrinkled forehead with his napkin, "My thoughts are with the Marines' families. How can you say that LtCol Warden didn't crack, General? You were not present that night." He dropped the napkin in his lap and picked up his water glass. He swallowed, hand trembling. "What was LtCol Stoner doing while his Commanding Officer was poking our neighbor to the south? Rest assured, as I'm sitting here, if Warden is alive and in the custody of the Mexican authorities, our State Department will bring your rogue Marine back rather quickly."

Slick reacted as Verbie's head leaned over his muscular forearms, preparing to lash out, as any good wingman would do, covering lead's ass. Slick pulled up a chair borrowed from a pair of striking blondes, who displayed astonishment and disappointment that the dashing officer did not join them but, rather, changed tables. "Excuse me for interrupting, General. Bear, how are you doing?" Adjusting the chair, he turned to receive the Senator's slimy handshake. "Senator, Colonel Mislick."

Reluctantly, Jourdan extended his hand. "I know who you are, Colonel."

Thirty minutes later, Mislick handed the Commandant his cover at the front door. The driver of the staff car held the door. Snapping a smart salute, the corporal closed the door behind Verbie then walked briskly around the back of the car to open the other back door for Slick.

The olive green car with small white USMC emblems on both front doors turned right, speeding north towards DuPont Circle.

Verbie looked at Slick. "How quick can you get to Andrews? I want you in El Centro."

"I have a couple sets of fatigues in my locker. Ten minutes and I can be on the way to the airport, General. My mission, Sir?"

"It's this uneasy feeling in the pit of my stomach. I had a conversation with LtCol Stoner twelve years ago that I'm afraid might lead him to do something that I, myself, would consider under similar circumstances. Monitor the situation and report back to me."

There was nothing else to say for the short ride to the 8th & I barracks. Colonel Mislick USMC knew what was required. *Semper Fi.*

Thursday 2130; Naval Air Facility El Centro CA
Nomad Flight Line

The sun had set behind the Laguna Mountains and the Imperial Valley floor was plunged into darkness. Nightfall brought a beehive of activity along the Marine Squadron's flight lines. Young Marine mechanics in soiled blue coveralls responded to the encouraging expletives from barking noncoms.

Friday's flight schedule called for a max effort and the Nomads' maintenance department responded to the call in flawless fashion. Hap walked among the Marines, beaming with pride. With the ass beating the unit had taken earlier in the week, the Nomads were out for blood. Hap sensed that during the upcoming fight, if the bad guys asked for quarter, they would get it. However, if they resisted, only God would be able to help.

Picking up his gait, Hap stuck out his chest a bit more than usual. Damn he was proud of these Marines. Stopping in his tracks, he watched as a tug towing a yellow genie sped by, bringing a wave from LCpl. McConnell, who hailed from Shiner, Texas. "Howdy, Colonel," he said, still smiling from ear to ear after being on the job 14 hours.

Some of the Marines would be going into battle. All participating in the Strike Package would be concluding their Marine Corps careers with an exclamation mark. Dereliction of duty and actions unbecoming of a Marine Officer were only two of the charges that came to Hap's mind as he approached the F-18 line.

Lit up like Wrigley Field on game night, the Cowboys maintenance personnel crawled over the F-18A Hornets like ants. Moving between the fighter-bombers, ordnance followed orders barked from irritated NCO's, loading Mark 82's and 4 shot Zuni rocket pods. Flight line personnel wiped down canopies, while others conducted pre-flights, holding flashlights and craning necks to see inside open panels.

Not particularly excited with the ordnance mix, the Marines would do what Marines have done throughout their lineage --do the most with what they have. God would sort out the rest. What Hap would do for a couple of M272 missile launchers laden with 4 AGM – 114 Hellfire Missiles in each rack. Instead, the only guided munitions in the strike package would be the 8 TOW missiles spread between 4 Snakes. Cobras launching without TOW would carry two 4-shot pods of Zuni along with one 7-shot pod of 2.75 and 750 rounds of .20mm.

Having to take the auxiliary fuel tanks decreased rocket delivery by 25% across the flight of Cobras. Running his hand along the Hornet's round snout, he almost butted heads with Swamp who was making his way down the line.

"Whoa, Cowboy," Hap said, putting his friend in an amiable headlock. "How are you feeling?"

Swamp pulled away, rubbing the bottom of his lower lip. "Hap, if your boys give us a good mark, we will blow their shit off the map."

Hap smiled. "I never had a doubt, my friend. Fellow Cowboys feel the same?"

The jet driver scratched the back of his head, yawning. "They do. That said, I would be remiss if I didn't tell you that to a man, there is concern about the unfamiliar feeling of being handcuffed and facing prosecution by court martial. We are invading a sovereign nation."

Hap nodded, his expression firm. "We will be represented by the best criminal defense attorneys available, Swamp. I will foot the bill, but suspect donations will come from around the country. People will give money for our defense, not for who we are, but for what we did: putting it all on the line to do what was right."

Swamp shook his head chuckling. "I will leave all that crap for you to work through, Hap. You're the business guy. Hell, I'm just a frigging airline captain when I'm not leading Marines."

37

Colonel "Slick" Mislick shifted restlessly in the seat flipping through the last of the three issues of Marine Corps Gazette. The Citation's APU was humming, but the hatch remained open, and neither pilot was strapped in behind the controls. Movement through the portal next to his seat caught his eye. Shank had arrived to board his jet to return to Atlanta for the night, and pick up more staff for the investigation. Slick expected the Group Commander to arrive at El Centro by noon tomorrow. "Bout frigging time," he said to himself, but that still didn't explain why his bird wasn't buttoned up and calling ground control requesting to taxi for takeoff.

Slick watched as Colonel Shank exited his dull green staff car, and turned to meet a black limo behind him. He was surprised to see Senator Jourdan step out of the limo and exchange a few words and a handshake. Walking to the rear of the car, Shank reached into the open trunk and pulled out the Senator's luggage. They both disappeared in the direction of Shank's waiting jet.

Fumbling to release the buckle, Slick jumped from his seat. Bent at the waist, he stuck his head out the open hatch. Both pilots wearing blue flight suits waited at the base of the steps, as if the President himself would be boarding.

"Major. We should have been in the air 15 minutes ago, any particular reason for the delay?"

Both pilots came to the position of attention. The aircraft commander responded, "Sir, we received an order to wait on an additional passenger."

"Who gave the order, Major?"

"Hey, Slick," Shank interrupted. Dropping his bag at the feet of the copilot, Shank clambered up the steps.

Slick stepped back, watching Shank ease by to drop into the seat across the narrow aisle from his. The pilot slid into the left side of the cockpit, donning a headset, while the copilot stored Shank's suitcase. Engine Number 1 spooled to life. Settling into his seat again, Slick looked across the aisle toward the new passenger, "So what am I missing, Bear?"

Cleaning his glasses, Shank perched them on his pelican-like snout. "Just following orders, Slick. The Commandant ordered me back to El Centro. The Senator has a meeting at the Los Americanos Hotel in Mexico and authorized the use of my plane."

"Isn't that decision a little over both of your pay grades?"

Shank shook his head. "You have a problem with the decision?"

Tapping a quick text on his cell, Slick depressed the send button. Moments later, the phone vibrated General Verbie's response: *What in the hell is Shank up to?*

Typing, he depressed the send button: *Your guess is as good as mine is.*

He was attempting to turn off the device as the plane approached the hold short line, but the phone vibrated. *Find out what the hell is going on with Shank.*

To many of his subordinates and peers, Shank was "Niedemeyer" of the United States Marine Corps. Having ruined many a Marine officer's career with the stroke of a pen, no one dared to get in the way of his General's star. To do so was at one's own peril. Slick would love to be a fly on the wall as Bear confronted Hap. It would be a lively debate for sure. Texting back: *Crossing hold short. Out.*

"Saying good bye to your girlfriend?"

Slick stored the phone. "No. Communicating with the Commandant why the fuck you're on this bird."

Shank chuckled. "Little over the General's pay grade on that one."

Reeling with that remark, Slick leaned into the aisle. "Shank, when I find out what the hell is going on, mark my words, I will shove it up your skinny ass."

Colonel Mislick settled back in his seat to grab some sleep. Like the Commandant, he sensed something big was about to go down, and he wouldn't be getting much sleep for the next few days.

Friday 0015; El Paso International, Cutter Aviation,
Team Jethro Insertion

Settling back in the Sikorsky helicopter for the two-hour ride
to the LZ, Captain Simmons tightened the harness clasping
his arm and rib cage together. Since leaving the hospital,
Simmons felt a "quart light" O-positive. The key to preventing additional bleeding was to immobilize the shoulder, and
he knew that once he left the chopper, the team would be
moving fast. For now, the ride was smooth and the pain
manageable. An aura of blue light radiated from the cockpit,
allowing Schlonger and the other pilot to read the instruments
by looking underneath their goggles. Simmons didn't know the
crew chief by name, but had seen him working around the
hanger during previous insertions. The team members were
fast asleep, their cammo'd faces relaxed. Collectively, the men
on this team had seen multiple tours, experiencing many
firefights. Staff Sergeant "Beer Can" Lyncher was the senior
citizen and active duty Marine at the ripe old age of 29 years
old. At this moment, Simmons, 27, could only wish he had
Lyncher's energy.

Multiple deployments overseas pushed Corporals Smitty,
Slaughter, Rock Carver, and Beaux to sixth-year-seniors at
University of Texas at San Antonio. Growing up outside the
back gate at Camp Pendleton, Simmons's dad always told him,

"Marines are the best the United States has to offer." He could think of no better group than this to be first to the fight.

These boys could be floating the Guadalupe, throwing back beers, and pursuing coeds in thongs, he thought. But, they chose a different path. Biting his narrow lower lip, he marveled over his Marines. They had been so lucky to survive previous firefights, if they were fortunate enough to survive this decision, all knew to a man, the UCMJ would shove their service up their ass. They faced a high likelihood that "graduation" would take place while serving their time at Leavenworth.

If the Captain's dad were alive, he would bless his son's decision to lead the patrol. If MC, Simmons' mom got wind of this, she would immediately question the legality of the matter, and then her motherly instincts would kick in. If she knew the depth and breadth of the mission, she would have LtCol Stoner on the phone rationing out crap no different from when Captain Simmons was growing up.

With Simmons' thoughts turned back to the mission, he could only hope everything played out relatively close to plan, a rarity in war. Simmons knew that as their boots landed on Mexican soil, a contingent of Raiders would insert into the FARP. Any Marine Corps Force Recon Captain would be envious of their method of insertion: Team Alpha would step from a C-130's rear ramp from an altitude of 1200 feet. Two swings in the chute and the heels of their boots banged the ground. Beats the hell out of stepping from a stationary helo in a cold LZ to meet Blad, he concluded.

He remembered Blad hanging around the house on Sundays, taking in a Dallas Cowboys game, and biting into his Dad's BBQ. Dad's pitfall was his belief that the Cowboys would return to their glory days, the days of his childhood. Blad made it a point to get under Dad's skin with dry one-liners after each Cowboy loss. "Maybe next year, H.D." or "when are they going to start playing football in Dallas?" The Cowboys seemed to suck year after year, but like his love for his three children, Dad's unconditional love for his Cowboys never once waned. Just as if it were yesterday, Simmons could see Blad handing him and the younger siblings candy or some other gift like a beanie baby, football, basketball, or baseball.

Hap had briefed Simmons that Blad would leave with the helo returning to the FARP. Team Jethro would then E & E approximately five clicks. The team would meet up with one of Blad's agents manning the OP, "Hawk."

The Rio Grande had passed out of sight a half hour earlier. Team Jethro was launching on their last mission as members of the U.S. Marine Corps. The fight was on. *Semper Fi.*

Friday 0415; On Approach to Mecca II MX

"Take point, Lyncher," Captain Simmons said through his voice-activated headset.

Staff Sergeant Lyncher moved past Rock Carver adjusting the mic on his headset to assume point. Goggled up, he led the team toward the high ground in the distance. Simmons trailed Lyncher by thirty feet. The balance of the team trailed, maintaining fifteen to twenty feet separation between each Marine. A slight breeze carried the howl of a pack of coyotes, moving parallel to the Marines.

Simmons kept the team moving at a rapid but silent pace dodging shoulder-high vegetation along the rock-covered path. The ruck's shoulder strap dug into the wound and blood mixed with sweat oozed through his bandaged shoulder, leaving a ghoulish purplish stain across the woodland blouse. Smitty would stitch him back up at Hawk; his battle now was to remain conscious.

OP Hawk was a 200-year-old home built into the side of a cliff overlooking the river. Vegetation covered part of the one wall and chimney that remained. With the trail carved into the cliff questionable, Blad had suggested during their brief conversation at the LZ that they hump to Hawk.

Going up a slight rise, Lyncher raised a clenched fist, and then quickly followed with an open fist and hand parallel to the ground, the signal to stop and take cover. Simmons telegraphed to the others, pain shooting through his shoulder as he repeated the motions. The team faced outboard. As previously rehearsed, Smitty faced left, while Slaughter looked right. Rock and Beaux covered the patrol's rear. Taking a knee, Simmons observed Lyncher, who gestured with two fingers, pointing toward his goggles before giving a victory sign, *two unknowns approaching.* Simmons moved almost soundlessly up the line until he came alongside Lyncher.

"Two bogeys just beyond the curve," Lyncher said softly. The breeze, coming from their front, carried the perfume of potent cannabis. Two men walked into view and stopped on the trail. One of the men took in a deep toke, exhaling into the AK-47's open bolt. Standing at the barrel, the other figure deeply inhaled the smoke flowing out of the end of the assault rifle. Their dress was loose fitting. Though their outfits appeared green through Simmons' night-vision lenses, he determined they were wearing black pajamas and scarves loosely wrapped around neck and shoulders, Middle Eastern style. Simmons' thumb crossed his throat. He used his good arm, pulling the Ka-Bar from the scabbard. Lyncher shook his head. "Smitty, up," he said softly, in his head set. Seconds later Corporal Smith took a knee next to them.

Simmons's left thumb ran across his throat. Resting his M4 on the ground, Smitty pulled his Ka-Bar and silenced 9 mm Beretta. Bent at the hip he passed into the foliage. Lyncher, clutching a Ka-Bar, followed Smitty. Simmons watched as the targets eased off the trail out of sight. Minutes passed. An audible tussle followed, then silence.

"All clear," Smitty reported quietly. Lyncher stepped onto the trail, waving the team forward with his hand clutching the bayonet.

"Move out," Simmons ordered across the headset. "Smitty dispose of the bodies." Lyncher returned the bloodied knife to the scabbard strapped to his right ankle. Gaining his bearings, he retrieved his long rifle from Simmons and took off at a trot vanishing around the corner.

Simmons passed Smitty, who was dragging a corpse off the trail. Slowing for a quick look at the second corpse, Simmons handed over his weapon and kept moving, having seen dead jihadis before. "Only one thing was better than a dead jihadist, two dead jihadists," he murmured under his breath. Simmons concluded that the two must have strayed far from camp to indulge in the mind-altering drugs.

Thirty minutes later, "Patrol coming from out front," Lyncher said.

Turning, Simmons gestured, pointing left and right. He and his team evaporated into the vegetation on either side of the trail. Simmons drew his Ka-Bar and knelt behind a stand of mesquite trees 6' from the trail. Each member of the patrol wore all black—jacket and trousers and balaclava head-cover exposing eyes only. This type of dress typically distinguished suicide bombers from the other jihadis. The leader wore a long beige jacket belted by an ammo chain. Simmons could see that all wore night-vision goggles and carried AK-47s. They're learning, he thought, pressing his face against rough bark in his attempt to become one with the tree.

Obviously leading a training excursion, the instructor grabbed the point man by the collar, pointing at something on the trail. Taking a knee, the instructor touched the ground, rubbing his fingers together. Standing, he placed his fingers underneath the man's nose, walking in a circle attempting to locate the blood trail.

"Stand by. We may have to take them."

"Eight souls," Lyncher said.

The instructor approached the stand of trees as the coyotes wailed nearby. He pulled the bolt back on his AK, letting it go with a sound that all within earshot recognized. Motioning the others to follow, he began moving forward slowly, as if hunting quail.

Minutes passed. "I counted eight souls," Beaux reported, guarding the team's back door.

"Point, move out," Simmons ordered. "Back door, join when the bad guys are clear."

"Will do," came the reply.

40

Carla's cell phone cut to voice mail after the fourth ring. Dropping the phone into his ankle pouch, Hap walked with Spanky towards the Q. Hell, at least Team Jethro had made it into the LZ.

Minutes later, he was in his living room, sprawled on the couch, flight boots still on. He weighed slipping into the shower, and nuzzling up to Carla. Good sex would be great. But, the need for rest outweighed his carnal pleasure.

"She will have to get over it," he said to himself, punching the speed dial. Unlike the earlier call, he could hear the ringing through the closed door. He hung up before the phone cut to voicemail. Bouncing from the couch, he crossed the room, putting his ear to the door. Slowly, working the knob, he pushed the door open to see an empty room. He sat on the bed. The sheets were cold to the touch. She had obviously left before he returned. Her car keys were nowhere around and the rental car was gone. The absence of a note and the fact she left her cell phone made him question whether she was in a hurry or simply pissed off.

Slipping off the musky flight suit, he flipped it into a corner of the room. He stepped into the shower without bothering to wait on the hot water. Within seconds, the cold water brought him out of the funk.

Wiping steam from glass, the man in the mirror didn't question a first in Marine Corps chronicles. Marine lieutenants in O'Bannon Hall's "Hawkins Room" would talk about the next 24 hours for years to come. Slipping his shoulder holster over a fresh flight suit, he did a quick check of his weapon to ensure the chamber was clear. He slipped his flight jacket on, concealing the heavy iron. Without packing away his personal gear, he flipped the room key onto the bed next to the cell phone, slipped on his piss cutter, grabbed the flight bag bulging with maps, and stepped out into the morning air.

He walked towards the flight line, joining Spanky and Love Doctor. He was counting on Will and Blad procuring 10,000 gallons of JP–4, spread-loaded across three operable fuel trucks. At the end of the day, he would take one truck with 6,500 gallons. The more trucks available at the FARP, the quicker the turnaround would be. Damn the torpedoes! Warden was coming out of Mexico with the Nomads.

The three Nomads returned a smart salute to the same Marine security guard he met first day on station. Stepping onto the tarmac, the officers slipped off their covers. "Good luck with OCS," Hap said, passing through the narrow entrance.

"You won't be returning today?" the corporal asked.

Hap stopped and turned, slipping off his cover. Spanky and Love Doctor continued toward the hangar. "Something tells me we will not be returning to El Centro."

"Sir, have a safe flight home."

Hap nodded, smiling faintly. Walking down the line of waiting birds, he considered God's grace and mercy as the weight of the decision lay heavy on his shoulders. Death would follow his order to launch the mission. Hap knew the alternative would be easy. He could walk into the Ops Shop and issue a stand down order. And going forward, they could spend countless hours throwing back Black Label while bad mouthing the Administration for allowing a Marine to rot in some hole in Mexico, or worse die on a YouTube video in the Middle East.

"FUBIJAR!" Hap said aloud, abbreviating "Fuck you buddy, I'm just a Reservist" Spanky and Love Doctor had joined Big Alabama, Goose, and Dick. They all turned toward Hap before filing into the hangar. Hap continued down the line of Hueys and Cobras. He couldn't wait for Warden's wrath, but only after he removed Warden's flight boot from his own ass for risking Marine lives to save him.

Turning toward the sound of a fixed wing on short final, he stopped dead in his tracks. His heart sank. The Commandant's private aircraft's main mounts burped smoke, touching the El Centro runway. Shank was minutes from cock-blocking the operation. Hap's jaw locked. No effing way, not now.

He watched the Citation proceed down the runway, turbo fan engines throttled up, nose gear rotated into the air. Instead of turning downwind to begin approach, the aircraft made a turning climb to the northwest, accelerating towards the mountains. Hap took in a breath and nodded sharply to himself, wondering how many lives did this mission have? Opening the small door built inside the large hangar door, he ducked inside.

"SQUADRON! Atennnn...HUT." Spanky's bark echoed through the hangar. "Reeeeeport."

Standing out front of the officer contingent bearing side arms, Big Alabama snapped a smart salute. "All present or accounted for." Spanky returned the salute.

The same protocol followed for the enlisted and staff NCO formations. Spanky saluted each senior Marine standing in front of the formations. Initiating an about face, the acting Executive Officer fixed his eyes on an anonymous object to the front. Hap could not help but notice that the aircrew wore shoulder holsters. Stopping long enough to drop his flight bag and cock the piss cutter over his narrow brow, he walked smartly, facing Spanky.

Spanky snapped a salute. "All present or accounted for. Each Marine in formation is on board, and all other Marines were given a 96 under one condition."

"And what would that be, Major?" Hap asked.

"They had to remain off base. I thought you would be OK with the decision," Spanky said, still holding the salute.

"Very well," Hap replied.

"And if I may be so bold, Colonel. Launch now. Personnel showed at 0400. Eight birds pre-flighted, fueled, and loaded for bear. The second flight was cancelled to let the boys enjoy their 96."

Hap snapped a salute. "Do it."

Spanky snapped his arm to the side. Hap did the same. Initiating an about face, the acting Exec belted out, "We launch in an hour. Disssssssmissed!"

Standing in front of an open locker, Hap slipped two magazines into the ammo carrier attached to his shoulder holster. He dropped another magazine into his ankle panel. Grabbing the trusty Bowie knife, he let it fall below his right armpit. Throwing on his survival vest, he used the toe of his flight boot to push the door closed.

Entering each of the maintenance shops, he shook each Marine's hand, thanking them for their service. LD Hicks had signed for the aircraft, so Hap shook hands with each of the Maintenance Control personnel. He took a pass reviewing the maintenance log.

Thirty minutes later, he walked down the line of aircraft, with maintenance and ordnance personnel gathered at the Hueys. Flight line personnel stood in front of each aircraft, outside the rotor arc.

Hap's extended right forefinger spun above his head. Eight starters initiated seconds from each other. Rotors started turning slowly counterclockwise, as engines spun to idle, slowly turning the rotor blades. Ducking underneath the rotor arc, Hap opened the canopy, removing his helmet resting on top of the TSU. He carefully slid around the scope and strapped in. Closing the canopy, he attached the ICS cord to his helmet. "You got me, LD?"

"Loud and clear," LD replied through the helo's intercom system. As the second engine came on line, throttles rolled to fly. Up and down the line, the rotors spun up to hundred percent.

"Kang Flight check in," Hap said, across the interflight frequency. Responses came: "Two, Three, Four, Five, Six— Seven needs two minutes—Eight."

Minutes passed, Hap became anxious. He needed every bird for the mission and with engines running, they were burning fuel. "Come on, Wrapper," he said to himself through clenched teeth.

Wrapper's voice came up on the net. "Seven Ready."

Hap didn't hesitate. "Kang flight. Roll ground." Hap punched in ground frequency, waiting a few seconds to ensure the entire flight switched over to ground. "El Centro ground, Nomad 22 Flight of 8 taxi for takeoff."

41

Friday 0500; Mecca II

No doubt about it, it was a Hap Stoner laugh, deep in Warden's subconscious state. He could feel the weight of Steve Smith's bloody and battered cranium resting against his throbbing shoulder. Guards standing by the entrance to the cave were speaking Spanish at a brisk clip. Their voices were easily recognizable as one of the guards had a distinct stutter, and his Executive Officer was only a pebble's throw distant.

Warden never doubted Stoner's resolve. Hell, Hap would take on a rescue solo. And, Warden looked forward to the fight; he wanted to visit El Tigre, reversing roles. It didn't appear that Steve Smith could contribute to any fight at this particular moment, but no doubt, he'd try anyway.

Hovering on the edge of consciousness, Warden overheard his captors speaking in Spanish, trailed again by that belly laugh, Hap's for sure. The laugh meant one of two things: all was well in Denmark or somebody was about to have his head ripped off.

The bad guys usually gathered around the entrance prior to a beating. Like John Wayne leading a cavalry charge, Hap Stoner had arrived in Warden's dream state just in the nick of time. Warden's head rolled slowly left, and then jerked back to the right as he fought to regain consciousness. The battered crown of his head continued to grind into the limestone leaving a trail of blood oozing down the wall.

The sound of the American girls crying out for their parents continued from the next grotto. Being a father, he knew that the girls' parents were crying in agony many times greater.

Warden's eyes snapped open. Had Hap Stoner arrived? Tilting his eyelids up, he gazed through a slit of an engorged left eye as the fat ass Gator driver and his skinny sidekick, who he and Steve knew some of the men called "Abbott and Costello," back-stepped carefully down the steps.

"Come on, Hap, come and get me!" Warden screamed, only half-conscious.

He watched Abbott propelling a boot into Steve's ribs, wedging him between the steps and wall. Now, with no regard for Warden's separated right shoulder, Abbott and Costello stood one at each side, working a looped rope under both his armpits. He could feel the slack in the line and knew hell was coming his way.

"*Ascensor*," Abbott called out in Spanish. He heard groans of effort coming from above them. With the rope cinched up around his shoulders, they dragged him up toward the entrance slamming his back against the steps. Coming to, he was face down in the bed of the Gator, wrists bound taut, snug in the small of his back. Little blood circulated to the extremities of the hands. The Gator began to move fast, and the rough ride jarred his bones and his skull hit the metal bed. He slipped back into unconsciousness, but not before he remembered, they were taking him to the chair.

He came to as they dragged him from the Gator and propped him on the metal chair, elbows strapped to bars. He heard the familiar hum of the air-conditioning vents, smelled the strong aroma of cleaning solvents he knew all too well.

Abbott was last to leave the room, turning off the light, slamming the door shut. Entombed in darkness, Warden flexed his fingers, attempting to regain feeling. Just before his chin dropped to his chest, he cursed the administration again for letting him rot. A snapping click and a floodlight blinded him. He turned his head away from the beam and it dawned on him that he was living a training scenario from the interrogation portion of his SERE school training.

"Bottom line," as Captain "Cutcha Cock Off" the Marine Staff NCO instructor, said repeatedly to the class, "is to remain calm, and keep your wits about you; do this, and you may live to see the next day. You may have to do this for a few hundred or God forbid, a few thousand days."

Warden suddenly felt hunger pains in the deepest part of his stomach. He had to keep his wits about him so he could stay alive. Had it been three days, or maybe four? He knew that whatever he had endured, Steve Smith had it ten times worse. That last kick to the gut may have done him in.

He wondered what the purpose of this encampment was. He'd spotted the Mexican cartel thugs, along with the men and women clad in jihadi attire speaking Arabic and Spanish. It was clear that the "jihadists" were operating in Mexico with the help of local drug cartels.

A voice snapped him back to what was about to begin. A male Mexican voice speaking broken English read from the Quran. This was a first.

"Slay the unbelievers wherever you find them
Make war on the infidels living in your neighborhood
When opportunity arises, kill the infidels wherever
you catch them

Kill the Jews and the Christians if they do not convert to Islam…"

* * *

The flood light went black. Seconds later, the overhead light lit up the room. His bloodshot eyes struggled to focus. He saw two men in Middle Eastern attire, faces masked. The taller and more muscular of the two, with the diamond earring was unmistakably El Tigre. Warden struggled, attempting to free himself.

"Save your energy, Colonel. You will need it."

"You and your pork belly friend can eat pig crap."

He saw the open palm just before he felt the stinging slap that wrenched his head to the side. When he could look up again, he saw a third figure, slight, cloaked in a purple burka. A woman? Why would they want her here? Another male, this one fat, followed the woman into the room. He began setting up a video camera. Not good. The woman moved beyond his line of sight, but not before he saw the gleam of a large butcher knife in her hand.

He spat spittle and a tooth toward the camera. "Let's get it over with, you cowards!" He had to find a way to stay alive; otherwise, the girls in the adjoining grotto would vanish into the abyss.

The fat man behind the camera laughed loudly. "You ready to be famous, Colonel?" he said with a thick Arabic accent.

Waiting for the knife to slice into his throat, Warden delivered his best F.U. stare through swollen slits. "Frigging pussy," he said slowly, spitting blood between his remaining teeth.

A feminine hand raised his chin and the blade touched just below his Adam's apple. He could feel his executioner's breath on his ear. As her breath quickened and hardened, Warden tensed and looked straight to the front. She whispered so only he could hear her message. "Hap Stoner said, 'Live. *Semper Fi.*' Marines are close." She pushed him and the chair to the floor. Shocked, Warden gasped for breath as the three men laughed. He was alive, and Hap Stoner was on his way.

Warden looked up from the floor as one of the figures stepped toward him, removing the black hood. "Colonel Warden. You just witnessed the rehearsal for your execution. It will not be in Mexico though, Colonel. Some Saudi prince is going to pay $15 million to have you delivered into Syria. More people will witness your death than watched the last Super Bowl."

The man looked Mexican, thought Warden, but his English was perfect. *So, the Islamo Fascists had made it to the southern border of the United States.*

Though beaten and battered, Warden showed his best poker face to the coward. He hurled as much saliva as his dry mouth could muster. Retaliation did not take long. Even with a foggy brain, he watched the boot's toe come in like a fastball.

Friday 1100 Hours; Los Americanos Resort MX

Settled comfortably inside the confines of Scorpion's private suite, Danny Lee Boyd enjoyed the Scorpion's Jado Steel Style Gold Bed comfort, technology, and luxury. It was easy to appreciate the Ferrari of mattresses' unique spring system, and its horsehair and wool stuffing. Interlocking his fingers behind his head, he could see the Senator in the mirror, clasping a guest towel with Los Americanos scripted on either end. The Senator seductively tugged and pulled the towel across his pale skin and plump body.

Boyd always anticipated each rendezvous with Jourdan, who he considered one of the U. S. Senate's finest. They both found their encounters stimulating. Their gazes met. Boyd returned Scotty Jourdan's smile as his towel slid to the floor.

＊　＊　＊

Slipping a navy blue sport coat over a white oxford button down, Boyd checked out his silhouette, ever mindful of his appearance. He looked across at Scotty, who sat slumped in a chair on the balcony, clad in a flowing Los Americanos terrycloth robe. With his reading glasses perched on the end of his prominent nose, Jourdan slowly turned the pages of the *Wall Street Journal*, occasionally stopping to sip Nicaraguan coffee from a delicate porcelain cup.

The phone rang, and Boyd entered the study, crossing to Scorpion's desk. He picked up in the middle of the third ring, and the front desk informed him that Charif Alawa and his entourage had entered the lobby. The Egyptian banker had arrived.

"Thank you," Boyd said, "Send Mr. Alawa up." He returned the handset to its gold plated cradle.

Minutes later, he crossed back through the bedroom to the living room to greet Charif, as the banker stepped out of the polished nickel elevator. The bellhop didn't carry himself like a typical hospitality industry employee. His red uniform jacket fit snugly around his muscular chest and shoulders, but it hung loosely around the waist. His jet-black hair, slicked straight back, just brushed the shoulders of his jacket.

Boyd could only assume that Scorpion had assigned Charif a Black Stone guardian. The man positioned himself just inside the elevator door, hands clasped at the belt; chin tilted back, exposing the neck of a Sumo wrestler.

Charif greeted Boyd with a firm handshake. "Where is the Senator?" the banker asked.

Boyd gestured with his head toward the next room.

"Balcony?" Charif asked.

Boyd nodded, stepping out of the way. Charif walked past him, moving with confidence and ease, as if he had been in the suite before. Trailing him to the balcony, he watched Charif approach the Senator, who remained seated, offering a limp handshake. Boyd could tell that Charif was not perturbed in the least by the Senator's arrogance. Though as crooked as the day was long, the Egyptian banker was all business. It was all about the deal and getting it done. Boyd knew that as far as

Charif was concerned, he was working with another crooked U.S. Senator, just a means to an end. Boyd was perfectly happy with the financial scraps.

"It's so nice to see you again, Senator," Charif said.

Jourdan continued reading the paper for several seconds before he made a show of folding it and setting it down. He took a very slow sip of coffee. "So do you have your part of the funding?"

Charif grinned. "Of course, Senator, I own the bank."

"How could I forget, Mr. Alawa? Do you have something for me?"

Reaching past three gold blings into his coat pocket, Charif flipped an envelope like a Frisbee on top of the paper. Jourdan accepted the envelope gracefully, sliding a manicured fingernail across the top.

"Don't bother, Senator. The wire confirmation is there. As before, the balance will arrive when the guarantee is in place."

Boyd smiled, watching Scotty slide the envelope into the robe's over-sized pocket. Without giving the banker a look of 'thanks' or 'go to hell,' he returned to savoring his coffee. "You will have your guarantee within three months."

"Any sooner? I have the capital on my end lined up," the banker said in a no nonsense tone. "There is a lot of money at stake, Senator."

The Senator looked up, the cup balanced in front of his generous lips. "As if you didn't know, Charif Alawa, Washington is a bit distracted these days. The crap going on along the border is making it tough."

Nodding, Danny filled Charif's cup, until the banker gestured with extended fingers to stop. He freshened up the Senator's cup, before finally refilling his own.

"That was unfortunate, but it should all blow over in due time."

"Let me see. There are dead Marines and a LtCol MIA. Even with our weak president, he can't just call the LtCol rogue and expect the American people to take it after a swift kick to the balls, followed by an upper cut."

Charif leaned over the table. "Senator, you just received two million dollars cash. I'm thinking this guarantee comes within the month. When will the Scorpion arrive?"

"Within the day," Boyd said, watching Jourdan glare over his cup at the Egyptian banker.

"If you would excuse me, I will be leaving now," Charif said.

Paying no attention to the banker, Jourdan went back to reading the paper.

"I will escort you out, Charif," Boyd said, gesturing toward the elevator.

Minutes later, Boyd put his hand on the paper, lowering it so their eyes met. "Why do you have to be so rude to Charif? He is our partner and more than generous."

"As is the Scorpion, and I no more respect that thug than I respect road kill."

Boyd's lips turned down slightly. "I wish you would drop your, uh, attitude when we are in the company of our business partners. We all need each other."

He watched in amazement as the Senator pointed to his half-empty cup and then returned to the paper, rustling its pages. Boyd stepped close and ripped the front section out of the Senator's hands. Wadding the newsprint into a ball twice the size of a softball, he backhanded it through the open door to the suite. Settling into a chair next to his business partner and lover, he crossed his legs and began taking large pulls of coffee. "Scotty."

The Senator picked up the money section.

Boyd swung out with his arm, again ripping the paper from Jourdan's hands. "Do you have any clue what could happen if the loan does not come through? You're just another Senator to these people. I'm just another damn developer."

Jourdan set the cup on the table and dabbed a napkin against his puckered lips.

"What are you saying, Danny?"

"You and I walk this earth today only because they want us alive."

Senator Jourdan gazed at Boyd with an incredulous look. The napkin fell from his plump fingers to the polished marble surface. Neither man spoke for several seconds. Boyd's lips pursed. It amazed him how the man he loved could be both so jaded and so naïve. He did not want to say the obvious but the situation called for plain speak.

"Scotty," he said, slowly. "I'm afraid if the guarantee is not delivered the only way out is in a casket."

Jourdan paled for several seconds before a look of determination altered his expression. "They can't kill a United States Senator."

Boyd chuckled, shaking his head slowly. "You have to think of your family, Scotty."

Scotty furrowed his bushy brows. "They would hurt my family?"

43

Friday 1100; Kang Flight En route to Douglas Municipal Airport

Peering through a darkened visor, LtCol Hap Stoner looked over his right shoulder, and then slowly left. The sky was clear and the flight flew into a rising sun. Dash 2 and 3 maintained a loose spread, passing over the ground at a brisk 145 mph. Ambassador and Waco strapped into Dash 2 while Chew Boy and Killer Koch manned Dash 3.

Departing El Centro, the flight maintained tight formation for the benefit of Station personnel manning the tower to confirm a flight of eight Nomad helos departed as per schedule. The flight of three Hueys, led by Big Alabama, trailed with 15 miles of separation. Spanky's flight of two Cobras trailed the Division of Hueys by another 15 miles. To have such a small flight spread out across the countryside was not sound Marine Corps doctrine. But, leaving El Centro's airspace, Hap wanted the casual observer on the ground or airborne to believe the U.S. Military had launched three separate flights of helicopters.

Crossing the dunes west of Yuma, Hap's flight accelerated, steering north of I-8, gaining separation from Big Alabama's flight. Passing over the dune buggies and dirt bikes rolling over the undulating sandbanks, their maneuvering looked like business as usual.

With the snouts of the helos pointed due east, LD passed north of the city of Yuma. Remaining clear of airspace owned by ATC, Yuma Tower, or any other reporting authority along their route, Hap wanted the flight to maintain anonymity. Ambassador and Chew Boy sucked their Cobras within two to three rotor-lengths separation between aircraft. Off their left wing, the Chocolate Mountain aerial and gunnery ranges were beehives of activity. Fixed wings and helos, operating out of MCAS Yuma, wing flashes sky-lined above the ridges, passed out of sight, darting below another ridge. "Stay on the edge, boys," Hap said to himself.

"Keep Yuma off the right wing," Hap said, over the ICS. Keeping Yuma city limits to their right, crossing I-8 to the south, the Cobras dove for the ground.

Spanky had confirmed the Moving Sands and Cactus West gunnery ranges were cold until 2100 this evening. Unlike previous times they had entered this space, there would be no checking in with (TACTS) range control. Hap knew that, after passing Yuma, the Huey pilots would give the gunners a good platform, allowing them to work together to remove the Ma Deuce 50 Caliber machines guns from their saddles. They would strap the guns to the aluminum deck for the remainder of the flight to Douglas. Any eyes on the three Hueys would think it was a cross-country flight.

Exiting the Nogales Ranger District of the Coronado National Forest, north and west of Nogales, the Cobras roared towards I-19, scooting 150 feet above the ground.

"I have the controls LD," Hap said.

"You have the controls, Hap," LD replied.

Hap heard LD tap the dash fixed above and behind his head, telegraphing Hap was flying the aircraft.

Hap could see several cars transiting between Nogales and Tucson pulling into a rest area south of their flight path to take in the air show. "Let's give the taxpayers a little show," he said.

"Roger that," LD replied, chuckling.

"Kang flight…Break right 180," Hap transmitted over the UHF radio.

Maintaining level flight for a few seconds, LD reported that Ambassador was passing their six o'clock from left to right. Hap's rotor tips pointed towards the sky, as Hap worked the aircraft around, passing Chew Boy's six o'clock. Chew Boy cranked the Cobra into a ninety-degree bank turn, orienting their turn out on the pre-announced 180-degree heading. The three Cobras were now traveling south in Combat spread, Hap's bird between Ambassador and Chew Boy.

Hap waited until the flight drew abeam of the rest area. Cars were now parking on the side of the road, parents lifting small children to sit on top of the vehicles. The rest area contained three picnic tables and parking for five times that many cars.

"Kang flight. Break left. 090." The sequence repeated itself, the observers getting an ear full of snapping rotor blades and growling turbo shaft engines. The snout of Hap's Cobra passed directly over the center picnic table, while Ambassador and Chew Boy passed on either side of the rest area. The audience raised hands above their heads, all cheering and many video-ing the event with cell phones, as Kang Flight screamed past 75 feet overhead.

"Not bad, Hap," LD said.

"What do you think the chances are the folks will be able to say they witnessed the same flight that entered Mexico to rescue their Colonel when the mission hits the newswire?"

Hap wouldn't divert Big Alabama and Spanky's flights to fly over the rest area. Half hour east of Yuma, LD had crested a ridge, passing close over a home built on the leeward side. Noise complaints were problematic, and could trigger a process whereby the military would realize that eight armed Marine Corps helicopters were flying an unscheduled mission. To avoid this "game over" scenario, Hap made sure that the flights behind LD altered their course to avoid that home. If in the owner complained, it would take the military time to work through where the flight originated and the name of the unit before they could notify the chain of command. As far as anybody was concerned outside of El Centro Tower, nobody had seen a flight of eight and no Hueys had guns protruding from their open cabins.

Forty-five minutes passed and Hap could see Highway 80 appear off the left wing. Veering left, Hap passed north of the last intersection of 80 and another roadway before 80 entered Douglas from the west. Avoiding the population center, Hap arced right with the flight in tight formation. The first low fuel light lit up the panel. With ten minutes of fuel remaining, he flew straight to the city's Municipal Airport.

44

Friday 1330; Douglas Municipal Airport CA

Built two miles east of the Douglas business district, construction of the airport facility began in June 1942 for the United States Army Air Corps. The government seized ranches under the authority of the War Emergency Powers Act, and 2600 acres went to the War Department, which became Douglas Army Airfield. The airfield's primary mission encompassed training aviation cadets to receive pilot wings, commissions, and advanced training for future bomber pilots who would carry the war to Japan and Germany.

Hap hung his vest across the barrels of the Cobra's .20mm, as he walked across the WWII era tarmac, towards a parked C-130. Tied into the receptacle forward of the crew entrance door, a Genie provided external power to the aircraft.

As Hap rounded the C130's bulbous nose, he continued underneath the left wing. He followed the scent of good grease and shook his head at the sight of three aluminum fold out tables, piled with a smorgasbord of Kentucky Fried Chicken and stacked pizza boxes splayed in no strategic order. Tables and chairs were set beneath the C-130's large tail section and in front of the open ramp to screen the sun.

Roach rested casually, cross-legged, in a lounge chair. If the half-buttoned purple Hawaiian shirt, worn over shorts, didn't grab your attention, the price tag protruding from the collar would. His scrubby flight boots put the exclamation on the scene. Holding a thick cigar Jackie Gleason style, blowing smoke rings over huge, silver-rimmed sunglasses—in the style preferred by porn directors—Roach flipped a stripped-down chicken leg into an open 55-gallon trash drum.

Drawing closer, Hap watched Roach reach into one of the dozen buckets of Kentucky Fried Chicken. Not bothering even to look at the chicken leg he'd snagged, he flipped it, so it tumbled end over end. Hap caught the errant throw, just as Roach retrieved another piece, quickly tearing into a plump chicken breast. Hap was happy with the still warm piece of extra crispy.

"Have you washed your hands today?" Hap asked casually.

"Eat me," Roach replied, continuing to devour the capon.

Roach looked over the mangled portion of yard bird. "You still want to go through with this LtCol Stoner?"

"Do I want to, you ask? No. I have to," Hap replied, dropping the bone into the trash barrel.

"Then this can be your last supper," Roach replied, laughing with his cigar in one hand and the half-eaten chicken breast in the other.

"Thanks a lot, dickhead. Is that a new shirt?" Hap inquired.

Roach pushed out of the chair, reaching into a flat box holding Canadian bacon and pineapple pizza. "As a matter of fact, it is," he said, stuffing the thick slice down his throat as nonchalant as Jabba the Hutt throwing down a frog. Leaning over, peering into another box, he belched, before looking quizzically back at Hap. "That obvious?"

Easing over to the table Roach used for grazing, Hap ripped the tag from the back of his brightly colored collar, stuffing it into Roach's left breast pocket. "Any new G2?"

"Slick took Shank to old MCAS Tustin of all places. Damned if the place was minus a fuel truck. They are waiting for a truck to come over from Orange County. Slick said Shank is on the warpath and wanting ass."

"That would be my ass," Hap replied. He thought of General Verbie and the cost to his career. He shrugged himself back to impending action. "So what else is new?"

Hueys chopped at the air with noses slightly raised, decelerating in formation down the duty runway while Big Alabama pedal-turned, taxiing onto the midfield taxiway. LD stood on the taxiway wearing sunglasses with an arm raised above his head. Gesturing with his hands, he pointed to where the recently arrived birds were to set down.

Ambassador and Chew Boy congregated in the shade, serving themselves without asking. All side arms and shoulder holsters remained in the aircraft, though Hap's trusty Bowie knife hung below his left armpit.

The fuel truck driver, who appeared to be in his early seventies, worked the knobs on the fuel truck, as Waco pumped the gas into the Cobra. If asked, the aircrew would say, they were fueling for a cross-country trek to MCAS New River. Any more questions, ask LtCol Stoner. If the fuel truck driver had any experience with fueling cross-country aircraft deploying to ranges, he would have seen missile racks and rocket pods void of ordnance, except for an occasional blue Stinger's simulator mounted on the end of a stub wing. Hopefully, he would not take an interest in the pods bristling with rockets, or with the green warheads attached to each.

Roach gestured with a hand cupping a pizza slice. "Come on in and see your airborne CP. I'll brief you on what we know."

Grabbing a slice of cheese pizza, Hap followed Roach up the ramp. The techs previously installed a high-tech automated airborne command and control center against the starboard bulkhead. Though the four console seats were empty, the computer-generated color-displays had powered up, along with the digitally controlled communication-and rapid-data-retrieval panels.

Techs, wearing wireless headsets and carrying iPads, grazed over the food while remaining linked to the equipment by Wi-Fi connections. The port bulkhead had two 84-inch screens, with maps of the target area on one screen, and the route on the other.

"Did Will see this?"

Throwing back the last of a Coke, Roach let loose with another belch, tossing the can in the trash to the right of the TV's. "Yes, he did. Explained to him this set up is the smaller version to the USC-48 "ABCCC" III Capsule. Raytheon lets me carry this around the world showing it to 'friendly customers.' They pay me twenty percent gross on each transaction."

"Nice," Hap said.

"Thought you could use the additional support. Blad said Shadow Services would clear the airspace. Do you mind?"

Hap chuckled and a grin appeared on what otherwise had been a stern face since entering the Hercules. "We can use all the help we can get."

Roach relaxed into one of the empty console seats. "Is Swamp still on board?"

A wider grin appeared. "The Cowboys are on board. We will get Hornets with dumb MK-82's, Zuni, and .20mm."

"Old School?"

Hap nodded. "Old School, Swamp and I already had the discussion." In the era of smart munitions, the Hornets would be dropping munitions dependent on the target being in eyesight, and the pilot diving in and releasing the explosives at the precise moment, to wallop the intended target. To acquire the target, someone with a visual must talk them onto the objective. Another way would be to mark the target and have the fighter-bomber make a high-speed approach, pop up, and gain a visual on the mark, and then adjust onto the target by the air controller.

Roach leaned over a small table near the forward bulkhead. "To the best of our knowledge, Tuna Man is still in the target area." He pointed to an empty Milk Duds box representing the house Warden had been seen entering and leaving a little roughed up. Cut up strands of blue recycle bags placed in the middle of the mockup represented the river. Pointing out the cabins (matchboxes) he noted Cabin 2, which had a large pavilion extending from the right side, the facility's kitchen. Stacked up behind the matchboxes, large mounds of mud signified the cliffs, rising approximately 250 feet above the meadow.

Roach gestured with hands now free of food. "Tuna Man is somewhere in these cliffs, kept in one of the limestone caves. Trees blanket the area, so we have not been able to gain eyes on the specific cave. Let me tell you, there's a lot human traffic moving in and out of the cliffs. A human trafficking operation of some sort is running out of this target area. Not sure what this has to do with one Marine LtCol." Roach frowned. "Up river, in the meadow, they've rigged a frigging training ground. Reports are that jihadists are training out of the target area."

"They intend to sell him, Roach." Hap's voice echoed grimly. "Tuna Man is going to be on YouTube somewhere, getting his head cut off. Question for us: is the execution in the target area or overseas?"

Roach shook his head. "The cartel leader may be dumb, but he is not stupid. Just like the Monarchs in the Middle East, they will only go so far, so they can keep their power. Play both sides, if you know what I mean. Warden dies in this compound, this dickhead is finished."

Hap cut his eyes to Roach. "You've been talking to Blad."

"A little bit. He is getting a constant stream of intel from Team Jethro. H.D.'s boy is doing a hell of a job, Hap."

"Hell, Roach, he has a hole in his shoulder the size of a ping pong ball." They heard Spanky's section of Cobras taxiing in.

Roach's round face half-turned, life glinting in his brown eyes. "Fruit doesn't fall far from the tree, Hap."

Hap nodded, grimacing. "I miss the son of a bitch."

Roach's gaze returned to the TV. Using his index finger, he drew a circle around Simmons' position. "Let's ensure we get his boy and the team out of there in one piece. Hap, you know his mother, she will kick all of our asses if we don't."

Hap nodded in agreement. "Know all about that, Roach."

"And you know, Hap, Blad has an agent embedded with Team Jethro."

Both turned as Ambassador and Chew Boy joined them, each clutching a chicken leg in one hand, and a folded over piece of pizza in the other. Ambassador attempted to speak, even as the cheese swelled in his mouth, and with nothing to wash it down. "Any change since we left El Centro?" he asked, smacking his gums.

Roach shot a laser covering the red circle on the TV moments before. "Shadow's intel is reliable, and Simmons is in place, feeding us info. OP Hawk has a great view of the target area. He is concerned about defending the position if exposed." Roach pointed the laser toward the feather on the screen marking OP Hawk.

Hap noted a first grader would have gotten a "D" from his teacher for the art effort.

Roach continued. "Supposedly, Simmons has two Marines on the bluff behind them to guard their rear but we could be looking at over 100 combatants."

Hap cut a glance to Ambassador. "Spanky and I have a 7 shot pod of WP." Spanky and Yukon walked up the ramp, each carrying chicken, and a soda in either hand.

"What's up Boss?" Spanky said.

"Welcome, boys," Hap said, pointing at the feather. "I will take my Division and anchor south near OP Hawk." He looked up at Spanky and Yukon. "You two cover the north side. Do we have any idea on a ground scheme of maneuver?"

"Fluid situation, Hap," Roach said, looking around for something to drink. Spanky reached into his ankle panel, pulled out a bottle of water, and flipped it in his direction. Roach caught it, twisted off the top, and took a quick pull. "I would argue the head of your GCE will probably tell you when they board the Hueys. The bad guys appear to be a bunch of jihadists. Not sure what you have stumbled into, Hap. Whatever it is, it's not good and needs to be snuffed out."

"Where's Warden?" Spanky asked, choking down the last of his chicken.

"In one of the caves carved out of the bluff. That's the good news. The bad news is OP Hawk has observed at least a hundred trainees, mostly male, mostly young line up for chow. Chow hall seems to be the second cabin farthest downriver."

"So the one hundred fighters are what have been identified by Hawk."

Roach nodded. "There has to be some sort of human trafficking operation going on. Just can't put my finger on why the jihadists are running around."

"What's going to be the ROE, Hap?" Ambassador asked. "We going to light these fuckers up?"

The sound of H-46 rotors approaching the line drowned out the ground generator running the electrical and cooling package inside the Hercules aircraft. Hap pondered the question, but the answer was obvious. "If they are armed or wearing jihadist garb, it is free fire."

"Right" Spanky chimed. "The boys will be glad to hear the news."

Minutes later, Big Alabama walked up the ramp carrying a box of pepperoni pizza. "Whatever secret mission we thought we were on, the Phrog drivers heard about it."

"What the hell," Hap said, helping himself to a couple of slices.

"Sons of bitches were ferrying the birds to the bone yard. They diverted, Hap, and they're offering up their services if you want them."

"Norfolk boys?" Hap said.

Big Alabama nodded. "Bastards were hungry, too. If you want something to eat, you had better hurry. LtCol 'Blob' Herman is flight lead. He said you would know him."

"I have side arms, holsters, magazines, and ammo for the crews," Roach said.

Spanky and Hap eyed each other. "How in the hell did this get out?" Hap blurted. "Who else knew? Who was talking?"

Hap knew the birds on ferry were probably carrying internal tanks, giving the birds legs, with room to spare. "Inform the Blob, the Nomads would love to have his company. He does recognize the risk?"

"Well, no shit, Hap," Big Alabama replied, walking back towards the food line.

Roach turned slightly, hands up to both ears, straining not to miss a word over the frequency he was monitoring. Looking up as if he just lost a best friend, Roach's dark eyes cut to the TV screen. "OP Hawk has been compromised. The team is pinned and has casualties."

"Shit," Hap blurted.

45

Friday 1415; Douglas Municipal Airport CA

Adrenaline drilling through his gut, Hap pulled out his cell and hit speed dial for Swamp, but not before seeing he had missed six calls from an unidentified caller ID. Whoever it was would have to wait. Swamp picked up the phone halfway through the first ring. "Swamp, how quick can you get airborne?"

"Within the hour, what's up?"

"Our OP has been compromised. We have wounded Marines. Ground assets, call sign Jethro will control you. Button Blue. Launch only half your assets and divert the balance to Douglas. Cross the border over Douglas. Don't have the time to explain but the airspace will be cleared south of the border to the target. See you over the target."

Technicians hustled back to their seats, plugging directly into the respective consoles. "Jerry, throw the communication over the squawk box," Roach said.

The bald-headed tech in the middle seat nodded. The staccato sound of sporadic small arms discharge reverberated through the cabin. Simmons' voice was calm under fire. The Marine would have made his father proud.

"Blad and Will are driving in a mid-1960's VW Bug, followed by half of Will's contingent in two old Chevy trucks. The balance of Will's team deployed around the FARP."

Saying nothing, Hap clambered up the ladder to the Hercules' flight deck. He flopped into the pilot's seat and dialed Verbie's home phone. Ruth Verbie answered on the second ring.

"Mrs. Verbie, Hap Stoner. Is the Commandant in?"

"You do not have to tell me who this is. Even after all these years, how could I forget Hap Stoner's voice? Russ is in his study. Let me warn you, the General is agitated."

"Yes, ma'am, I probably have a little bit of responsibility contributing to the General's angst."

Through the line, Hap could hear her slide open a door, and then her voice, more tentative in tone now. "Russ..." she paused, "Excuse me, honey, but Hap Stoner is on the phone. I thought you would want to visit with him."

Seconds passed before General Verbie's voice came across the line. "LtCol Stoner. What gives me the pleasure?"

"General. We found him."

"What do you mean you found him? Hap, the CIA, NSA, DEA, DIA and last but not least the fucking Mexican Government said our Marine was nowhere to be had." Verbie's voice reached a pitch that made the line vibrate.

"General. I want you to know I'm about to lead Marines on a mission that many inside the beltway will consider brainless and some say treasonous."

"You found Warden, right?"

"Yes, General," Hap heard the General sigh in relief. "Tuna Man is still alive and we are going into Mexico to get him."

"So I'm assuming that in your best judgment, running the info up the chain of command is out of the question?"

"General. I believe if we wait for the Administration to

make a decision, Tuna Man will be on a one way trip to Southwest Asia for a beheading party."

"Regarding the mission, I trust your judgment, LtCol Stoner. It should have never come to this. For the record, I do not condone your actions. Off the record, I have held NIS off about as long as I can. By close of business tomorrow, they will be on station looking to crawl up your ass."

"General, by that time, Warden should be on the U.S. side of the border. I will gladly drop my trou and grab my ankles."

The Commandant laughed. "Stoner, that's a picture I have a problem framing."

"General, I want to thank you for taking my call. And General, keep Shank off my back."

"I understand Colonel Mislick is doing a good job in keeping you and Shank apart."

"And General, this conversation never took place."

"Hardly, Colonel," Verbie said, laughing again. "Bring Warden and your Marines home safe."

Hap heard the audible click of the Commandant hanging up the telephone. He couldn't see the General swivel around to his computer or his fingers run across the keyboard like a concert pianist. His resignation would be effective at 0800 tomorrow morning.

＊ ＊ ＊

Hap climbed down the ladder to the cabin of the Hercules, and walked in on a catfight: Spanky, Roach, Ambassador, and Jim Bob—between bites of chicken and pizza—were in disagreement over next steps.

"I say go with a max effort now," Big Alabama half-squawked, half-drawled.

Roach jutted out his lantern jaw, shaking his head. "I don't like it, B.A. We need to get the boys out of Hawk or at least secure the position. At the same time we can set in roadblock points north and south along the hard surface road."

"Blad has Will and half the San Andres Warriors en route to Hawk," Spanky said. "The balance is being held in reserve. If we want them in the fight now, I suggest we get them moving! Hornets will be on station soon enough, and only God knows what will happen after that."

Hap watched Roach rub his thick bottom lip, while staring at the topo map displayed on the left side of the 84-inch flat screen. The Operations Status, displayed on the right side of the screen, showed all the moving pieces.

Roach turned to Hap, "Let's insert the Reserve." He pointed to the intersection where the dirt road and hard surface road came together. "Drop a fire team at the intersection. They can block anything trying to *di di mau* up the dirt road to gain the hard surface road. They will also be covering Simmons' left flank." He'd clipped through the Vietnamese, but Hap caught it, knowing it roughly translated as "hurry the hell up."

Roach ran his right index finger along the map, moving upriver; with his left index finger, he followed the hard surface road. His two fingers met at a low water crossing. "This is where we put two teams to block runners moving down river by foot or escaping up the hill from behind the house. Gaining the hard surface road, they will be moving in a defilade position from the team at the gate."

Hap studied the topo embedded on the screen. Walking over to it, he pressed the finger-activated annotate button and drew a circle on a knoll behind the bluff. "This would give eyes north and east of the main house, on the back side of the bluff. Insert a team northeast on this knoll. If we withdraw from Hawk moving upriver the team at the gate will have their pants down."

Roach nodded. "I like that idea, Hap. What about the team at the gate if we retreat from Hawk?"

"Let them fall back into the ground between the river and hard surface road," Hap said. "This way they continue to cover Simmons' left flank."

"Let's go with it, CO," Spanky said, looking at Hap, then to the Roach.

Hap looked over to Roach, who nodded. "Make it so, Roach," Hap said.

Roach used his finger to draw a triangle at the dirt and paved road. To the right he wrote "Hammer." Drawing another triangle at the low water crossing, he wrote "Falcon." To the right of the triangle Hap had drawn across the river, he wrote "Owl." A print screen appeared on the TV. Roach walked over and touched the bottom left portion of the screen and an admin page appeared. He punched the print button, advanced the arrow to thirty copies, and touched the print button.

Hap turned to the console to see the same marks were now on the console operator's screen. "Gotta love technology," he said to himself as the printer began spitting out copies of the updated target area.

Roach tapped the console operator farthest to the right. "Have Reserve move immediately to set up positions at Hammer, Falcon, and Owl until relieved. Two teams in Falcon."

Writing notes as fast as Roach barked out the commands, the tech began transmitting orders to the FARP.

"I will launch with the division now," Hap said.

"You're fueled, Hap," Spanky said. "I suggest arm-on-site."

"Concur, will fly to the fight, kicking off our external fuel tank before engaging. Spank, bring your section with the Phrogs." Cutting a glance to Roach, Hap said, "Have a hospital on standby."

Roach nodded and handed out maps to the aircrews. "I can brief the Hornets en route to the target area and wrangle a hospital with a reputable trauma unit."

Hap turned. "You sure, Roach?"

"Wait until the invoice lands on your desk," Roach said, with a wink. "I live for this shit."

"Blad has assured me Big Shadow is in Mexico City clearing the path for no resistance from the Mexican Military."

"Shit, Hap, let's kick all of their asses," Big Alabama said.

"At ease, B.A., we have enough on our plate as it is."

"B.A., bring your division in tail end Charlie. You will bring the ordnance men. Get the ammo and ordnance out of the C-130 and loaded. Fly into the FARP, fuel and stand by."

Big Alabama nodded, dissatisfied. Tuna Man was a friend, probably more so than any other Marine in the outfit was.

Hap looked into each of the officer's strained eyes. "Questions?" He watched all shake their heads, almost in unison. "Very well, then. I will see all of you over the target area. God speed, boys!"

Hap turned to walk down the ramp, giving Blob, who was standing over the pizza, a slap on the back. "Now I understand why I lost to you in the nacho eating contest. See you over the target. Save the gas in the external. We can provide hot pump from the FARP but you may have to fly a while to get the wounded to a hospital."

Blob nodded, giving a thumbs-up due to the pizza sticking to his gums.

Little Ray walked towards a bucket of chicken, speaking in Cajun tenor. "Pardon me, Colonel, your Division is fueled."

"Very well, Ray. Inform Ordnance we will arm at the hold short. Let's get moving," Hap responded.

Once Hap slid into the gunner's seat, LD Hicks, seated in back, threw the starter switch, followed by Ambassador and Chew Boy. Seeing a commotion down the flight line, Hap saw a car speeding down the taxiway as LD rolled the throttles to fly. To his amazement Carla, wearing her noted oversized dark sunglasses, was swerving the rental between Marines and parked aircraft.

Screeching to a stop by the nose of the C-130, Carla leapt from the car. Little Ray pointed her toward Hap's bird. Removing her sunglasses, she took off sprinting towards the turning aircraft.

As Carla passed the buffet, Big Alabama intercepted, easing her wriggling body across his broad shoulder. She thanked him by pounding his lower back with both fists and screaming. LD lifted up into a hover and began taxiing to the centerline, before initiating a pedal turn to move to the arming area. Hap watched until Big Alabama and Carla, with arms flailing, passed from view. He could not see the tears flowing down her high set cheeks.

What do you wanna do?" LD asked.

"Let's go get our Marines," Hap answered, finally.

"She's going to kick your ass if you live through this."

Hap chuckled, dropping the dark visor. "You're probably right. But, she is probably going to have to wait in line."

"Roger that," LD replied, turning the bird slightly with his pedals to ensure that Grumpy's and Waco's birds were in trail.

During arming, LD kept the cyclic wedged between his legs, and both pilots kept their hands raised clear of switches and triggers. Both returned the Ordnance NCO's salute, as he raced over to the next Cobra. LD took the controls.

"You know what happened hundred forty miles or so east of here in 1916."

"Not really, Hap, but something tells me you are about to enlighten me."

"Pancho Villa's guerillas raided Columbus in 1916, intent on knocking off the National Guard Armory."

"No shit," LD replied. "What a small world."

"Old Pancho failed at taking down the armory but killed a bushel of U.S. citizens in the process. Black Jack Pershing led a retaliatory expeditionary force into Mexico to hunt him down like a dog. Never caught the bastard. Son of a bitch should have waited 90 or so years for the river of weapons to flow south through Columbus. The Black Stone and Juarez cartels are slugging it out for control of drug trafficking in the State of Chihuahua."

"Hope we have better luck finding Tuna Man."

Hap watched the hand salute before the ordnance team backed away from Grumpy's bird. "Dash 3 is armed. Let's go."

46

Friday 1415; OP Hawk, Mecca II MX

Captain Simmons USMCR grimaced, rolling his injured shoulder away from what remained of an old limestone wall. The ache continued to get in the way of sleep, which suited him. Pop had always told him how invigorating a 15-minute fighter nap could be. But, he didn't want to wake the Shadow agent who was manning the OP when they dropped in.

The ancient structure, or what Mother Nature hadn't worn away, had to be a hundred and fifty years old. Not that he was an archaeologist or anything close to the sort, but the old dowel holes cut into the lime stone blocks fit the era. Shelving, benches, or even tables could be supported simply by stabbing pegs—attached to the specific fixture—into holes that were hand-drilled into the rock wall.

This structure, built into a ledge twenty feet above the river, was on a bend on the southern side of the Concho. He couldn't fathom the number of years of careful observations, shared and passed down the generations that went into selecting this specific site. The canyon inhabitants chose a location with a steady supply of running water, and yet they were high enough to have never been flooded by a rising river. In addition to water, the location provided an excellent vantage point to spot the approach of marauding Comanche Indians. If need be the OP could become the Alamo. For now, the Marines and their guest had an outstanding view of the compound.

The best Simmons could guess was that the roof and most of the walls had eroded decades earlier. Vines, trees, and bushes had overgrown what was left of the structure. From his resting spot, Simmons could see the rock chimney of the fireplace rising up through the thorny growth, but anyone on the outside would have a hard time spotting any sign of the structure. SSgt Lynch stood next to the hearth, sweeping a chaw of tobacco from his square jaw into the firebox.

Simmons extended his canteen cup. "Hey, Beer Can, can you give a broke dick captain a hand?"

The Marine turned smiling, stuffing a fresh chaw of Beechnut into the back of his cheek. "No problem, Cap," he replied, grasping the cup. He held the cup above the hollowed out rock sink and watched it fill with water bubbling from the rock wall.

Simmons traded a green scarf for the water. Lyncher flicked his fingers, sweeping the algae onto the limestone floor. Ringing out the scarf, he gave the balled up cloth an extra half twist before dropping the moist wrap into Simmons's lap.

"You going to be okay, Cap?" SSgt Lynch asked.

Simmons nodded without a word.

He thought about the two jihadists they'd killed on the way in, and he wished they had time to bury them. It wore on the Captain to think of the corpses exposed to buzzards, a dead giveaway, even to city slickers. After hours observing camp activity, he needed no convincing that the Marines had stepped into the middle of something big. If discovered, the camp's occupants would come at them like pissed hornets protecting their nest.

Clearly, training was a big part of the camp. Before the sun crested the big bluff, the obstacle course filled up with masked jihadists carrying AK-47's slung across their shoulders. When one platoon-sized unit moved on to the pistol range, another of equal size appeared from the cabins to fill the obstacle course again. After the pistol range, the units moved in rotation to hand grenade pits and then to scaling 250-foot bluffs with ropes. No doubt, four of the cabins were makeshift barracks for the would-be warriors. But, for what purpose?

Simmons closed his eyes, picturing the night patrol with whom they'd almost rubbed noses. Do these shitheads ever sleep? He thought about the lines of teenage boys and girls filing from the cliffs to the second cabin that they used as a chow hall. Paneled trucks would pull in, off-loading human cargo.

Whoever the hell the Shadow agent was, she grabbed his attention. She had carefully tended to his wound before falling off to sleep. It took a while but eventually she came to rest her head against his good shoulder. He couldn't resist letting the side of his head relax against the top of hers, so her hair tickled his cheek. She smelled good, even after days in the field.

Lyncher had made sure Big Shadow was on the receiving end of their observations, blow by blow. He returned to his perch, prone and peering through the scope of his M-14 sniper rifle. Smitty squatted behind the observation scope previously used by the Shadow agent. The scope would do her no good, as she was sound asleep.

Two Marines dug in twenty feet above their position. Simmons already decided they would retreat west up river if the opportunity presented itself, but he wanted their flank covered.

Lyncher spoke without taking his eye out of the scope. "You seeing what I'm seeing Smitty?"

"Fuckin' A."

"Hey, Cap, you gotta see this."

Simmons opened his eyes from another two-minute fighter nap. "What's up," he asked, only raising his head slightly, so he wouldn't disturb the woman sleeping against his shoulder.

"The jihadists appear agitated. The Gator pulled up and the passenger is tossing out banana magazines like cans of beer at a high school beach party. They are locking and loading, Cap. One of the jihadists is going up the bluff with a ruck spilling over with magazines for the trainees on top of the bluff. Could be problematic for the good guys, if they move up river."

"They must have found the bodies," Simmons said.

Smitty broke in, "It looks like all eyes below are staring directly at us."

"Top watch, join on us," Simmons said, speaking through his headset.

"Roger, Cap," Sergeant Slaughter said. "Give us a few. We have good cover."

Beaux eased behind his scoped M-14 as the tension elevated.

"Easy, Marines," Simmons said.

The Shadow agent stirred, rubbing her eyes. "What's going on?"

Simmons looked over and said, "We are about to be in the shit."

"Our friend is halfway up the bluff. Appears now he has a friend with him." Crack! A round ricocheted off limestone, splintering over the Marines.

"Not sure if they're trolling or they have us pinpointed," Lyncher said.

"Cap, we have three men toting RPG's running down the trail to join the men around the Gator."

"You have the RPG's, Beaux?" Simmons said.

"Got em, Cap," Beaux replied.

"You got our friends on the bluff?"

"Got em," Lyncher replied.

Simmons glanced to see Rock Carver follow Slaughter into the structure. "Slaughter, I want your gun on the troops around the Gator."

"Roger, Cap," he replied, dropping the bipod on the sawed-off M-240. Resting the bipod atop a level rock, he was able to sit on his ass with legs crossed, between Lyncher's and Smitty's firing positions.

Corporal Rock Carver inserted a .40mm round into the breech, quietly seating the round in the M203. "Where do you want me, Cap?"

"Rock, get your ass upriver twenty-five yards or so. Set up and cover if we have to haul ass out of the OP. Take the girl."

Roger, Cap," Rock replied, pushing the agent under the vines. "Stay low, we don't want to silhouette between the animal trail and river."

The Shadow agent glanced back and hesitated staring into Simmons' eyes.

"Get her out of here Rock."

Rock nodded and grabbed her by the collar. Both crawled down the trail on knees and elbows.

Smitty turned. "Cap, the sons of bitches are setting up a mortar position in front of the chow hall."

"We have at least a squad-sized unit on the bluff. Fuckers appear to be looking right at us," Beaux reported.

"Take the climbers, Beaux," Simmons ordered. Two muffled shots followed, toppling lifeless bodies off the ropes.

"Give em hell, Beer Can." Simmons said. "Hey Beaux, reposition with Rock."

Lyncher squeezed off a 700-yard-shot, took a breath, and squeezed off a second. The lead RPG man threw the tube into the sky, thrown back into his loader. Tail-end Charlie caught the second round square in the chest, dead before hitting the ground. Slaughter cut loose, spraying the area around the Gator with two long bursts. Smitty blew one of the antagonists off the bluff, sending the others to cover. Thunk. Beaux lobbed a .40mm round across to the bluff, hurling two jihadists straight off the rim on a one-way journey to Allah. More importantly, the surviving men retreated. Snapping in another round, he lobbed it into the meadow.

"Go, Smitty," Simmons barked. "Broken Arrow! I say again Broken Arrow," Simmons screamed into the handset.

Limestone exploded just above their heads, as the volley of fire from the meadow cut through the vines. "Move, Beaux," Simmons said, during a short lull before the next barrage raked their position.

Fire into the OP died down. Taking advantage of the lull, Lyncher raced over, bent at the waist. He pulled Simmons by the collar, dragging him over the rocks, eliciting obscenities from his Captain. "I was going to give cover, Staff Sergeant!"

"Maybe next time Cap," Lyncher screamed as they positioned along a line oriented upriver. Lyncher worked along the line on his belly ensuring the team threw accurate cover fire. Thunk. Another .40mm went down range, landing in the middle of four men moving rapidly through the pistol range.

Simmons, now on his feet, moved past the team, grabbing the female Shadow agent to pull her temporarily from harm's way. "Rock, you're with me, now move your ass!"

Simmons discerned the leapfrog tactics would continue until help arrived, or, if Lady Luck was really on their side, they evaded the threat. Deep down, he knew the reality. Rounds snapped overhead and around their positions. The jihadis were not aiming, but throwing reckless rounds down range. Only a matter of time before a round found flesh. A Marine leaves no one behind. When the time came, they would Alamo-up and fight down to the last Marine able to offer resistance.

Slaughter raced by, bent at the waist, moving rapidly to the next position. Minutes passed and Lyncher and Smitty provided cover fire for Simmons and the Shadow agent to move upriver. Slaughter and Beaux passed behind, as Simmons pressed the handset against his ear. The agent balled up against his hip as he listened for help.

Slaughter screamed. A volley from below slammed him against a boulder and deposited him across Simmons's legs.

"Smitty up! Slaughter is hit!" Simmons yelled.

Beaux slung his weapon across his shoulder. Picking up Slaughter's M204, he directed short bursts into the meadow, shooting from the hip like Rambo. Hot brass from the 204 fell onto Simmons and the Shadow agent. Smitty crawled over, handing his first aid pouch to the agent, then kept moving, Lyncher close behind.

"You're going to have to be the Medic," Simmons told the wide-eyed agent who began fumbling through the pouch. Finding a bandage, she tore away the package with her teeth and bandaged Slaughter's hip. Reaching around Slaughter's back for his medical kit, she pulled out another bandage.

"Shot clean through the hip, Cap," Slaughter groaned.

"Can you move?"

"No, Sir, my hip is broken," he said, grimacing in pain. "I can still fight though," Slaughter half-yelled.

Simmons grabbed Slaughter by his harness, pulling him painfully into a firing position. Beaux tossed the weapon to Simmons, who placed it in Slaughter's hands. Limestone exploded all around them as incoming fire intensified. Seconds passed and the weapon was back in action.

"Alamo, Marines!" Simmons shouted.

Lyncher yelled, dropping the M-14 and clutching both eyes. Blood spurted between the fingers of his left hand. Simmons watched the SSgt reach around for his medical kit. Pulling out a bandage the SSgt wiped away the blood.

"I'm good, Cap, they only got one eye," Lyncher growled, wrapping the bandage around his head, covering the left eye. Picking up the M-14, he squeezed off three quick rounds.

"Jethro Six, this is Trixie," came the radio call. "Will be handing over a flight of three Hornets in ten minutes."

Simmons dropped to the ground, thanking God in between his rapid breathing. "Bring them in from Chevy, 220 degrees, offset right, 7.5 miles, 3400 feet. Infantry in the open. WP. Danger close southeast, right pull and circle the wagons. We will throw the mark when they report IP inbound. Pass this on, copy."

"Copy," a voice from the C-130 replied. The transport's turbines whined in the background.

"Hang in there, son," Roach cut in. "We will pull all of your asses out of the fire or die trying. You copy?" Roach's voice had not changed in the all these years.

Simmons' blouse was soaked in blood front to back, and the Mexican sky began spinning around him. Bringing the handset up to his mouth, he replied weakly, "Copy that, Trixie. Don't be late to the party."

Simmons dropped the handset, no longer hearing the cursing, the shouts, and the gunfire. He managed to call out, "Rock, take the handset, Hornets in 10 minutes. Bring em in."

Then, sinking back, his flushed face came to rest across the Shadow agent's lap. He was swathed in silence.

47

Friday 1500 Hours; Kang Flight

Departing Douglas Municipal Airspace, the three Cobras making up "Kang" flight winged their way toward San Bernardino Ranch. Fifteen miles east of Douglas the old ranch had been converted to a United States Army Camp in 1911. Soldiers manning the outpost encountered Mexican bandits carrying out raids along the border during the Mexican Revolution.

Initiating a right turn, west of the old ranch compound, Hap didn't rock a rotor, give a hand signal, or transmit over the inter-flight frequency to announce the maneuver. Flying a loose cruise off Hap's five o'clock position, Ambassador slid over, and, crossing Hap's six, snap-rolled 90 degrees, kicking in left rudder, to skid into Hap's seven o'clock. Looking over his left shoulder, Hap caught Chew Boy initiating a wingover, climbing over the fur ball going on between Hap and Ambassador. Seconds later, Hap looked through his dark visor, confirming that both Ambassador and Chew Boy had worked into position.

Hap extended his left hand above the TSU, gesturing like a seagull diving for its next meal. LD was at the controls, leading Kang flight into Mexico at a brisk 155 knots. The flight crossed the barbed wire fence just above 50 feet over the flowing waterway.

After crossing the border north-to-south, the landscape shifted discernibly and quickly. Rooflines changed from shingle to cheap metal, the brick and stucco facades replaced with cinderblock, lawns and gardens vanished leaving dirt yards and few paved streets. Hap had traveled over this part of Mexico years earlier. As far as he could see, not much had changed. In the previous encounter, departing Douglas single ship after a fuel stop, he and Waco unknowingly crossed into Mexican airspace, penetrating 50 miles, before noticing the change in landscape. This type of navigational error was something a Marine Corps Aviator avoided talking about if possible. Hap shook off the incident. No harm, no foul, but it always made good fodder at happy hour. Semper Fi!

Hap glanced briefly at the GPS. The flight was an hour from the target area. Roach kept him abreast of the fluidity of the situation through a data link. It was clear the Marines had stepped into the middle of Shadow's investigation. Not surprising, the U.S. Administration missed the storm that Hap Stoner and U.S. Marines were about to enter. He snickered beneath his visor knowing that, one day, Hollywood would write one hell of a screenplay about this operation.

Roach's voice across the tactical net interrupted his thoughts. "Kang. Trixie, over."

"Go Trixie," Hap said.

"So you don't pop out of your seat and decapitate yourself later, I will break the news. Bear landed in Douglas and arrested the three Cowboys pilots."

"You catching this, Hap?" LD said.

"What in the hell happened to Slick?" Hap transmitted.

"Funny you ask," Roach said. "Slick was not on the bird that landed in Douglas, over."

"Move the rally point to Columbus," Hap said.

"Already did that. You copy that, Kang?"

"Roger," Hap said.

"Was looking to make the move anyway, Columbus has a great trauma unit at the local hospital. Something told me we are going to give the ER some business tonight. By the way, we contacted Carla and she is en route. She is one pissed off lady, Kang."

"PAN, PAN, PAN, Nomad 69 has been intercepted by Mexican Air Force T-33's. Can any Nomad flight copy this transmission?"

"Hap," LD said. "What the hell."

"Sit-Rep, over," Hap said, thinking, did Blad's boss not make it into the President's office?

Roach jumped the conversation, "Trixie copies."

In a voice as calm as if he were conversing on the shitter next to eight other guys during a morning sabbatical at Twenty-nine Palms, Spank replied, "A section crossed over the flight. Bastards came out of the sun. They had us dead to right, Kang. They didn't fire and now loitering to our six. Our weapons are not armed. We look good but we can't fucking fight—46's are unarmed.

Hap contemplated reversing course to cover Spanky's fight, even turning around Swamp's division of F18's. What a turd hunt, he said to himself. Now the Mexican Government is aware of the invasion of their airspace. Ambassador and Chew Boy stayed silent. "True warriors," Hap murmured.

"Hap," LD said, quietly.

Hap nodded once. He loved LD's level head. Nothing ever got the man excited. "We continue to press. We need the Hornets. Everyone knew the risk." Keying the UHF, he said, "Spank we are pressing to target. Acknowledge."

Silence followed. "Hap, if the turds engage. We will scatter and padlock these bastards. It will drive them crazy. Then the suck and blow guys will run out of gas attempting to maneuver into position for a shot. Just hope they don't run us out of fuel in the process."

"Kang, state intentions," Roach inquired.

"Pressing to target."

"Understood. You know they cannot defend themselves."

"Well no shit, Sherlock," Hap said. "They are Marine Aviators and will adapt. Has it been that long?"

"Putting it that way I, uhhhhhhhhhh, agree. Jimmy will be coming up their ass in those extraordinary Huey war birds. Kinda feel sorry for those Mexican shooting star pilots."

"Concur. Where are the Cowboys?"

"Kang Cobra, is that you?" Swamp said, in his Southern Mississippi drawl. "We were kinda hopin' you would let us take care of those interceptors."

"Eat ca-ca, Swamp. Go drop steel on some Islamo Fascists."

"Swamp, flight switch Green," Swamp instructed.

"Kang, flight go button Green," Hap said. Listening intently, he waited for Swamp to report IP inbound. Minutes now seemed like an eternity.

"Swamp is IP inbound."

"Continue," said a female voice that clearly wasn't Captain Simmons'. Where in the hell had she come from? He could hear a faint voice in the background. It was Simmons' barely audible voice. The female parroted his commands into the handset.

"Roger," Swamp replied, his voice distorted by the O2 mask, his Mississippi twang sounding as if originating from the bottom of an empty tennis ball can.

Hap waited anxiously; concerned that Simmons was not on the handset. A sick feeling began at the pit of his stomach. Simmons' mother would never forgive him if her son were KIA. First her husband, and now their oldest.

"Mark out," the woman's voice called out.

"Roger," Swamp replied.

The same voice began transmitting seconds later: "Mark on the ground. Hit the mark."

"In the pop," Swamp said, inverting the fighter-bomber and attempting to put eyes on the smoke. Straining against G-suit-pressure constricting around his torso and legs, he transmitted while battling the "G" forces pulling the bomber's nose through the horizon. Arching his neck back to single out the mark, he snapped wings level. "Wings level."

"Clear hot," the woman replied.

Hap grinned, hearing the distinct sound as Swamp pickled two Mk 82s. "Pulling off right."

"Dash 2 in the pop," the second fighter driver said.

Barely audible over the gunfire and the 500-lb bombs' impacts, she said, "Dash 2 continue. Good hits, Dash 1. Dash 2 hit 1's smoke. "

"Roger. Wings level."

"Cleared hot 2."

Seconds passed, and then two tweaks came across the net, pickling a pair of Mk 82s into Swamp's mushroom clouds. Exploding almost simultaneously, a crump…crump filled Hap's headphones.

"Dash 3 is in the pop."

"Continue, Dash 3. From Dash 2's hit 100 meters south. Infantry moving along the bluff."

"Roger. Searching.........OK, tally ho. Wings level."

"Cleared hot 3." What seemed for all listening on the TacAir frequency to be an eternity, was only seconds before the explosions.

"Good hits 3,".the female voice said. "We have them on the run."

"Looks like Swamp and the Cowboys are kicking a little bit of butt, Hap," LD said, anxious to get into the fight.

"You think?" Hap replied.

Swamp's voice broke the silence over the net. "I have back blast in the area of the barn. Deploying flare. Flight scatter. Rally at Chevy, right hand turns, Angels 20. "

"Any eyes on the MANPADS?" Roach asked.

"Negative," a faint voice said. It took Hap a moment to recognize Captain Simmons, half whispering, "We will not be moving from our position. We are Alamo."

Roach transmitted, "Swamp, lay waste to the barn. Do not touch the main house. Copy?"

"Roger, Trixie. We will expend all ordnance; 30 minutes from bingo fuel."

"Understood. Divert to Columbus. Copy."

"Roger that."

"Jethro, can you get eyes on the barn?"

"Negative. We have wounded and are securing the position," Will Kellogg said.

"Hell, yeah," Hap yelled over the ICS.

"Hap............Spank, over."

Using his left foot, Hap depressed the foot transmission switch beyond the ICS détente. "Situation?"

"Fast movers have left the area. We are pressing to FARP."

"Understood."

"Trixie," Will's voice silenced the conversation. "We have teams moving north up hard surface road. Will leave one fire team at Hammer and squat the balance at Falcon."

"Roger," Roach said. "Hap, time to target?"

"Twenty minutes," LD said over the ICS.

"Ten minutes, Trixie," Hap replied.

"Get off your ass, Hap. We have wounded on the ground. Insert one team at Owl with Blad's bird—"

"Negative," Will cut in. "Two serious wounded. They need a hospital."

Piloting Mayo, Schlonger chimed in, "We can be in the zone in three minutes."

"Hold. We have a hot LZ," Will replied. "Trixie, we have two squads moving up the hard surface. I'm going to have all units hold at Hammer. On my order they will flank the main house upon the snakes arriving on station."

"Roger," Roach replied.

Hap listened to mortar rounds exploding, small arms fire snapping, ricochets, and human cursing across each of Will's radio transmissions. He hoped to God he didn't bring a knife to a gunfight—two WIA and no closer to gaining Warden's release.

"Kang copies," Hap transmitted. "Five minutes ETA."

48

Friday 1600; Mecca II MX

Another wave of gunfire bounced between the canyon walls signaling that the jihadists had begun another assault. A staccato at the outset, the sounds began building as both sides worked to gain fire superiority. If his memory served him correctly, Jorge figured this was their fourth assault.

Feeling beneath a stack of folded white T-shirts, Jorge used both hands to scoop out six loose magazines. He rested three magazines by each of the polished nickel-plated .45's. Each weapon glistened in the sunlight flooding through the windows. Fixed at ground level, the windows were set horizontally with steel frames encasing bulletproof glass rising five feet above the cedar hardwood floors. The glass slid open left to right to bring in a southern breeze or to provide excellent fields of fire to repel attacks from Black Stone adversaries.

Four windows wrapped the two outside walls of Jorge's sleeping quarters. An unmistakable sound stepped over the gunfire. Screeching in from the south, an F-18 jet thundered directly over the house, followed almost immediately by the cruuuumph cruuuumph of bombs exploding. Jorge watched a second jet pass at bluff level down the center of the river. He couldn't believe his eyes as a third F-18 flew in trace of the second fighter, bearing the same unmistakable markings of a U.S. Marine Corps fighter-bomber.

It had been 45 minutes since the jihadists initiated their first assault.

Picking up both .45's, Jorge inserted a magazine before racking rounds in each. He eased the weapons into holsters that he wore in the small of his back on either side. This allowed the loosely fitting *guayabera* to fall below a bulging gut. Reaching back into the open drawer, he removed an ankle holster containing a 380 ACP.

Two wireless earbuds rested inside rather outsized ears. His left earbud allowed him to listen in to Scorpion barking orders as he attempted to organize resistance from afar. The other transmitted a continual feed from Shadow. The good guys were taking the worst hits despite delivering heavy casualties to the jihadists.

Scorpion would execute the Marine and the other American if he did not see a way out of the ambush. Stepping out of his quarters, Jorge stopped at the bottom of the stairs, allowing a half-dozen armed Black Stone men to pass. Gaining the stairs, he continued around a corner to the kitchen where more armed men gathered around the large island. Busily stuffing rounds into magazines, they passed the loaded magazines along until each had a full vest. From outside the house he heard men running and calling out to each other. A sure indication Black Stone security forces were in disarray.

With Scorpion now halfway to Los Americanos, the snake was missing its head. Two guards stood outside Scorpion's empty office giving Jorge anxious looks as he crossed the hall, moving toward them. Through his earbud, Jorge now heard Scorpion speaking with Mexico's President.

"Enrique. Bombers and infantry are attacking my installation. Why?"

"Gregorio, these are not Mexican assets. I have assurance on this. The American Ambassador has been called to my office."

"I pay you and your family too well to deserve this."

"You have to believe me, Gregorio, our air force intercepted helicopters with Yankee markings in the last couple of hours."

"Is it DEA or CIA, Enrique?"

"How would I possibly know?"

"You're the fucking President of Mexico, Enrique! I would hope the President, of all people, would know if his country was under invasion. You sold me out," Scorpion hissed. Jorge could visualize the spittle spraying across the vehicle's wet bar on the last statement.

"If you do not call off this attack, Enrique, I will have a tweet down line leaking this to the press within minutes." A click followed by silence.

Jorge watched from the shadows as three dozen Black Stone soldiers gathered around Carlos Garcia, one of Scorpion's lieutenants. Carlos barked orders, while gesturing wildly. The soldiers prepared to move south, orienting between the hard surface road and the river. They paid no mind to Jorge as he slid behind the wheel of a Gator generally used to haul trash to the incinerator. There was a load in back now.

Scorpion had just hung up on Mexico's President. El Maestro and his lieutenant were across the river, rallying the jihadists. Denied money from the Saudi Prince, Scorpion would take the Marine's head. He would probably video the beheading and then attempt to sell it for a few million to a number of radical Islamist groups to use in their recruiting videos. Knowing Scorpion, Jorge believed he would dress Black Stone soldiers in jihadi attire. Who would know the difference?

Jorge was surprised when half a dozen Black Stone soldiers motioned him to stop. As he braked, the men moved to the bed of the Gator tossing bags of trash onto the ground. Twisting around, Jorge was surprised to see a portable MANPAD resting in the bed.

"What is this?" he asked with a firm tone.

The tallest of the group appeared to be in charge. "We are moving the SAMs across the river," he said, in rapid-fire Spanish.

Jorge nodded. "You can deploy the weapon from here! But if you insist, I will take this one across."

The Squad Leader pointed to the smallest of the group. "Sabino will go with you to shoot down the Yankee airplanes."

A short scrawny kid, who couldn't have been more than 18, launched himself into the passenger seat. Jorge watched one more soldier fall back into the bed, ending up next to the weapon. Leaning over the wheel, Jorge cranked the engine, which turned over immediately. He looked over at the Squad Leader. "I thought you said this man would come with me."

"Sabino would never go anywhere without his A Gunner," he replied.

Jorge gestured with both hands, as if to say whatever. Shifting into drive, Jorge slammed down on the accelerator, whipping around to the front of the house. Making the right turn leading to the riverbed, he and Sabino exchanged looks, ignoring the rounds snapping over their heads. They came to a section where the road dipped, temporarily concealing the

Gator from the house and the cabins below the bluff. Sabino ducked down as rounds continued to snap overhead. A fighter shrieked past demanding the passengers' attention. Jorge cut the engine leaving the key in the starting position. The vehicle slowly rolled to a stop.

"What is wrong?" Sabino yelled, still hunkered down in the passenger seat. Ejecting himself from the bed, the A Gunner circled around from the back.

"I have no idea. Son of a bitch must be out of gas," Jorge replied.

The A Gunner opened the gas cap. "It's full of gas!"

Jorge rested his forehead into his fingertips, acting as if he were contemplating the problem. Out of the corner of his eye, he saw the A gunner rush over to Sabino, jabbering at a hundred miles an hour. Sabino nodded and jumped from the passenger seat, and both men prepared to walk the weapon into a firing position.

Busy preparing the weapon, neither paid any attention as Jorge eased himself from the Gator. Removing one of the nickel-plated .45s, he turned, aimed, and fired twice. Both soldiers slumped to the ground from deadly accurate head-shots. Stepping over their splayed bodies, Jorge broke down the MANPAD. He tossed the reloadable grip stock in one direction, underhanded the missile into a patch of small tightly packed junipers, and lobbed the thermal battery over the high ground on the other side of the road.

Returning behind the wheel, he turned the key and the motor roared to life. Another volley of rounds cracked overhead. Splintered rock and clipped weeds from his right settled across the two soldiers' lifeless bodies. He floored the accelerator and the Gator leapt forward, throwing up a bow wave as it crashed into the river. Jorge ducked low over the wheel for the short bumpy ride across the river. Gaining the concrete drive on the opposite bank, the vehicle accelerated but he remained low. He saw men spread out along the meadow, moving in between obstacles in the training area. Some were armed and shooting; others wounded, and still others apparently in the throes of dying. Jihadists with blood-stained clothing howled with terror, while others yelled in confusion as bullets shrieked overhead. They gathered in front of the cabin closest to the training area. Rounds hitting the ground around them kicked up dust, while the air was full of rounds ricocheting off the bluff, hissing, snapping, and travelling down river.

It appeared that Shadow's allies continued to give as much as they were taking. The jets had retreated briefly but Jorge hoped it was only a matter of time before they were back. He had to make the cover of the bluff to have any chance of avoiding the carnage beginning to grow along the meadow. Even while rounds snapped close overhead, the jihadists set up a triage station in front the cabin farthest from the fighting.

Jorge eased the Gator downriver of the triage station and parked next to the centuries-old Indian midden: earth ovens once built, opened, and later rebuilt in the baking pit. Fist-fractured by heat over the years, the Indians tossed the spent cooking stones to the sides forming a debris ring. Over time, the process created a midden twenty meters across and two meters in height—in this instance, enough cover to conceal the Gator.

Gaining the steps leading up the bluff, he took them three at a time. Just as he was about to collapse, unable to catch a breath, he reached the third level where Warden and the

Shadow agent were captive. Breathing heavily, he continued, unaware that someone was following him. He stayed on the path and approaching a bend ran into a cartel soldier coming the other way. Old Jorge suspected Warden and the Shadow agent were in the grotto where Scorpion imprisoned high value captives. Moving toward the soldier, Jorge waved. The soldier stepped aside for Scorpion's chief servant, and Jorge wheeled right, clutching the soldier's H-harness and then slinging him off the ridge. Gunfire and the shrieking of the Hornets' twin turbojets drowned out the death cry. Helicopters were close, and the noise of their rotors reverberated, dancing back and forth across the canyon walls.

Jorge kept his quick pace, moving rapidly toward another bend in the path. As he rounded the curve, he saw two guards ducked down on their knees, moving their heads as they conversed intently. Even from a distance of 75 feet, Jorge could see their eyes blinking rapidly and heads scanning in all directions, especially up through the foliage as they attempted to follow the Hornets' flight path. He chuckled, knowing that the thugs had no idea how to react now that they were on the receiving end of combined arms.

As Jorge leaned around the corner for one last look before making his move, one of the sentinels put a hand to his ear. Through his earpiece, Jorge heard the same order from Carlos to kill Warden and the agent. Around the corner, he saw the grotto entrance and the missing Shadow agent about 25 feet away with a guard on each side. As Jorge raced to close the distance, he pulled both pistols free from their holsters. The guard standing closest to the agent brandished a switchblade from his right rear pocket. Before the guard had time to depress the button to spring the blade, Jorge placed a well-aimed .45

ACP slug into the man's forehead. The round's impact sent him spinning and tumbling down the path.

Jorge's fellow Shadow agent dropped to the path as the other guard released his grip, fumbling to unsling an AK-47. Jorge squeezed the trigger rapidly four times, and the resulting wound pattern on the guard's chest was tight enough for a silver dollar to cover it. Jorge thumbed the release, and the empty magazine clanked off the rock path, dropping down the bluff and out of sight. As he fed a fresh magazine into his .45, another guard appeared around another small bend just beyond the grotto entrance. Jorge let the slide slam shut, seating a round.

Jorge's sixth sense finally kicked in. Someone had a bead on him. The air around him cracked, shooting splintered rock against his face. Reeling away, he dropped to a knee sending two wild rounds over the fallen agent further down the path. Jorge pulled the trigger two more times, aiming at a figure he could barely make out through the gush of blood in his eyes. A round entered his right thigh. He pivoted to the rear, raising the gun in his left hand. Continuing to shoot, he was only spraying and at the mercy of his assailant's shooting abilities. Another round hit his right shoulder, spinning him around and down, his back pressed against the bluff that provided scant cover.

He tried to clear the blood from his eyes to check the severity of his wounds. The leg bled profusely, but the femur artery was still intact. The wound was clean. He twisted to get a look at the damage to his shoulder. His right arm was useless. Worse, he couldn't find the pistol he'd been holding in his left hand before taking the bullet in his shoulder.

Jorge knew the soldier was either reloading the pistol or shifting to his AK because he was still alive. Either way, the end of the road in this life was at hand. Grimacing, he bent over to remove the 380 from the ankle holster. He could already feel the onset of shock. His head flopped back and he could barely make out a blurred figure stepping over his unresponsive limbs, shielding him from the guard. His head fell to the left, and the peripheral vision began closing in as if he were peering through a small pipe. He couldn't feel the 380.

Had he saved the Shadow agent and the Marine? Gunfire erupted, the exchange brisk. Jorge felt shards of splintering rock sting his face. There was no more adrenaline to ward off unconsciousness. He closed his eyes just as another of exchange of gunfire erupted.

49

Friday 1600; Kang Flight arrives on station west of Mecca II

"Kang anchored at Chevy with three snakes left hand turns," Hap said, over the tactical frequency. "Have friendlies south of Hawk in sight. Flight jettison externals." Empty external fuel tanks tumbled from each Cobra.

"Roger, Kang. Welcome to the fight," Roach replied. "Maneuvering force, move out."

"Ambassador, hook around our six and protect left flank. Chew Boy, anchor, and cover our back door. I'm popping up for a look-see."

"Moving into position," Ambassador said, dipping the helo's pointed snout, simultaneously feeding in left pedal. Hap watched Ambassador and Waco drive off his left wing 75 meters anchoring in a 50-foot hover. LD pulled in the collective, leveling at 150 feet. "Going into the bucket," Hap said.

"Roger," LD replied.

Hap worked the joystick, sweeping the ground south of Hawk to the main house. He could make out the activity in the meadow in front of the cabins and the war going on in the training area. What little structure was left of the barn continued burning. He swept back around, overflying the bluff on the opposite side of the Conchos.

"Twenty minutes to bingo, Kang," LD reported.

"We will leave the Cobra's in this hell hole before leaving Warden."

"All righty then," LD chimed in.

"Swamp, it appears the bad guys are congregating around the northernmost cabin. A line is forming, and a mortar is being set in to the front of the southernmost cabin. First pass hit the southernmost formation and take out the mortar. If you can give me one more pass, I will throw a mark on the northernmost group."

"Kang, is that you?" Swamp said.

"Who did you expect, the Bear?"

"IP inbound," Swamp reported.

"You have the initial target LD," Hap said. "Ground in front of the southernmost cabin."

"Tally ho," LD answered.

Swoooooosh—a rocket carrying a White Phosphorous (WP) warhead ejected itself from one of the Cobra's 7shot rocket pods streaking toward the meadow.

"Mark out," Hap said. *Bam—Bam*—the fuselage was taking hits.

"What the hell, Hap," LD said, in a calm but firm tone.

"Drop us out of the line of fire for a few seconds, LD," Hap said. He dropped the Cobra like an elevator ride at a Tail Hook convention in Vegas. "Slide right."

"Will do." LD said

Hap watched his cyclic mounted on the right hand console move right. The Cobra tilted over its roll axis, moving rapidly sideward, staying masked below the crest. "Anchor in front of the saddle and take it up for a look."

"You sound like a submariner, Hap," LD said, whipping the cyclic left of center, continuing to dance on the rudder pedals.

"Dash 1 is in the pop," Swamp said. The oxygen mask muffled the Mississippi resonance.

"Twenty seconds we pop," LD said, stabilizing the Cobra in a ten-foot hover.

"We gotta go now," Hap said, inflecting urgency.

"Our ass is going to be hanging out if we pop now, Hap."

"Now," Hap ordered. "Ambassador, give us fire suppression on the mark and rake the meadow to the north." Out of the corner of his eye, Hap could see Ambassador and Waco pop, squeezing off 5- and 6-round bursts from their M61 Vulcan nose gun, lobbing rounds before achieving their perch.

Firing M56A3 HEI rounds, the nose-fused round would explode above ground, creating a fragmentation hazard out to 20 meters against troops in the open. As each round arched towards the target, a great puff of smoke could be seen in the distance discharging just above the evenly cut meadow. LD answered with two clicks across the ICS.

"Going into the bucket," Hap said. The Cobra shot up, as if out of a cannon.

"Kang, there's a platoon-sized element moving south from the burning structure to our ten o'clock. They look to be sweeping the bluff west of the river, orienting to hard surface road," Ambassador said.

"Understood. Keep suppressing the target area, cleared hot," Hap said with his head down in the scope. "Chew Boy, swing around to Ambassador 9 o'clock and clear to engage." The thought of leaving the back door wide open by repositioning Chew Boy did not sit well. They hadn't had time to inspect the small structure west of the ridge to their rear.

"Did anyone notice smoke coming from the creek bed two clicks west of the shack?" Chew Boy reported.

Peering over the scope looking out to his 2 o'clock high, Hap said, "Tally ho."

"Swamp is wings level," LtCol Stenson reported.

"I got 'em, Hap. Friendlies are clear," LD said.

Switching between the tactical and inter-flight frequencies between transmissions, Hap worried about making the wrong call. His cockpit and brain were juggling a lot of balls.

"Wings level. You're causing me to press, Kang."

Hap's head moved along with the speeding jet measuring the drop angle would clear the friendlies heavily engaged in a life and death fight. "Cleared hot Dash 1," he said.

"Cleared hot," Stenson parroted.

Ambassador and Chew Boy's six-barrel .20mm spun death in longer bursts, spilling empty brass casings onto the ground, attempting to kill—but more importantly to suppress—the target area.

Working the joystick, Hap swung the scope towards the burning barn. Chew Boy's rounds cut the formation like a hot knife through butter. The advancing line of infantry wavered with the initial casualties. A couple of additional bursts sent the only living aggressors to ground, hiding behind rocks and old tree stumps. This group wore civilian jeans and sweaty green T-shirts. Must be Cartel, Hap thought

As Stenson pickled two Mk82s, he could hear the sound of the bombs leaving their racks over the tactical frequency. "Dash 1's off cold, right pull. Son of a bitch, I took hits coming from the face of the bluff."

"Anybody see where the fire came from?" Hap asked the flight.

"Dash 2 is in the pop," the second F-18 pilot reported.

Hap turned his head, catching the glint from the Hornet's wing. "Continue Dash 2. Fire is coming from below the bluff. Do not press the target. Acknowledge. LD dropping into the bucket. Keep eyes on the Hornet." Swinging the scope to the right he saw bodies hit by Chew Boy's gunfire twisting in agony. In Marine Corps lingo, enemy combatants twisting on the ground were 'kickers.'

"Copy not pressing the target," the pilot of Dash 2 said in a muffled tone.

Punching with his left hand, Hap locked the scope on the meadow just as Stenson's two Mk82s exploded the ground. The barracks, two structures to the right of the kitchen, disintegrated. Enemy combatants vanished in a cloud of dust and steel shrapnel, casting out arms, legs, and limbless torsos.

"Dash 2 is wings level."

"Clear hot two. Aim south of Dash 1's hits," Hap said. "Kang flight mask."

Hearing the *crump* of Dash 2's hits, Hap raised both thumbs-up on either side of his green helmet.

"Unmasking," LD replied.

Ambassador and Chew Boy took their cue, bringing their Cobras to position. "Kang flight is cleared hot," Hap said. Amazingly, through the carnage, he could see the white phosphorous round burning midway from the river between the first and second cabin, counting right to left.

"Dash 3 is in the pop."

"Continue," Hap said, just as a muffled bang rang out, and a projectile tore into the Cobra behind LD's head. "Son of a bitch. Where's the fire coming from?" Hap asked broadcasting over the tactical net.

"That was close, Hap," LD said stoically.

"I got the son of a bitch," Chew Boy announced. "Ten o'clock just below the crest of the bluff. Ambassador, I will mark the cave opening with cannon fire. We don't have TOW."

Adjusting his head to the tracer fire opening, Chew Boy squeezed the switch located on the cyclic with his index finger. The gun's six barrels slewed left. Squeezing the trigger, the rounds hit left and low of the cave opening. Using Kentucky windage, he tilted his head up and right, sending a long 30 round burst down range.

"Tally ho," Ambassador announced.

Hap watched the TOW leave the rail off Ambassador's bird, trailing a large back blast of swirling smoke.

"Missile on the wire," Waco announced over the radio.

"Keep our ass covered LD, I'm going into the bucket." Hap set up a TOW shot, sending it off the port outboard station depressing the transmission button with his left boot.

"Kang's got a missile on the wire."

Waco's shot blew a massive hole into the side of the bluff. Hap's missile followed seconds behind exploding in a ball of yellow flame and black smoke. Comfortable no more fire would come from that gun position, Hap went back to his role as FACA. "From the initial mark, 100 meters north cleared hot," Hap said. "Take us down, LD"

LD positioned cumulus granite and dirt between the Cobra and the shooters.

"Dash 2, pulling off right," the Hornet pilot said, grunting to ward off G-forces pushing blood from his brain into his polished flight boots.

"Wings level and cleared hot. 100 meters north of 2's hits," the Dash 3 F-18 pilot reported.

The cannon's barrel encased by the nose turret slewed slowly below him, moving in sync with LD's head, keeping their right flank covered.

"They are coming at us again, Kang," Will Kellogg said calmly.

Listening in on the third radio, the AH 1–W carried on board, Hap knew that the attack had to be coming from south of the meadow.

"Kang," Ambassador said, returning to the perch. Chew Boy popped up, hammering away with the cannon at the infantry advancing south between the hard surface road and the western lip of the gorge.

Hap switched to Radio 2. "Swamp, can you blow the shit out of the training area south of your last attack?"

Silence, and then, "Semper Fi, Kang."

"I will throw a mark to the southern boundary. Walk it up to the meadow from there."

"Roger," Stenson replied. "IP inbound."

"Ambassador and Chew Boy anchor," Hap said over radio one. "You know where we're going. LD, I got the gun and you shoot the WP." The Cobra's nose swung right as LD fed in right pedal. Tucking the nose, the Cobra accelerated, paralleling the hard surface road. Located on the other side of the high ground off their left wing, the road was not in their field of view. Hap's head was out of the cockpit and on a swivel.

"I'm popping, Hap," LD said.

"Do it," Hap replied. The snout of the Cobra climbed 45 degrees above the horizon, then snap-rolled to 90 degrees left wing down.

"I got it," LD said. Pulling the nose through the horizon, LD rolled wings level. Feeding cyclic and pedal pulling military power, the helo raced down the slot towards the intended target.

Hap took in the show. "Cleared hot LD. Make it a good one."

The first rocket came out of the pod, tracking for a moment. Going stupid, the rocket arced up, making a hard climbing turn to the left. Without hesitation, LD squeezed off a second round putting the rocket just inside the boundary between the training ground's end and the beginning of the river's rocky basin.

"Mark out," Hap reported, keeping his eyes on the first F-18 popping in a hard left turn. Rolling wings level, Stenson reported, "Wings Level."

"Cleared hot," Hap said. LD peeled off in a right turn, moving slowly upriver.

"Cleared hot," Stenson said, rippling off eight 5-inch Zuni rockets, traveling at over 1600 miles per hour. Stenson expertly walked the round across the meadow. In seconds, the meadow erupted in smoke and shards of limestone and chunks of rock, as the 80-pound rockets raked the target area.

"Dash 2's in the pop," Dash 2 said.

"Hit Dash 1's southernmost hit."

"Tally ho. Wings level."

Hap waited. "Cleared hot."

The jihadists regrouping to advance now vanished in smoke and flame.

"Dash 3 popping," the pilot said, between grunts.

"Change of target." LD whipped the nose around, and Hap let off a long burst into the meadow. "From the northernmost cabin, hit between river and burning structure."

"Roger. Wings level," the Hornet pilot said.

Seconds passed, the small arms' fire had come to a stop, and Will's team was moving upriver. "Cleared hot 3."

Hap watched the small telephone poles blast away from their four shot pods like Atlas rockets leaving a Cape Canaveral launch pad. The meadow erupted again in smoke and flame. The smell of Cordite now filled the cockpit.

"Dash 3's off right."

"Jordy, make a hard turn to the southeast and we will be at your ten o'clock in right hand turns," Stenson said.

"Tally ho," Jordy, the second F-18 Cowboy, replied.

Roach interrupted the melee, "Kang. Spank is in the FARP with two toads. Big Alabama's flight is on short final."

"Kang," Will's voice broke in calmly. "Taking defilade fire from the ridge opposite our position. Those stiff wingers have any more ordnance? We pushed upriver but have hunkered down until suppressed."

"Ambassador, anchor. Waco, stay with Ambassador. Keep the infantry from advancing south. We're going to button-hook in from the south to check out the threat," Hap said. "You have the targets, LD?"

"Got em, Kang," LD replied. "Maneuvering." The Cobra dipped its nose as the tail swung around to the north. Flying low, the bird passed over the assault unit on the western bluff setting up an echelon right formation while taking fire from the bluff. The unit would provide mutual support for Will's advance, all the while proceeding north towards the burning barn and main house.

"Roger," Ambassador replied in his slow Texas drawl. "Chew Boy, you have our left flank and keep our six clear."

"Will do," Chew Boy replied. Allowing Killer Koch to unleash 2.75 rockets armed with HE warheads, Chew kept his head on a swivel, ensuring that the bad guys were not allowed a cheap kill by attacking their six. With a flip of a switch and depressing a switch on the cyclic with his pinkie, Chew Boy let the gun slew where his eyes fixated. As Killer depressed his left thumb, a rocket left the inside station on the Cobra's port side. The Cobra's black box sensed that the barrel of the cannon wasn't fixed forward, and delayed the release of the rocket. During the delay, the barrel automatically swung forward to the point that saw the rocket clear the aircraft. The barrel then slew back to where Chew Boy was looking. Chew Boy would then simply have to pull the trigger to would neutralize a surprise threat with the .20mm.

"Swamp, you have the targets on the south bluff? Infantry in the open."

"Got em, Kang. Will attack in a flight of three and go Winchester. And, we are bingo fuel. TOT two plus zero-zero."

LD swung the nose around a slight rise, masking the bird from the jihadist on the bluff. "Taking a lot of fire, Swamp."

"No mark required, Kang. TOT in thirty seconds."

"Roger, Swamp. Continue."

"Pop up, LD. Let me throw a few rounds to keep the bad guys' heads down." LD squeezed in collective. Seconds later, Hap had 2.75-inch rockets and .20mm rounds sweeping the ridge. As the third 30-round burst went downrange, the ridge erupted from the three Hornets' .20mms. Without planning, the Marines had pulled off a perfectly orchestrated "L" attack. Within seconds, 600 rounds of .20 mm and seven 2.75 rockets had raked the ridge, encasing it in smoke and flying debris.

Outside of a few kickers, jihadists lay strewn about the ridge, their cadavers twisted and mangled. Incoming fire from the ridge ceased.

"Team Alpha is cleared to advance. Do you copy, Trixie?"

"Copy, Kang," Roach replied, as he paced back and forth in front of the console.

"Team Alpha is on the move," Will reported. "We have two urgent medevacs and one priority. Get on it."

"Swamp is off. See you on the other side, Kang. I'll have the authorities save some of those handcuffs for you and the Nomads. Semper Fi."

50

"Medevac ETA in fifteen minutes, Will," Hap said. "Let's do a quick sweep of the ridge, LD."

LD pulled the collective into his armpit, giving two clicks on the ICS, clawing over the ridge. Dead jihadists littered the ground below. "Kang, Trixie. We have confirmation on both hostages."

Hap cringed and waited for the inevitable, the pressure building in the pit of his stomach. "Those motherfuckers," he yelled, loud enough for LD to hear without need for the ICS. Had he just killed Warden? Had his actions signed Warden's death warrant?

"Both confirmed alive. I repeat, they are alive but in tough shape. Sorry about the delay, Kang. Dropped my Kit Kat on the deck."

Hap's forehead pressed heavily against the rubber headrest as he attempted to regain composure.

"Kang, Shadow Services is pulling two WIA off the bluff. One Shadow WIA, urgent surgical," Roach said.

"Fifteen minutes and we're bingo to the FARP," LD said.

Hap acknowledged, pressing the foot switch two times. Spanky's section crossed overhead. The Boeing H-46 Sea Knight was on short final to the green smoke grenade thrown minutes before by one of Will's soldiers left to care for the wounded.

Hap watched Will's squad moving along the meadow, guiding on the river, capturing any of the wounded jihadists that Blad judged had a very good chance of living. Shadow Services needed somebody to interrogate. Others received a coup de grace shot to the face.

"Kang…Trixie. One Phrog down at the FARP. Couple of hours to repair but it's out of this fight."

Hap's awareness returned to the situation at hand He knew the Phrog was a tired old aircraft that needed to go to rest in the boneyard at Davis-Mothan AFB in Tucson. "I want the Phrog to push our wounded and KIA to the hospital in the vicinity of alternate LZ on the U.S. side. Schlonger, I need you to push to FARP and top off when you have a handle on your situation. Spank, cover the advance in the meadow, moving south to my front."

"Do we have any positive ID on Scorpion or El Maestro?" Roach asked.

"Negative," Will said.

Hap maintained an over watch position north of the river, moving along the bluff. Will's advance pushed past the southernmost cabin. Two arm movements and the four remaining Recon Marines peeled off behind the cabins steering clear of the destroyed yet still burning fourth cabin. Systematically, the Recon Marines searched the caves at ground level, with surprisingly little fanfare. The occasional shot rang out, and for those still alive, Blad had their hands tied roughly behind their backs, regardless of their wounds.

A human chain appeared from behind the northernmost cabin. Six men struggled to carry a weighted blanket, gripping each corner and either side along the middle. Hap observed another group of eight men gripping a second blanket.

Whatever they carried dragged along the rocks as the team muscled the load toward the meadow. A third group of six laid down yet another blanket and its contents in line with the other two. The sun cast its last light upon the bluff, a panorama, thought Hap, worthy of a National Geographic cover.

"Do you see Warden?" LD asked.

"Can't tell," Hap said. "Blad is busy securing prisoners and shooting others in the face."

* * *

Will raised a clenched left fist and pumped it vertically up and down. Double-timing while maintaining line and separation between each team member, the squad rapidly closed the hundred-and-fifty-yard gap. The squad rushed around the blankets, setting in a defensive position oriented south and west across the river.

Will pushed through the crowd with Blad close on his heels. Dropping to one knee, he threw back the blanket only to meet what appeared to be a corpse's stare. It took seconds before he heard fragile signs of life—air wheezing in and out of lungs. The stranger dressed in tattered civilian attire, spattered in blood, needed immediate medical attention. He moved quickly to the next blood-soaked blanket and with Blad looking over his shoulder, dropped to a knee, and began tending to Jorge's wounds.

The Shadow agent knelt next to Will and tended to the wounds. Will patted her on the shoulder and moved to the last blanket, and even from a distance, Hap could see that whoever was in the blanket was struggling to escape. Will went to a knee to peel the blanket back. "We have your Lieutenant Colonel. Hap, we need a Medevac—*now.*"

Hap's head came out of the bucket as a big sigh escaped his lips. "Get down there, LD. Warden can have my seat."

"You sure, Hap?"

"I've got the aircraft, Major." Hap tucked the nose-lowering collective, letting the bird fall into the riverbed. Before reaching the meadow, he stood the bird on its side, banking hard left, feeding in left pedal. Picking a path clear of craters, he conducted a sliding landing between the wounded and the river. Rocking precariously to a stop, the rotors came within a hair of striking the ground to their front. Hap breathed a deep sigh of relief and gave the controls back to LD.

Removing his helmet sight, ICS cord, and harness, he leapt from the gunner's position, and rushed around the nose to Warden. Will grabbed Hap hard by the collar, bringing him to a sudden stop. "He should be okay, Colonel. My guys are stabilizing him.

* * *

Looking over the medic's shoulder Warden painfully opened his swollen eyelids but they were still only slits.

"What fucking took you so long, Hap?" Warden asked, chuckling, spitting up blood.

"You look like shit, Boss," Hap replied. "The Administration was going to leave you."

"I figured that out after 24 hours. Something told me you would throw your life and career away to say otherwise. Anybody on our side hurt?"

"We've had a few on our side pretty shot up. Simmons went down again. We have one more confirmed Marine KIA."

Warden blinked, tears welling up.

"Can he travel?" Hap asked the Corpsman.

"Let me sit him up and wrap his ribs. They're pretty broken up." Hap dropped behind Warden and eased him up.

Warden let out a shrill yell. "Damn you, Hap, that fucking hurts!"

Freeing his Bowie knife, Hap cut away the top of Warden's flight suit and the corpsman cinched a tight wrap around his rib cage. After wrapping the ribs, the medic stuck a Syrette of morphine into Warden's arm, attaching the empty device to the injured Marine's dog tags.

Will bent over to support one shoulder, and, with Hap under the other shoulder, they lifted Warden to his feet. Carrying his limp body to the aircraft, they both stepped into the ammo door Hap had just opened. Hap grabbed Warden's lower torso, guiding it into the seat, as Will muscled the CO's upper body into place. Hap quickly strapped him in. Connecting the ICS cord to his helmet, carefully, he began to work the form-fitted head protection over Warden's tender cranial area. Warden kept tapping Hap's arm signaling that the morphine had kicked in and Hap should stop pussyfooting around. Gently patting the top of Warden's head, he closed the canopy and raised the ammo door.

Hap looked to see Blad waving him over.

"We've got to get my men out," Blad said, yelling over the roar of the Cobra's twin turboshaft engines and spinning rotors.

"Twenty minutes for the medevac to arrive, big guy," Hap replied, yelling in his ear. Then he realized that he owed Blad big time for Warden being alive. He remembered SERE school and Cutcha Cockoff emphasizing that to live through captivity, you must work in teams. That must have been what Warden and the Shadow agent did.

"Raise him up," he said to Blad and Will. They lifted the almost lifeless figure, with energy only to moan. Hap took off his vest, letting his pistol and Bowie knife fall below either armpit, and carefully slipped it around each shoulder. Dropping to a knee, he connected the two straps coming through his legs.

"Bring him to the bird," Hap yelled, pointing at the Cobra. Dragging him to the starboard stub wing, both Will and Blad stared at Hap, as if he'd just downed a dozen shots of hard liquor.

"You said you wanted him out of here," Hap shouted. "Let's go!"

"Enjoy the ride, Steve," Blad yelled. All three heaved his dead weight face down on to the top of the stub wing. "Hold him in place," Hap yelled. Removing one of Will's carabiners, he hustled around the stub wing, connecting the vest to a tie-down bracket. Removing his earplugs, he pushed one into each of Steve's ears. He banged the front canopy with his fist, wishing he could enjoy the view of the wild toad ride that Blad's agent was about to experience. Then he dropped, joining Will and Blad flat-faced on the ground as LD pulled max power, taking off in a no-hover maneuver that left a dense cloud of dust.

51

Friday 1645; Mecca II MX

The first to pick himself up off the ground, Will helped Blad and Hap to a standing position as the roar of whirling rotors and spooled turbines vanished to the west. Silence settled over the meadow except for the groaning and crying of the wounded.

Will walked over to a dead jihadist, rolling the body to free a vest. He grabbed one of the few AK-47s in workable condition, and tossed vest and weapon to Hap.

Hap caught both midair, rifle in his right hand and vest in his left.

"He won't need those," Will said.

Hap waited while Blad walked over to the medic who was busy stabilizing Jorge's shot-up body. The Shadow agent had gone a ghostly white from loss of blood. As Blad knelt close to Jorge, one of Scorpion's prisoners rushed up to deliver blankets. Jorge reached up, and Blad leaned close so he could hear his agent.

"I'm freezing my balls off," Jorge said weakly in Blad's ear, struggling with each word.

"What about my guy, Hap?" Blad asked. "He needs plasma and a surgeon, without blood he's a dead man."

Will removed the handset from his ear, "Trixie says 20 minutes for the Hueys, Colonel."

Hap placed a hand covered in Warden's blood on Blad's broad shoulder, "We are going to have to keep him alive ourselves for now. Nothing we can do regarding air assets."

Blad looked back over his shoulder. "Understood, Hap, this crap kinda goes with the job description."

The roar of rotor blades chopping air filled the meadow. It wasn't a Huey and Hap knew it. Mexican Military or a cartel bird, maybe? Whoever controlled the bird wasn't talking to Trixie. The sound continued to grow louder. Roach instructed Spanky to mask, oriented to the northwest. The now freed prisoners rushed for the tree line, running behind the cabins.

Will barked into the handset to the squad leader across the river: "Move to the reverse slope west of compound and set a defensive position. Orient northwest, possible air threat inbound. Get on it!"

He gave two arm signals, and the remainder of the squad quickly set up under the canopy of pecan trees growing along the river.

Hap joined Will standing over Jorge; the medics had gone as far as they could to stop the bleeding. Hap removed the magazine from the AK. It was light. Tossing it aside, he inserted a full magazine. Pulling the bolt to the rear, he ejected a round to the ground. He let the bolt slam home.

"What are you thinking, Colonel?"

Hap laid the barrel across his shoulder, the way he would if he were duck hunting. "What in the hell did we step into?"

Will opened his mouth to answer, but the abrupt sound of the turbine engine along with small arms' fire west of the hard surface grabbed everyone's attention. Hap dropped to one knee. Will stood behind him, his M4 at the ready. Blad stood clutching .45's in both hands. Schlonger blew past the northern rim at fifty feet.

"Break," he said. "Platoon-sized element moving across the pasture west of the hard surface road."

Hap grabbed the handset from Will's blouse pocket, "Spanky. Clear to engage."

"I would attack from the north," Schlonger said. "Rising terrain will mask you until you pop."

The two Snakes dropped their snouts, moving to the northeast and paralleling the hard surface road and the riverbed.

Will walked over to the mortar tubes, hoping to put them to work. But, after kicking the bodies off the top, he saw that neither tube was good to be a flower vase. Each tube lay bent, with shrapnel holes drilled up and down the length.

Gunfire rang out to their right rear. Instinct kicked in and Hap ran toward the sound of the guns, racing in front of the kitchen cabin. Will broke off in the rush, taking the left side of the cabin. Hap slowed to move cautiously around the side of the pavilion. Peering carefully around the corner, he kept the BBQ pit between him and any potential threat lurking behind the cabin. Two of Simmons's Marines, who had split off earlier, were dragging a figure wearing the black jihadist uniform from between the cabins. One of the men did a quick body search throwing a pistol and knife to the side. Blood poured from multiple wounds as the figure writhed on the ground.

Hap looked over at Will, who had already slung his rifle across his shoulder, giving a thumbs-up. Will took his 9mm from his holster and put a round in the jihadist's forehead.

The two Marines acknowledged Hap and Will before moving to search another cabin.

"Just helping him along a little quicker to make the acquaintance of the 72 virgins, Colonel," Will said stoically.

Sounds of a scuffle coming from a grotto caught their attention. One of the Recon Marines and a woman, apparently friendly, were using the barrels of their rifles to prod two men out of the same grotto the other Recon Marines had just vacated.

Hap recognized one. He'd seen a photo with his alias scrawled in Sharpie across the 5x7—"El Maestro." He and the other man moved forward reluctantly, following the prodding of their guards. They stopped and then knelt, as ordered, their knees cut by rocky ground, their hands zip tied behind their backs.

Hap stepped in front of both prisoners, removing his Bowie knife. Passing intentionally behind El Maestro, Hap stepped to the other man and cut his hands free. Tall and muscled, weighing at least 200 pounds, with a pierced diamond earring, he looked like one of Scorpion's special employees, with all the charm and skills of a horror-movie sadist. He shook his arms, trying to reboot his circulation, his piercing gaze never leaving Hap.

"Nice jewelry," Hap growled, jerking his chin toward the man's very big diamond earring and imagining it on Carla's finger.

While the strong man made a show of warming up, Hap tossed Will his AK and Belgium Browning Hi Power, and then he threw the knife into the ground sticking it blade first.

"Let's go shit-bird," Hap said. "If you kill me, they'll let you go." Hap broke down into fighting position and began moving counter clockwise around the knife.

Mirroring Hap's movements, his opponent asked in broken English, "Why should I believe you?"

"Because you will die painfully and very slowly if you do not give me the pleasure of killing you fast."

Hap knew a haymaker was coming his way, and sure enough, before long his opponent telegraphed his move. Lunging forward, he came over the top with the right. Hap stepped aside and the punch met air. Clearly, from his moves, he never before had to consider if a punch might throw him off balance. Hap would take all bets that he really was a sadist, and a pro at that, especially with his victims' hands tied behind their backs.

Hap let the brute's momentum carry him out over his front foot. Using his right hand to cock his wrist, his left hand pushed on the shoulder, creating an arm bar wrestling move. He learned that move from Roach, a former champion college wrestler, who always laughed when he said the fun part of this move was separating the shoulder.

Hap's left elbow came down with all 212 pounds just below the shoulder joint, producing a howl from his victim. He grabbed the knife with his left hand and the terrorist's vest with his right. Dragging the 200-pound man into the small moat running around the cabin, Hap stood him up against the wall. With all his strength, and screaming at the top of his lungs, Hap drove the Bowie knife into the sternum and through, penetrating the wood wall behind him. Pinned to the wall with the knife, the body went limp, eyes staring into the abyss.

Hap turned to El Maestro, who knelt in silence before him, eyes fixed on the ground. "Cut the turd loose."

"Stand down, Hap," Blad howled, coming fast around the corner. "I need El Maestro alive."

Cradling his M4, Will appeared to enjoy the show. "Colonel, dead or alive works for me. Shit, just kill the bastard. The world will be a better place."

Blad wielded a .45 in his right hand. Will countered, allowing the M4's barrel to fall, stopping as it aimed directly at Blad's midsection.

"I have one seriously wounded. The Colonel has one KIA. Warden is on his way to safety. Let's get the hell out of here," Blad said. Walking over to Hap's knife, he worked the handle of the Bowie knife back and forth cutting away from bone. The corpse fell to its knees, fixed in death facing to the east. Blad tapped the diamond with the tip of the knife, as if asking, You want this? Hap shook his head.

Blad tossed the blood-soaked blade slowly into the air toward Hap. "Something tells me you're going to need this." Blad shoved the body to the ground with his boot. Catching the knife by the handle, Hap reached for the closest piece of cloth, ripping away El Maestro's turban to wipe off the blood.

"Fucker bleeds a lot," Hap said to himself. He refrained from crushing El Maestro's skull. Instead, he dropped the bloodied cloth into El Maestro's lap.

Will pulled the handset away from his ear, "Spanky said there's a convoy that could cross New Jersey end to end. It's coming our way from five miles north. There's a figure dressed in a burka between the convoy and us, standing in the middle of the road like a roadblock. Spanky is asking permission to blow the bitch to hell."

"Cleared hot, Spanky," Roach said from his perch on Trixie circling overhead.

"Roger, Trixie. It will be my privilege."

Blad lunged, ripping the handset from Will's hand. "Abort, abort, abort. Acknowledge! Trixie, abort this mission! She is one of ours!"

El Maestro looked back over his shoulder, both brows coming together. His eyes drifted forward, his head shaking slowly, without saying a word.

Silence followed while Blad stood with clenched fists.

Finally, the voice came through: "Spanky off cold. Good timing: came within a nanosecond before the burka became Swiss cheese."

Blad flipped the handset back to Will. He looked over to Hap. "I have to get this piece of shit to the Gulf Coast. Hopefully, with the treasure trove of intelligence we get out of him and a bit of coercion, he may be allowed to wear another turban.

Hap retrieved the AK and 9mm. "What's so important that this worthless pile of crap breathes?" Hap asked.

Agent 22 approached from behind the first cabin herding six teenage American girls toward their position.

Blad smiled, reaching into his shirt pocket. Pulling out a cigar and lighter, he popped the stogie into his mouth. Stepping back, inhaling a few long drags, he said, "Can't talk about it now, Hap. With any luck, you may find out one day. Besides, you want Scorpion, and Jorge was able to tell me that you will have to track him and the Caliph to Scorpion's resort, Los Americanos. He also mentioned something he heard on the wind, something called 'Fer-de-Lance,' no intel, but it sounds important. Keep your ears open."

Hap grunted his thanks. "Small world. Took Carla on a fishing excursion last year and played a couple of rounds of golf at Scorpion's resort."

Blad took another draw on his cigar, exhaling smoke and words. "We have to take the girls out on the Mayo, Hap."

Hap returned a questioning look. "Going to be tight, Blad, and way over max gross. They just took a full bag at the FARP."

Blad shrugged. "Shit happens, Hap. Between Schlonger and Scharver at the controls, we are in capable hands."

Hap's head half-turned as Shadow's yellow Sikorsky flared, preparing to set down in front of the first cabin. He nodded, the sides of his mouth turning up.

"It is what it is. We need to get these girls back to their parents."

Hap tapped Will on the back and they double-timed it to assist the Marines carting Jorge inside the bird. Blad walked under the rotor arc leading the turban-less man by the cuff of his robe. His hands remained zip tied behind his back as Blad shoved him into the far corner of the helicopter's cabin. The female agent stood outside of the rotor arc ensuring each girl bent at the waist to load. The helo was leaning slightly right rotor low.

Blad pointed at Hap and Will, and then circled his finger vertically next to his right ear. Both took Blad's cue, approaching on either side. Reaching his arms around their shoulders, moving his head left and right to their ears, he tried his best to yell above the idling engines, "As soon as the assault to the west is repelled, have your men surrender to the Mexican authorities. The Recon Marines go out with us."

Will recoiled, shaking his head. "They will be shot!"

"What the hell are you thinking, Blad?" Hap yelled. "You're issuing the men that remain behind their death warrant, and we're going to need a catapult to get the helo into the air."

Blad looked at both of his friends, his expression resolute. "You have to trust me on this, Hap. These are your men, Will, but they'll be released by tomorrow morning. Have them lay down their arms to a Colonel Rodrigo Falto. No other. Got it?"

Will gave a curt duck of the chin as Hap nodded slowly to his old friend. Will turned to Blad with an expression that said he best not be wrong, before he walked over to his men who were guarding the jihadi warriors. Hap pointed to Rock, Beaux and Smitty, motioning them into the bird. Moments later Blad squeezed into a cabin growing more cramped by the 'man'—reminiscent of the history of the evacuation of the Embassy in Saigon.

The female Shadow agent recognized the dilemma. Plucking an AK off the ground, she ejected the magazine for weight. Satisfied the magazine had sufficient rounds she stepped back, kissing the fingers of one hand away at Blad. Smiling at Hap, she ducked under the rotor arc, double-timing to join Will's commandos, making one stop to relieve a jihadi corpse of 7.62 ammo.

Rock prodded El Maestro, poking the barrel of the Marine Corps-issued M4 in his chest, motivating him to move farther into the corner.

Minutes later, Will paused before stepping into the aircraft. Looking back, he pumped a clenched fist. His teammates and the female Shadow agent came to attention with their rifles running up along their right legs. Will slammed the cabin door shut, falling back into the middle of the girls huddling on the cabin floor. The girls recoiled and tried to move to the other side of the cabin but the wounded Shadow agent and the medic kneeling over him blocked them. By their dress, they still wore the garb they were kidnapped in. Knee high skirts, soiled blouses, and knee socks with pumps. Gaining a knee, Will slid into the seat across from Hap.

Hap nodded and placed both hands on two of the girls' shoulders. Both recoiled away leaving traces of Hap's handprint on their shoulders. He raised both hands and very slowly, his lips formed the words, You're safe now. He nodded to ensure they understood. *You're going home now.* One of the girls nodded her head rapidly and began to speak in each of the girl's ears. As she spoke to one of the girls, the girl turned and smiled before beginning to cry.

Hap spun an extended finger above his head signaling Schlonger: *Get a move on.* Craning his neck to observe the human refugees packed in the cabin, Schlonger acknowledged Hap's directive with a nod. Reaching over, he tapped Scharver on the shoulder. Both turbines' governors began dumping JP into the hot section responding to Scharver beeping the turbines to max.

Hap could see the collective coming to a stop just under Scharver's armpit. The Mayo's engines made a lot of noise but the bird refused to budge an inch. He had all the confidence in Jeff Scharver's skillset, having gone through flight school with him. Hap received orders to Camp Pendleton on the west coast while Scharver's orders were to MCAS New River on the east coast. Since they shook hands congratulating each other on the day the Wings of Gold were pinned on their chests, they lost touch. It was good to see he was doing well in his next life.

Not surprisingly, Scharver lowered the collective and each pilot looked to the other, deliberating over the ICS. As they set their eyes front, the engines spooled up for another go. The nose began rocking as Scharver nursed the cyclic forward. Mayo started to inch ahead and his fingers darted across the engine gauges, continuing to bump the cyclic forward. The engines raced but stayed in their mounts.

Still, Scharver nursed Mayo's over-weighted fuselage. The helo's tires slowly rolled across the ground. Working to gain translational lift, the aircraft vibrated violently as the wheels cleared the ground by only inches. He tucked the nose slightly, feeding in left rudder until hitting the stop. Mayo responded, gaining another foot of altitude.

Hap glanced at the girls and they seemed ok. Will's medic, Benjamin Sherry removed his blouse and ripped a strip from the t-shirt. He quickly laced the makeshift bandage around Will's head, and then returned his attention to the wounded Shadow. The Recon Marines showed no emotion, staring straight ahead. Hap knew these boys were the best of the best, combat veterans who'd enlisted at eighteen or nineteen to earn enough money to make it through college, and, who now, only a few years later, wouldn't think twice about the Spring Break they were missing.

Hap felt Will's gaze. His old friend sat with head pressed back against the bulkhead, one half-open eye staring at him. Hap cut a reassuring nod, and Will's eye slowly shut. Squeezed to Hap's left on the other side of Doc, El Maestro sat pressed into the back corner of the cabin. His eyelids squeezed tight, and the fear of God written across his face—no interpreter needed. No doubt, El Maestro expected the cabin door just to his left to open and to feel himself pushed overboard. Hap scribbled a note, wadding it up before passing it overhand to Blad, who sat catty-corner.

Now Hap turned his attention back to Scharver, who was feeding in left pedal, taking power from the tail rotor, and transferring the additional drive back to the transmission in a classic Chicken Hawk maneuver, named for the famous book by Robert Mason on the bravery and monumental skill of helicopter pilots in Vietnam. The Mayo's nose pointed thirty degrees left of the line of flight. Vibrating violently, the aircraft's rotors strained to keep the helicopter from rolling up in a ball of twisted metal and flames. The girls huddled together with their arms to their side, eyes closed, and heads tucked.

With the rotor's turns drooping severely, Hap didn't take comfort from the fact he could count each rotation. It didn't take a rocket scientist to understand that the rotor's droop was one or two percent away from being unable to provide further lift to the overloaded aircraft.

Scharver allowed Mayo to sacrifice precious altitude measured in feet in order to gain airspeed, which in this case was life. It was a monumental struggle to maintain flight a mere few feet over the Rio Conchos.

Hap and Blad each looked at the other knowing this could go either way. Reading Hap's note, Blad dialed the satellite phone to call Carla's cell. Both knew whatever was going to happen, crash or flight, would happen in seconds. Whether the Mayo broke up violently in the water, or whether the nose straightened down the line of flight, lifting the aircraft to safe harbor, Hap Stoner was proud of all involved in the Operation...damn proud.

52

Friday 1615; Road to Los Americanos MX

Just hours before fighting broke out at the camp, Scorpion left Mecca II for Los Americanos with the Caliph by his side. Since speaking with President Fuentes, Scorpion was in no mood for scenic driving. From his right rear bucket seat, Scorpion eyed his driver as he guided the Chevy Suburban between a new convoy of speeding Federales police escorts. They were clearly visible on the Suburban's digital screen. The recently relieved escort initiated a U-turn shutting down their mounted emergency lights and gunning their motors for the return trip to Torreon.

So far, the Federales had delivered on their promises when it came to speed, and the Suburban with its Vortex 5.3 Liter V-8 had no trouble keeping up. The armored Suburban had been a gift from a man who lived in constant fear. He had added turbochargers to boost the power plant beyond the advertised 355 horses necessary to handle the weight of supplementary protective armor and bulletproof glass necessary to protect Mexico's President and First Family.

A quick glance at his Rolex confirmed that he'd been imprisoned inside the vehicle for six hours with thirty minutes to go. Why the hell hadn't he taken his Cessna Citation jet? His gut told him that his business partner had screwed him, ironically the same man who had given him the Suburban. The waters of the Presa El Cuchillo came into view. He massaged both eyes with thumb and index finger. Had the US Administration grown a set of balls in the last twenty-four hours and launched an invasion of their southern neighbor? But maybe, just maybe the President was telling the truth and the Americans had acted unilaterally.

Scorpion's phone rang. Tapping the back of the passenger seat, he knew who was on the other end. Someone had attacked Mecca II and if the Mexican people knew their President was involved with Jabhat al Mahdi operating inside the borders of Mexico, another revolution was not far behind. All communications from the compound had gone silent. He had received information that soldiers guarding the methamphetamine processing plant west of the compound had mounted an assault. After 15 minutes taking heavy fire from ground forces and Cobra helicopters, the few soldiers still alive had straggled into the factory with various wounds.

Jorge was nowhere around. The big guy would be sorely missed and as sure as Scorpion swore on his father's grave, Jorge's killers would surely wish he'd found them dead. Oh, how he hoped the Marine and other agent were dead. Nothing good would come from their testimony. Besides, he'd lost a king's ransom, plus the payday with the American virgins.

Continuing to tap his fingers, he answered the phone. "Yes, Enrique."

"Gregorio, you have to believe that neither the Mexican Government nor US Government is behind this aggression."

Removing a recently lit cigar from his lips, Gregorio pressed the phone against his clenched jaw, "Enrique. Let's act as if I believe you because I pay you a lot of money, you crooked piece of shit. But, based on the Yankee Marine markings on all the aircraft, who am I to think is behind this aggression, fucking Martians? Then, I have to ask how in the hell did they find Mecca II? Maybe it was the Ouija board. Or maybe you sold me out."

The President interrupted, "I'm oblivious Gregorio. My intelligence resources are clueless. The Yankees are not talking."

"Not my problem," Scorpion interrupted. "You are Mexico's President."

"Gregorio, the United States Ambassador has been called to my office. I have advised my Ambassador to the United Nations to call an emergency meeting of the Security Council."

Scorpion leaned back in his seat laughing uncontrollably. It was too easy picturing the US Ambassador attempting to explain the unexplainable to Mexico's President.

When he caught his breath, he said, "And why should possible United Nations interest impress me? They do nothing. For Christ's sakes, Enrique, the UN diplomats—80 percent of which come from barbaric nations—don't even pay their New York City parking tickets."

Turning off Highway 400, the three-vehicle convoy sped through downtown China Nuevo Leon, a city of ten thousand. With police cruiser lights flashing and horns blaring, the convoy sped through the city's few red lights.

"Gregorio, you cut out. Are you there?" President Fuentes asked nervously.

Scorpion rolled his eyes, shaking his head in disgust. "Yes Enrique. Despite the fact what I'm about to say is going to cost all of us money in the short term; I'm going to activate Fer-de-Lance within forty-eight hours. We must deflect whatever is going on with the Yankee Administration and push it onto the Radical Islamist movement."

"Gregorio, are you sure Fer-de-Lance is the right course of action at this time?"

Scorpion weighed the President's words as if Black Stone's existence depended on them. If just by chance the President of Mexico was being honest, a snake with who knows how many heads existed within the Black Stone organization. He knew who the vipers were. "I'm sure, Enrique. Execute Fer-de-Lance on my order."

"I will order the Army to depart for Mecca II immediately," the President said with authority. "The entire Mexican Military and law enforcement will be placed on alert within the next fifteen minutes. As agreed, all additional forces will move the moment you initiate your plan, Gregorio."

Scorpion nodded, hanging up. Letting the phone drop into his lap, he turned to gaze out at the city's day-to-day activity. Street vendors, waving trinkets and other wares, coaxed potential buyers closer to their carts. Sparsely clad ladies in skintight outfits cut three-quarters above the knees, stood on street corners negotiating a different catch with the tourists, who, hours before, had been fishing on the lake.

Chewing on the smoldering cigar, Scorpion ran through what he knew. Jourdan would deliver the guarantee and Charif would cough up the cash. Danny Lee Boyd would build the resort he designed months earlier on the Pacific Coast. It was time to look west.

Initiating Fer-de-Lance would abruptly end Jabhat al-Mahdi's expansion in Mexico. Shame, he thought—a few more tens of millions before corking the bottle would have been like taking candy from a baby. He chose the name Fer-de-Lance for the deadly pit viper. Like Scorpion himself, excitable and unpredictable when disturbed, the most venomous snake in Mexico could move quickly to flee danger, but could also make a sudden reversal to defend itself. Fer-de-Lance would rid the country of all remnants of the Jabhat al-Mahdi. Black Stone soldiers would work side-by-side with Mexican military and law enforcement during the eradication process. Despite the bastard's lies, Scorpion would allow President Fuentes to be the hero and drive the assault. If Enrique played his cards right, the U.S. government might even foot the bill, leaving Mexico's military and Scorpion the saviors of Mexico. The U.S. military were right now in the process of neutralizing Mecca II.

At Gregorio's order, Black Stone soldiers would go to work. Similar to Hitler's Night of the Long Knives, bureaucrats, politicians, upper-ranking military and law enforcement officials who took Black Stone money and were associated with the movement would disappear. The depth and breadth of the Operation's reach would force Western Hemisphere leaders to follow Mexico in the fight to destroy the menace once and for all.

Scorpion's motorcade made a right turn into the quarter-mile stretch emptying into the gated entrance of *Los Americanos*. The Federales escort maintained position but muzzled the siren and light show before motoring under the resort's arched entryway. The armed guards waved the vehicles through, closing the gate as the rear cruiser rolled past.

53

Friday 2045; Shadow's Yellow Bird crosses the US Border

Settled back into his seat, Schlonger piloted Shadow's yellow Sikorsky 175 miles per hour flying north out of Mexico. Scharver twisted around in his seat, taking in the mayhem of the overloaded cabin before returning his attention to the task at hand. Maintaining 125 feet above the ground, the altitude remained constant except when crossing above electrical transport lines. Leaning back in the jump seat, Hap watched both Schlonger's and Scharver's heads turn slowly, left then right, as if mounted on swivels. Sighting an obstacle, old habits from flying medevac kicked in as they gently eased around cell towers splayed out like trees in a lush forest. Remaining clear of guide wires, Schlonger maintained a steady platform for Doc to move around the cabin stepping over and around the girls to treat the agents' injuries.

With his back to Hap, Bennie knelt beside Jorge, and pumped up a blood pressure cuff wrapped around the unconscious agent's upper left arm. He'd cut much of the agent's clothes away and what was left was tie-dyed red with his blood. Bennie brought the stethoscope from around his neck and inserted the ear tips, placing the diaphragm on the comatose patient's chest. Hap could tell by Blad's drawn features that Doc was working hard to keep the giant of an agent alive.

Wearing a headset, Blad continued jotting down notes, communicating through a satellite link to God knew where. El Maestro was pinned against the bulkhead by Blad's right boot. Staff Sergeant Lyncher sat next to Blad, a bloodstained scarf covering one eye. Beaux sat next to Hap, his right arm in a sling; on the other side of Beaux, Smitty had his right arm taped snugly to his chest. Smitty had been first to meet the guy with the earring. To hear them tell the story, the man stood between a pissed off Marine and El Maestro. The subsequent melee left Smitty with a separated shoulder and the barrel of Lyncher's M-14 pressed against the man's earring, all of which happened before Hap arrived.

Now the helo dropped with a thud, as if driving over a chug hole, sending grimaces of pain across Jorge's face as the girls huddled and cried out over the whine of the engines. Blad leaned over, yelling into Doc's ear. Cocking his head, Doc replied with a shrug. Hap didn't have to hear Blad's question. He knew.

Rock Carver sat next to Blad, having made it through the fight without a scratch. Sleeping soundly, the young Marine's head had come to rest against Lyncher's broad shoulder on the last bump. The Staff Sergeant let the young Marine sleep. Blood seeped out from beneath Lyncher's saturated bandage and trickled down his forehead. He didn't bother wiping away the blood, allowing it to drip onto his soiled vest. Also asleep was Will Kellogg, across from Hap, snoring as if he was in his own bed and today had just been another day in the park. What made him do what he did, Hap wondered? Adventure? Certainly not money. Boredom? Or, the creed Hap lived by: doing what is right despite risk and consequence?

Hap knew Will had spent years as a Force Recon Marine before the CIA recruited him to do the same work at five times the pay. A decade followed as an independent contractor with a host of clients. He protected coffee products in Columbia for the Coffee Buyers of America, and did a stint for the DIA purchasing Soviet communications hardware taken from overrun Sandinista outposts.

They met at a bar while attending the Marine Corps Ball in New Orleans. Luck or fate, either way, the two became fast friends, business partners, and now brothers in arms, with a common belief in doing what was right and letting the man upstairs sort the bullshit

A headset landed in Hap's lap. Blad gestured to put the headset on, mouthing: You gotta hear this.

Hap donned the headset, and listened to the chatter cross-ing the net. It was clear Shank had arrived at the Alternate LZ, and with a star in his sights, he was not going to let a crisis go to waste. Hap could visualize Shank making a spectacle as the Sikorsky hot pumped for the return trip into Mexico and Los Americanos. U.S. Marshals and FBI had set a secure perimeter around the airfield. Shank controlled access. He allowed cable news vans inside and the regular cast of ho-hum newscasters had set up shop on the tarmac, broadcasting non-stop to the world. Blad had piped in a Shank interview with one of the cable networks, one of dozens he had given, assuring the world that Colonel Ted Shank was in control. He could picture Verbie watching the spectacle on Cable television.

Blad also piped in a recorded Sat call of the President of the United States, crediting Shank with preventing a global crisis. Hap was sure General Verbie was hours from being called in to the Senate Intelligence and Senate Armed Services Committees and a face-to-face with the Chairman of the Joint Chiefs.

Blad peered down at his agent, and then slowly raised his head to look towards Hap. "Looks like Shank rolled out the welcome mat."

"If it wasn't Shank, it would have been somebody else," Hap replied.

"If he has his way, we will be wearing jewelry the moment we land at the Alternate LZ."

"Five minutes out from the hospital, Hap," Schlonger reported. "Running with lights, will light up the bird like a Christmas tree as we cross the border. Hospital has been alerted."

"Understood," Hap replied. Unbuckling, he touched Will's knee, a strong hand clamped down on his, and Will's wild eyes snapped open. Hap tapped Will's pitted cheek holding up five fingers. He fell back towards his seat. Will quieted.

Blad returned his notepad to the side panel of his fatigues, withdrawing each of the nickel-plated .45s. Thumbing the release, the magazine fell into his lap. Replacing the weapon into the shoulder holster, he did the same with the second .45.

"LZ looks clear except for medical personnel," Schlonger said, flying now with the goggles. Scharver called out altitudes as goggles provided no depth perception. Ten feet...three, two, one, wheels on the ground.

Hap and Blad slid open the respective doors, jumping to the ground. The Recon Marines took up positions on either side of Jorge's blood-soaked blankets as Hap helped each of the girls from the bird, keeping them together underneath the rotor arc. A sixth sense kicked in, and as the last girl touched the ground, he came face to face with Carla. She looked as good in a cranial as without. Reaching up with both hands she pulled his face to hers, giving him a big kiss. Although much appreciated, he knew his breath would drop a water buffalo. Seconds passed and she pulled away pursing her lips. She yelled over the idling engines and whirling rotor blades. "All the parents have been contacted and are on the way to the hospital."

Hap watched Carla lead the girls under the rotor arc. Moving rapidly, like a mother goose she hustled her little goslings down the sidewalk towards the emergency room entrance and the waiting arms of the medical staff.

"One, two, three," Doc called out. All lifted the blood-soaked blanket at the same time, inching Jorge's large frame across the cabin deck. "One, two, three," Doc repeated. Only a few feet away, the starboard door seemed yards away. Outside the door, Hap and Will reached in to grab the foot of the makeshift litter. With the help of the hospital staff, they gently strained to transfer Jorge onto the gurney.

Will walked with his arm around Doc's shoulders toward the ER entrance. Yelling into Doc's ear, he patted him on the back, dropping an empty ruck to the deck. Doc moved to the side of the gurney now rolling through the automatic ER doors. Will stopped, knowing he was of no further assistance; he peeled back toward the helo.

Hap signaled for the Recon Marines to exit from underneath the spinning rotors. Each followed the other bent at the waist until clearing the rotor tips. Hap leaned into the cabin, grabbing Lyncher by the cuff, yelling in his ear. "Take your Marines in for medical attention. That's an order, Marine!"

The Staff Sergeant eyed the ground, and his head turned slowly to the team. Turning back toward Hap, his bloodied face drawn, he issued a reluctant nod—Yes, Sir! Hap looked into the Marine Staff NCO's teary eyes. Dried blood now stuck to the stubble on both cheeks. Each shoulder held a slung weapon.

"Safe up those weapons, Marines," Lyncher said. Rock Carver worked his way around the spinning tail rotor and reentered the aircraft from the opposite door.

Lyncher turned slowly, handing Hap an M4 last touched by Slaughter. Hap nodded looking straight into the Marine's eyes. Both knew what the other was thinking, but Hap's order dictated otherwise.

Will pointed at his ruck, "leave the ammo," he shouted.

The Marines peeled off bandoliers and emptied their magazine pouches into the bag. More than a few grenades came to rest into the top of the ruck.

"Now the pistols," Will said next.

The Marines dropped their spare 9mm magazines into the bag. As they unholstered their Beretta 9mms, each dropped the magazine before clearing the chamber, ejecting a single round onto the ground. Hap reached down and placed the three 9mm magazines into his pocket.

"You going to get the Rock out of the bird or am I?" Hap asked.

"Something tells me he's not going to obey any of our orders regarding standing down now," Lyncher said.

Will laughed. "Why would he, Hap? All he has looking in front of him is life in Leavenworth with hard labor."

Hap pursed his lips. He reached down and picked up the bag. "Let's go get some gas, Will."

Blad jogged up the sidewalk yelling into his cell phone with the Medic in tow, ducking underneath the rotors. Stepping in, they joined Will, Rock Carver, Hap, and El Maestro. Sliding the door closed behind him, Blad returned a reassuring look and a thumbs-up after buckling in. A bang on the door followed. Blad cracked the door back and two small hands clutched the edge of the door pushing it open. Carla planted her ass, sliding over the bloody cabin floor. Realizing there was no way she'd vacate, Hap gestured to Blad to pull the door closed.

Putting on his headset, he squeezed the ICS trigger. "Northeast side of the airfield, there will be a fuel truck. Shank has every fuel stop within 100 miles under lock and key. I had an agent entice a driver to move to the northeast side after the sun set. Let's go."

"Roger that," Schlonger replied. The S-76 conducted a no-hover takeoff, the nose ducking for a few moments before Schlonger fed in left cyclic and pedal until the nose pointed toward the rotating beacon located at the airfield. White flash followed green flash as the beacon spun slowly, directing traffic towards the airfield.

"I have IR sticks on the northeast side of the field," Blad said. "That's the fueling point. Let Scharver gas the bird."

"Roger that," Schlonger said. All the activity was occurring on the southwest side of the airfield. It was lit up like a county fair with all the news outlets illuminating the tarmac. "Damn it, Hap. They have the Marines under armed guard behind concertina wire lit up as if they were going to try to escape."

Hap knew Hancock was already working with some of the best defense lawyers in the country. He would join them soon enough, but there was more work to be done this night. If he had his way, those responsible for the past few days were going to get payback with dividends. Many had paid with their lives, Shadow Services had El Maestro, but the brains behind this crap still ran free. Placing his hands on Carla's shoulders, Hap nuzzled her as she sat between his knees for the short ride to the Alternate LZ.

* * *

The moment Schlonger touched the wheels to the ground, Hap, Will, and Blad followed Scharver under the spinning rotors. Breaking away, Scharver grabbed the fuel nozzle stretched out to the edge of the box outlined by IR sticks. Hap watched Jeff pull the nozzle under the rotor arch as two sets of headlights approached from the other side of the field. The vehicle's high-mounted headlights were unmistakably U.S. issued Humvees. Chasing two hundred yards in trail were two additional sets of headlights.

Blad looked at Hap. "It's Shank. We're not going to be able to lift off in time. "

"What took them so long?"

"One of my agents had a van mocked up as a news van. When we launched from the hospital, he had Shank in front of a camera that didn't work, and a Mr. Microphone. Couldn't last forever though."

The vehicles, two military, and two civilian screeched to a stop in line, their headlights cast the entire scene in bright lights.

The three men covered their eyes and turned away from the blinding light, but not before Hap identified a figure with gangly legs atop a pigeon-toed gait. Eight men in civilian dress with dark windbreakers followed close behind, deploying on line.

"LtCol Stoner," Shank called out. "These U.S. Marshals and FBI agents will relieve you and your men's weapons."

"Colonel Shank," Hap said. "How nice to see you." A news helicopter circled overhead providing additional light.

Blad chimed in, "Evening, Colonel."

Shank tilted his head off to the side. "I thought that was you, Blad. It's been a while. You should choose who you run with more wisely. Your weapons, gentlemen."

Slightly turned to avoid the lights' glare, Hap saw Scharver drop the nozzle beside the Sikorsky's back tire and walk around the front of the aircraft.

Hap took the cue, nudging Blad. "We will be departing now."

"Not so fast, LtCol Stoner. I have been ordered to take you and your party into custody." Shank slowly un-holstered the military issue Beretta 9mm from his right hip. "You'll never know how much this pleases me—to throw you and the rest of your law-breaking scum into chains."

A figure darted from behind, stopping midway between Shank and the three warriors. Digital cameras were rolling, overhead and off to the side. All eyes went to the figure standing alone like the Statue of Liberty.

"Would you go so far as to shoot a woman, Colonel Shank?" Carla asked, in a raised voice. Shank did not have a chance to reply.

Rock Carver barked, "Drop your weapons—now!" Approaching from the back of the chopper, he advanced with short jerky steps. Following in trace, mimicking Rock's movement, Doc moved the barrel of his M4, dancing the night-sight laser from one silhouette to the other.

Blad filled both hands with unloaded .45 caliber pistols, while Will and Hap unslung their weapons, drawing a bead on Shank. Shank immediately lowered his pistol, folding a weak hand. The sidearm slid from his index finger to the ground. Slowly stepping back towards the waiting vehicles, his eyes went from Hap to the barrel of Rock's M4. Shank's deputies dropped their weapons, backpedaling without argument.

Carla walked forward seductively in her bulldogging alligators and bent over with a certain flair to retrieve the weapon. Using her ring finger, she depressed the button, dropping the magazine into her hand and then inserting it into her cleavage, leaving the ball ammo visible. When she jacked back the bolt, the round in the chamber flipped to the ground. She used her forefinger to depress the release sending the bolt home.

Hap nodded with a smile.

Keeping both .45's pointed at the aggressors, Blad said, "Impressive, Hap." He reached into his pocket and reinserted the magazines in both pistols. He looked at Hap and shrugged.

Carla moved deliberately to the spot where the agent farthest to the left had abandoned his weapon. Inserting the magazine into her tight blue jean pocket, she ensured the weapon was safe before letting it slide next to Shank's weapon dangling on her index finger. Doc walked over to her, carrying the ruck that held the Recon Marines' magazines and bandoliers. Rock joined them with the other pistol and magazines. Retrograding back to the waiting helo, Hap was last to board.

Carla stood motionless staring at Colonel Shank and the men who were beginning to congregate around him. She turned as the helo lifted into darkness.

She tipped her head and said, "Go get 'em, Hap," as two agents clasped her arms from behind. The smaller of the two began speaking. She understood what the female voice was quoting through the whir of the helicopter's fading sounds. The agent was reading Carla her Miranda rights.

54

Friday 2100; Flight Line, Colonel Shank

Stepping out of the car, eyeing the scuff on the toe of his spit-polished combat boot, Colonel Ted Shank wanted butt. Frustrated to no end, he looked up and down the line, then back to the cage. He was enraged that Hap Stoner and his renegades had taken off just minutes before with the help of some curvy, cowboy-booted female desperado who kept Shank at gunpoint while news-cams rolled! He wanted everyone on this airfield to understand who was in charge.

At least the girl was in cuffs, and as he was contemplating how to get Stoner, he found himself staring up at the whirling rotors and quickening turbines of two Cobras flaring at the far end of the line. Almost simultaneously, a rotating beacon and the noise of a Citation's turbofans throttling down caught his attention. He homed in on the Citation just as the pilot cut engines to flare the aircraft's nose an instant before the main gear squeaked onto the runway.

"Major Smith!" Shank barked. "What are those two Cobras doing and who the hell just landed? Did somebody miss my meaning? Nothing in, nothing out!"

The group's maintenance officer trotting towards the arm/de-arm area with four U.S. Marshals in tow stopped dead in his tracks. "Last two Cobras are going through de-arm, Colonel. Have no fucking idea who the plane that just landed is. And Cobra's Hueys are on the line. Outside the Phrog hard down outside of CONUS, all birds accounted for.

"Have the Cobras shut down after de-arm and take the treasonous bastards into custody. And, for Christ sakes, secure this airfield. No traffic in or out unless I authorize it. Understood?" Ducking back into the car, he tapped the driver on the shoulder. "Drive over to the Hueys."

"Which ones are Hueys, Sir?" the private asked.

Shank rested the weight of one arm heavily across the young Marine's right shoulder. "For Christ sakes, son, the two helos with the flashing brights, straight ahead."

"Got it, Sir. Sorry. Graduated from boot camp three weeks ago, Sir. Waiting for 'A' School." Dropping the shift to drive, the young Marine accelerated in the direction Shank had pointed. Parked F-18's, and a H-46 Cobras, winged past the Hummer's windows.

Federal authorities looking to get their faces and opinions on the cable networks gathered along with reporters around the helos and Hornets, bee lining for those aircraft showing the most dramatic battle damage. U.S. Military aircraft, now parked inside the U.S., with holes very recently punched through their airframes by enemy combatants, counted as breaking news. Portable light towers supplied by the cable networks and the U.S. taxpayer lit up the line like a Fat Tuesday parade after sundown.

Colonel Shank nodded to himself, vowing to turn this lump of coal into a star.

The Hummer skidded to a stop out front, midway between the two Hueys' rotor arcs. Shank saw the pilots of both Hueys reach up with their left hands to pull down their respective rotor brake handles. Shank hit the tarmac while the rotors still turned. Dipping below the drooping blades, he stopped in front of the pilot's door of the port side Huey. U.S. Marshals walked in behind as the hub groaned to a stop. Stepping between the pilot's door and Shank, the crew chief palmed his military issued 9-mm, shoulder-holster snug under his left armpit. Reaching forward, Shank rested his hand on the door handle.

The pilot lowered his head, slowly loosening the strap on the form-fitted helmet with flipped-up goggles. "Evening, Colonel," Big Alabama said, speaking through the open window. "You missed one hell of a night," he said, winking as he turned to the over-stimulated crew chief. "Foxie. Stand down. You're one hell of a Marine, son."

The crew chief stepped back, as the pilot removed the goggles from the helmet mount, letting the unit rest around his neck. Swinging out of the cockpit, Big Alabama touched his unpolished flight boot to the tarmac. Shank moved to the side as the major fell back, resting his ass on the edge of the cabin. Slowly removing the helmet he reached back, letting it rest on the jump seat, center aft of the pilot and copilot seat.

"You are under arrest, Major," Shank said. "These Marshals will relieve you of your sidearm." Shank would take no chances with this one.

The Big Alabaman had earned his reputation on both coasts and on every airbase in between. Big Alabama would hang upside down like a bat from the ceiling at Davis-Monthan AFB Officers Club, displaying camaraderie while chugging beers with A-10 pilots. Or, he would throw rabbit punches into some poor soul's face who was screwing with a Nomad. It just didn't matter.

Shank knew what had happened at the officers' party at the Squadron GP tent in Jubail, Saudi Arabia. In the unit's Marine Corps lore, the "Flail at Jubail" was legendary. RAF pilots, under the influence of spirits, heard that the Nomads had invited many of the nurses from the British hospital to their mixer. The Brits' point of agitation reached its peak upon hearing the line used to ensnare the lovely ladies: "The Ghost of Elvis was in country visiting U.S. Military personnel and would be in attendance." Along with Elvis, free booze and all the steak and potatoes the lovelies could throw down would be available. Barging into the tent, a British Squadron Leader with the best of intentions demanded the nurses leave the Yanks and join their party.

What followed became another legendary Big Alabama story. With one of his Elvis sideburns peeled off, and his Elvis wig tilted halfway off his round head, Big Alabama challenged the jet puke. As the story goes, confused looks splayed across the Tommie pilots' faces. Both lenses of Big Alabama's large sunglasses (worn to entertain the ladies) had gone missing. The Tommie pilots relaxed their clenched fists.

To add insult to injury, another Elvis stepped out with a Brit nurse on each arm. One of the nurses sported Elvis's sunglasses and sideburns, while the other had donned the Elvis wig. Big Alabama's missing sideburn was now an improvised moustache worn by the wigged nurse. Like any gentleman, Ambassador excused himself from the ladies, leaving the short blonde his Elvis scarf as a parting gift. The two Nomads would rather have partied with their allies, but instead, reluctantly threw the Brits out of the tent, knowing at least that their fall was cushioned by Saudi sand. Not one of the U.S. allies attempted to reenter.

The party continued until the sun shimmered on the Persian Gulf.

* * *

Shank glanced across the taxiway at a Marine leaping from the back seat of the Cobra. Taking a Taser blast from a U.S. Marshal, the Ambassador of Goodwill went to the ground, quivering for several seconds before going still. Shank would not give the big Huey pilot the same latitude.

"Step out of the aircraft. Stand down and allow yourself to be taken into custody, Major."

Big Alabama pulled out the 9mm tucked below his left shoulder. Tilting his head with a smirk, he ejected the magazine into his lap. Pulling the bolt to the rear, the chambered round clinked across the tarmac. He locked the bolt to the rear. Shank froze as the weapon spiraled lazily in the air. One of the Marshals reached out to catch the pistol by the grip just before it creased the bridge of Shank's prominent nose.

Big Alabama stepped onto the front boot-rest on the skid. Slowly turning, he said, "No disrespect to the Marshals or yourself, Colonel, but you can kiss my ass."

"Take him down," Shank barked, stepping back quickly. Both Marshals discharged their M-26 Tasers. Big Alabama fell like a sack of rocks, flailing his arms and legs against the tarmac. He would wake up inside the wired compound a half hour later with bloodied knuckles and surrounded by fellow Warriors.

The Marshals led Staff Sergeant Fox, aka Foxie, away with hands cuffed tightly behind his back. Refusing to remove his vest or body armor, the Marine Air Crewman walked erect, eyes front, as U.S. Marshals clutched his forearms leading him to the cage. 'Uuuurah's' erupted from inside the barbed wire as the Warriors welcomed another comrade in arms.

Shank eased into the Hummer as three silhouetted figures approached. He couldn't help but notice the swinging hips and cowboy boots on one of them. *I thought the bitch was cuffed and hauled away an hour ago.*

Two ladies with brief cases strolled by Carla's side.

Thirty feet from the Hummer, Carla spoke. "Colonel Shank. Can I have a minute of your time?"

Shank rested one boot inside the Hummer. "You have exactly one minute."

As they closed the distance, he thought the tallest of three looked familiar. The woman was striking even in the shadows: tall, shapely, with a full mane of dark hair. Only one woman like that would have the balls to walk on his flight line.

She held out her hand. "Colonel Shank. It's been awhile."

Not bothering to return the gesture, he looked around for law enforcement. Spanky passed by handcuffed, making his walk of shame with the other cuffed pilots of his section.

"Good morning, MC," Spanky called out. "H.D. missed one hell of a show today."

MC turned, tossing her hair close to Shank's face. "Spanky," she called out. "Excuse me, Colonel," she said, walking toward her dead husband's good friend.

Shank took the opportunity to duck into the Hummer and roll up his window. Carla moved swiftly around the Hummer sliding in through the other passenger door.

Shank looked over, both sides of his narrow mouth turned down, lips quivering in anger. Patting the driver on the shoulder, he said, "Transmitter, Private."

Confused about who was in charge, the young, impression-able PFC held up the mic. Only after a nod and wink from Carla, did he reach back, nervously handing it back to Shank. Shank keyed the mic, "Operations, this is Colonel Shank. Can you get some law enforcement over to the Hueys? The perimeter has been breached."

"Roger, Colonel," came the reply. "Number and description."

"Three ladies. Be quick."

Carla chimed in, "It's not going to be that easy, Colonel. The Luna County Sheriff is on his way with the County's entire complement of Sheriff's Deputies."

Shank gave his best pissed-off-Colonel look, hoping she would notice. His brow tensed as his narrow jaw tightened. His bony right hand clutched the bill of the Marine Corps utility cover sporting an Eagle rank insignia, as he scratched the top of his thinning hairline.

"Between the Marines, U.S. Marshals Office and FBI, Carla, I believe we have the situation well in hand. If you haven't forgotten, your Miranda rights have already been read to you."

"The County authorities own this matter and the State Department of Public safety is en route," Carla retorted.

"So what in hell is MC doing here?" Shank snapped back.

"Major Hancock requested that her law firm represent the Marines. Her partner is outside, if you would like to meet her."

"Ahhhhh, Major Hancock. I will have him in custody in due time."

"You better have wings, Colonel Shank," she replied.

Shank watched a corporate jet accelerate, rotate its nose, and lift off the runway. "So I am to assume that this is Major Hancock?"

"You are very perceptive, Colonel. Now, will you please let us inside the concertina wire to begin interviewing our clients?"

Shank gave pause as four US Marshals trotted up, stopping outside the vehicle. Rolling down the tinted bulletproof window, he looked out at what could have been the starting four for the Dallas Cowboys. Looking back to his guest he said, "I believe your escort has arrived."

"Where do you want them, Colonel?" one of the Marshals asked.

Looking back towards the Marshals, he said, "Get them the hell out of my perimeter."

Carla's door opened and an arm reached in and pulled her from the car. One of the Marshals had MC's partner in tow. The remaining two Marshals walked swiftly to break up the reunion between MC, Spanky, and his flight.

Colonel Shank pressed speed dial for Senator Jourdan's cell phone, but the call went to voice mail.

55

Friday 2100; Crossing the US/MX Border

The yellow Sikorsky crossed into Mexico with five pissed off passengers. The 440-mile journey left little margin for a navigational boo-boo; even travelling as the crow flies; they would be running on fumes and a prayer when landing.

Boarding the aircraft at Columbus, New Mexico, Rock Carver tried to explain to Hap why they called the yellow helo 'Mayo.' Hap stopped him. No need, Mayo was a Marine Lieutenant killed in a flying accident years earlier. Although in different Squadrons, Hap had shared a bunch of beers with Mayo, rolling bones across more O'Club bars than he cared to count. Good son of a bitch, Hap said to himself. Only Marine Aviator he knew who was a member of the 'Mile High Club,' as well as a distinguished member of the 'Simulated Mile High Club.' Hap grinned at the thought as the Mayo streaked lights out into Mexico.

Hap knew whose blood belonged to the rifle-resting barrel between his legs. It carried the marks of the previous day's firefight, streaked on both sides of the weapons stock and hand guard in Sergeant Slaughter's blood. Reaching between Will's legs, Hap pulled the bulging flight bag into his lap. He flipped the snaps of the blood-soaked vest to exchange AK mags for M4 magazines. His fingers found a couple of grenades and attached the explosive pineapples to his vest.

Rock hooked his bloodied combat boot inside the bag's handle and slid the bag across the deck to peruse the ammo smorgasbord.

Blad, passed glossies between Rock, seated next to him and Doc relaxing comfortably across the cabin. "Refresh your memories, "Blad said over the intercom. With any luck, you'll see some of them before the sun rise."

Hap retrieved a trifold pamphlet advertising Los Americanos amenities resting between his flight boots. He grabbed a couple of 8 x 10's from Will with his other hand barely able to make out the illustrations with the dim lighting. Blad removed a poncho liner and tactical flashlight from his flight bag. He flipped the items one at a time into Rock's lap. Rock pulled the liner over his head as the lights of El Paso and Juarez passed by the Mayo's port side windows.

56

Friday 2315; Biggs Army Airfield; Ready Alert Shack,
El Paso TX

Reluctantly, Captain Slam Jackson tossed the only heart in his hand onto the queen lying on top of the other two hearts. With a case of Shiner Premium resting center on the card table, Captain Jackson knew he would be the lucky buyer. With one hour remaining of their 24-hour shift, the crews continued to maintain a fifteen-minute alert status. Both MH-6's parked outside the Quonset hut were fueled and armed. Being part of the 160th Special Operations Aviation Regiment (Airborne), their Company was in the middle of a 30-day training exercise, flying and shooting at night, high speeds, low level, and on short notice.

WO3 Chuckie Schmidt laughed. "Way to cover my queen with your cowboy, Slammer."

Captain Jackson grinned, cutting his gaze across the card table to his wingman. "I take it your queen was dry."

Schmidt's eyebrows raised. "I will never kiss and tell, Skipper. Maybe it was just intuition."

Jackson rolled his eyes just as the duty desk BAT phone rang. "You are a son of a bitch, Chuckie." Leaning over he removed the old black handset from the cradle on the third ring. "Captain Jackson."

He could hear the anxiety and sense of urgency in the female voice on the other end of the line. "You are cleared to launch immediately, Captain. Urgent mission. Contact Sky Hawk on Button Green departing tower frequency. Repeat, call sign Sky Hawk. Heading 170 degrees to I-10 and parallel southeast."

Jackson nodded, writing feverishly. The others placed their cards face down on the table, slipping on the safety vests hanging on the back of the chairs. Hanging up the phone, he scanned his scribbles, shaking his head.

"Okay, gents, we are on," Captain Jackson said.

"What's up, Skipper?" Schmidt asked. "You got 'trouble' written all over your face."

"That obvious?" Jackson said, slipping on his vest. Both pilots and their co-pilots stood, zipped up vests, and pulled the torso straps through their legs to connect in front

"If I didn't know better, I'd guess we'll be ordered to cross the border."

"Button Green on the tactical freq." Jackson walked over to a 4-drawer filing cabinet behind the duty desk and pulled out two maps, flipping one to Schmidt. Pawing through another drawer he picked out two more, and tossed one to Schmidt's co-pilot. "Let's go," he said, leading the flight out of the shack to the waiting birds.

Scanning the airfield, the Captain didn't feel right about this mission. There was something going on. The entire airfield's runway and taxi lights were low, plus the hangar doors closed, outside lights secured, and there were no flight line personnel walking the line, and no vehicular traffic. This was unheard of for stateside deployments. But, he wasn't complaining. It made taking off goggled up a hell of a lot easier.

"Slammer 23, cleared to switch Sky Hawk," the tower operator said.

"Roger tower. Slammer flight, go green," Jackson replied across the tower freq. "Go green," Jackson said to his co-pilot.

"Good to go," the co-pilot replied extending his right arm with a thumbs- up for Jackson to see.

"Sky Hawk, Slammer 23 is with you with two killer eggs. Southeast bound at the intersection of 375 and I-10."

"Roger, Slammer 23. Radar contact, fly heading 155 degrees."

"Roger, Sky Hawk," Jackson said, dipping the rotors right to pick up a more southerly heading. Through goggles, Jackson and his copilot exchanged a tense look before shaking their heads. "How long do you want us to remain flying last assigned, Sky Hawk?"

Silence followed except for the whine of the lone turboshaft power plant and six blades cutting air just above their heads.

"Sky Hawk. Do you copy?" Jackson repeated.

"Until advised otherwise, you are to cross the border. We have you on an intercept course. Your target is a yellow rotary wing aircraft south of your position. The aircraft is hostile. You are directed to take down this aircraft."

The Rio Grande passed out of sight. "Copy. Where is authorization for this direction coming from?"

Another voice broke in on the conversation. Whoever it was spoke in a no nonsense kind of way. "Captain, are you disobeying a direct order?"

"Copy, Sky Hawk. For the record, I'm following this order, but in dispute. Do you copy, Sky Hawk?"

"Just fly the mission, Captain. The aircraft is chock full of known terrorists. The aircraft is at your four o'clock and twenty miles. Time to intercept, five minutes."

Jackson ground his upper and lowers together.

"Slammer, Chuckie on squadron common."

"Go ahead Chuckie," Jackson said.

"This stinks, Captain. Nothing on the board and the only thing on cable news is that ruckus west of El Paso. The bird I saw departing Columbus on TV was piss yellow."

"That would be our terrorist, Chuckie."

"Bull shit, Captain. We are being asked to become assassins."

"Slammer 23, your target is one o'clock and two miles."

"Tally ho," Captain Jackson replied.

"Target in sight," Chuckie chimed speaking on squadron common. "Damn it, Slammer. Look at this guy. He's flying about as straight and level as an aircraft taking a trip can go."

"He doesn't have any lights on, Chuckie."

"Yes, Sir, but neither do we."

Jackson, torn between a direct order and his gut and wingman asked, "What the fuck is going on?"

"Chuckie, I will take the target six o'clock. Hook 'em to the north."

Jackson watched Chuckie stand the bird on the left rotor, peeling off to the north.

"Captain!" Chuckie shouted. "Are you sure?"

"Commencing attack, Sky Hawk," Jackson transmitted.

"Understood, Slammer. Commencing attack," the man who had interrupted their conversation earlier said.

"Let's go hot," Jackson said to his copilot. The copilot flipped the arming switch on the console extending another thumbs-up.

"Captain?!" Chuckie cried, his urgency-level 50 decibels higher than the previous transmission.

"Screw it," Jackson said. "Go guard now." He waited for the thumbs-up. "Putrid yellow Sikorsky, you have been intercepted. State your intentions." Silence followed. They were travelling over an inhabited area. Jackson raised the nose slightly to gain altitude and let loose with a short burst from his minigun ensuring the rounds would pass to the targets starboard killing only rattlesnakes. Tracers arced across a dark Mexican sky.

The yellow bird broke hard left entering the trap. With nowhere to go, the target was dead meat with Chuckie closing from the north. Jackson entered a climbing left yo-yo and began the path down the chute aiming at the helo's glowing exhaust.

"Aircraft shooting up northern Mexico, you are firing on U.S. Marines. Call sign Nomad."

"Captain," Chuckie said over the squadron freq.

Jackson knew of the Nomads, having thrown back beers with several of them over the years. He knew the Marine at the controls of the yellow bird. "Schlonger! What in the hell is going on?"

"Slammer, I thought that was you. You still owe me money from that last dice game in Tyndall."

The firm voice from Sky Hawk broke in on the tactical frequency. Jackson knew whoever Sky Hawk was had been listening to the call over the Guard frequency.

"Slammer 23, I order you to blow the target out of the sky."

Jackson shook his head. Whatever the Nomads were up to, they didn't need to be shot down by the U.S. Government. These sons of bitches deserved a medal. "Slammer flight. Abort, Abort, Abort," Jackson said over the squadron freq., attempting to put Sky Hawk off for as long as possible. The yellow helo broke hard right continuing the turn until picking up a southeastly heading.

"Join on me, Chuckie. Let's go home."

57

Friday 2330; Inside Mayo Cockpit

A steady stream of 7.62 tracers blew past Mayo's starboard quarter coming from their six. "Break left, Scharver," Schlonger said, cool as a cucumber.

Jeff Scharver, Shadow's pilot, had already initiated a diving left turn before Schlonger spit out the first syllable. "Little late on the call aren't you, Schlonger," Scharver said, flashing a wide grin. "Need eyes on the shooter."

"Clear left," Schlonger said without hesitation. "Bogey ten o'clock going to twelve same altitude."

"Tally ho," Scharver said continuing the dive. "Maybe I can padlock this fool. Need to know where his buddy is, gents. Get on it."

Throwing in with the crew, Hap's eyes darted left, right, up, and down scanning the starboard windows' 150-degree field of view.

"No joy port side," Blad reported, pushing to the deck the prisoner who ended up in his lap on the last maneuver. "Will somebody buckle these fuckers into their seats?"

"No joy starboard side," Hap parroted. Scharver's initial maneuver proved that Schlonger had an experienced combat helo pilot next to him. Not only did he break azimuth with the hard turn left, he had the Mayo break plane, initiating the hard dive for the deck.

Mayo's sudden turn garnered the attention of everybody in the cabin. Hap watched the tracer fire fizzle out over Scharver's right shoulder. A second burst melted into the stars. The moment Mayo snapped wings level, Will released his seatbelt, repositioning into the empty seat across from Hap. Quickly locking the seatbelt in place, he pulled back the charging handle on the M4, sliding the barrel across his left knee. Firmly clutching the pistol grip, the veteran warrior's right thumb rested on the safety, prepared to shoot it out.

Hap knew the pilot had shot across the Mayo's proverbial bow. Whoever it was, even on his worst day, could have blown the Mayo out of the sky. He sank down in his seat, extending his right leg to kick Will's boot. Turning away from the window, Will locked eyes with Hap's bloodshot eyes. Palm facing outward, Hap's hand ran up and down in front of his face. Will's chin turned ever so slightly, returning a questioning nod. Hap followed with a long nod and-up. Having listened to the inter-flight radio communications, Slammer Jackson had a conscience and God bless his wingman. Coming out from under the poncho, seemingly oblivious, Rock handed the photos and cloak over to Will.

Listening to Scharver and Schlonger discuss resuming course, Hap, with arms crossed, flipped a thumb towards the cabin roof in response to Will, who gestured he was going beneath the poncho liner. Slammer's flight had not strayed, navigationally speaking, to take potshots at a piss yellow Sikorsky. The Dog Face Pilots had orders, "Shoot to kill!"

Hap glanced at Blad, who was pressing his left hand against the left head pad, while jotting down notes on a scratchpad balanced on his knee. Doc and Rock had fallen asleep. El Maestro lay motionless in the middle of the cabin, sprawled on his belly. Blad had him firmly hogtied, legs and wrist secured in the small of his back. "Damn it," he said, "Thought I told somebody to strap El Scumbag in."

Mayo turned gently right to resume course towards Los Americanos. Will popped out from underneath the poncho liner like a turtle head from its shell and ran his hand alongside the outside of his right ankle. He pulled out a small sharpening stone housed in a nylon pouch and strapped to the outside of the Ka-Bar sheath. Removing the knife made famous by the Marine Corps, he slowly began working the Ka-Bar's 7-inch carbon steel point blade slowly across the stone. All the time he fixed his steely gaze on El Maestro

Blad's voice came over the ICS. "Ok, Hap. Here is what I know. The Los Americanos Resort is on full alert. Scorpion is on site." Blad ran the flashlight end of his pin alongside the list of notes. "You may find this detail interesting: a certain U.S. Senator is registered and present at the hotel. The despicable son of a bitch is residing in Scorpion's private suite."

Hap wondered what in the hell the head of the Senate Armed Services Committee was doing in Scorpion's private suite. A wide grin splayed across Blad's round face. He cocked his head slightly to the side, as if asking, *Is it beginning to make sense now?*

Returning a dubious look, Hap said. "About as thick as mud."

The space between Blad's thick brows tightened. "Thought I had it all tied together but the Senator is throwing me back to square one."

58

Saturday 0015; Insertion into Rally Point MX

Blad flashed a pair of thick leather gloves, and then tossed them into Hap's lap. He dropped a pair into Bennie's lap, and another into Rock's. Will paused his honing process on the Ka-Bar to reach across the sleeping Rock Carver still clutching the knife and honing stone.

"I'm not a proficient fast roper," Blad said. "We'll drop into the parking lot of a roadside cantina in the middle of nowhere."

"We'll?" Hap said, shaking his head. It was becoming apparent that Blad was planning on going in with them.

Blad grinned, "Something tells me you are going to need all the help you can get. Schlonger, we are going to need a crew chief."

Schlonger worked his way around the copilot's seat, squeezing between Rock and Blad to enter the cabin. Blad rested his hand on the fast rope attachment bar assembly. "You know how to use this?"

"I always flew 'em, Blad. Never was much in doing the James Bond crap."

Blad pulled back the spring-loaded locking pin, swinging the bar left and right. "Swing it out to the 90 degree stop, and the hole you are looking for is right there. Let it go home and we are off to the races."

Schlonger nodded, "Got it."

"After last man is on the deck, swing the bar inside." He pointed to El Maestro head down against the cabin deck. "Shoot this son of a bitch if he even thinks about a fart."

Schlonger looked back at the motionless El Maestro and issued a thumbs-up.

"Five minutes out," Scharver reported.

"Five minutes, Hap," Blad said.

Hap gave Will a kick in the boot, raising five fingers. Will elbowed Rock. Blad reached over, shaking Doc's leg. Hap raised his hand extending five fingers. "Five minutes," he yelled.

Schlonger stood by the cabin door. "One minute. One van in the parking lot." He threw back the door allowing the night air to swirl around the cabin.

Scharver eased back on the cyclic to raise the Mayo's nose, setting a decelerating profile as the airframe descended towards the DZ. As both turbines rapidly decelerated, Schlonger swung the arm out, allowing the spring to push the locking bar into place. Each of the jumpers gave the other a quick once over. Will stepped across El Maestro and was first down the rope. Hap ensured his gloves were snug and then stepped across the hog-tied figure.

Schlonger grabbed Hap's vest, pulling him close, and screaming over the whining engines and rotors, "You know I would go with you if let me, you bastard."

Hap gave a quick nod and a pat to Schlonger's broad shoulder, and then vanished down the rope. Will pulled away from the rope just as Hap began his spiraling descent. The moment his boot touched mother earth, Will inserted the M4's stock into his shoulder scanning the DZ for uninvited guests. Hap spiraled down and landed hard, the shock beginning inside both boots, travelling up both legs, and finally quaking both hip joints. The jolt sent him flying backwards just as Rock's boots passed where Hap's head had been just a second before.

Hap eased onto both elbows and watched Rock move away from the rope, unslinging his M4 and running bent at the waist to the base of a fence. Rock scanned over the five-foot fence then moved to the front of the bar. Doc followed in trace. The scene of blowing dust, trash, and howling turbines was suddenly quiet as the bird lifted up and away.

Hap followed Will through the gate into a beer garden. Will attempted to move stealthily up the rickety stairs, but Hap, frustrated with the squeaking, quickly bounded up. Reaching the top, Hap saw Will go to a knee while directing the barrel of the M4 at a shapely figure standing in the shadows.

The death dot traveled fifteen feet from the EO Tech Laser to the bogey's chest. Will called out over his shoulder to anybody within earshot. "I have something here."

59

Saturday 0020; Rally Point at the Cantina

The rap of boots hitting wooden stairs followed Will's announcement. Hap raised the M4 to his left shoulder, bending to a knee, covering the adjoining door on Will's left flank.

Hap Stoner would always look back to his childhood days with Pop Stoner hunting the East Texas Piney woods. He learned stealth, because a clumsy placement of a foot or swinging an arm on a half-rotten limb would wake a quiet forest. Pop Stoner's rebuke would be an immediate thump to an ear, or, upon returning to the farmhouse, a verbal dressing down. "Son, if you don't care enough about the hunt, don't waste your time or mine." The scenes with Pop Stoner remained vivid to Hap, even while leveling the barrel covering Will's flank.

Blad rushed past, breathing hard, stopping in front of the target. Will's death dot remained rock steady between Blad's shoulder blades. Hap looked out of the corner of his right eye to see Blad light a cigarette held in the figure's left hand. The light from the Zippo revealed a female dressed in black pants and long white blouse fitted to show every curve. Hap could just make out a red sash hanging loosely around her waist before the lighter snapped shut.

"Showers are down the stairs to the left," she said. Her accent sounded Puerto Rican to Hap. "Employee uniforms are on the table next to the shower. Let's move, gentlemen, you have a ride to catch."

"Glad you made it," Blad said. "Things were getting a little hairy at the river."

The double doors joining the cantina to the porch swung open and Rock Carver's chest appeared in Hap's scope. Will drew his 9mm Beretta, cocking the hammer, pressing it near the startled Marine's forehead. Hap raised the M4's barrel towards the porch ceiling, placing the weapon on safe.

Will's thumb rode the hammer home before holstering. "Gentlemen, besides the old Ford van parked out front, we are it. Doc is keeping watch out front."

"Roger that, Corporal," Hap said.

The female strutted, grabbing the Recon Marine by the ear. "Beat feet down the steps and the shower is to the left," she said. "Clothes are on the table next to the shower. Find something that fits."

Will nodded. "Checked out the place, saw the clothes but didn't see anything else but an old water hose."

"That's your shower," the Shadow agent said. "This isn't New York."

"Get a move on, Corporal," Hap said, motioning his head towards the steps.

"Yes, Sir," Carver said, bounding down the steps.

"Gentlemen," Blad said, "if you care to join me, I believe it's time for a little toast."

Hap followed Blad into the cantina, and asked himself what kind of organization Blad was running. The agents he had the privilege of meeting had been beaten and shot. Between the two, there had been no complaining, and now, here was the Puerto Rican beauty.

Striding behind the bar, Blad eyed the stock, stopping in front of several bottles of tequila. He turned to the men, the fingers of one hand extended into the open ends of four shot glasses. Like a Third World dictator, he raised a half-empty bottle of tequila above his head then poured the Don Julio Real. "The best the house has to offer."

Picking up a glass, Hap looked around the bar as if looking for Mama Stoner. "Speaking of the host, where is the owner?" he asked.

Blad's agent grabbed a shot glass. "Son of a bitch is a Black Stone sympathizer, or should I say was." She threw back and drained her glass in the blink of an eye. Returning the glass to the table, she walked over to the light switch to the left of the screen doors that opened to the porch. Flipping the switches with the tips of her fingers, she turned. "From what I can tell, the proprietor had trouble catching his breath and expired. Turns out he was the Caliph's younger brother."

Hap couldn't take his eyes off the knockout agent—worthy of a Playboy centerfold—with ebony eyes that matched her dark mane of hair. She vanished through a door adjacent to the bar, a Glock .40-caliber seductively strapped to her right hip.

"Next," Rock called out, swinging open the double screen doors. "Water is frigging great. Where are the towels?"

She reappeared carrying an armful of bar towels. She dropped one at the Marine's feet. "Water appears to be cold."

Rock's face flushed pink, his hands dropped to cover the shrinkage. She vanished through the screen doors to marry the towels with the uniforms.

"Can't a man get some privacy around here?" he moaned.

"I'm next," Will said, bounding through the screen doors. "I want her to see a real man naked!"

Hap and Blad followed, stopping on the porch.

Will blew by the agent, taking the stairs three per stride. She turned ever so slowly, her elbows resting on top of the rickety rail, her back to her new admirer. Rock walked sheepishly down the stairs, wearing the bar towel like a fig leaf. Will stripped as if performing in a cabaret. Diplomatically dropping his weapons to the side, the vest, and armor formed another pile. A stubborn combat boot had him feverishly hopping around on one foot. Adorned in his baby ensemble, Will stepped underneath the hose held overhead in one hand while the other hand lathered his muscular frame.

"Miss, can you help me with my back?" he asked.

"That's okay. I have seen better backs on pigs that I roasted on a spit after slitting their throats."

Not giving up, "Those pigs couldn't make you squeal at the top of your lungs. Do you have a name?"

She did a 180 until she was looking at Will in all his glory, her hands on her hips. "The pigs give a short squeal when I make the cut. Give me your number. When I get back from this mission, maybe I will need a long vacation. My birth name is Zaida."

Hap bounded down the steps, passing Rock who was now clad in a black coat, black pants, and red cummerbund over dirty combat boots. "Relieve Doc." Glancing at the boots, Hap's eyes reflected concern.

"Will do, Colonel," Rock replied.

Eyeing the boots, Zaida shrugged. "Missed that one, Boss."

Blad chuckled nervously. "So we store side arms and assault rifles where?

"I brought along laundry bags which will hold all the heavy hardware. We simply store them underneath the cloth on the food cart or drop them inside a laundry cart if one is available."

Will topped the stairs a bit out of sorts, struggling with an outfit a tad tight. Minutes later, Hap followed Will, his jacket threatening to split down the back if he took one more breath. He shrugged.

"James Bond's clothes always fit. What in the hell happened here?"

Zaida laughed a low seductive purr. "So now we know. Jihadi warriors are not as large as Big...Bad...American Marines," she said, smiling. "Our van is outside. As soon as my boss and the medic finish up, we need to roll. We have a party to bash"

Blad walked up, speaking into his Sat Phone, looking as goofy as the others did. His head raised as he wrapped up his conversation.

"So she is not much on picking clothes sizes but one hell of a cook and one of our better agents," he said. "Good news to report. The Mexican President capitulated, allowing Trixie to land and pick up your Assault Team, Will. Trixie will be overhead within the hour."

"Go ahead, Blad," Hap said. "You were about to say something else."

Blad hesitated adjusting his collar. "Funny thing, the Mexican Government ran some of the serial numbers on the weapons used at Scorpion's training facility. Damned if they weren't part of the weapons sold in the Fast and Furious operation. Isn't it a small world?"

60

Saturday 0200; The Road to Los Americanos Resort MX

"Let's get a move on, gents," Hap said, ducking inside the passenger seat. Rock jumped behind the wheel. Zaida reached through the open door grabbing the Recon Marine by the ear, just like a bossy schoolmarm cuffing an unruly student. She guided Rock to the open back seat and then she eased into the driver's seat.

"The area is crawling with Black Stone and Jabhat al-Mahdi operatives," she said. "The owner let us use his van."

Glancing back over his shoulder, Hap watched Rock slowly slide the door forward, looking like a kid who'd just had his candy taken away. Doc eased into the rear seat followed by Blad. Will settled in behind Hap, pushing the door until the latching bar locked.

Turning on to the hard surface road the Mexican Government called an Interstate; Zaida pointed the beat up Ford towards the Los Americanos Hotel and Resort for the twenty-minute ride. Inside the van, conversation was scarce. The V8's leaky exhaust manifold clattered, and wind howled through the open windows, blessedly cancelling out some of the engine's rattle and, more importantly, evacuating exhaust fumes seeping into the van through the firewall.

Hap knew they were all lost in their own thoughts as they approached what they were fairly certain would be another firefight. He figured he'd gleaned enough of the picture to know it stank. Senator Jourdan's presence at a meeting with those of questionable integrity was more than problematic. Blad reported that many of the weapons at the river sold to Black Stone came from none other than the current U.S. Administration. Throw in Shank and U.S. Army helos taking pot shots at the Mayo. Events going back to the cover-up of Warden's disappearance seemed to revolve around one of the most influential men inside the beltway.

The World would be waking up to what some could legitimately call a U.S. invasion of Mexico. General Black Jack Pershing had led a punitive expedition into Mexico almost a century earlier. Unlike that expedition, LtCol Hap Stoner was going to find his guy and kill him.

Since Simmons' rescue at the LP, activity based on Hap's orders over the last twenty-four hours had seen WIA and KIA of the U.S. Marines. Blad's group had taken hits but no deaths. If the bad guys won round one, the good guys gave them a drubbing on the Rio Conchos. He had to ensure the good guys won the rubber match. Overall, and despite tonight's outcome, the story would give Major Hancock the subject matter to write about in his next career. Hap's play-by-play analysis (like any armchair quarterback lazing in a recliner) did not explain why Scorpion would want the might and power of the United States coming down on Black Stone. If all went well, Hap would go face to face with Scorpion and ask him personally.

Blad had reported that employees at the Los Americanos included both Black Stone and Jabhat al-Mahdi operators. Who was who would be anybody's guess, but collateral damage had to remain at a minimum. In the big scheme of things, Jabhat al-Mahdi operatives would depart the resort in time to infect soft targets. Madrassas teaching Wahhabism would continue to spread their toxic doctrine like poison ivy throughout the Americas. Profits from the resorts funded by U.S.-guaranteed loans would bankroll blackjack dealers, security officers, janitors, bellhops, and maids, as the *Hijra* of Muhammad slowly migrated across the continent. The irony of it all remained hidden behind the smiles.

Zaida turned onto a road leading to the resort. Hap remembered fondly nine months earlier when he surprised Carla by kidnapping her moments after a client meeting. The driver delivered a quizzical Carla to Addison Airport, where Hap had the corporate jet waiting in front of Million Air with the APU running. Exiting the limo, she walked straight across the tarmac. Obviously, this was an adventure and she was ready. At the top of the Citation's stairs, she pressed the switch to lift the hatch, lowered the handle securing the door, and entered the cockpit, giving Hap a quick peck on the cheek. She strapped herself into the copilot's seat and ditched her heels, tossing them back into the cabin. She then removed the Pro Pilot Lightweight Headset resting over the yoke. She then fitted the unit over her head, adjusted it to cover her ears, and initiated an intercom check.

"One, two, three ICS check…do you copy, Hap?"

Hap remembered looking across the cockpit at her gorgeous brown eyes and seductive smile. "Loud and clear, Toots," he said.

"Ready one, Hap."

He initiated the starting sequence, which was followed by golf, world-class bass fishing, and a dozen restaurants from which to choose. Then came the massages, haircut, nails, twenty-four hours of nightclubbing. Los Americanos never slept.

Now, still ten miles away, the resort lit up the night sky. The two-lane road was superior to the highway that Zaida left behind at their last turn. Minutes later, she wheeled into the employee entrance. Recognizing the van by its rumble, the two guards kept their AR–15s slung low and waved Zaida on without a second look. Too easy, Hap thought, or was this woman that good?

Thinking back to his visit with Carla, the indicators were present. There was no bacon on the menu. When he asked for ham the waiter replied, "There is no pork served here, Sir." Hap had just shrugged it off then and ordered beef fajitas to go with his three over easy and short stack. Based on the large parking lot filled to capacity and few vacant seats in the restaurants and the casino, the absence of pork from the menu didn't hurt bookings. The hotel had a five-star rating and Peg had to make their peak season reservations two months in advance. Clearly, Los Americanos was a cover for something more sinister. Depending on your source, some said World War III had started. Civilians of all nations continued to die all over the world, the U.S. Military buried their dead lost in the fight against terror, and the Veterans Administration continued giving the wounded half-assed care. Life went on for most in the grand old U.S. of A.

Zaida guided the van into the service roundabout. The area was a beehive of activity and no one gave them a second glance. Four 18-wheelers backed up against the loading dock. Forklifts vanished into the trailers, reappearing in seconds with full pallets. She parked the van to the side as men dropped bundles of linens wrapped in plastic into large hampers on wheels. Zaida killed the engine.

"Give me a minute," she said stepping out. Moments later, she returned. "Let's go. Exit right."

Hap, Will, and Blad were first, followed by Doc and Rock. Men working on the loading dock vanished. They found Zaida standing over the hamper, both arms locked around packaged linens and one hand clutching a wad of twenty-dollar bills. She gestured with her head toward the half-filled carrier. The five men quickly dropped body armor, rifles, side arms, and the bag of additional weapons retrieved at the Alternate LZ into the carrier.

"Old man," Zaida said, eyeing Will. "You push the cart up the access way. We will meet you at the top."

"Excuse me, young lady."

"Let's get a move on, Will Kellogg," she replied with a head gesture. Amused by her boldness, Will cocked his head, and pushed the cart up the ramp. Hap led the rest of the team trailing Zaida. She guided them into the warehouse through a side door.

"Quickly," she said pointing towards doors to their front. "The service elevator to the executive suites is in the kitchen through those double doors. Look like you belong. Stay close."

As they entered the kitchen, a handful of employees glanced their way, zeroing in on the worn combat boots. Zaida greeted and joked with the few employees they passed as if she owned the establishment. Several employees acknowledged Zaida with a different name and she answered in rapid Spanish.

Hap and the team followed her along an aisle lined with polished commercial kitchen appliances. Rock pushed the cart stuffed with the long rifles and vests from the back. A chef hovered over a room service cart being readied with various covered dishes and a vase of roses. Zaida walked up to the pudgy man wearing a tall white hat. She spoke to him in sharp-toned Spanish. "Gregoria Moya wants room service now."

The chef, who obviously enjoyed eating his creations shook his head rapidly and blurted back in rapid Spanish. "This tray was for Room 645."

Refusing to take "no" for an answer, Zaida nudged the chef aside, pushing the cart to the kitchen's service elevator. On the way, she lifted an expensive-looking bottle of cabernet from a counter, and set it next to the roses on the cart.

Hap grabbed the chef by the collar, hissing in his ear "Ssshhhhh. Vamos."

Hap pushed the frightened chef into the service elevator joining the others along with the two carts. Zaida pointed to the small panel. "Acceso de codigo a la Gregorio suite... pronto." The chef hesitated. Hap pulled his Belgium Hi Power from beneath his red vest and pressed its muzzle into the soft flesh of the man's third chin.

"Sit," he said, gesturing sharply to the floor.

The chef slid awkwardly down, filling one corner, where, shaking uncontrollably he choked out numbers in broken English: "47983."

Will entered the code, the doors shut, and the car began its smooth, fast ride upward. Hap reached down, patting the chef on one of his rounded cheeks. "You are doing fine. *Stay or I'll shoot your head off!*"

When the elevator reached the top floor, Hap locked the doors open. The vigilance level of Los Americanos' security force would determine how much time they had before all hell broke loose. So far so good, Hap thought.

Reading suite numbers on the wall, Zaida gestured they should move right to find the two suites, one occupied by Scorpion and the other by Senator Jourdan and companion. She pushed the cart into the hall, with Hap and Doc close behind single file. Blad and Will loitered with Rock and the weapons cache to cover the rear.

As she approached the next corner, she stopped and raised her left fist to her ear. Hap did the same. She raised two fingers to her eyes, and then gestured with three. Hap parroted her hand signals to the others. As she moved forward, Hap sneaked a look and saw the cart heading for a room guarded by a grim-looking man with a week's worth of beard. The man stood between two boys dressed as if for prep school. Neither boy was more than twelve years old. The man's jacket bulged under his left arm, and he had a radio and a pistol on his belt. From his vantage point, Hap could see the boys staring straight ahead and trembling while their escort kept his hands firmly attached to each collar.

Zaida maneuvered the cart between the boys and their escort. Good job, Hap thought. The escort frowned at her, but his dark eyes widened in approval as he gave her a very slow once-over. The brown-haired girl with the Puerto Rican accent, a girl on first appearance any man would want to introduce to his parents, bent down to pick up the fork she intentionally brushed to the carpet. Standing erect, she revealed the Mossad weapon of choice, a silenced .22-caliber LRS that must had been in her ankle holster. Two rounds entered the escort's right eye before he could blink.

61

Grabbing the dead man's collar, Hap dragged the corpse away from the door and the peephole. Pressing his back to the wall, he gestured to the wide-eyed boys to be quiet and waved the team forward. Both boys trembled uncontrollably. Rock and Doc moved low and swiftly, pushing the weapons cache to take a strategic position on the other side of the door. Blad stayed to Hap's rear. Zaida moved to the side of the door and the food-laden cart, using her body as a shield for both boys. Will anchored at the corner of the hall with one of his hands attached to the chef's collar. A voice from the other side of the door questioned, "Did we order room service?"

"Compliments of your host, Señor Moya, Sir," Zaida said with authority.

Silence followed, presumably while the room's occupant eyed through the peephole the cart's covered dishes, the single bottle of wine, and the vase with two perfect roses.

Hap's jaws clenched. The boys, whom he guessed might be Honduran or Guatemalan, continued to tremble. Zaida gave each a reassuring squeeze, snuggling them against her bosom. Their expressions conveyed confusion and fear. Looking back at them over her arms, Hap saw two sets of round, dark eyes pleading for help. Well, the Marines have landed, Hap thought fiercely. What human vermin was low enough to traffic children to perverts? Hap wasn't in the mood to listen to pundits, politicians, or pontiffs rationalize misery. Those responsible would pay.

"Señor Moya asked that we deliver your late snack with a select French cabernet from his private cellar," Zaida said, keeping the rising tension from her voice. "He thinks you will appreciate the wine, and he sends his regards."

At the click of the lock, Hap moved around to the back of the cart.

"One moment," a male voice said through the still-closed door.

Zaida wedged the pistol between the small of her back and pants. She quickly returned her arms around the boys' waist. Hap saw that the boys now realized that nothing good would have come from entering the room.

The door opened. A man who could be anybody's friendly uncle stood silently in the doorway eyeing the delivery. He wore a finely woven terrycloth robe and both his hands rested in the plush pockets. A Los Americanos logo stitched across the right breast depicted the silhouette of the resort's lone tower, with two arcing bass at the "two" and "ten" positions leaping toward the tower.

Hap fought back his rage and the urge to grab the man by the throat and squeeze the life out of him! Was this soft, spoiled man who would pleasure himself with children the same man responsible for a Marine's death and Warden's kidnapping?

The man opened his arms to the boys, gesturing with his long supple fingers that everything was okay. Recoiling, the boys pressed to hide behind Zaida's hips.

"Come now," he said, still playing the role of 'nice' uncle. "It will be fun, boys."

Hap had seen enough angling between Zaida and the robed male to screen the boys. He palmed the pervert's angular face, sinking thumb and forefinger into his temple, increasing the pressure as he yelped shrilly.

"How's this for fun, dirt bag," Hap growled barely audibly.

Zaida turned to allow the boys to bury their faces into her midsection. Hap pressed forward, pushing the man back into the doorway so he stumbled and his robe fell open.

The son of a bitch was naked!

Hap pushed the man headlong into a short couch, where he crumpled into a quivering heap. Weapons drawn, Blad followed close on his heels, providing cover. Rock followed pushing the cart with the weapons.

With the situation secure, Blad reached around the open door and grabbed the chef from Will who had move from his position to the door. He pulled the wide-eyed chef to a closet left of the polished elevator doors and pushed him inside. He silently ordered the terrified man to be quiet by laying a finger across his lips. "Hush," Blad whispered, shaking his head as he slowly closed the closet door.

Hap heard a click and pivoted low toward French doors on the far side of the suite. One of the polished brass handles turned and three side arms aimed directly at the door as it opened slowly. "Danny?" a man's voice asked. He was pale, bald, pear-shaped, and naked except for silk boxers. "Did our order arrive?" he asked, rubbing his eyes sleepily.

Hap lowered the Belgium Browning, peering through cold eyes. "Senator Jourdan? You're with…?"

Jourdan's eyes fluttered wide and his arms pressed across his belly. He stared at the tableau in front of him in disbelief. "May I inquire who is asking?"

Hap gestured with the pistol toward the couch. "Park your ass next to your buddy."

Still stunned, the Senator hesitated only an instant. Rock and Doc quickly pushed in both carts trailed by Zaida and the boys. Will brought up the rear, backing into the open doorway.

Blad's satellite phone buzzed. He listened and nodded, pursed his lips as he contemplated what he was hearing, then lowered the phone and gave a grunt of approval. With a sly grin, he reported. "Trixie is on station. The Mexican Government was kind enough to loan parachutes and gas. Roach says the team is ready for a night jump at 500 feet. He is asking our intentions."

Hap kept one eye on the partially shaded window that looked out over the resort's ground floor swimming pool and outdoor lounge. Rock manned the door to the suite, keeping watch on the hall through two inches of space. Will's pitted face remained taut; his right eye partially closed weighing options.

"Something tells me we are going to need a diversion to get out of this place alive," Hap said, looking at Will.

"Shit, Colonel, We can insert my team and they will shoot their way in. We can fight our way down to the lobby and drive out of here in Los Americanos courtesy vans."

Jourdan whimpered, "Danny," as if pleading for help.

Speaking urgent Spanish, Zaida walked the boys past the Senator, and into the room he'd just vacated. She seated the boys on the bed, and both dove to hide under pillows and covers. Before leaving them, she spoke softly in Spanish, reassuring them all would be okay. And, with that, she shut the door.

She took a breath that sounded to Hap like a sigh. Then she began to unbutton her red coat. She took it off and set it on the arm of the couch. She continued removing her outer garments until she was down to bra and panties that did nothing to hide her amazing body. She flipped the .40-caliber to Will, and then reached around her back to return the .22 to the ankle holster.

"What are you up to, young lady?" Will asked.

"Let her go," Blad said. "She knows what she has to do."

Looking into Will's bloodshot eyes, she spoke in a matter-of-fact tone. "You want the Scorpion, don't you," she said, sighing.

Will gestured to Doc, "Go with her."

Bennie nodded pulling the slide of his pistol back slightly and cocking his head, ensuring a round chambered. Rock leaned into the hamper, slinging linens randomly over either shoulder. Straightening, he held up a vest. Will motioned it was his. Rock lobbed it underhanded. Zaida gestured to Doc towards the service door. "Follow me!"

* * *

With Zaida and Doc out of the room, Hap looked with disgust at the men on the couch. He rubbed his forehead with the barrel of his Belgium Hi Power Browning. "Senator, may I ask what brings you to Mexico?"

Senator Jourdan said nothing. He shifted nervously on the couch.

"You don't have to say a word, Scotty," his guest said.

"Shut up, Danny," Jourdan hissed.

Hap looked at the Senator's companion, who had been kind enough to retie the robe. Danny sat erect, legs crossed aristocrat-style. His brown eyes shifted focus as he eyed the room. The men were probably trying to measure the threat level.

"Do you have a name?" Hap asked. "Oh, right, it's Danny. Do you have a last name?"

Danny's chin shifted up slightly. "Fuck you."

Will and Rock donned their tactical vests while listening intently. Blad removed his red service coat and leaned cross-armed against the wall. His shoulder-holstered pistols, now exposed, could have just as easily fit in a scene of *The Godfather.*

"What do you two have to do with this mess?" Hap asked.

"Refer back to my previous response," Danny said arrogantly.

"Careful, Danny," the Senator warned. "This has to be LtCol Hap Stoner. I would have thought you'd be in custody by now."

"In due time, Senator," Hap replied.

Danny gave a casual flip of his well-manicured fingers as he turned to the Senator. "Scotty, this murdering fool will not kill a U. S. Senator. Since he will not shoot you, you become a witness. He will not kill me with you as a witness."

A popping sound came from outside the room, near the service entry. Will vanished first out the door, followed by Blad and Rock. Danny leaned forward appearing relaxed.

"Looks as though your plan is already unraveling, Colonel Stoner." Sitting back, he crossed his arms as a smirk spread across his angular face. Danny looked directly at the Bowie knife hanging under Hap's left shoulder and the empty holster dangling under the right. "See Scotty, what did I tell you? This LtCol Stoner is not going to do a thing."

Hap removed the Belgium Browning from inside his red vest and leveled the barrel at the space between Danny Boyd's brown eyes. Pulling back the hammer on the single action weapon, he shifted aim at the last second, squeezing a round into the man's right shoulder. Danny screamed, fainting into the Senator's lap. Dumbfounded, Jourdan covered both ears wailing in disbelief. Slapping with his hands and kicking out like a child, the Senator attempted to push his friend's unconscious body onto the floor.

"Wha—wha—what is it that you are looking for?" he blurted.

Hap pushed his boot against Danny ensuring the shoulder wound bled out into the Senator's lap. Will rounded the corner carrying the dead body of a young female in his arms. He set her gently down into the oversized armchair to one side of the couch, covering her with a decorative afghan. Danny moaned, still unconscious, and Jourdan whimpered, attempting to pull away from the bleeding shoulder. Will stared into the Senator's rapidly blinking eyes.

"Is the burden getting heavy Senator?" His voice, hard with barely contained rage, was almost a growl. "This girl can't be more than fifteen years old, you son of a bitch."

Scotty B. Jourdan, U.S. Senator, fidgeted as blood poured through the opening of his boxers. "Ok, Colonel. What is it you want to know?"

"*Why.*" Hap said it flatly.

"Why what?" Jourdan replied, beginning to hyperventilate.

"Why did they need you?

His breathing turned into a pant. "The guarantees," he replied, shaking his head. "I don't want to die."

"Guarantees?" Hap repeated. He pressed the barrel of the Belgium Browning against the Senator's sweaty, balding head.

"The U.S. Treasury-backed loan for the Los Americanos Resort. I've had similar projects I inserted into major legislation. Don't let me die."

Jourdan was still pleading as Doc rounded the corner with a fit, muscular man in his mid-thirties, a man that Hap recognized from photographs as "Scorpion," leader of Mexico's most powerful drug cartel. Doc pushed Scorpion along with the other man, cuffing their collars. Hap recognized the second man from Blad's confidential dossier as Geraldo Moya, Scorpion's nephew, who considered himself the Caliph of Latin America. Doc had tightly secured both men's hands behind their backs with medical tape.

Teenage girls wrapped in sheets and nothing else raced past the open doorway. Seconds later, Blad passed by the doorway, weapons in hand.

"Shut up, Senator," Scorpion uttered harshly. "Security will have this floor in minutes."

Doc pushed Scorpion and his companion to the other end of the couch with the warning, "Don't even sneeze."

"Senator?" Hap snapped the fingers of his left hand. "What about the Fast and Furious weapons?" Hap held his pistol by his side, aimed at the floor.

Jourdan's perspiring head shook slowly back and forth. "I—I—I want to go home to my wife and children."

"If you don't answer my question I'm sending you to hell," Hap said. He felt an odd sense of peace, as if everything happening around them was part of another world.

Gunshots rang out from somewhere down the hall, and seconds later a muffled grenade erupted from the left end of the hall. Senator Jourdan squeaked in alarm and Scorpion's buddy flinched. Scorpion kept a stone face.

"Tell me about the weapons," Hap said, slowly raising his pistol.

Trembling, Jourdan leveled his eyes with the barrel of Hap's Belgium High Power. "Scorpion needed weapons and I just happened to know where he could get his hands on truckloads of them."

"Courtesy of the Grand Old U.S. of A.," Hap replied.

Jourdan lowered his head mumbling, "If I ever thought innocent people would be killed, I would never have reached out to Justice."

* * *

Fire erupted from the right. Blad dropped two jihadis attempting to access the floor via the service elevator. Blad raced into the hallway towards the fire escape, Will followed close on his heels. On the chance the fireproof door would be unlocked; Blad pulled the pin to a grenade letting the spoon fly ten feet from the door. Pushing down on the locking bar, he put a shoulder to the door opening it enough to underhand the grenade down the stairwell. Another muffled explosion followed.

Will pulled back the charging handle of his M4. "You're going to have to shit or get off the pot, Colonel."

Zaida rounded the corner, staring at the men with crazy eyes, the .22 resting in the palm of her right hand. Will flipped her the blouse, and she slipped it on without buttoning. "I'm going right to cover Blad. The children—?"

"The boys are safe. We'll get them out. Count on Hap." Will nodded. "You'll need this." He tossed her the Glock.

Catching the pistol, she looked quickly down both sides of the hall.

"I'll go left, Zaida," Will said. "You might need these."

She'd barely turned back but her free hand caught the two grenades the way a juggler catches tangerines. Gunfire erupted from both fire escapes, the exchange heated. A muffled grenade followed a few moments of silence, and then it started all over again.

• • •

Hap watched coldly as Senator Jourdan collapsed back on the couch, with his breathing increasingly labored. His pal Danny was still slumped unconscious in his lap. Covered in other people's blood seemed apropos, the weight of the consequence, fitting. Scorpion sat with his expression as immobile as granite, while the self-appointed Caliph whimpered.

The Senator struggled to say the words, "I can't breathe."

Hap placed fingers on the Senator's carotid artery. He could feel a slight pulse. The asshole would probably live, he thought. Danny would, too, at least for the moment. Reaching into his pocket, he turned off the recording on his mobile phone and began snapping pictures.

62

Huddled on the couch, the Chairman of the Senate Armed Services Committee whimpered like a child, his white and pasty figure smothered in sweat and coagulating blood. Seated tightly between the Senator and Geraldo Ponce Moya, the self-appointed Caliph de México, Gregorio Moya, a.k.a. Scorpion, glared at his captor.

Hap didn't spare any of them more than a glance as he passed the couch on his way to the suite's private elevator. Once inside, he turned the key, locking the car in place. He stepped out of the elevator to turn his full gaze on the man who carried as much power as the President of Mexico. Hap's lips turned up in a mean smile and then he winked at Scorpion. Though the thug wanted a piece of his ass, Hap could not hold back one of his classic lines. Moving to the front of the couch, he casually stuffed a stick of Wrigley's Spearmint into his parched mouth. "Take a picture dipshit, it will last longer."

Scorpion lurched forward grunting like a bull attempting a shoulder tackle. With his hands taped securely against the small of his back, Scorpion was two steps slow. Hap reached out stiff-armed like a running back and palmed Scorpion's forehead, launching the leader of Mexico's largest cartel into the Caliph's lap.

Senator Jourdan's constant whimper had slowed to an occasional snivel. His ashen face indicated he might be moments away from entering shock. Danny Boyd still bled heavily from his shoulder wound. His eyes blinked open, and he stared up at the slowly turning ceiling fan.

Sounds of sprinting boots on carpet resonated through the hallway. Hap reached into the hamper to grab his M4. Blad rushed through the open door holding a nickel-plated .45 in either hand, looking a lot like famous pictures of Billy the Kid. He spoke between fast inhalations. "Security was obviously napping. Unfortunately for us, the turds never touched REM." He pointed one of the nickel-plated .45's toward the open elevator door. "Elevator locked out?"

Hap nodded. "Sounds like they're throwing the kitchen sink at us."

Blad chuckled. "Fuckers are trained. They're not running around like the Cub Scouts at Scorpion's river camp."

Hap retrieved the vest, tossing it over his shoulders. Left-handed, he pulled back the blood stained M4's charging handle, releasing the T grip. The bolt slammed home.

"Where do you need me?"

"On the roof, we have a ride, ETA 5 minutes."

Hap stepped carefully out into the hall; perturbed he would leave not knowing Shank's involvement in all this misery. "Where's your girl?"

"She can take care of herself," Blad said. He was standing in front of the couch, pistols at his sides. He gave Hap a sharp look. "She stays. We have to get the hell out of here."

"Got it." Hap nodded. "Leave those two," he said, gesturing toward Jourdan and his companion. The Senator stared back at him with glassy eyes, any protest mute. "They'd only slow us down, and we got what we need."

Blad nodded. "But this one is going with us," he said, placing the barrel of one of the .45's against Scorpion's temple. "After you, Gregorio."

Scorpion stood slowly.

"And let's not forget your friend, the Caliph," Blad said, nodding as Gregorio's plump cousin struggled to stand. "Let's move!"

Just outside the door, in the hallway, Hap caught movement to his right. Raising the M4, he drew a bead center mass on a purple burka. Blad's hand slapped down on the barrel. The figure waved with one swipe of her open palm, then vanished around the corner.

"I'll tell you about it later, Hap," Blad said.

Hap trotted to the bedroom giving Scorpion a forearm shiver in passing. Turning the handle to the door, he found it didn't budge. The boys had locked the door. Stepping back, he gave a half turn donkey kick crashing the double doors open. Both boys covered their heads with pillows reacting to the crashing sound.

Hap hesitated, unsure what to say. He had begged his 9th grade Spanish teacher to give him a "C," promising himself to "never, ever take Spanish again." Now giving it his best, he bent low, trying to make himself smaller as he coaxed the boys out from under pillows and off the bed. "Muiii Prontooo."

One set of eyes, then two, peeked up from behind pillows.

"It's okay, it's okay," Hap said, waving them over with a thumbs-up.

They hesitated but then jumped in tandem from the bed and raced into his open arms just as he slung the M4 over his shoulder. Scooping them up, he carried them from the bedroom to the service hallway.

"Move it, Hap," Blad said.

Looking left, he saw Blad pushing his newfound human shields down the hall. They could hear the sound of boots around the corner of the hall. Hap eased the boys to their feet, swinging around to cover them and unholstering the Belgium Browning in one motion. It was Will, bounding down the hall shouting, "We got some bad guys on their way up."

Muffled explosions resonated from behind the fire escape door that Will had been guarding only moments before. Hap holstered the pistol, ushering the boys toward the roof access. Will was pulling a grenade from his vest as Hap rushed the boys on.

Doc and Blad were just ahead and already through the door, herding the prisoners up the staircase toward the roof. One of the boys caught the fire escape door just before it closed and moments before Hap's shoulder slammed the steel door against the wall. Hap nodded to the boy as he nudged both upstairs. Rock stood bent over on the down stairwell, rigging a booby trap across steps.

"Right behind you, Colonel," Rock called out, tying off the last knot. He rushed up to the landing to cover Will as he booby-trapped the heavy door. Pulling the grenade's pin, Will wedged the grenade in between the handle and the door. When the handle turned, the spoon would release as the grenade dropped to the floor.

"Corporal, get your ass up the ladder well," Will barked. Rock vanished up the steps, with Will hot on his tail, knowing any moment the booby traps would be spraying hot shrapnel up and down the ladder well.

Blad pushed Scorpion and the Caliph across the threshold to meet Mayo's whirling rotors. Schlonger, covering the team's egress, was standing outside the Mayo's cabin, waving them over with the AK in his hands. Blad prodded his prisoners forward with a pistol, nudging the small of each man's back.

Almost to the top of the stairs, Hap heard the Mayo's rotors and the high-pitched whine of the twin turboshaft engines. Pushing past the boys, his body was now their shield if they took fire from the roof. Schlonger waved Hap forward while, next to him, Doc fanned his M4 across the expansive rooftop. With Scorpion and the Caliph now loaded on board, Blad turned to add cover for the team's final rush to Mayo.

Hunched down, Hap motioned the boys to stay low and dash toward Schlonger, but they clung to Hap. With a quick glance back, Hap saw Rock let Will pass through the door. Rock slammed the door shut and dropped to one knee to rig one final Hallmark greeting card to their attackers. Schlonger yelled frantically, gesturing for the boys with his free hand, while Hap guided them toward the safety of the bird offering cover with his body. They were just a few feet shy of Mayo when the first crack of an AK-47's 5.45x39 mm round passed by Hap's left ear. Pivoting, he saw three shooters tactically deployed in a wedge formation. "Bastards made it up the other stairs," he realized. "Sons of bitches. Will should have set one more before *di di mauing*."

Will had dropped to one knee, returning fire, while Rock finished rigging the booby trap. Schlonger and Doc unleashed a burst joining Will's suppressive fire, sending the man to the left of the formation spinning to the ground. Overhead, Trixie orbited low over the grounds, aiming to create a diversion. Hap stayed where he was, keeping his body between the boys and the shooters. Pain seared across his abdomen but he didn't break his focus on the two shooters while backing the boys toward the helo. Blad banged away like Outlaw Billy returning heavy fire.

Now, with one magazine emptied, Hap dropped the piece to the ground and pivoted enough to sling both boys up and into the cabin. Next to him, Schlonger groaned, dropping doubled-over to one knee. Hap drew the 9mm pushing past the pain. He shuffled forward, firing at the point man in the wedge as the aggressor fumbled for a fresh magazine. Rock wrestled the third aggressor to the ground trying to stick him with his Ka-Bar.

Even as two of Hap's rounds ripped through the point man's torso, the bad guy got off a round just as Hap's third round entered his forehead. The man jerked straight back with arms splayed as Hap spun to the ground. Resting on all fours and fighting off shock, Hap looked over at Will sprawled face down. He didn't feel the abdominal wound anymore. Two new holes had punctured his body, just below his right shoulder. The rounds' impact had felt like somebody slamming him with a mallet.

Hap stumbled toward Rock doubled over and clutching his waist. The aggressor had gained the advantage and was trying to stick Rock with his own Ka-Bar. No time to unsling the M4, he mustered all he had left. Drawing his Bowie knife, he rushed Rock's attacker. The aggressor trained the Ka-Bar toward Rock's chest, using weight and strength. Rock gripped his attacker's wrist, straining to push back and keep the knife from impaling his heart.

Just as the charging Hap was within feet of Rock's attacker, the top of the aggressor's head blew into pieces. The warrior was a corpse before falling sideways to the concrete floor. Hap made a mental note to thank somebody later. Rock gained a knee reaching for his M4 and returning the Ka-Bar to its scabbard.

Doc grabbed the back of Hap's vest, but Hap gestured with his head—*Tend to Rock*. Doc's hammer-like fists hefted Rock to full standing. He let the wounded Marine fall over his shoulder just as Blad rushed past carrying Will to the Mayo. Hap pushed to a knee as a new wave of pain rolled through his body. Slumping down, he splayed out on the roof just as he heard the sound of rapidly approaching footsteps. Unable to get out a warning, Hap turned possum, weighing options.

As Doc turned with Rock sprawled over a shoulder to follow Blad, the attacker ran full stride to make a tackle. Hap used his last reserves to throw out a kick sending the aggressor the size of a Brahma bull tumbling over himself. He attempted to raise on all fours, but it seemed as if a grand piano had somehow attached itself to his back. He didn't have to be a combat surgeon to realize the loss of blood had taken its toll. He kept the Bowie knife drawn to his side.

Having tucked and rolled, the thug snapped to his feet and charged Hap, who could only raise the blade of his knife chest high. The attacker closed the distance at full stride, and went strategically airborne, pile-driving Hap to the rooftop with a groan. Pinned down by the sheer weight of the aggressor, Hap knew resistance was futile. He waited for the inevitable.

It never came.

The weight suddenly lifted and Doc's bad breath filled Hap's nostrils.

"You okay?" Doc stood bent over, clutching the corpse in one hand and his M4 in the other. The handle of Hap's Bowie knife jutted from the dead man's chest.

Doc released his grip on the corpse and placed his boot to its chest, removing the knife. Hap reached up for the knife.

"You'll be fine," Doc managed, breathing heavily. Hap grunted, sheathing the bloodied blade. He painfully unslung the M4, and wavered for a moment. Doc dragged Hap by the collar toward the Mayo. As the two crossed under the spinning rotors, Hap saw the blur of the fire escape door swinging open. Hap shot one-armed but the barrel barely cleared his foot, ricocheting harmlessly towards the lake. The first man through the door jammed back against the wall. A second aggressor, who appeared to be female, vanished in smoke and shrapnel. The moment Hap fired off his second burst from the M4, both went to ground. Shock waves washed over them as the grenade exploded. Hap felt Doc's big paw grab the back of his vest dragging him to the helo, and heaving him inside.

As Hap lay on the blood-covered deck, both boys huddled together, their screams drowned out by the helo's howling turbo shaft engines and spinning rotors. Hap managed to raise an arm to give the boys a reassuring squeeze. He barely heard the cabin door slide shut and the wheels broke ground. Scharver cleared the edge of the resort's rooftop, diving for the ground, building speed to put terrain and space between the Mayo and Scorpion's would be rescuers.

Hap blinked, refocusing to see out of the cabin window. The moon rays shimmered casting Trixie's broad shadow across the speeding helo as the C130 roared by with two hundred feet vertical separation.

63

Mayo's harmonics resonating through the aluminum deck sent Hap to a restless slumber, the throbbing of his wounds trumped temporarily by the aerodynamic phenomena unique to rotary aircraft. The vibration's amplitude, as transmitted through the airframe, soothed better than a fistful of painkillers for Hap Stoner. Minutes after Scharver dove Mayo away from the roof of Los Americanos, Hap's eyelids closed.

As soon as the vibrations ceased, Hap's eyelids snapped opened in time to see the underside of Trixie's rear empennage passing overhead. His head lifted slowly, he took in the scene: Four Mexican Marines held the handles of his stretcher and were moving him quickly across a busy tarmac to Trixie. Rotating his head, he found what he was searching for—the two boys struggling to break away from a fifth Mexican Marine.

"Let the boys go," Hap growled.

"Do what he says." The voice belonged to Roach, who stood at the top of the Trixie's ramp holding two Cokes and a dozen day-old donuts.

As the Marine released the boys, Roach gazed down at Hap and said, "Welcome to General Roberto Fierro Villalobos International Airport, LtCol Hap Stoner."

"That's a mouthful," Hap said gingerly, gesturing for the boys to join him. But, they were already positioned on either side of the stretcher, each clutching one of Hap's thumbs, creating a procession up Trixie's ramp.

Shadow Services had obviously pulled a rabbit out of a hat arranging for the Mayo and Trixie to land at the airport in Chihuahua, Mexico.

As if reading Hap's thoughts, Roach said, "We got a full platoon of well-armed Mexican Marines who set a 300-foot-buffer around the Mayo and Trixie. Nothing can enter or exit except for fuel trucks."

Hap raised his head enough to see Blad placing hoods over Scorpion's and the Mexican Caliph's heads before their feet touched the tarmac. He was about to call out to Blad when he noticed stretcher-bearers carrying Will and Schlonger up the ramp and into the cabin.

"They're tough, they'll make it," Roach said. Gently placing the Cokes and donuts between Hap's knees, he grinned. "The treats are for the boys."

The moment Hap's stretcher settled into the rack hanging from the bulkhead, he handed each boy a Coke. He gestured for Roach to find a place for them to strap in, and then he gave each a pat on the back. "Enjoy the feast," he said.

Roach seated the boys side-by-side in a jump seat across from Hap and they promptly opened their Cokes. He dropped the box of donuts between the two and nodded his approval as they eagerly bit into powdered sugar and grease. He moved back to stand over Hap's stretcher. Hap reached out with his left hand.

"Tough night?" Roach asked, loosely palming Hap's hand. Hap nodded. Roach clenched his hand with both mitts. "You going back to the Alternate LZ?" Roach asked.

"Would you expect anything less?" Hap responded groggily.

Roach shook his head laying a hand over his heart. "Nah, Hap. Figured you would go and take the first bullet."

Hap gestured with his head a silent *Thank You*. Doc wedged between the two men, cutting away Hap's vest, boots, and flight suit. He pulled Hap's nametag and Nomad Squadron patch from the flight suit remnants, he held them out and said, "Need a little help here."

"I'll take those, Doc," Roach said.

Tossing the bloody rags to the side, he began applying alcohol to the wounds. "You're pretty fucked up, Colonel," he said wedging a knee behind Hap's back. Looking at the shoulder wound and down to the mid-section he shook his head. "Both clean, Colonel. You're one lucky son of a bitch." Doc applied compression bandages covering the two wounds in the shoulder and one abdominal wound giving the tails an extra tug before tying them off. "Can I make a suggestion Colonel?"

Hap's head fell to the side gazing through heavy eyelids. "Sure. What is it?" he asked, forcing a smile without the help of morphine.

Doc spoke while working on the shoulder bandages. "As soon as you get out of hack, go buy a lotto ticket and get me one while you're at it. You are one lucky son of a bitch."

Grimacing, Hap said, "Doc, can you be any rougher? Your bandages hurt like hell."

"Surprising words coming from a man Will Kellogg claims to be the toughest bastard in the world," Doc said.

Roach motioned to the crew chief standing by the ramp. Closing fingertips together like jaws coming together, the ramp began rising. Seconds later the hatch lowered sealing the Hercules.

64

Saturday 0500; Trixie Transporting Wounded,
En route to Columbus

As Trixie rose to altitude, Hap propped up on his right elbow. As uncomfortable as it was, he counted heads while looking for a pittance of relief from the nausea wreaking havoc on his insides. Trixie's litter configuration provided ample headspace with stretchers stacked three-high to the bulkhead aft of the command module. Doc worked back and forth between Schlonger and Will, stretched out motionless in their litters. Rock sat across the fuselage playfully attempting to con donuts from the boys. The Mexican Caliph sat slumped in a jump seat, his hands cut free from any restraint. He now wore a parachute.

Doc sidestepped to his left, dropping to a knee by Hap's rack placing the ear tips to his ear to check Hap's heartbeat. When he finished he removed the earbuds and said, "You're still alive."

"Where's Blad?" Hap quizzed.

Doc shook his head. "He met some Ichabod Crane-looking fellow at the airport. This guy looked old but well preserved. The two definitely knew each other. They talked briefly with the Caliph, before prodding Scorpion and El Maestro with leg kicks up the portable stairs and boarded Ichabod Crane's corporate Boeing 737. Excuse me Colonel, this might hurt a bit." Doc gingerly cinched a blood pressure cuff around Hap's right bicep. He pumped up the pressure as he spoke. "The plane was a beauty, polished aluminum with red and blue markings, the tail number just happened to be the last four of my social, Sierra Mike 1638. Blad talked briefly to Roach and next thing I knew Trixie's aircrew strapped a parachute to the Mexican rag head wannabe. Then the 737 blew Dodge."

Releasing the pressure on the cuff, he continued, "The Mayo shut down and the Mexican Marines escorted the bird to a hangar."

Hap turned his head to Roach, who was speaking to two of the aircrew, while he sat with arms crossed, chewing on a cigar as round as a small tree branch. The hand pinching the cigar pointed to the Caliph. The cigar swung towards the ramp, drawing laughter from both.

Hap fell back struggling with the pain. The morphine Syrette dangled above his head. He slowly pushed Doc's bear-sized paw aside. "No, Doc. Need a clear head when we hit the Alternate LZ."

Doc stared down at Hap with a questioning look, mimicking John Belushi in *Animal House* except with a crew cut. "Stop it, Doc. Laughing hurts and you look like Belushi in *Animal House* at the toga party."

Doc palmed the Syrette, his square jaw fixed, "Just trying to help, Colonel. And by the way, I don't do toga parties,"

Hap nodded, trying to hold back another bout of laughter. "How are Will and Schlonger?"

Doc leaned in close, speaking into his ear. "Will needs to be by your side when you buy your lotto ticket," he said, touching his sausage-sized fingers on Hap's carotid artery. "He caught a ricochet off the side of the head that knocked him out cold. Outside the blood and a killer headache, the old buzzard will be fine."

Hap reached out grabbing Doc's Popeye forearms. "Schlonger?"

Doc's gaze rotated towards Schlonger lying still in the middle litter. "Ya know Colonel, after a little rehab, he will be fine. Not sure if you know this, Sir. I washed out of med school," he said wiggling fingers deserving of a diesel mechanic. "Always dreamed of being a proctologist. Enlisted in the Army Medical Corps instead and ended up in Delta Force."

"Scary thought, Doc," Hap replied. "What do you do when you're not blowing up shit?"

Doc grinned. "Colonel, you may find this hard to believe. I'm a black jack dealer at the Buccaneer." Hap chuckled realizing the fight to keep his eyelids apart was a losing proposition.

"Damn it Doc, I'm tired." His mind drifted on the edge of consciousness. The legal maneuvering soon to begin would be the lead story on cable news for the foreseeable future. The Administration would press Justice to appoint a special counsel attempting to wrestle the matter from DOD. Looking ahead, they would treat the Marines worse than the Islamo Fascists in Guantanamo. The Justice Department's attempt to make a spectacle by conducting the trial in New York City would be an attack on the few true warriors remaining in the higher echelon of command within the U.S. Military. The whole world would soon witness a country crucifying its own behind a facade of justice. LtCol. Hap Stoner would be the tip of the phalanx spending his last dime to ensure the Marines received a proper defense.

The deceleration of Trixie's turbines and the pilot turning on the cabin lights woke Hap from a restless sleep. He squinted through barely open eyes. Instead of a Jump Master barking, *Stand up! Hook up! Stand in the door!* Roach, chewing the now emasculated stick of tobacco, shoved the clueless Caliph to the rear of the aircraft. The two struggled to maintain balance as the hatch and ramp separated, air swirling around the cabin like a tornado and Roach without a safety harness.

"Hey Caliph," Roach screamed, patting the Caliph's bearded cheek. "When your sandals hit the ground…tuck and roll. You'll thank me later!"

The moment the light went green, Roach pulled the Caliph's rip cord deploying the chute into the swirling air. 1/1000, 2/1000, 3/1000. 4/1000 and in the blink of an eye the Caliph vanished into the night. Roach gestured with his thumb to raise the ramp.

Only God and the Caliph knew that the moment he touched down on Mexican soil, he stripped off the parachute, continuing until he was down to sandals and stained boxer underwear. His career as a Caliph had ended. The Ichabod Crane-looking guy had told him in no uncertain terms to find a different religion.

• • •

After landing at Columbus, Trixie taxied toward the tarmac. As the Hercules C-130 came to an abrupt and premature stop,

Roach bounded up the cabin ladder entering the cockpit. Flight line helos tied down with intake pillows, exhaust covers, and pitot covers in place. Bright yellow barrier tape, strung across the taxiway, blocked the Trixie's path.

"Go through it," Roach said, patting both pilot and copilot on their shoulders. Both looked back at him, questioning the order. FBI agents and U.S. Marshals rushed forward wearing prominently marked windbreakers. Reporters swarmed out of nowhere like cockroaches flushed from an unkempt pantry.

Roach wedged himself into the engineer's seat and the pilot eased the four throttles forward. He gripped both pilots' shoulders with his claw-like grip. "Don't touch those fucking brakes or maybe I'll just break both your necks."

Following Roach's matter of fact directive, the pilot nervously looked to his copilot as Trixie rolled through orange pylons and taped off perimeter.

"Keep the taxi lights on and throw on the landing lights. We are going to light up like a Christmas tree."

Roach was laughing like a brazen sailor as the wall of Federal agents rushing from the Nomad line towards Trixie broke to either side of the taxiway to clear themselves of the spinning props. The pilot cranked the nose wheel, steering Trixie into a hard right turn to pick up the yellow centerline to remain clear of the parked helicopters and F-18 Hornets.

Cable news cameras placed their reporters between the fixed and rotary wing aircraft, using Trixie as a backdrop. Col Ted Shank strode to the centerline. Shielding his eyes with one hand, he gestured toward Trixie to stop. Roach leaned over the pilot's left shoulder, pointing toward the concertina wire.

"What about the traffic cop," the pilot asked.

"Trust me. The dickhead will get out of the way." The pilot and copilot tried to hold back their grins but it was too late. "Do a 180 in front of the concertina wire," Roach directed, "there's plenty of room. I'm going to drop the ramp, guys."

The pilot nodded, steering Trixie past the last Huey, turning about its left main mount. Both of Trixie's air crew chiefs stepped from the crew entrance door. Walking between the Number 2 engine and Trixie's fuselage, the older of the two set up to act as taxi director while the other positioned himself off the right wing to act as wing walker. As the APU spooled up, Roach hovered around the ramp control panel adjacent to the left hand paratroop door. Seconds later Trixie's auxiliary hydraulic system opened ass-end to a horde of camera lights and reporters.

Corporal Rock Carver USMCR walked down the ramp wearing the full complement of combat gear over Los Americanos service attire. In need of a shave, both service uniform and vest soiled with sweat and human blood, Rock was a combat Marine coming off the line. Holding the weapon above his head as a gesture of surrender, he slowly went to his knees lowering the weapon to the tarmac.

US Marshals and FBI agents closed the distance, sidearms drawn. Rushing forward, the Nomad's crusty old Sergeant Major Matthew Biggs, who looked grizzled enough to have served with Chesty Puller on the frozen Chosin Reservoir, stepped between Rock and the oncoming Feds.

"Stand down!" he barked at the Feds in a full Boston accent. "This Marine is surrendering."

Built like an inside linebacker, the taller of the two US Marshals stepped forward to remove the Senior NCO Marine on site. Biggs gave two quick left jabs, sending the pistol flying as the Marshal flopped on his back. The second Marshal drew his Taser and fired. The electrode dropped the Marine like a sack of potatoes. Additional federal agents within the perimeter closed in on the melee. A dozen Marine MPs carrying 12-gauge shotguns and three leashed barking German shepherds charged the scene. The MP OIC removed the electrodes, pulling his military Beretta 9mm.

"Staff Sergeant Jones," he said, cutting his eyes toward the Feds, "the Sergeant Major is going to need a medic."

The Staff NCO raised a handheld radio to his lips, shielding his eyes from the glare of camera lights with the other. "Need a doc in front of the holding cage. We have a Marine down!"

Inside Trixie, Roach reached down, yanking Hap up and out of the stretcher by the arm of his good shoulder. "You look good in bloodied tighty whities." Roach thrust a cell phone into Hap's hand. "Doc said you'd need this. He found it dropping your bloody shit into the trash."

"Doc is perceptive." Clasping the phone, Hap returned a half-grin. "You would look the same after a good undressing by Doc."

Hap hobbled down the ramp, using Roach's broad shoulder as a crutch, as Roach shielded their eyes from the bright lights. Doc loped by with the medical bag slung over his shoulder, and then kneeled over the downed Marine. Checking for a pulse, he shook his head and initiated CPR. Between short thrusts with the heel of his hand, Doc barked, "Stay with us, Sergeant Major!"

"You're too mean to die, Sergeant Major," Hap yelled, leaning over in time to see the color vanish from the Sergeant

Major's grizzled face. "Your nephew will never forgive you if you punch out."

The Marine MPs jacked a round into their shotguns, remaining at order arms. "You want a fight?" the Captain barked.

The Nomads within the wire began to vocalize their discontent as Doc opened up the Sergeant Major's blouse. Hap stepped away to let Doc place the paddles.

"Clear!" Doc yelled. The Sergeant Major's upper cavity lurched. "Again, clear!"

An Alabama yell came from inside the wire. Three Nomads wearing flight suits leaned their bodies over and across the single strand of concertina wire. Getting a head of steam, Big Alabama's size-eight-boot landed squarely between one of the Marine's shoulder blades, launching him toward the melee like a raging bull. Other Nomads followed, spilling across the wire just as Doc yelled, "Clear!"

This time the Sergeant Major's body lurched up, followed by a large intake of air. One of Trixie's crew handed Doc a portable oxygen bottle. Doc placed the small mask over the Sergeant Major's nose and mouth. A few seconds later, the injured Marine's eyes blinked rapidly and he began taking in long slow breaths, slowly coming back to life. Hap went to a knee resting his hand on the Sergeant Major's shoulder.

"Settle down Sergeant Major. You'll be fine and your nephew will be relieved."

Sergeant Major's eyes fluttered open. "Jeez, Colonel, get in uniform," he said weakly.

Turning to Doc, Hap said, "Get a stretcher." Breathing hard, Big Alabama leaned over his uncle. Behind them, the corral was void of previously incarcerated Marines.

Hap tapped Big Alabama's shoulder. "Fire up one of the Huey's. Let's get your uncle to the hospital."

Big Alabama nodded. "Roger, Colonel. Goose and Little Ray, on me." Goose and Little Ray broke away, following Big Alabama, racing toward a Huey parked down the line. Hap walked alongside the stretcher, propped up by Ambassador and Spanky. Ahead, the rotors on the Huey began slowly turning.

Doc held the Sergeant Major's hand until the stretcher was loaded. As the stretcher slid across the deck, Little Ray took Biggs' hand as tenderly as if he were the Sergeant Major's son. The cabin door closed. The Huey's engine spooled. The entourage went flat to the ground as Big Alabama lifted rapidly using a hoverless takeoff maneuver into a cloudless New Mexico sky.

*Saturday 0530; Alternate LZ, Columbus Municipal
Airport, NM*

Shank approached Rock Carver from the rear, followed
closely by two MP's carrying shotguns at the port. Coming to
attention, the MPs' left hands crossed their war belts, touching
the barrels of their shotguns.

"Corporal Carver," Love Doctor said, pointing. "You owe
these Marines a salute."

Turning at the waist, Corporal Rock Carver immediately
straightened, level hips, body erect, shoulders square. Both
arms hung at his sides stiffly with both thumbs touching the
seams of his torn and blood-covered black pants. Bringing his
right boot behind his left heel, he initiated a smart about face.

"Atennn huuuut!" Love Doctor barked. The Nomads
snapped to attention. Love Doctor tossed Rock his utility
cover. Placing the cover low over his brow with the back
resting high on the crown of his head, Carver returned a
smart salute. Receiving the salute, the MP's cut their hands
back to their sides. Rock cut his left hand slowly to his side,
then, with the same hand, flipped the cover back to the Love
Doctor. The cable news mini-cams captured the scene for
viewers worldwide to witness.

"Detail, riiiight face," one of the MPs said. Conducting a
right face, the same Marine issued a call for port arms. The

MPs raised the shotguns across their chests, their left hands snapped onto the pump mechanisms, while their right hands simultaneously dropped to the stock. "Forward…huuuuuut." The Marines marched to rejoin their unit.

Flanked by two FBI agents and with the shiny 737 as a backdrop lazily orbiting the airfield, Shank approached, visibly grinding his jaw. Both Federal agents pulled badges, leaving sidearms holstered.

Hap came to attention wearing only tighty whities, bandages with growing red splotches, and clutching a cell phone.

Shank's upper lip appeared to quiver at the site of Hap. "LtCol Stoner, consider yourself under arrest."

"Colonel Shank," Hap said, one eyebrow raised, tipping his head. "If you'd be so kind to accompany me down the flight line, I have something for you." The Nomads who had been behind the concertina wire now formed a line separating the press from Hap and Shank.

"You've got to be shitting me, Stoner," Shank replied, lips curling in a mocking sneer. "Look at you, appearing half-dressed right this instant on every fucking cable news network in the nation."

Hap maintained firm eye contact, holding up his cell phone between thumb and forefinger, attempting to suppress the flutter deep in his empty belly. "Colonel…shall we?"

Shank turned to both Federal agents, holding up a fist. "Hold your ground, gentlemen."

Hap shrugged away Spanky and Ambassador's assistance. "I got this," he said, struggling to continue forward.

"You sure, Kang?" LtCol Stenson came to a stop next to Spanky and Ambassador. "You sure?" he said, breathing hard from his recent sprint. Hap inhaled deeply, and breathing sent a wave of pain through his body. He returned a slightly shaky nod. The two Marine officers' paths aligned, so Hap and Shank moved slowly down the flight line shoulder to shoulder. Shank walked, watching intently, as Hap pushed the volume on the cell to maximum.

The voices were clear. Senator Scotty B. Jourdan, head of the Senate Armed Forces Service Committee speaks. "Colonel Shank, I need you to confiscate any and all Soviet-made weapons found on site. Don't ask questions, just do it. You *do* want to make general?" And, Shank responds "Yes, Sir." Shank's shoulders fell, as his breathing intensified.

"Where the hell did you get these private conversations with a U.S. Senator? They're classified, Stoner."

"Colonel, you can take your 'classified' and shove it up the Senator's ass." Hap stumbled to a knee, spitting up a small bit of blood onto the concrete.

Shank offered no assistance. Spanky and Ambassador rushed forward. Hap looked around his good shoulder, a small dribble of blood spilling to the concrete. "Stand down, Marines," Hap coughed out. "I got this one."

The two Marines froze in their tracks. Maybe it was time they tell Hap Stoner, "Kiss my ass." Still they did not move. Shank stood over Hap, hands on hips, his angular face telegraphing disgust. "What the fuck do you want from me, Stoner?"

Hap chuckled, struggling to gain his feet. Working to control the trembling, he held up his phone. "I have more, Colonel. Wait 'til you see the pictures."

Hap's thumb slid photos across the cell phone screen. He held the phone at the belt line to shield the sun just below the eastern horizon. There they were, the Senator sitting in boxers next to Danny Lee Boyd on the couch and Zaida comforting the two boys outside Scorpion's private suite. Scorpion and the Caliph had their hands secured behind their back. Page 444 of the Los Americanos register showed the distinguished U.S. Senator's signature, a memento for the world to see, a U.S. Senator enjoying guest privileges, the perks of his stay in the private suite of one of Mexico's most notorious drug cartel leaders.

"Didn't you let the Senator take your plane into Mexico, Colonel?"

Silence. Hap gestured with his left hand down the flight line, "After you, Colonel."

Shank took the first step and Hap hobbled along by his side. Spanky, Ambassador and Stenson, joined now by Doc holding two military issue wool blankets, trailed the two Marines by fifteen to twenty feet. Holding the line, the Nomads kept the reporters at bay and out of earshot. To Hap, Shank's body language said surrender, neck, and shoulders hunched forward as he stared down at the tarmac. The only thing missing in Hap's mind was the frigging white flag.

"So what now?" he said, sounding less than confident. "What do you want from me, LtCol Stoner?

Suddenly Hap heard a new voice, female, Carla shouting at the top of her lungs. He gave a painful half turn in time to see her about 100 meters away, running toward them.

Now Hap heard her words. "Let the 737 orbiting the airfield land and take the Nomads back to New Orleans!"

Hap shook his head. "What is she trying to say, Major Hammer?

"If I didn't know better, she is saying to let the 737 land and take the Nomads back to New Orleans."

Shank's lips pressed together as he deliberated the request. He shook his head. "Colonel, I just can't let everybody go."

Shank pulled the radio from his belt, raising it to his mouth. "Shut the girl up, damn it. That's an order!"

A howl followed. Carla was pissed. At least now, Hap had an alibi. Shank was the one who ordered her apprehended. Meanwhile, the audio on Hap's phone played on, and now the Senator was explaining his involvement with Black Stone for the past twenty-four months.

Hap eyed Shank pointedly, tipping the cell. "Colonel, can I call the plane in?"

Shank stopped abruptly, grabbing Hap's good shoulder. "You will assure me not one Marine will attempt to go AWOL?"

Hap returned a crisp nod, coming to a position of attention. "You have my word as a Marine Corps Officer standing in skivvies."

"Excuse me, Colonel." Shank raised the radio to his narrow lips. "Major Wilson. What is call sign of the aircraft that's been trying to land for the past half hour?"

"Sierra Mike 1638," the Major replied.

"Crap," Shank said, shaking his head. "Give them permission to land, Major."

"Roger, Colonel." Seconds passed and then Major Wilson's voice came through the radio again. "Colonel Shank, the aircraft will be on the ground in ten minutes."

Hap turned. Spanky, Ambassador, and Doc stood motionless on line. His peripheral vision went gray, similar to the body's reaction to pulling out at the bottom of a loop. He began hobbling slowly. Shank stayed put, staring into a New Mexico sky at the 737 turning final.

Carla blew between Spanky and Stenson in full stride, almost bowling Hap over. He wanted to give her a congratulatory peck on the lips but his breath smelled like crap and his vision was now completely gray.

Burying his head into the base of her soft neck, he held her close. "I'm going to drop, Carla," he said. "I'm freezing my balls off." Shank stepped aside, as she cradled his head, allowing his weight to bring the lovers crumpling to the ground.

"You okay, Hap Stoner?" she purred, tears running down her cheeks.

"Passed out cold," Spanky murmured, as he, Stenson, Ambassador, and Doc closed on the two. Nobody cared Shank had turned to walk to the other side of the airfield.

Doc wrapped Hap's body in both blankets, checked his pulse, and then lowered his ear to Hap's chapped lips. Looking up he said, "He'll be okay. But he's lost a lot of blood."

"I know he will be okay. He's Hap," she said, nuzzling her chin against Hap's bloody shoulder.

Three weeks later, White Cliff Ranch, outside of Hunt Texas

After talking with Warden for over an hour, Hap signed off and sat back on the covered porch of his ranch house. He pitched slowly back and forth in a rocking chair constructed 85 years earlier, still going strong and beautiful. He thought of Warden resting peacefully in Brooke Army Medical Center in San Antonio, Texas. Warden would be honorably discharged from the Marines when well enough to walk out the doors. Neither he nor his wife knew how much longer that would be but both knew he would keep his hard-earned pension and benefits.

The fresh air of the Texas Hill Country gave Hap the lift he needed. This was where he could go to cut a business deal if need be or just put distance between himself and the rat race. The undulating terrain, the sheer cliff formed tens of thousands of years earlier, the flowing Guadalupe River, the peace, the quiet. Normally there would be several other couples enjoying a lazy life on the river, banging dominoes in a tenacious game of 42, gathering around Hap's large smoker built years earlier, or working in an evening hog hunt. A half dozen 4x4 ATV's and three multi-seat crew sports vehicles were waiting in the barn. The five guest houses were all small two-bedroom cottages, fitted out in Texas Hill Country décor.

Hap, with the help of good friends, constructed the four-bedroom home around the original cedar structure built in the mid-1800s. Farmers had poured sweat and probably blood into the cabin, built smack dab in the middle of Comancheria.

Carla walked out of the enclosed dog run, guiding the screen door shut with her bare foot while balancing cappuccinos in both hands. Wearing one of his Marine T-shirts cutting her midway between knee and thigh, she bent over to kiss Hap on the cheek. Taking the cup, Hap rocked back, closing his eyes, offering a toast, "To the boys: *Semper Fi.*"

Glancing around uneasily as if taking in the surreal scenery, he pulled her into his lap gingerly guiding her hand clutching the cup away from the chair.

Smiling, she blushed, kissing his forehead. "Hap," she said clasping his face in both hands. "I never told you, but your deployments to Iraq and Afghanistan were long and tough for me."

Hap listened silently to every word she said, all the while thoughtfully nibbling his lower lip.

"But those few days between California and New Mexico were the hardest." Hap's body tensed, as he shifted their combined weight in the seat. Hap looked down at each of the rockers, wondering if they would hold the added weight. The old chair creaked but held.

She leaned into his good shoulder dreamy-eyed. "I have something to tell you, Hap," she said, purring. Hap looked into her soft brown eyes. He turned his head to the side, silently questioning her. Kissing his cheek, she whispered, "I'm pregnant, Hap."

Hap rocked forward spitting a mouthful of coffee and spraying the cedar floor. She patted his back then kissed him on the cheek again, whispering, "Just kidding."

Hap sighed, nuzzling his nose into her breast. He knew the pitter-patter of little feet was the music to which she wanted to dance. "You know I love what I do, and I do what I love every day."

Carla laughed aloud. "Well at least you are done with the Marine Corps. Now you can concentrate a little more on the company and a whole hell of a lot more on me," she said, pulling back with a grin.

He slowly nudged her head until their eyes met. "I want to thank you for what you did for the Marines. Getting them all off with an honorable discharge is worth something special."

Her eyes widened at his words, just as the sound of rotors cutting the air broke the moment. The yellow Sikorsky H 360 came into view, breaking over the top of the house, as it traded altitude for airspeed to clear the bluff. The Mayo landed moments later between the house and the tennis court thirty yards across the lawn.

Hap pushed Carla up, giving her a swat on her shapely posterior. Gingerly stepping off the porch, he could see Scharver was behind the controls with his trademark shit-eating grin. What a great Marine, Hap thought. The main mounts set down on the plush grass followed by the nose gear. The door slid back and Blad swung out carrying a leather satchel as Scharver idled the twin turbines. Ducking underneath the rotor arc Blad greeted Hap with a firm handshake followed by a man hug. Blad helped Hap up the three steps to the porch.

"So, you do own this thing," Hap said, eyes bright, looking past Blad's shoulder at the added ventilation covered by green squares of 100 mph aviation tape. "Tough being you." Hap pursed his lips. "You could have picked up the phone or shot me an email."

Blad grinned. "Have a little more than anybody will ever know, Hap. Just wanted to drop in to say thanks before continuing to Colorado. Don't worry; this isn't an invoice for the recent aircraft upgrades." Blad reached into the satchel pulling out a brown envelope.

"After you read this after-action report, shred it, burn it, I don't care. Just make sure it's destroyed." He handed Hap a second envelope. "Don't open this one," he said, pointing at the markings in Sharpie that read, "Don't Open, Dickhead."

Hap extended his hand for the folders. "So we did good?"

"Ending Senator Jourdan's political career is one thing. Rescuing Warden is another. The contents in the envelopes are a totally different matter and will hopefully be useful in the future."

Hap tore off the end, browsed through the dozen or so pages of the report, and asked, "Really?"

"The brunette is a Shadow agent and was the same lady in the burka. She is now on her way to North Africa. Scorpion has turned and now works for Big Shadow. I understand the Mexican Caliph is entering the priesthood."

Carla stood arms crossed with a questioning gaze. Blad gave her wink, nodding all was kosher.

"We worked through back channels to ensure U.S. Intelligence circles were aware of our coup. How else do you think you and your Marines got off so light? Life in Leavenworth would have been kind."

They stood in silence except for the idling engines of the helo and then Hap finally asked. "You didn't come all this way to tell me this."

Blad smiled and said, "Hap, the world is a crazy place and there are a lot of opportunities. Just wanted to look you in the eye to be sure."

"Be sure of what?"

Blad laughed placing one hand on Hap's shoulder. "You will know it when it hits you."

Hap was tempted to ask, but Blad twirled his right index finger above his head. Scharver spooled Mayo's engines to fly. Reaching out Blad gave a firm handshake and walked away, ducking underneath the rotor arc before stepping into Mayo's cabin.

Hap stepped to the edge of the porch coming to a position of attention. He and Scharver looked at each other both knowing how each felt about the other. Hap cut a sharp salute. Jeff returned the salute. Both knew the ground where the other stood. Clutching the envelopes Hap walked back to Carla who was standing seductively in the doorway leading from the porch to the dog run. He didn't flinch as the Mayo clawed its way over the house. The two embraced. He could barely feel the pain in his waist now but her embrace tweaked his left shoulder.

She nuzzled into Hap's left side to allow his arm to slip around pulling her close. Entering the house, the double screen doors banged shut behind them as Hap's cell began to ring. The two of them stopped in front of the master bedroom door. Carla knew by the ring who was on the line and gave Hap a coy look.

"Hey, Will," Hap said.

"What in the hell did you do to Doc at Columbus? Son of a bitch has been on Cloud 9 and wants to visit Dallas."

"Your guess is as good as mine, Will. How's your head today?"

"Migraines come and go but getting better every day," Will said. "How about yourself, Colonel?"

"First of all I'm out of the Marines and damn lucky not to be cleaning heads and ladder wells in Leavenworth."

Carla leaned against the doorjamb; arms crossed giving out a little snort and said under her breath, "You gotta be kidding."

Hap continued the conversation, turning away from Carla's irresistible eyes. "I'm doing fine, Will. But, you knew that because nothing has changed since we spoke last night. You miss me already?"

"Not really, Colonel, but you're not going to believe this?" Will said, sounding like a teenager keeping a secret. "Besides you owe me one."

Hap had to take a second to process what he just heard. The man who had almost taken a shot through the head three weeks earlier was bubbling over with excitement. He knew that Will Kellogg had something brewing and it wasn't tea. An awkward grin appeared as Hap heard the two boys playing in the background.

"You going to keep them?" he asked.

Will chuckled. "Hap, the little fuckers are growing on me. I'm thinking about sending them to military school after a year of tutoring."

"Good for you and the boys, Will. I'm sure as they grow to the next shoe size, they'll help you grow up. It's been a long time coming. If you don't mind, Carla is signaling if I don't hang up this phone in thirty seconds…"

Will interrupted, his tone coy, "Give the young lady my regards, Colonel. If you don't mind, let's continue the conversation later. Be thinking about the Caribbean in the summer."

Dropping the call with a press of a thumb, he stood staring at Blad's package wishing for Superman vision to peruse the manila envelope's contents. Then again, why would he want to do that? Though healing, he did have four new body piercings by Kalashnikov and he needed to get back to the office.

Carla stepped up and took the phone from his hands, snapping him out of his contemplative state. Flipping the phone onto a neat stack of bath towels, she reached up to spin one of two spurs hanging on the breezeway horseshoe hat rack with the lone star fixed on top. The spur whizzed with a sexy spinning sound as she pulled Hap into the bedroom, pushing the door closed with a gentle donkey kick.

—The End—

Glossary for Borderline Decision

7 shot pod of WP: LAU-68 Rocket POD
AH-1W Cobra: Marine attack helicopter
Azimuth: Horizontal angle measured clockwise from any fixed reference plane
BGM-71C TOW missile: Tube launched, optically tracked wire guided missile
Bogey: Something that is not identified as either friend or foe
BOQ: Bachelor Officer Quarters
Collective: Controls increase or decrease in overall lift in helicopters
Cyclic: Tilts rotors forward and back or sideways in helicopters
FARP: Forward Arming and Refueling Point
Fer-de-lance: Latin American poisonous viper
FLIR T620-25: Thermal imaging infrared camera
G2: Division Level Intelligence
Grunt: Slang for Marine Infantry
HMLA 767: Marine Light Attack helicopter squadron
HMLA XO 767: Executive Officer, second in command to Commanding Officer "CO"
HUD: Heads up display
Humint: Human intelligence
JTF-6: Joint Task Force
Laze for a Hellfire shoot: Designate target with laser for a Hellfire Missile to guide on.
LEA: Local Enforcement Agencies
Locked up: Standing in the position of attention

LZ: Landing Zone
Ma Deuce: Fifty-caliber machine gun
Marine Close Air: Integration of Marine air and ground combat efforts
MAW: Marine Air Wing
MFD: Multi-function display
MRE: Meals Ready to Eat
NOMADS: New Orleans Marine Air Detachment
ODO: Operation Duty Officer
Pax: Passenger
P-Bags: Parachute bag
Phrog: CH – 46 Sea Knight helicopter
Piss cutter: Marine foldable military cap with straight sides and creased hollow crown
Portable MANPAD: Shoulder fired surface to air missile
Posse Comitatus Act: Willful use of the US Military to enforce domestic laws
PRC: Combat – net radio transceiver used to provide short-range two-way communications
ROE: Rules of Engagement
RPG: Rocket Propelled Grenade
Run the trap: Look into
SA: Situational awareness
Snap-rolling: High-speed rotation on a helo yaw axis – the line perpendicular to the wings
Syrette: Disposable injection unit of morphine
UH-1N: Huey helicopter

Acknowledgments

To Sarah Lovett and Cynde Christie, you grabbed me by the collar and continued to bang the proverbial frying pan to the side of my "jar head' moving me past being a "story teller" to "writer" and now "author". You make me better.

To my Beta Readers, Thank you for your brutal honesty. You made me better.

To those I had the honor to serve beside—WHAT A RIDE! SEMPER FI.

To the Warriors who gave and will give the ultimate sacrifice, I weep.

.

About the Author

Hugh Simpson has worked for over 25 years in the Telecommunications Industry and Family Law Firm. Prior to entering the Telecommunications Industry, he served in the U.S. Marine Corps retiring as a LtCol serving in 3 overseas deployments including Operation Desert Shield/Storm. He lives in Richardson, Texas.

After 33 years of writing stories in the closet, *Borderline Decision* is the first in the Hap Stoner series to be published.

To learn more about 3Span Publication and Hugh's writing career, visit his website at 3SpanPublications.com.

Coming Winter / Spring 2019

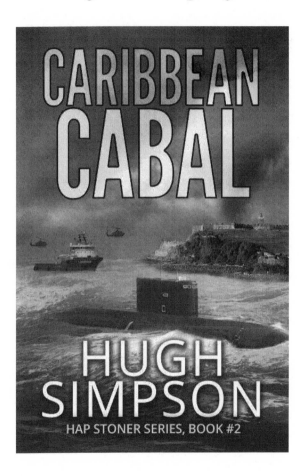

85592208R00253

Made in the USA
Middletown, DE
25 August 2018